What Took You So Long

Pamela S. Williams

WALNUT SPRINGS PRESS

For Roger—
my friend, my hero, my other half

Walnut Springs Press
4110 South Highland Drive
Salt Lake City, Utah 84124

Printed in the United States of America.

ISBN-13: 978-1-59992-958-3

This is a work of fiction. The characters, names, incidents, and dialogue are products of the author's imagination and are not to be construed as real, and any resemblance to real people and events is not intentional.

Acknowledgments

Although creating a story can be a solitary experience, you're never alone when interesting characters inhabit your heart and mind. I'm grateful for so many friends who have encouraged my literary efforts: Tristi Pinkston, my ANWA sisters (American Night Writers Association), particularly the Wasatch Writers chapter, Provo Parkway Fifth Ward book club, my long-lost and highly valued Saturday morning critique group (I miss you!), Bobbette Shepard, Marie Turner, Stewart Shaver, and Caren Liebelt, as well as my pep squad/family, especially my thoughtful daughter-in-law Heather Wheelwright Williams, and Linda Prince, my editor and touchstone on this serendipitous adventure. Thanks for believing in me.

One

Tuesday, December 5, 1995, Provo, Utah

"I thought you said this guy was Mr. Punctuality." Lainie checked her watch again and frowned at Carrie. "I have things to do this afternoon." They waited in the foyer of Magleby's restaurant for Carrie's lawyer friend John Marchbanks to join them at lunch to discuss making their business partnership official.

Carrie shrugged. "I don't know what's up with that. I just know he's an excellent attorney, and he said it wouldn't be hard to incorporate a family-oriented business in a family-friendly town. We're about to be a roaring success."

"Now that your aunt Sophie has agreed to sell us her house," Lainie said, "I don't want some goofy lawyer to mess things up." She and Carrie planned to start a reception center in the elegant old Victorian home.

Carrie explained that her husband Morgan and his classmate John had started Marchbanks & Burke in 1981 right out of BYU law school. "They specialize in business, corporate, and family law. Best in the valley, and I'm completely without prejudice." Estranged from her husband since August, Carrie was on the verge of reconciling with him.

"What about the other half?"

"John can be exacting and fussy, but his attention to details makes him reliable. You'll like him. He's madly active in the Church. I told you before—he's the brother my parents never gave me, so don't be shocked if we act like siblings. He calls me Sassy Lassie sometimes."

Lainie laughed. "Who even talks like that anymore?"

"Well, I've been known to be irreverent sometimes, but John is always a gentleman."

"Hey, I'm meeting an attorney, not going on a blind date."

"Did I mention he's single?"

"I promise not to hold that against him."

At the door again, Carrie looked into the parking lot. "He's usually so prompt." She returned to Lainie. "He does have good work habits, and he always does his homework." She folded her arms. "Just think. You passed the five-year-cancer-free mark, you're submitting your resignation letter, and we're becoming partners, all in the same week."

"Am I crazy to be so eager to leave my secure, predictable life to plunge into the unknown of business ownership? I've always wanted to be my own boss, and now it's here."

"Yeah. This is the dream that kept you going."

John Marchbanks rushed in and made no excuses for being twelve minutes late. He kissed Carrie's cheek. "How's my girl?" He pushed a loose lock of blond hair off his forehead.

"Glad to see you at last."

"Who's your friend?"

Carrie introduced them, and John took Lainie's extended hand. She knew it was no accident that his shirt was the same blue as his eyes.

"Lainie McGuire," he said, glancing at her red hair. "Irish?"

She shook her head. "Scottish."

"Me too."

He smiled, and her mind went blank as she tripped and fell into the deep dimple that interrupted his left cheek.

~

Observing Carrie and John behaving like siblings almost made Lainie forget this was a business meeting. Most of the relationships she'd had with males were strictly board room, nothing as fun as this. She felt a twinge of envy as she listened to their witty, easy conversation.

After the meal, when the server brought the check, John said, "I'm in the mood for dessert. Can't have lunch at Magleby's without chocolate cake."

"I can," Carrie said. "At the present time my jeans fit just fine. But maybe I'll have one bite of yours."

He ordered the dessert and put his credit card in the server's folder, which she took before she walked away. "When Carrie first told me about this business you want to start, I was frankly surprised," he declared, looking at Lainie. "Isn't life good enough for both of you the way it is? Why do you want to complicate your lives with owning and operating a business as demanding as a reception center? Seriously. Neither of you have owned a business before. That's a huge risk."

"Didn't Morgan tell you about the great Single Adult party we organized?" Carrie asked.

"Yes, and it did sound like fun," John admitted. "Almost made me wish I'd broken my own rule and come to it."

"What's your rule?" Lainie suspected she wouldn't like his answer.

He rolled his eyes. "I don't get involved in dating services."

"I don't want to hear this," Carrie muttered, holding her head in one hand.

Lainie's preconceived notions crumbled. John was clearly a misogynist, satisfied with being perfect and superior, not unlike what she'd discovered her former fiancé, Max, to be. "What do you mean, dating services?" she asked, giving him a little more rope.

"Isn't that what Single Adults is all about? Matching people up?"

"Forgive me, John," Carrie interrupted. "And I'm only saying this because you're an idiot—you're a *colossal* idiot."

John frowned as the server put the cake, receipt, and credit card in front of him. "Speak right up, Sassy," he said as he signed the paper. "Don't be afraid to say what you think." He gave Lainie an innocent look and shrugged.

"No, it isn't a dating service," Lainie corrected. She didn't like being thought incompetent, especially by a man she'd just met. "It's a divinely inspired support group."

"I stand corrected." He put his hands up in a defensive pose. "Boy, now I've got another sassy girl on my case."

"I'm not sassy," Lainie retorted. "I have a reputation for being a nice girl." She bit her lip. *What a stupid thing to say.*

John picked up his fork. "Sorry. My mistake."

"Our point is," Carrie stressed, "if you *had* come to the party, you would have seen what a spectacular, fabulous event we put together. That's not bragging. That's a fact."

"True. We developed a great working relationship, and it was so satisfying we didn't want to stop," Lainie said. "Besides, I've put four years of groundwork into this enterprise already. I've thought through every detail of every possible scenario."

John frowned at her, obviously still bewildered. "You're really determined to do this."

Lainie smirked. "I'm so sure I quit my other job."

"Whoa. That's gutsy."

"We're not wasting your time, John." Carrie gave him a wilting look. "When do we get to the part where you take us seriously?"

Only a reassuring glance from Carrie kept Lainie from bolting for the exit. Mentally reviewing the names of other attorneys on her contact list, she began to smolder at John's dismissive conceit. "We have the funding. It's all here in the prospectus I put together." John's eyebrows went up. He took the portfolio Lainie handed him and stared at her. "I have a degree and a strong business background." She sat back in her chair, named a couple of the companies she'd worked for, and put on a bland smile that said "So there, Mr. Always Does His Homework."

"Aunt Sophie's selling her house for a very reasonable price," Carrie told him as he thumbed through the document. "Her daughters don't need the money, and they knocked off a considerable chunk just to thank me for being there when Sophie got sick." Carrie's aunt, adjusting to a pacemaker, had been in Arizona since October with one of her daughters and now planned to make a permanent move.

John looked perplexed. "So this isn't just some fanciful Relief Society whim?"

What was your first clue? Lainie thought, reclaiming her serenity.

Carrie leaned over and patted his hand. "John, it's going to be hard to finish that cake with both feet in your mouth."

Lainie spoke with a smile. "Just put my name on the papers, Mr. Marchbanks, and I'll sign them. Or would you rather we find another attorney? We can do that, you know."

John's eyes flashed. "Look, as your legal advisor, I don't want you getting involved in something that could overwhelm you. This puppy may be cute and cuddly, but it has to be fed, and it might grow up to be a Saint Bernard. Are you ready for that?"

"Wouldn't that mean we're successful?" Carrie asked. "Nothing wrong with that."

"Surely you've been listening for the last fifteen minutes," Lainie said as if he were a six-year-old with attention deficit disorder. "This isn't a complex concept."

"We're not doing this on some mindless impulse," Carrie explained. "We found a passage of scripture that describes exactly what we want Sophie's Place to be. This earth was created for the use of mankind, and all the beautiful and pleasant things were put here 'to please the eye and gladden the heart.' That's our mission statement."

Lainie held John's eyes now with hers. "That's what people want when they celebrate important events in their lives. We have the creativity and imagination and business sense, *and* now a fabulous place to make the magic happen."

"Lainie and I are both at a place in our lives where we can settle into the thing we love and keep it up until we're too feeble to walk in the door." Carrie smiled. "If you're reluctant to help us because you think my husband might not approve, let me handle that."

Watching him absorb what Carrie said, Lainie knew it was time to go in for the kill. "John, you love the law. It's obviously your passion. You devoted three years to learning it."

He nodded. "That's true. What's your point?"

"What are we here for if not to make life better for somebody else? That's what Sophie's Place will be."

He caught his breath and stared at her.

"Well?" she demanded.

"Yes, I do love it that much." He put down his fork.

Lainie knew something had clicked. "Then you understand."

"I have a question for you."

"What's that?"

John leaned toward her, his pen poised over a paper he took from his coat pocket. "What's your legal name?"

"Now we're getting somewhere," Carrie said, rubbing her hands together.

"Elaine Thomas McGuire." She spelled it all out for him.

"Thomas?" Carrie picked up John's fork and sneaked a bite of cake.

"My parents were sure I was going to be a boy," Lainie explained, "and I was born on my grandfather's birthday, so they named me after him anyway because he was a redhead too."

They both frowned at her and glanced at each other. "Really?" Carrie asked.

"My dad calls me Tommy sometimes. But it's okay. My grandmother's name was Elaine, and she always called me Lainie."

"That's really something." John chuckled, put the pen and paper in his pocket, and retrieved the fork from Carrie.

"It's not as interesting as some other Southern Utah names I know. I grew up with twin girls named Relvadeen and Revaleen."

John winced. "Clearly, the parents' baby-naming privileges should have been revoked. That's egregious. But I once had a client named Chance Dakin. Stockbroker. True story."

"Are you two going to spend the afternoon one-upping each other, or are we going on to the next step?" Carrie said. "I'm ready to sign something."

Finished with the cake, John took a sip of water and wiped his mouth with a napkin. "I couldn't have known it until we talked, but this prospectus might alter the partnership agreement in some way, and I want to read it first, in case something needs to be amended."

Meticulous. Lainie liked that. Maybe he could be pardoned for his conceit. It surprised her when he squeezed Carrie's hand, a sweet, reassuring gesture. "Are you interested in telling Morgan about this, or do you want me to talk to him when I get back to the office?"

Carrie shook her head. "I want to tell him myself. He doesn't know it yet but we're having dinner tomorrow night. Just tell him he can read the prospectus."

"Okay, and I'll send a review copy of the partnership agreement to the house tomorrow afternoon by courier." They pushed their chairs away from the table. "Call me by noon Thursday if you're unhappy with anything in the document. Then Friday, you can sign the papers at the same time you finalize the sale with the title company. I think I should be there for that." He shook Lainie's hand again and she thought she saw admiration in his eyes. "See you then." He kissed Carrie's cheek. "I miss you, Sassy, but not as much as Morgan does."

"You know," Carrie mused as they watched him walk away, "I'm glad he wasn't my brother. I might have murdered him by now."

"You'd probably have to get in line," Lainie muttered.

~

Driving to her office to deliver the resignation letter, Lainie considered John Marchbanks. She could see why some women might find him attractive. Blond, about six feet tall, he wore no pretentious lapel pin or gaudy school ring. His watch was gold, thin, and inconspicuous, and his straight, very white teeth sparkled when he smiled. His exquisite dark-blue Glen-plaid suit might signal that he was a clotheshorse, but she decided to delay judgment.

Still, Lainie saw him as possibly a pathetic veteran of the romance wars, haggard and stupefied by an exhausting social life, too picky to make a choice and settle down, or maybe the staggering survivor of a grisly divorce. It didn't matter, because he had "dating disaster" written all over him. Dating was a non-issue anyway; she'd given it up five years ago when Max, that sorry excuse for a fiancé, walked out of her life, taking his cowardice and disloyalty with him.

Reflecting on the events of the last few months—chairing the Single Adult party, meeting Carrie and discovering their compatible talents, making plans to buy the vintage Victorian home in Provo— made her think things had fallen into place so fast it was like some force in the universe seemed to say, "What took you so long?" This business partnership was meant to be. One by one the obstacles were falling.

Lainie was glad Carrie's personal life would be sorted out soon. During the separation from her husband, Carrie and her two teenage daughters had lived in her aunt Sophie's basement apartment. When Lainie called Bishop Kendall last summer to ask who in his ward could help with the regional Single Adult party, he had given her Carrie's name. "She's talented, and she needs to be involved," the bishop had said, "even if it's behind the scenes as an honorary committee member. If you can talk her into it, this kind of service would bless her life."

When the two women met that September day, it took about ten minutes for Lainie to discover that in addition to being the perfect committee member, Carrie was also the business partner she'd been looking for. Little by little, over the next two months, as they planned and executed that memorable event, Carrie recognized it too.

Lainie smiled as she pulled into the parking lot of her office building. *Life is full of sweet serendipity.*

Two

Friday, December 8

John was on time for the meeting with Ron, the title company officer, and Tina, the real estate agent, at three that afternoon. Lainie and Carrie took them through the house, explaining all the changes they would make. With peppermint tea and a plate of cookies, they sat in the kitchen to discuss the building inspector's report and reviewed its major points.

"This place is in very good condition," Ron said. "A few things need to be repaired—there are some loose boards on the back porch, you need a new roof, the bathrooms need to be remodeled, and the garage is a fixer-upper—but the bones are good and with the right maintenance, this house will probably last another hundred and fifty years."

"And this is a sweet price," Tina commented.

John took the partnership agreement out of his briefcase and offered to answer any questions. Lainie and Carrie assured him they understood everything. He pushed the papers across the table for Lainie's signature. "By the way, that was a very impressive prospectus."

"I worked for a company where proposal writing was in my job description," she said as she signed. "And you've done an excellent job with this document."

He tipped his head in a gracious nod. "Thanks for saying so."

"I'm always truthful. You can count on that." She pushed the papers to Carrie.

John smiled at his friend. "Morgan thinks this is a good idea."

"I knew he would. We discussed it at dinner Wednesday night."

Then Ron opened his portfolio, and Carrie and Lainie signed more papers. "This fabulous house is now yours," he said. With handshakes all around, the meeting ended.

"What's next?" John pulled on his gray topcoat.

"We'll set up the office next month and start remodeling," Carrie said. "Our advertising campaign begins in March, we'll have an open house the first week of May, and we'll schedule events after that."

"While the carpenters are at work, I'll interview for caterers and photographers," Lainie explained as Ron helped her with her coat. "I already have a reliable accountant."

"We're hoping the weather cooperates with the landscapers," Carrie added.

John looped a scarf around his neck. "And my work here is done. Welcome to the happy family of satisfied customers at Marchbanks & Burke. You can expect my bill next week." Carrie punched his arm and he laughed.

"You can send it here." Lainie handed him the accountant's business card.

He put the card in his pocket. "He's excellent. You've made a good choice."

"I know," she said.

He raised an eyebrow. "Of course."

Carrie put an arm around John's waist for a sideways hug. "Thanks for everything, Johnny. You're my hero."

He kissed Carrie's cheek and grinned. "Go home soon, Sassy."

"When the time is right, I will."

Wednesday, January 3, 1996

Just before noon, John stood at the front desk in the offices of Marchbanks & Burke discussing his schedule for the rest of the week with Maggie the receptionist when Morgan came in, a faraway grin on his face. "Good morning," John said, but Morgan, oblivious, continued smiling and went to his office to take his place behind the desk. John followed and sat in a chair.

Finally Morgan looked up. "Oh, hi, John. Didn't see you come in."

"Everybody's here but you."

Morgan laughed and threw his arms into the air in a victory gesture, spinning his chair around. "They came home. We're a family again."

"I'll be glad to close the file on that case."

"I can't tell you how much I appreciate your help, John. You kept us both from going completely nuts."

"What can I say? You're an A-list client."

"We burned last year's calendar on New Year's Eve."

"Very symbolic and appropriate. It was a rotten year for both of you."

"Sophie and her daughter will be here this afternoon to start packing. They should be ready to go by Saturday, and on Monday the house becomes a business. Lainie's coming over to our place tonight so she and Carrie can bring me up to speed on the whole enterprise."

"Mind if I drop by to welcome Carrie home?"

"She'd love it."

"Think you'll be able to pay attention?"

Morgan laughed. "I plan on coming back down to earth sometime this afternoon."

"Too bad," John remarked as he left the office. "I kind of like the goofy you."

~

That evening when John rang the bell, Carrie opened the door and accepted the bouquet of flowers he brought. She took his arm and led him to the family room. "Look who's here."

"It's nice to see the sassy lassie back in her native habitat," John said. He nodded at Lainie, seated in an armchair. "Nice to see you again too." He took the hand she offered.

Lainie smiled. "I haven't known her very long, but I don't think of her as sassy, not in the mouthy-teenage-brat sense of the word."

Carrie turned toward the kitchen. "I'll put these in water. Talk among yourselves and choose a place to go to dinner where we can celebrate."

John leaned back and crossed his legs. "I haven't been to Los Hermanos for a while."

"Sounds good to me," Morgan said. "Carrie loves Mexican food."

John looked at Lainie with raised eyebrows. She shrugged. "I don't want to crash the family reunion."

"Don't worry about it," Morgan told her. "Business partners are family too."

They were on their feet and ready to go when Carrie returned with the vase of flowers. "Better leave the girls some money," she said to Morgan. "They can order pizza."

He muttered something about high-maintenance children and went to find his daughters while Carrie got into the car in the garage.

John guided Lainie out onto the front porch and pulled the door shut. "Want a ride?"

"I live in west Provo, out by Utah Lake."

He nodded. "Oh. I live on the east side. Quail Valley."

"Never been there. Let's take our own cars so we won't have to backtrack in this basketball-game traffic."

"Makes sense."

"Yes, I'm quite predictable and boring that way. I wear sensible shoes, and I don't wear earrings because they get in the way when I talk on the phone."

John held the car door for her and followed her to the restaurant.

Over appetizers Morgan regaled them with the story of his frustrating scavenger-hunt adventure on New Year's Eve, part of the reconciliation with Carrie at the basement apartment in Sophie's house. Over dinner, Carrie and Lainie explained their business plan, described the products and services they intended to offer, and answered questions. John and Morgan made a few suggestions.

Later the conversation went to topics both serious and silly. John insisted Lainie's short stature was evidence of leprechauns in her family tree and nicknamed her "Irish." It was after ten when the spontaneous party broke up.

⁓

John smiled all the way from the restaurant to his condo. Whatever she did during those four months away had made Carrie a more confident woman. It was gratifying to see her together with Morgan once more, and both of them so happy. With his best friends reunited, John's world was right side up again. Maybe Carrie had come home because of the influence of Lainie McGuire.

No one could be unimpressed by that red hair, but John also remembered her insight and perception when the three of them discussed the Sophie's Place partnership over lunch a month ago. He felt like he'd been hit by a runaway locomotive and then trampled by a herd of stampeding buffalo that day. It unnerved him to admit it even to himself, but she'd opened his heart and mind and read verbatim. No one had ever done that before. And he had to confess—that little cleft in her chin beguiled him.

While stopped at a red light, John changed the radio station to his favorite jazz program. At first this party-planning business had seemed like a cockamamie girly thing, but if wit and brains, chutzpah and moxie counted at all, Carrie's creativity and Lainie's business acumen would make it a huge success.

A horn honking behind John intruded into his thoughts and he realized the traffic light was green.

From what he knew about her so far, he liked Lainie's approach to life. She was assertive without being obnoxious and showed a breathless, take-no-prisoners attitude. He didn't admire wimps, marshmallows, or chameleons; he found straightforward, independent women much more interesting. He sighed as he turned up the hill toward Quail Valley, wondering how Lainie felt about plays and concerts. She was a client now, and she might find the occasional social event appealing. He wouldn't go to dating purgatory—his life was full enough without that aggravation—but this redhead could be a good friend too, like another sister.

Monday, January 8

"Imagine the brilliant schemes for weddings and parties we'll dream up here." Lainie grinned as she and Carrie admired the two-person workstation in their sitting room office. "I think Aunt Sophie is right—we've both found our glitch in life."

They laughed and Carrie checked to see if the car in the street might be Morgan. He had a few things to finish at his office before they flew to Houston this afternoon. Tomorrow morning they'd board the cruise ship in Galveston. She pulled some folded papers out of her purse and put them on the desk. "I typed up Aunt Sophie's cookie recipes so we can start practicing."

"I look forward to learning how to make our signature specialty."

Carrie glanced out the window again. "Here he is." She grabbed her coat as Morgan pulled into the driveway. "John will probably call you about that zoning question."

Lainie shook her head. "I don't know why he's fussing over that. I checked with the landlord at the other end of the block and he told me we won't have a problem."

Carrie paused at the door. "John fusses because that's what John does. Besides, it'll keep him busy and out of your hair, and we won't make any mistakes."

"I'm reassured," Lainie said as Carrie turned to go. "See you next week."

Wednesday, January 10

Lainie looked up from her desk mid-morning, guessed the accumulated snow on the front walk to be three or four inches, and knew she was going to have to remove it the old-fashioned way since she didn't know how to use the snow blower Sophie had left in the garage. She turned from the window when the phone rang.

"Hi, it's John Marchbanks."

"Hello, Counselor. How are you this snowy morning?"

"Glad to be indoors. Listen, you and I need to take care of a little business, and I thought maybe we could do that at dinner tomorrow night."

"Another evening of madcap revelry, I suppose, like last week at Los Hermanos. Shall I meet you somewhere?"

"No, I'll pick you up at six thirty."

"What are the dress standards?"

"Casual, I guess, but you always look good."

"That's incentive. I'll try not to disappoint you."

"See you tomorrow."

Maybe he settled the zoning question, she thought. *But he could just tell me that on the phone. Is this some kind of silly lawyer game?*

She picked up the phone when it rang again. "Lainie, it's Angela Cavanaugh."

"Hi, pastry lady."

Angela laughed. "I guess my reputation's made, but I refuse to have it tattooed on my forehead." She and the bakery where she worked had provided tasty rolls and luscious French pastries for the Single Adult party Carrie and Lainie had organized a couple of months ago.

"That party wouldn't have been the same without you," Lainie said. "What can I do for you?"

"I have an emergency. My niece is engaged to a Marine, and they just found out his orders have changed. He's going overseas, leaving the end of February, so they've decided to get married on Valentine's Day. They'd have forty or fifty guests, and they want it very low-key. I know you're technically not open yet, but it's such a beautiful place. Can you help us?"

"Well, it isn't torn up with remodeling yet, so I suppose we could do a small event. Can you come and talk details with me today or tomorrow?"

"Today on my lunch hour. Perfect. We'll be there at quarter to twelve."

Lainie finished shoveling snow just as a car drove up and Angela, two other women, and a Marine got out. After brief introductions, Lainie guided them into the sitting room.

Tiffany, the bride, took in all the details. "This place is gorgeous."

Lainie sat at the desk and smiled. "We're very lucky to be here. Now what do you need for this Valentine wedding?"

"We definitely want to keep it simple," said Karen, the mother of the bride.

"If you need kitchen staff, Carrie and I can recruit our daughters, Jane and Julie, and they have some dependable friends," Angela put in. "I'm planning to make the cake. It's a wedding gift for my niece."

Karen added, "We want to serve the cake, too."

"It doesn't really matter what the refreshments are," the bride said. "You can choose something easy that everybody will like. I have other things to think about."

Lainie looked up from making notes. "That simplifies a lot. I'll get back to you in a few days with ideas, estimates, and some samples for you to taste. Let's go into the parlor now and I'll show you what we're thinking about doing for wedding decorations."

Lainie pulled open the pocket doors to the parlor, and the women and the groom, Lance, followed her inside. The clergyman could stand in front of the fireplace at the opposite end, Lainie suggested. Clear leaded-glass windows flanked it, giving the room a church-like feel. Without the sofas, they could set up plenty of chairs. She also explained that wedding photos could be taken on the staircase or on the furniture from the parlor, which would be moved upstairs.

As they returned to the office, the bride's mother asked, "What do you think—is February 14th going to be okay, or is it too soon?"

"No, this is doable," Lainie assured her. "And you can have a rehearsal the day before. We're planning to turn the main-floor bedroom into a bride's dressing-room suite. It has a bathroom, a vanity, and a large cheval mirror. We'll clear some space upstairs for the men."

When they left they seemed pleased with the plans, and Lainie thought about the decision she'd made without her partner. They'd targeted May to open their doors because the wedding season accelerated then, but it wouldn't be hard to modify that to accommodate a friend's emergency. This would be a small event, and preparation was mostly a matter of setting up enough chairs, fixing a few easy refreshments, and arranging some flowers.

She spent the afternoon making sketches, developing some menu choices, and pricing out everything. About four o'clock the computers arrived, and she stayed late to get acquainted with the new system and applications.

Three

Thursday, January 11

For the business meeting with John, Lainie wore a chestnut-brown pantsuit with a beige pinstripe, and a silk blouse the color of dandelions. *Casual enough,* she thought as she grabbed her coat and glanced in the mirror again before answering the door. He led her through the slush of the soggy snowstorm that had dribbled on all afternoon, opened the door of his silver-gray Lexus, and waited while she slid in. Once he was settled in the driver's seat, she asked, "Where are we going?"

He smiled and raised an eyebrow. "How do you feel about surprises?"

She laughed. "At the moment I'm buckled into your car. How do you want me to feel?"

Driving away, he gave another hint. "We're going to have excellent food in a relaxing atmosphere. What more could you ask?"

"Just interesting company, and I see you've provided that too."

John grinned as he pushed a button on the instrument panel, and some cool jazz spilled out of the rear speakers. They talked of the day's activities and he hummed with the music as he drove east, turning north finally at University Avenue.

Lainie tried to think of restaurants in this part of town that weren't noisy student hangouts. Slowing as he approached the country club, he pointed out the offices of Marchbanks & Burke in Jamestown Square just north of the golf course, and then turned east at the traffic light, going up the hill past Canyon Road. At almost the top of the very steep winding street, he turned at a sign that read "Welcome to the Village of Quail Valley." Now she understood. He'd told her he lived in Quail

Valley, but she hadn't known exactly where it was. Disappointed, she thought maybe he'd send out for pizza while they talked business.

He turned off the car and smiled at her. "Here we are—Chez Marchbanks."

Something smelled delicious when Lainie walked into John's condo. Definitely not pizza. He flipped a switch to turn on the gas flame in the brick fireplace dominating the wall beyond a baby grand piano on the right.

Over the mantel, a large watercolor-and-India-ink painting brought Mt. Timpanogos indoors. A potted tree stood in front of a wide, floor-to-ceiling window next to the fireplace. It reached up to the open beams of the dark cathedral ceiling. A burgundy leather sofa and two armchairs with ottomans huddled around a large tree-of-life area rug, accented by sturdy Craftsman-style end tables and reproduction Tiffany lamps. Chocolate-brown hardwood plank flooring complemented the leather and the off-white walls.

"You have a beautiful place." Handing him her coat, Lainie noticed at the far end of the room a small dining table, with four spindle chairs, already set with two placemats, a basket of rolls, and a butter dish.

John hung her coat with his in the closet just inside the door. "It's the right size for me. There isn't even space for a dog or a cat, but I'm allergic to pet dander anyway." He pointed out the library wall behind the piano as he rolled up his sleeves and tucked his tie inside his shirt. "Make yourself comfortable. I have to check on dinner."

Lainie stared after him, stunned by this unmistakable invitation into his world. He was her attorney, and at first she trusted him because Carrie did. Then she discovered he was actually a first-rate professional. They didn't know each other very well, except for that nearly disastrous lunch a month ago, and that impromptu dinner at Los Hermanos last week. Whatever was going on in the kitchen wasn't cold cereal or Spaghetti-Os.

Absently inspecting the Timpanogos painting, but distracted by what John's possible motivations might be for this business meeting, Lainie considered their professional relationship. Sophie's Place was her focus now, although he could be a friend, as long as it didn't interfere with her goals. Carrie liked him, so he was probably okay—almost certainly safe. First impressions began rearranging themselves in Lainie's head. It might be nice to have one more brother in her life.

Titles in the library seemed to indicate he'd been an English major. That had been Lainie's minor in college. She studied the four watercolor landscapes, the same scene in different seasons, dominating the wall behind the dining table. With an open, assertive style, the simple and uncluttered paintings appealed to her. All the art was signed "jtm." She wondered what the *T* stood for. Travis? Troy? Terwilliger?

She went into the kitchen and stood by the island while he tended something in the oven. "These watercolors are all by the same artist."

"That would be me," John confessed, wiping his fingertips on the apron tied around his waist. "My studio is the guest room."

He paints, he cooks, and there's that piano. What else? "They're very nice. What smells so good?"

"Game hens with rice—brown and wild." He gestured to some dishes and cutlery on the end of the counter. "Want to set the table?"

"Sure." Lainie put the simple silverware and plain, pale-gray silver-rimmed china on the placemats. It was masculine, with a notable lack of pretentiousness. "Modest" hadn't been a word that would have come to her mind if asked a month ago to describe John Marchbanks.

When she finished and came back to the kitchen, he handed her a bowl of mixed greens with sliced almonds and orange sections, some tongs, and a bottle of poppyseed dressing. "Would you toss?" She did so while he stirred butter and honey into steamed carrots. "One minute to dinner," he announced, grating some nutmeg over the vegetables.

"How long have you lived here?" she asked.

"A little over eight years. It's a great neighborhood—kids on all sides. In good weather we play kick the can almost every night."

She carried the salad and the carrots to the table, chuckling to herself. *He's just a great big kid. I can deal with that.*

He followed with two chilled goblets and a liter of ginger ale. When he returned with the serving platter—two golden-brown birds resting on a bed of rice, garnished with fresh chopped chives—Lainie stared in amazement at the meal. John helped her with the chair and sat across from her, smiling as if he'd executed some complex prank. "Welcome to my table." He rolled down his shirtsleeves and buttoned them.

"I'm honored to be here, Counselor." *Carrie never mentioned he was such a handsome man,* she thought, spreading the napkin on her lap. "But you said this was a business meeting. Somehow it doesn't feel very businesslike. You haven't misled me, have you?"

His smile broadened. "I like to multi-task if I can. Getting acquainted is very important business too, don't you think? I see it as the 'discovery' phase of the friendship."

"So I'm on trial."

He laughed. "You and Carrie are going to be my clients for a long time, and I already know her pretty well."

"All right. I'll admit that into evidence, but I'm not convinced."

"Give me an hour." Then he bowed his head, said a prayer, and served the food.

"Where did you learn to do this?" she asked. "I suspect none of it's takeout."

"I read, and when I can, I watch cooking shows on TV."

"Self-taught—that's extraordinary." She cut into the hen.

"That's survival." He opened the ginger ale and filled the goblets. "When I was a kid, while my brothers and cousins were out playing guy games, I was in the kitchen cooking with Grandma. Carrie taught me quite a bit too. She's as good as anybody I know."

"What's the glaze on this bird? It's superb."

"Orange marmalade thinned with melted butter and white grape juice, my secret ingredient for everything."

"Would you sue me if I stole this idea for Sophie's Place?"

John laughed again. It was throaty and genuine, a sound she was beginning to like. "What do you do when you're not Lainie McGuire, Girl Party Planner?"

"Mainly I'm a people person. I've always had jobs in companies that help people, and I like activities and projects that support good causes. It drives my parents crazy."

"You mentioned Southern Utah earlier. Is that where they live?"

She nodded. "Cedar City. My dad is a retired math professor. He's the patriarch now in the stake where I grew up. I'm the youngest by seven years. My brother Glenn is a high school principal in Montana, and my sister Gayle is married to a firefighter in Seattle."

John looked up from buttering a roll. "Really. I'm from Portland."

"They used to live there, but they moved several years ago."

"Have you ever been there?"

"A couple of times," she said. "It's a beautiful city. Actually, I had a mission call to Portland, but I got some mystery virus in the missionary training center and they reassigned me to Tennessee. I only lasted a few months because I still wasn't strong enough to keep the missionary schedule. It was disappointing."

"My folks still live there, and I have a little getaway place on Gleneden Beach."

"Right on the beach?"

"It's modest, second tier, not nearly as upscale as the fancy place Mom and Dad have in Newport, but it has a good ocean view and easy beach access. I bought it from my grandparents' estate and I've made a few improvements."

"What's second tier?" Lainie asked.

"Houses across the street from me are beachfront, but I have a more panoramic view."

"What's an Oregon boy doing in Utah?"

John took a drink and wiped his mouth with the napkin. "After I joined the Church, which displeased my Roman Catholic family in a big way, I felt drawn to Utah. I did well enough on the LSAT to be admitted to BYU Law. Their mission statement is to teach the laws of men in the light of the laws of God. As a fairly new member of the Church, that appealed to me."

"That's taking a chance—coming here without knowing anyone."

He shrugged. "Security is always good, but I do risky things occasionally, when I'm convinced it's right. I met Morgan and we clicked, and some excellent mentors guided us into corporate and business law when we were second and third years. Things worked out for us to establish the firm, so we started as partners as soon as we passed the bar in 1981."

"Why is it Marchbanks & Burke instead of the other way around?"

"We agreed that whoever finished highest in the class would get top billing when we hung out our shingle. I was ninth and he was tenth, but he should have been ahead of me. Their daughter Jane was a toddler at the time and got meningitis, so he spent the last three weeks of the term, including finals week, at the hospital with her. No sleep, worried sick."

"You've obviously been a member of the Church for quite a while now."

"I was twenty when I was baptized—junior year at the University of Oregon. I got to know some great LDS guys who helped me through a rough patch and taught me the gospel."

"So you're Morgan's age."

"Two years younger. He served a mission and I didn't. I'm forty next June."

Lainie watched John sip ginger ale and tried to imagine him as a new convert, finding his way in the LDS world. "It must be hard when you're single and forty and a good cook," she commented. "People are bound to wonder about you."

"Yeah. They've got you pegged as a playboy, hooked on porn, or gay."

"None of which you are."

He cast her a look of gratitude.

"Why didn't you go on a mission?" she asked. "You were young enough."

John put his fork down. "When you come from a big, traditional Catholic family, there are expectations," he explained with a frown. "I'm the oldest son, and my parents wanted me to be a priest, or a doctor like my father—he's an anesthesiologist—but certainly not one of those reprehensible attorneys they were always reading about in the newspaper."

"Ouch," Lainie said. "Strike three."

"Uh-huh. It was bad enough that I chose to leave Catholicism. They couldn't suffer the disgrace of seeing me try to convert other people to this heretic church I found. I didn't want to disappoint them any more than I already had, so I decided to be a missionary in other ways."

"And have you been?"

He picked up his fork again and dug into his rice. "I guess you'd have to ask my Primary class, or my sister Margaret. I baptized her and her husband Jerry fifteen years ago, and we've been working on our brother Richard in Vancouver, Washington, for quite a while."

"A single man teaching Primary is so unexpected." Lainie pictured John in a room full of children, and more preconceived notions bailed out of her brain.

"I guess I like Primary because I never had anything like that as a child, and it keeps me grounded in the gospel. Just learning all those songs is a solid review of the basics." He stabbed a couple of carrots. "I really like kids. They tell it like it is."

"What age do you teach?"

"I've got seven- and eight-year-olds again this year. It's very satisfying to help prepare them for baptism. I'm teamed with a father of eight, a child psychologist, who's given me some helpful insights into the child mind, which, in many ways, is not really very different from my own." Lainie laughed with him. "In Primary I'm known as Brother John."

"I haven't been around kids a lot. As a teenager I was always too busy with service projects to babysit very much."

They laughed again, and the question on Lainie's mind popped out of her mouth. "Why aren't you somebody's dad?"

Clearly caught off guard by her candor, he put down his fork again. "I wish I were. In some ways, Primary teachers have more credibility with kids than their parents. Being a good influence, teaching gospel principles, helping parents raise their children in the nurture and admonition of the Lord—all that's a fairly satisfying role even if I never get to be a dad myself."

She sipped her drink. "I'm sorry. That was an unfair question."

"I'm not offended. I wouldn't have answered if I didn't want to."

"You're probably wondering the same thing about me. I'll be thirty-eight in May, and, well, I've spent a lot of time wandering around smelling the roses. I've had so much fun, met so many interesting people, and learned so much. I love life. This chance I have now with Carrie as a partner at Sophie's Place is something . . . well, is it too corny to say it's a dream come true?"

"Dreams are good." John studied her face. "It's ironic that the people person didn't find someone for herself."

"Ironic, yes, but I decided not to shed any more tears over it. Obviously, my life has a different purpose than most other women, and

I've come to terms with that. My patriarchal blessing is kind of vague on the subject. I know in my own way I'm still a nurturer."

He sat back in his chair, regarding her with a smile. "Lainie, if I were choosing up sides I'd want you on my team."

It was a startling personal statement. "So you think you know me that well now, do you." Enchanted by his eyes, the color of a clear June sky, she realized she and John could probably be comfortable friends. They sat for a moment in easy silence.

"Would you like some pie?" he asked. "I have apple and peach."

"I love peach pie. Did you make them?"

He laughed. "I'm not *that* good. I bought these at that little bakery on Second West."

"Do you shop there very often?"

"Quite a bit. They know what they're doing, and they do it superbly."

He put away the leftovers, and Lainie cleared the dishes and rinsed them in the sink. Then he brought the pie, with generous scoops of raspberry sherbet, to the table.

"Want to talk a little business, just to make this legitimate?" she asked when they were seated again.

John chuckled. "Okay. How's business?"

"We got our first booking yesterday."

"I thought you were remodeling first."

"We are, but that's mostly downstairs until the weather warms up. Doing a small wedding for Carrie's friend Angela seemed like the right kind of trial-run first job. Besides, Angela works at that little place on Second West and is going to make the cake."

"Boy, did you get lucky."

"It's payback in a way. Angela really helped us with the Single Adult party."

"Carrie probably would have accepted the job too, for the same reasons."

"I wonder where Carrie and Morgan are now," Lainie mused, savoring the dessert.

"Somewhere in the Caribbean."

"Well, with Sophie's free tickets, they didn't even care about the destination."

"I don't know why Carrie left last year, or what brought her home, but the magic is back," John said. "It's good to see her together with Morgan again, and both of them so happy."

"They're desperately in love."

"That's blindingly obvious."

A comfortable silence descended again. Lainie met John's gaze as she took a sip of ginger ale, and couldn't help wondering about his small, inscrutable smile. "What a marvelous end to a wonderful meal. It's been a relaxing, refreshing evening, John. Thank you."

"It's been perfect, but your eyes look tired. I think you'd like to go home."

"I hate to break up such a splendid business meeting, but I do have a lot of work facing me tomorrow, and I imagine that with Morgan away, you're busy too."

"I think there will probably be other times. Parties seem to be what we both do best."

"Even small parties, and we can always find something to celebrate."

As John drove her home, they saw stars, evidence the storm was over, and when he walked her to the door, they stood on the porch grinning at each other. He touched the cleft in her chin with his index finger, a simple but almost intimate gesture made without guile. "Good night, Irish."

"Thanks for a lovely evening. Good night, Counselor."

All the way back to Quail Valley, John alternated smiling and frowning as he tried to sort out his feelings. Lainie was a woman of substance with natural warmth many people didn't have. He'd never seen hair that looked like oxidized mahogany, but he'd painted autumn leaves almost that color and wondered if she'd be willing to sit for a portrait.

When Lainie was ready for bed she took a cup of chamomile tea to her room, intending to read for a while before she went to sleep. A few minutes later the phone rang.

"Hi," John said.

She waited but he didn't say anything else. *What's this all about?* "Hi."

"I really enjoyed tonight."

"So did I. Now remind me—it's orange marmalade, melted butter . . ."

"And white grape juice."

"I wasn't kidding. Without question, it's good enough for Sophie's Place."

Again he paused. "You know, I really enjoyed tonight."

"You almost sound surprised."

"No, I didn't mean it that way. I just meant it was great having you here."

"Maybe you'll come to my house for dinner sometime."

"I'd love it. You're probably a wonderful cook." There was another pause. "When?"

"When what?"

"Dinner at your house."

Lainie chuckled. "I'll check my calendar and we'll plan something."

"I'm looking forward to it."

"Me too."

He paused again. "Well, you're probably getting ready for bed. I'd better let you go."

"Thanks for calling, John. Good night again."

"I really enjoyed tonight."

"So did I."

"By the way, I checked on that zoning thing, and you won't have a problem."

She stifled a laugh. "It's good to be sure of that."

"Well, I just wanted to say good night. See you sometime soon, I hope."

"Sometime soon." Lainie smiled as she hung up, and went back to the food-service-industry magazine she'd been reading, but couldn't concentrate. John had manufactured a reason to get her to spend the evening with him, and that was catch-her-breath flattering. She hoped she *would* see him sometime soon.

Four

Monday, January 15

Due to a late plane, Carrie and Morgan didn't get home until midnight. It was noon Monday before she called Lainie.

"Hi. What's up?" Carrie said, and Lainie heard her yawn.

"We've got our first booking."

"Really?"

"It's on Valentine's Day. It's Angela's niece, and Angela's doing the cake."

"Sounds good."

"You know, I wish we could steal her away from that bakery. She's really talented."

"We definitely need to have that discussion."

"But we'll wait until you're fully awake."

"Thanks. Maybe tomorrow. Look, I have to reclaim my children in a few hours and then transfer Miranda back to her Orem school, but I'll be there in the morning for sure."

Lainie hung up, pleased for her friend's rediscovered happiness, but wondering for the first time what it would be like to be so close to someone that you would know things about them no one else had a right to know. She shook those thoughts out of her head when the phone rang.

"This is Alice Jensen, and I need a wedding for my son in a hurry. Can you do it?"

"How many guests?"

"About thirty. What you're doing for Karen's kids sounds like the event we need."

"I appreciate your confidence, but technically we're not going to be open for clients until May. We have volunteer help from the family for Karen's wedding."

"I don't care what it costs, but we can't wait until May. That's when the baby's due."

Lainie paused, briefly wondering if the baby was the bride's, or the mother of the bride's, or . . . "Well, that does make a difference. I'll put my partner on it. She'll get back to you in a few days with some ideas."

"Oh, thank you." Alice sounded relieved. "Here's all my information."

Making notes for Carrie about this new job, Lainie was interrupted by the phone again.

"Good afternoon, Lainie. How are you today?"

She was delighted to hear John's voice. "Well, hello. You treated me to such a nice evening, and I'm sorry we had to cut it short. I was hoping you'd play the piano for me."

"Next time for sure. I called to see if you could suggest some ideas for the Primary lesson I'm giving in a couple of weeks. It's about the Creation, and I need something visual and tactile to illustrate the creative process, so I thought I'd ask a creative person."

"You're an artist. You know about creativity."

"But I'm an amateur."

Lainie laughed at the thin veneer of his excuse, but she was flattered. "All I know is that the earth was created for the use of mankind, everything to please the eye and gladden the heart. But that's the fluffy stuff. I don't know anything about separating light from darkness, except when I'm sorting laundry."

"That's my problem. I don't fully comprehend 'let there be light,' so it's hard to teach it to seven-year-olds."

"Yeah, there was light because the Creator commanded it to be there."

"And the Creator *is* light."

"Let me think about it, Counselor. Call me at home later."

"I will. Thanks, Irish."

Lainie smiled and hung up. Nobody had ever asked her opinion about the scriptures or gospel principles except in a Sunday School class. John respected her ideas. What was it he'd said? "If I were choosing up sides I'd want you on my team." She spent the rest of the afternoon planning the Valentine wedding. Just before six o'clock, Angela Cavanaugh came in.

"Hi. I'm glad you're still here. I want to show you some ideas for this cake." Angela laid her drawings out on the desk.

Lainie studied them and sighed. "These are beautiful. Wedding cakes are so labor intensive. You must have a lot of patience."

Angela grinned. "Tiffany wants me to use fondant and I've only done it twice before. It'll be good practice."

Lainie opened a drawer and pulled out a file. "You have great ideas, but I researched Victorian Valentines today, and you can use these illustrations if you need more inspiration to refine your concept. This is what I'm going to do for the rest of the room."

"They'll love it." Angela glanced through the file. She took two pages and handed the folder to Lainie. "I'll bring these back tomorrow."

"Hey, I had some peach pie from the bakery last week. Really delicious." Lainie put the folder back in the file drawer. "And we just got our second job because of you. Alice Jensen called. We should put you in charge of advertising. Are you available for that wedding too?"

"Does that mean another cake?"

"Carrie's going to be the boss. You can work it out with her and Alice." They left together and Lainie locked the door. "Listen, if your soufflé ever falls at that place on Second West, let's talk."

Angela's face lit up. "Thanks. I'll remember that."

When he called that evening, John asked, "Did you have any brilliant ideas today about teaching a Creation lesson?"

"I'm just reviewing it now," Lainie replied. "As the Creation unfolded, it progressed from inanimate to animate to prepare the way for human life to survive when people came on the scene."

"Good point. Light, darkness, water, seasons all had to be in place before other life forms, and plants and animals had to be there before people."

"Yeah, natural physical laws set into motion in sequence would sustain life. Apparently it couldn't have happened any other way with the same outcome. Adam and Eve depended for their survival on the cycles of time set in motion, the days and seasons."

"It's all about life, isn't it," John mused.

"Isn't everything? Life is a gift."

"Yes, it is. How do I bring it right down to the kids themselves?"

"You could talk about ways they can be creative in their own lives, just like Heavenly Father is creative in His realm. Show them one of your drawings and what it looks like as a painting."

"That's good—the ideas come before the reality."

"Right. You could even make cookies. Talk about how individually the ingredients don't taste good, but when you know how to put the right amounts together, they can be delicious."

"Yeah. Food always communicates."

"Don't I know it. Good luck, Counselor, and tell me how it goes."

Tuesday, January 16

Carrie came in the next morning ready to work and started on the Jensen wedding. Don, the remodeling project manager, arrived in the afternoon with his crew. Their first task was to post the sign in the front yard. A secondary sign, "Open in May," hung from it.

"Did John call about that zoning issue?" Carrie asked as she and Lainie returned to the house from approving the sign placement.

"Yes. He said everything's fine. Then he called later to pick my brain about a Primary lesson he's giving. How long has he taught kids?"

"Since he moved to Quail Valley, I think. He loves it."

"You know, he doesn't seem like the vain, self-absorbed single guy I thought he'd be."

"No, he's anything but that. He goes home to visit his family for Thanksgiving but usually spends the day serving meals at a soup kitchen." Carrie reached for the ringing telephone before the shocked Lainie could respond.

Carrie fielded questions from Angela's aunt, who called about having a retirement party in March, and then Carrie and Lainie brought each other up to speed on their projects, now numbering three.

Noise from the demolition going on downstairs nearly drowned out conversation. "I guess I shouldn't be sentimental about it," Carrie said, "but a huge reminder of my past is gone now."

"You mean the apartment?" Lainie asked.

"It was the most important four and a half months of my life. It saved my marriage."

"It took courage to do what you did—to take a timeout and rethink everything to get yourself back on track."

Carrie smiled and returned to the task on her desk. "Well, you'll pardon me if I'm a little distracted. My mind is still on that cruise ship."

Sunday, January 28

John called Lainie late Sunday evening to report on his lesson. It had gone well, and of course, the cookies were a big hit. "Thanks for the help. I owe you," he said. "Do you teach something?"

"Relief Society every fourth Sunday. That was today, so I don't need help this month."

"Put me on standby then."

"Well, come to think of it, I could use your help with my other calling in a couple of weeks. I'm invited to a dinner with friends. Would you go with me?"

"Aren't you all partied out at the end of the day?"

She chuckled. "No danger of that. Occasionally I like to go to one I didn't plan."

"Is this at your house?"

"No, but we'll schedule that soon."

"Okay. I'd like to meet your friends."

"It's two weeks from Tuesday. I'll pick you up."

"According to my planner, I have a court date for a pro bono case. That could change, however, if our negotiation strategy works, but I'll call and let you know where I'll be."

Saturday, February 3

Lainie hired Carrie's daughter Jane and her friends Julie Cavanaugh, Mark Trumbull, and Dylan Gregory to help to help clean out the debris of Uncle Walter's workshop in the garage. When the work was done and the helpers' hours recorded, the kids got a bonus of milk and cookies.

"They're good workers," Lainie remarked once the boys went home and the girls sat at the kitchen table doing homework. "Maybe we can depend on them in the future."

"I agree." Carrie smiled. "They worked well as a team. Let's put them on the list."

Sunday, February 11

Lainie was just getting into bed when the phone rang.

"Hi. How was your day?" John sounded mellow.

She smiled. "Good. Very good. How about you?"

"My lesson went well."

"What did you teach?"

"Abraham and Isaac."

"Not an easy subject. How do you teach that to little kids?"

"A Primary lesson usually hits the high spots. There are the facts of the story, and then there's the major Atonement metaphor. When you don't have any big-time sins to your credit, it's hard to understand the need for repentance, but these kids are pretty perceptive."

Lainie settled against the pillow. "Abraham didn't volunteer for anything."

"Neither did Isaac, but they both had to be willing to take the test anyway."

"Just like with some of life's educational experiences. Submissiveness is everything."

"That's true." John paused. "Look, I called to let you know that my court date has changed and I'll be at home on the thirteenth."

"I think I can remember how to get there."

"Are you sure you don't want me to meet you?"

"No, it's okay. It's my treat."

"Well, it'll be a treat to spend some time with you."

"Thank you, John. I'll pick you up at six."

"See you Tuesday. Good night, Lainie."

She went to bed smiling. She'd never been so comfortable with a man before, not even Max, and she suspected she and John could talk for hours and still have more to say. Nearly all of her preconceived notions about him had been shattered now. She wondered what else she would learn about him at her Sweet Souls' Valentine's dinner.

Tuesday, February 13

Lainie rang John's doorbell at six o'clock.

"Right on time." He pulled on his jacket and followed her out to her car. "I like a girl who knows how to read a clock." He opened the door for her, then got in the passenger side and asked, "So where is this party?"

"At my ward meetinghouse." She waited for him to buckle his seat belt before she drove away. "You're in a good mood. Things are going well?"

"Extremely well. My pro bono client settled out of court." As they drove through the busy traffic to the other side of town, he told her about attending CLE seminars—continuing legal education—to gear up for expanding services at the firm. "Things have changed since Morgan and I were in law school, and we haven't dealt with some of these issues in our practice. CLE is bringing us up to speed."

As Lainie pulled into the church parking lot, John asked, "Now what kind of party is this?"

"Single Adults."

"Single Adults?"

"You say that like it's a bad thing."

"But I don't do Single Adults. I told you before . . ."

"It's a great group. You'll be pleasantly surprised." He frowned. "Oh, come on, John. It'll be fun." She got out of the car and he followed her inside.

In the cultural hall she watched John blanch when he saw old people, some chatting, some bustling around getting ready to serve the meal. Lainie's heart sank as he surveyed the room. His jaw tightened and his eyes asked, "What am I doing here?" She looked at the tables decorated with hearts, cupids, lacy valentines, and heart-shaped candies with pitifully stupid sayings printed on them, and realized it had been a mistake to bring him to this party. People greeted her with hugs, and John forced a smile as she introduced him. He shook hands and made small talk, but she could tell he felt more uncomfortable by the minute.

When there was a break, he whispered, "Yeah, this is fun."

Lainie rolled her eyes. "I'm the Single Adult leader in this ward, and these are my Sweet Souls. They invited the singles from the other two wards that meet in this building."

"What are you, the queen bee?"

"Well, yes. We'll have to sit in the middle because they all want to be next to me. It's kind of like elementary school that way. Sorry."

"But they've got valentines all over the place," John muttered, a smile pasted on his face. "You didn't tell me about that. A guy could easily find evidence of sabotage."

Now she realized people were watching him, sizing him up like judges assess beauty pageant contestants, weighing him in the balance, deciding if he was good enough to be here with her. Of course he was uncomfortable. "It's February, John. What did you expect—presidents?"

"I *hate* Valentine's Day," he replied just loud enough for Lainie to hear. "Stupidest holiday on the calendar. Dumber than Halloween."

"I'm sorry, Counselor. If you want to leave, I can make excuses."

"Not on your life," he said through his artificial grin. "If I took you away they'd hunt me down and beat me senseless with canes and walkers. I can see it all now. Not pretty."

As people found places to sit, Millie, the party committee chair, got everyone's attention. She welcomed them and called on one of the brethren to pray, which he did at length, and then she assigned the order of tables going to the buffet line.

Despite the good food, Lainie was now acutely aware that dinner conversation at the table—ranging from medical treatments and retired children to quilting and funeral expenses—didn't interest John, although she could tell he was trying to make the best of it, nodding and sort of smiling. Left-handed and seated in close quarters, he kept bumping elbows with Lainie. He accepted seconds of some pretty good homemade cherry cheesecake, a universal Valentine's or Presidents' Day dessert.

A tall, stooped brother with a full head of white hair accompanied himself on the piano as he sang love songs from the 1930s and '40s for half an hour. John applauded with what seemed like enthusiasm. When the audience called for encores, the man pulled out another stack of well-worn music, and John whispered, "I'm done, Cinderella. Unless we leave in the next ten minutes, I'll turn into a team of angry mice."

Lainie glanced at his face and knew it was prudent to surrender. Passing Millie at the end of the table, she hugged and thanked her friend for organizing the Valentine party.

Out in the hall, John sighed a deep sigh and looked at his watch. He said nothing until they got into the car, and when he finally spoke, the edge in his voice was unmistakable. "You know, this is practically actionable. I could bring you up on charges."

"What?"

"Failure to disclose. False pretenses. Fraud has many names. You should have told me where you were taking me."

"It's just a party, John." She gripped the steering wheel with both hands, as if taking a tight curve. "You didn't fully disclose that we were going to your condo when you invited me to a business meeting."

"Well, in this case, the judge might let you off easy if you plead *nolo contendere* and promise never to do it again."

She shivered in the cold. "Translate that to plain English."

"No contest. Guilty as charged."

Lainie frowned. "If it please the court, Judge Marchbanks, I object."

"Overruled on the merits," he growled. "Something you should know about me right now is that I don't like being trapped in a place where I feel this expectation to pair up."

"I'm sorry you didn't have fun. I did."

"You were too busy being the social butterfly to notice."

Lainie was bewildered. "Notice what?"

"Deaf people don't whisper."

"What did you hear?"

He sputtered for a moment as if trying to find words. "Look, my life is simple and uncomplicated and I like it that way. Let's understand that right now."

"They said something about us?"

"Now that we're gone, I'm quite sure we'll be the main topic of conversation when they break out the dominos."

Lainie started the car and turned on the defrost to clear the condensation on the windows. "John, that's really paranoid. Not very attractive at all."

He reached inside his coat to scratch his left shoulder. "Then I guess you just discovered what a petty little man I really am. Maybe you should take me home now. I'm sorry I spoiled your evening."

Too angry to drive, she stared ahead, calming herself. "What happens now?"

He took a deep breath and blew it out before buckling his seat belt. "I guess we need some dispute resolution. That's where I say I'm sorry for acting like a pretentious popinjay." Then he tried to explain himself. "Look, it was unfamiliar territory. Maybe I overreacted."

"You think?"

"I'm sorry if I embarrassed you in front of your friends."

Lainie didn't hold back. "Unlike some of your little lawyer friends, my Sweet Souls have no guile, and contrary to your personal preference it *is* Valentine's Day, and they want to celebrate and rejoice in the love they've known in their lives, and why not? Love is the best thing that can happen to anybody. To be honest, I envy them because they have memories of love that I'll never know." Her voice and her anger rose even more. "Henry, the piano man, lost his wife two years ago, and it brings her back for a little while when he can sing for somebody else the love songs he used to sing to her. Those three women sitting across the table from us are widows this past year, and this is their first Valentine's Day alone. What's your problem, John? Are you really such a snob?"

Leaning on his hand, he massaged his forehead with his fingers. "I try to stay in control and avoid these moments, but sometimes I hit the wall and come face to face with what I am and what I'm not. All those people are nice enough, I'm sure, but I'm extremely uncomfortable being reminded of where I'm headed. It's just a thing I have."

Lainie stared at him in disbelief, her anger unabated. "I'm not coming to that pity party, John. You're headed for death, just like everybody else, and sometimes it's tough getting there. I've already wrestled that alligator and it doesn't scare me anymore. That's what I have in common with these people. They're not afraid of it either."

"What are you talking about?"

She leaned back in the seat. She hadn't intended to bring that up, but there it was, and maybe he should know. It might make a difference. It mattered before. Maybe John was more like Max than she thought. How disappointing. If they were going to have this discussion, however, she wanted to be someplace warm. She put the car in gear and drove the few blocks to her house, regretting that Max was the standard by which she judged other men. Not waiting for John to help her out of the car, she hurried inside, dropped her coat and purse on a chair, and stood there getting her emotions under control.

John closed the door, put his coat on the chair, and waited next to her. "I'm ready to listen." She looked in his eyes and saw reassurance and trust. His voice was tender as he smiled and shrugged. "If you can't talk to your attorney, who *can* you talk to?"

She sat on the sofa and leaned back on the pillows to stare at the ceiling. He sat beside her. "Just now as we left, Millie said, 'Thanks for coming. You're our oxygen supply.' How ironic is that? I'm the life-giver now. I never thought . . ." Lainie sat up and pushed her hair away from her face. "Look, four and a half years ago surgeons removed a golf-ball-sized malignant tumor from the lower left quadrant of my left breast. I had chemotherapy to shrink the tumor, reconstructive surgery when they removed what was left of it, and then radiation. I was sick and bald and miserable, and it was months before I was certain of the prognosis." She turned to him, tears starting down her cheeks. "But I learned to believe in life before death. I have an eighty-five-percent chance of survival after five years, and a sixty-five-percent chance after twenty years. Every day is truly joyful for me, and I'm grateful to God for giving me another opportunity to get it right. So please don't tell me . . ." Her words dissolved into sobs.

"I'm so sorry," John murmured, taking her in his arms. "Oh, Lainie, it must have been terrible. That's a heartbreaking loss. I'm sorry."

She sniffed against his shoulder. "It's all right for you to be sorry for me, but I won't be sorry for myself." When she finished crying, she reached for a tissue in the box on the sofa table. "Who knew I had a full-service attorney? He creates my business, he fixes my dinner, and then I find out he has a nice comfortable shoulder to cry on."

"I left that part out of the brochure," John confessed. "It's just for my A-List clients anyway." He laughed with her. "Are you okay?"

"I'm okay." She sighed and straightened his tie. "I haven't cried about it for quite a while. You think you're finished grieving, and then you talk about it, and all the feelings come back again, even after all this time."

"I guess the worst thing that ever happened to me was breaking my leg the first time I went skiing my first year in Utah. It also fractured my enthusiasm for winter sports."

She laughed again and looked into his very blue eyes. Her smile faded and she whispered, "John, something about you inspires a return to turmoil."

"No, Lainie, I don't want to take you there. Look, I'm really sorry. I was wrong about everything tonight."

"And you're face to face with what I am, and what I'm not."

"I see a whole woman—intelligent, kind, and creative. I like what I see."

She took a deep breath. "I've never known anyone like you. I don't know what to think."

"I'm just an ordinary, garden-variety guy, obviously not too clever, not too bright."

"No, John, there's nothing ordinary about you at all."

"Well, it's what my sister told me when I was fifteen."

"Sisters can be wrong." Lainie paused. "You probably want to go home now."

She watched a range of emotions play out in his eyes before he asked, "Are you really okay?"

"You were really here to catch me when I stumbled, and I'm really okay now."

He took her hands. "If you need me, I'll stay."

Do I need him? Do I need anyone? If he stays, what happens next? I'm not sure I want to go there. I like the feel of his arms around me. That's unsettling enough. "It's sweet of you to offer," she said, "but I'm fine."

They said very little on the way. Light snow began to fall as she steered the car up the hill into Quail Valley, and when she pulled in front of John's place and stopped, they turned to look at each other. "You're terrific, Lainie. I was wrong about everything else tonight, but not that." He touched her chin. "Good night, Irish." He turned and reached for the door handle.

"What's a popinjay?" she asked, not ready to let him go.

He closed the door. "John Marchbanks. You'll find it in any dictionary."

"Thanks for clearing that up."

He sat back in the seat again, his hand on the console between them. "One of our crusty old first-year law professors used to call us that when our brains weren't in gear. He said it's usually cross-referenced with 'bungling bubblehead.'"

Laughing, Lainie took John's hand. "Thanks for being there, Counselor. We need to plan a time for you to come to my house for dinner."

"Yes, I'm really looking forward to that."

"I'll check my calendar."

"I will too." He squeezed her hand.

She couldn't think of anything else to say to hold him there longer. "Well, good night."

~~~

Reluctantly he got out of the car and watched her drive away. He put his hands in his pockets, wishing he could make a portrait of her, the way her face glowed when she talked about loving life. He forgot it was a cold, snowy night and walked around the neighborhood thinking about her, until squeaking sounds of his shoes in the accumulating snow drew his attention, and he went home to warm up with a cup of hot chocolate. When he was ready for bed, he got a sketch pad from the studio, sat in the living room, and began to draw her very appealing face—broad forehead, strong jawline, that tiny cleft in her chin, magnificent cheekbones, a well-proportioned nose, and a slight overbite in a mouth that smiled easily.

~~~

Driving home, Lainie realized she had seen several dimensions of John tonight. Caring and complex, he would always be a surprise. When they met in December, she thought getting to know him would be like peeling away the layers of an onion, but now she realized it was more like the rich, sweet layers of baklava, with honey and spices and a handful of nuts.

She got ready for bed, said her prayers, and then sat for a long time reflecting on the events of the evening. She was turning out the light when the phone rang.

"Are you all right?" It was John.

"Yes." She snuggled into the pillow. "I'm not hurt. Really."

"I'm honored that you trust me enough to tell me about your breast cancer. You didn't have to."

"I know some men are uncomfortable talking about things like that."

"I don't know why. It's a disease, and that calls for compassion."

Thoughts of Max skittered through her mind. "Some men aren't very compassionate. Some would say I'm damaged goods."

"Then they're idiots. I meant it when I said I look at you and see a whole woman."

"Thank you for that." Tears of gratitude started. John wasn't a bit like Max.

"It was impressive to see how much those people love you."

"Well, I love them. I'm sorry if you felt left out. I didn't mean to do that."

"There's no need to apologize. Once I stopped being defensive, I felt proud to be there with you. I do value our friendship."

"It's important to me too." She paused. "Do you like baklava? It's my favorite comfort food. Driving home tonight I started thinking about it."

"I've had it a few times. Kind of sticky, isn't it?"

"I serve it with forks. When you come to my house for dinner, I'll make some for you."

He chuckled. "I'm looking forward to that."

"Me too. Thank you for calling."

"I just wanted to be sure you're all right."

"I am." She waited, just listening to him breathe.

"Well, sweet dreams, Lainie."

"You too."

~

John hung up the phone and drew a few more strokes on the portrait. Having breast cancer wasn't like having the flu. He couldn't imagine

Lainie lying in a hospital bed, weakened by chemotherapy, losing that magnificent hair. She was meant to be up and doing, bringing good into the world. He remembered the scent of her hair and the startling warmth of her body, the way she melted into him when he took her in his arms. He hadn't held a woman that way in a very long time, but in those few moments, he had felt the strength of her spirit. It still shook him. When she stopped crying, he hadn't wanted to let her go.

He propped the unfinished drawing on the dresser, then sat on the bed and looked at it for a long time. It was a face he could get used to. He said his prayers and turned off the light. In his last moments of consciousness, he decided to follow the fascination.

Five

Valentine's Day, Wednesday, February 14

Arriving at Sophie's Place late the next morning, Lainie found Carrie and Angela in the kitchen admiring a vase of bright-yellow roses.

"They're for you," Carrie said.

Lainie pulled the card out of the little envelope and silently read, *I wasn't wrong about the most important thing.* He signed it with a simple, uncluttered *J.* She could almost feel his arms around her again.

Carrie and Angela, who had been there since seven finishing the cake and preparing refreshments, awaited an explanation. "It's just that . . ." Lainie began. "Well, he . . . Oh, I'll tell you later. It's . . . well . . . complicated."

"What kind of complicated?" Carrie frowned.

Lainie threw her hands in the air. "We'll talk later, I promise. Let's just get these kids married today." She picked up the vase and went to the sitting room.

"Who are they from?" Angela mumbled as she and Carrie continued stuffing tiny puff pastries with chicken salad filling. "Does she have a secret admirer?"

"John Marchbanks went to a party with her last night." Carrie looked at Angela and frowned. "Maybe something happened that required an apology."

"Or something good. Did you see her face when she read the card?"

"If he did anything . . . Well, I'm going to find out." She pulled off her plastic gloves and went into the sitting room. Lainie sat on the window seat holding the vase of flowers, wiping her eyes with a tissue.

Carrie sat next to her, a hand on her shoulder. "It's John, isn't it? Did he hurt you?"

Lainie sighed and turned to Carrie. "Did you know he hates Valentine's Day, and doesn't particularly like old people either?"

"No. It's never come up in our conversations."

Lainie squeezed her eyes tight shut, reliving the frustration of the night before. "It's so irrational and so disappointing. He's nice and smart and funny, and I didn't want him to be just another shallow guy, but he was." She shook her head. "I scolded him for it, but then he apologized, and then I told him about my cancer, and I started to cry, and he . . . well, he held me and comforted me and said he was sorry." Tears started again.

"John? Our John Marchbanks did that?"

"He was very sweet and humble about it. Gentle. And understanding." She put the vase on the corner of the desk and reached for another tissue.

Carrie followed her. "And this morning he sent yellow roses. That's a symbol of friendship. So why are you crying?"

Lainie turned and leaned against the desk. "Sorry about the meltdown, but no one has ever sent me flowers like this before."

"No one? That's odd."

"When I had cancer, a lot of people did, but this time it was different. Except for some of the men in my family, no other man has ever said he was sorry that I lost a part of my breast to cancer. John said he sees me as a whole person, and for the first time in five years, I felt like a regular, normal woman."

"That's a side of him I've never seen." Carrie shook her head. "Remember when he went to lunch with us and acted like such a dimwit?"

Lainie laughed and wiped her nose again. "You know, I fully intended to choke him with my bare hands that day."

Carrie put her arm around Lainie. "It would have been justifiable homicide, and Morgan would have cheerfully defended you in court. Just so you know. But if it makes you feel any better, I'm canceling my plan to hire a hit man."

"That's good." Lainie hugged her friend. "Come on. Let's do a wedding."

It went well, the bride and groom taking their vows with quiet confidence while the parents shed some tears. Later Lainie escaped to the sitting room to call John. She knew he was busy at work. "Thank you for the flowers," she said to his answering machine. "I wasn't wrong about you, either. Hope to see you again before the roses fade."

Sunday, February 18

When Lainie returned late Sunday night from visiting her parents she found a phone message from John. "Hi. Just wanted to tell you something one of my Primary kids said today. We were talking about friendship—David and Jonathan—and a little redheaded girl, who reminds me of you, said a friend is somebody you're not afraid to cry in front of. And I thought about us the other night. I hope that makes us friends." He paused. "I mean, I know we are, and this is getting more complicated than I meant it to be, but I hope we're better friends now. Sorry I missed you. I have CLE on Monday in Salt Lake, but I'll call you Tuesday night."

Hearing his voice, the sincerity in it, Lainie knew they were good friends, and friends pay attention to each other, take time for each other, each caring about what happens to the other. He called Tuesday, as promised, and several more times late at night over the next couple of weeks. Lainie had never experienced anything like this before, and she had to admit she enjoyed it.

Wednesday, March 6

"I'll get it," Lainie said when the phone rang. "It's my turn." At her desk, Carrie studied the proofs of posters for their advertising campaign.

"I got the part," John announced.

"What part were you missing?"

"I'm in a play at a theater in Orem," he said when he finished laughing. "That kind of part."

"When did this happen?"

"Auditions were last Tuesday. I'm playing Ed in *You Can't Take It with You.* It isn't a leading role, but music is involved, and the play is a classic comedy. We had a read-through last night, and I don't have a rehearsal until Saturday, so I was thinking maybe you could come over Friday night and help me learn lines."

"I don't know much about it, but I guess I could come to the aid of a desperate thespian."

"I'll pick you up at six. I can fix us something to eat."

"No, you won't. It's my turn. Remember?"

"Oh, yes, the baklava."

"You concentrate on learning lines, and I'll give some backstage support. Come to my place at six thirty with an appetite."

"Thanks, Lainie. I'm looking forward to it."

"See you Friday. And congratulations." She laughed as she hung up the phone and sat cross-legged in the window seat. "He got the part he wanted."

"What part?" Carrie asked.

"Ed in *You Can't Take It with You.* A theater company in Orem is producing it."

"That's one of my favorite plays. They made a movie of it back in the '40s, but it wasn't nearly as good as the play."

Lainie nodded. "It sounds familiar. I think I've seen it. So John's an actor too?"

"Mmm-hmm. He caught the acting bug when he took a class in college. Thought it might be useful if he ever went into trial law."

"There's yet another layer of John Marchbanks revealed. He's coming to my house for dinner Friday night and I'm going to help him learn lines."

"Sounds like an interesting date."

"It isn't a date, really, it's just . . ."

"Are you getting together to do something fun?"

"Yes, but . . ."

Carrie rolled her eyes. "Trust me, Lainie, it's a date."

Wide-eyed, Lainie stared at her. "Oh. Do you think he knows that?"

"Probably not. That man has been in denial about women since I've known him. He has dated occasionally, but never the same person more than two or three times."

Lainie frowned and pursed her lips. "Hmm. I guess that's why he called that dinner at his condo last month a business meeting."

Carrie chuckled. "Calling it a date might feel too threatening."

"Yeah, for both of us. He is attractive and so accomplished in so many ways. I'm surprised some ambitious woman hasn't caught him by now."

Carrie shook her head. "John is equipped with radar. He's always in charge, and he'll never be taken by the devious design of some ambitious siren's call. He finds that kind of stuff highly resistible."

Lainie sat back and folded her arms. "Okay. I've wondered about it since I met him, and now I'm going to say it out loud. What's wrong with him? Why isn't he married?"

"As a matter of fact, I asked him not long ago if he'd ever been in love, and he said something like 'been there, done that, didn't like it, don't intend to go there again.' He's very private." Carrie frowned. "Come to think of it, he also said some people weren't meant to be married. That's as much as I've ever heard him say about it."

"Now that inspires my curiosity. Did he have some spectacular, star-crossed romance?"

"I don't know. What's your excuse?"

Lainie shrugged. "I've just never been lucky in love I guess."

"Well, Morgan knows him pretty well, but I don't think even he knows what happened." Carrie answered the ringing telephone. Lainie knew it was Morgan when Carrie said, "*Va bene.*"

Lainie liked the way Carrie and Morgan spoke to each other on the phone. Carrie's face changed, her love for her husband evident in her eyes and her voice. When they finished a phone call, Carrie always said, "I love you more . . . *baci dappertutto.*"

"What does that mean?" Lainie asked when Carrie hung up.

"What, the Italian part?" She laughed. "Kisses all over."

"That's pretty intimate."

"Well, it's okay now. We've been married seventeen years, we finally had a honeymoon, and he's taking me out to dinner tonight at Firenze when the girls go to Mutual."

"What's the occasion?"

"He's teaching me Italian and I'm having my next lesson—making small talk with the waiter and ordering food."

Lainie smiled. "It takes a lot of trust to be married, doesn't it."

"Trust, and patience, and tolerance, and lots of other qualities that take a lifetime to develop. You have to be willing to surrender everything. That doesn't mean you'll *have* to. It just means you're open to the possibilities and it's okay. When you say yes across the altar, you say yes to everything—flu, snoring, bad breath, new cars, stolen kisses, roses on your pillow."

"Do you think John is afraid of intimacy, or he's just never found the right woman?"

"Good questions. Maybe a little bit of both."

"He's not afraid of touch. He's always kissing you or patting your hand."

"Yes, he's very affectionate and easy to love, but I'm safe. I'm Morgan's wife. John doesn't have to worry about getting tangled up with me emotionally." Carrie leaned her chin on her hand. "No, I think when John falls for someone—if he'll let himself fall—it'll be hard and it'll be forever."

A constantly ringing phone kept them busy and answering questions all afternoon. Two more calls, also from word of mouth, resulted in client visits for consultations that led to booking two June wedding receptions.

"I guess the 'Open in May' sign out there in the yard doesn't mean anything to anybody but us." Carrie laughed.

"It's okay," Lainie said. "We can be flexible for a little while. This is advertising."

With three new projects to think about, Lainie settled in the window seat to search through a few files, catalogs, and magazines for ideas, but her mind kept drifting back to the mystery of John Marchbanks.

Friday, March 8

Lainie made the spinach meatballs Thursday night, along with the baklava, and at lunchtime Friday, she went home to put minestrone ingredients in the slow cooker. After work at five, she picked up a fresh baguette from Angela at the bakery, and once she got home she added pasta, fresh herbs, and a can of cannellini beans to the pot.

When John arrived he tossed his jacket on the arm of the pillowed sofa and his script on the coffee table, then followed Lainie to the kitchen. "I really like your living room." He glanced at the deep-green walls, the picture window to the west framing a little stand of trees, and the forest mural on the adjoining wall. "It reminds me of Western Oregon."

While she sliced bread and set two places at the island, he paced the kitchen explaining the play. "It opened on Broadway in 1936, deep in the Depression. It's a comedy about a big extended family of odd characters, all unemployed, trying to survive bad economic times. They're all following their lunatic passions, as if a national financial crisis didn't exist. It has a great message about living simply and being happy with what you have."

Lainie invited John to take the stool at her left and say a blessing, which he did. Then he slathered butter on a slab of bread and talked and ate with enthusiasm.

"Ed doesn't have a lot of lines, but he has a lot of stage business and he's out there when other things are happening. That means if I lose my concentration I might miss cues."

"You said odd characters. What kind?"

John paused for a drink of sparkling grape juice. "Two of the men make fireworks in the basement, thinking there's a market for something so transitory in the middle of the Depression, and the women make candy that Ed takes orders for and sells around the neighborhood. A typewriter was accidentally delivered there, so his mother-in-law Penny is writing a novel. Sometimes they take in strays, which means more mouths to feed. That's how Ed met Essie."

"So they're generous, compassionate people," Lainie said. "Rugged individualists."

"Enablers, if you ask me. Essie wants to be a ballerina—never mind that she's too old and not that good to start with—so she takes lessons once a week from Mr. Kolenkhov, a ballet master who brings the latest news of Russian royalty, as if anyone really cares, and then stays for dinner. Ed accompanies the ballet lessons on the xylophone."

Lainie put her spoon down. "You play the xylophone?"

"Not as well as I play the piano, but I've started practicing and it's coming along. There's Grandpa Vanderhof—Martin, the patriarch of the clan—and Essie's parents Penny and Paul Sycamore, and Alice, their other daughter, the only person in the family with a normal, income-producing job. Alice falls in love with Tony, the rich boss's son, and that's where the romance comes in, and the conflict. Tony's mother is a strait-laced snob."

"Isn't there any romance left in Ed and Essie's marriage?"

John scratched his left shoulder blade. "Actually, they're thinking about having a baby."

Lainie raised her eyebrows. "So it's a juicy part."

"No, but the director wants to make it juicier than it's written." He frowned. "I'm skeptical. These characters are charming adult children a step removed from reality, and to introduce something as real as a baby doesn't make sense. I think that's why Kaufman and Hart treated it so lightly in the script, and a director shouldn't mess with that."

"Isn't the director the boss of this whole enterprise?"

"Yeah, but he also knows that maybe in rehearsals we'll find that the new interpretation doesn't work." John took another piece of bread and concentrated on buttering it. "I can play it any way he wants. You might find it hard to imagine, but I have played love scenes before. On stage, I mean. Bear in mind that it's only make-believe."

She questioned him with skeptical look.

"Let's just say I'm familiar with the procedure involved in kissing and leave it at that." He concentrated on dipping the bread in his soup.

"Well, that's not really the question. Mainly you're worried about playing a husband because you've never actually been one yourself." He nodded but didn't say anything. "Why don't you talk to Morgan? He's pretty good at it."

"That's true. When Carrie left, he learned not to take anything for granted. I wouldn't recommend separation as therapy for every marriage, but it worked for them. Now he calls her three or four times a day just to say he loves her more now than he did the last time he called."

"Yes, I've heard the other end of that conversation. It makes me blush sometimes. Did you know they write love letters to each other every week?"

"That honeymoon will never be over. I don't know how he gets any work done."

"What about your own parents?"

He paused. "They were respectful, courteous, and faithful, but they were never very affectionate with each other—at least nothing I ever saw."

"Maybe they were exhausted from raising five kids."

John chuckled. "Could be. Something made it easy for my sister Katie and my brother Brennan to take vows of poverty and celibacy and devote themselves to the Catholic Church. Marriage didn't appeal to either of them."

"Well, my parents were very affectionate, madly in love, and they didn't care who knew it," Lainie said. "They always kissed when one of them left the house or came home, not one of those sexless bogus air kisses, but a genuine, sincere, firmly planted smackeroo. Every night after dinner, Dad went into the living room to read the newspaper, and as he left the table, he'd kiss Mother and thank her for the meal."

John smiled. "Sweet. I can see how that would give a child a real sense of security."

"Once when I was in high school, one of my friends came to the house, and my parents were sitting on the sofa, Mother on Dad's lap, smooching like teenagers. It was no big deal to me—they did that all the time—but my friend was in shock the rest of the night. I felt sorry because her parents didn't even like each other anymore."

"You think Ed should be like your dad." John finished his drink, then wiped his mouth and put the napkin by the empty soup bowl.

"Sure. He's a good role model. It doesn't mean everything was rosy all the time." Lainie led the way to the living room. "They dealt with disagreements respectfully because they've always believed that God is a partner in their marriage." On the sofa she sat with her feet under her and leaned on a loose cushion. "What about you? Since you didn't become a priest, your parents probably expected you to find a wife."

John, seated in an armchair, bristled and drew back. "Do you kiss and tell?"

"I don't think I've ever really been in love," Lainie said. "I thought I was once, but I was mistaken. As a teenager and in college I was often in serious 'like.' There wasn't much kissing, so there isn't a lot to tell. I haven't dated at all in the last five years."

He stared ahead. "You do dumb things when you're a kid. You think you know it all. You think you have everything under control, and then you discover how incredibly clueless you are."

Lainie frowned at his sounding so bitter. He turned to her and asked, "So you never came close?"

"I was engaged once, about five years ago. I was over thirty and willing to settle for companionship in my old age. After all, life does require some compromise, doesn't it? A month before the wedding I was diagnosed with cancer, and—what can I say? He cancelled everything the next day and I never saw him again."

John shook his head in disbelief. "You're kidding. That's unconscionable."

She shrugged. "It doesn't matter now. My life is full, and marriage isn't the only way to be happy. If I'm alone in my old age at least I'll be in good company. Of course, no hopeful eighteen-year-old girl sits down to draw up a life plan that includes becoming a forty-year-old virgin, but after cancer, even that looks good."

"It must have been terrible going through that alone."

"I wasn't alone. I have friends and family who love and support me. And God loves me."

John smiled. "I really admire you, Lainie. I like your confidence."

"You're not so bad yourself." She gave him an impish smile and picked up the script. "Let's get to work." She read the cues he'd marked, and in the next hour he memorized the lines, pounded on an imaginary xylophone, paced, pantomimed, and entertained her with his antics.

When he could recite every line perfectly, she applauded, as much for his creativity and playfulness as for his quick memorization skill. He took a curtain call with the drapes and threw himself down on the sofa. "Thanks, Irish. Now I'm ready."

"This is exciting." She rubbed her hands together. "I've never been close to an actual theatrical production. I've never even met an actor before. What happens next?"

"We learn the blocking, which is how we move around on stage, which the director determines, and which is mind-numbingly tedious, but then the fun begins. Rehearsals and performances are energizing and creative. I especially like that part of the process."

"How often do you rehearse?"

"The schedule's in the back of the script. I'm only in the Tuesday–Thursday–Saturday cast, but I'm the understudy for the other Ed. That's sort of like being on call."

Lainie opened the script and found the page. "Fifteen performances is a huge commitment."

"This is a popular play and the producers expect it to sell out. In fact, they just added two more Saturday matinees I'll be doing."

"That's good. And bad. I won't see you very much."

"I'll be busy most evenings, but we have late phone calls, and we can sneak out for lunch now and then, can't we?" He reached around and scratched his shoulder again.

"You've been scratching all night. What's up with that?"

"I've got a mole back there that itches all the time. It's worse the last few weeks."

"Let me see it."

He undid a couple of buttons, turned his shoulder toward her, and pulled the clothes aside. She saw a dark-brown and black crescent-shaped mole, about an inch and a half long, next to his shoulder blade. Several coarse black hairs grew out of it. She touched it and found it crusty.

"Does this thing hurt?"

"Not particularly."

"John, you need to have a doctor look at this."

"Okay, I'll take your word for it." He buttoned his shirt.

"Don't put it off." Lainie got up to return to the kitchen. "Want some baklava?"

After she cut the servings, he sat at the island and savored the first taste. "Mmm. Delicious. How do you make it?"

She sat next to him, her fork poised. "I've combined a couple of recipes." She explained about stacking buttered layers of paper-thin phyllo dough, sprinkling them with spices and chopped nuts, and once the baklava came out of the oven, pouring rich hot syrup over it. "There are lots of ways to make it, going back to Greece and the Middle East and even some Jewish traditions."

"Maybe you could teach me how to make it." He swooned over another bite. "Is this going to be on the menu at Sophie's Place?"

"No, I don't think so. Angela's bakery makes it a few times a year, but it's too labor-intensive to be practical for us. We might consider it for a small party if someone specifically requested it. I don't know. Some things are so distinctive you just want to save them for yourself, and for private occasions with friends. Like I said, it's my favorite comfort food."

"I'm honored," John said. "And comforted."

She smiled. "A play seems to be a time-consuming commitment. What do you do about home teaching or your Primary class while you're committed to a production?"

"Troy, my partner, isn't fond of home teaching on Sundays because that's his day with the family, but it might be the only day we have, so I'll give him tickets to compensate for upsetting his life. It's only for a couple of months." John frowned and rubbed his chin. "But there is one boy in my Primary class I'm kind of worried about. I thought I saw a bruise on his arm. My teaching partner, Curtis, says the family is fairly new in the ward."

"Bruises might mean a lot of things."

"I know. He's the saddest child I've ever seen. His name is Will. He's there every week, but he doesn't smile or talk to anyone or answer questions in class. He always looks like he needs a good night's sleep. Two weeks ago when I was making a point about God's love for His children, I looked at this kid and there were tears streaming down his face. That haunts me."

"When it comes to the safety of children, it's best to speak up," Lainie said.

"Yeah, I know. Curtis and I decided to see if the bishop is aware of something going on." Finished with the dessert, John put down his fork and smiled at her. "Hey, you haven't told me how things are going at Sophie's Place."

"We're already getting lots of practice because people keep asking us to take on small events, and we can't say no. There's a bridal fair next week at the mall that coincides with the beginning of our ad campaign. We don't have time to spend there ourselves but we can display a poster and leave brochures."

"You can never get too much good publicity."

"Actually, we're finding that word of mouth is the best advertising. After those two weddings we did last month, we have seven definite bookings for May and June, and five more tentative ones. And we haven't even had our open house yet."

"That's great." He wiped his mouth with a napkin and looked at his watch. "Well, I've got an early rehearsal tomorrow so I'd better take off."

"It's been great having you here." She patted his hand and he kept it for a quick squeeze.

"I really appreciate your help with learning lines. It's so much easier when you have someone to toss cues."

"Is that what I did?" They got up and went back to the living room.

"Thanks for the great minestrone and the fabulous baklava. I really liked it with filberts."

"Filberts?"

"Hazelnuts. In the Northwest we call them filberts, after the guy who started the industry. Good choice for baklava." John put on his jacket and grabbed the script. "Anyway, I have to give up chocolate and dairy products when I'm in a play, so that was just right."

"What is it, Lent or something?"

"That stuff coats the vocal cords and I can't project my voice as well. I also have to let my hair grow. They wore it longer in the '30s."

"That's not such a hardship. It looks nice."

At the door John smiled again and put a hand on her shoulder. "Thanks for all the help understanding Ed. I think I've got it now. Good night, Irish." She smiled and started to say something when without any warning he bent down and kissed her, a warm, soft touch on her lips, as if it were routine. Shock waves flashed through her, a startling, intense feeling that she wanted to do that again. He opened the door and walked away about four steps before he stopped, slapped his forehead, and turned to her. "Did . . . did I kiss you?"

"Yes, you did."

"It . . . I don't know . . . It seemed like the thing to do."

She floated to where he stood. "It was. I mean, I didn't mind."

"I guess I got confused." She couldn't talk, but he couldn't seem to stop. "All this chatter about kissing is bound to jumble up a person's brain. Maybe that means I'm successfully getting into character, but you . . . uh . . . you probably shouldn't read too much into that. After all, actors kiss everybody, you know, and . . ."

With her heart still doing flip-flops, she reached up, pulled his face to hers, and stopped his mouth with a genuine, sincere smackeroo. It was sweeter than the baklava still on his breath. "Read anything you want into that," she murmured. "It wasn't make-believe. Good night, Counselor." She touched his chin, turned, and went into the house.

Half an hour later when the phone rang, Lainie still hadn't stopped grinning.

"How are you?"

"I'm fine. In fact, I can't remember when I've been so fine."

"Lainie, you're a remarkable woman, and I'm really glad I know you."

"You surprise and delight me every time I see you, John. I'm really glad I know you."

He was quiet for a moment. "Well, I just want to be sure you're okay."

"I'm very okay. Do actors really kiss everybody?"

"I suppose some do, but I'm a little more selective."

"I'm glad."

"Me too. Sweet dreams, Lainie."

"Good night, John."

She lay in the dark smiling, remembering how it was. It felt like a natural consequence of the whole easy, comfortable evening. And then her smile faded when she realized that things change when someone kisses you.

Six

Monday, March 11

"How was your date with John?" Carrie asked when Lainie came in.

"He's quick and memorizes easily. He has a very good mind."

"So it wasn't that bad spending a couple of hours with him."

Lainie put her jacket on the coat rack. "He's very pleasant and charming and funny and interesting. We're friends. You don't need to read anything into that."

"John's my best male friend right after Morgan," Carrie declared.

"Do you wish you'd met him first?"

"Oh, goodness, no. John may be pleasant and charming and funny and interesting, but I could never be married to him. Eeeww. He's practically my brother."

Lainie stared out the window, an amused frown on her face. "He talked about doing dumb things when you're a clueless kid. I'm still trying to figure that out."

"I don't know much about his life before he joined the Church."

"It was a little moment of mystery that puzzled me, that's all."

"Well, don't let it . . ." Carrie picked up the ringing telephone. "Hi, Angela . . . Oh, no . . . I'm so sorry . . . Can I help? . . . No. Do what you have to do, and I'll talk to you tomorrow." She hung up and sighed. "Poor Angela."

"What is it?"

"Her son Brandon spent the weekend in Park City with his dad, and nothing good ever comes of that. Sean doesn't believe in discipline, for himself or anyone else. Now Angela has to deal with some kind of trouble Brandon's in because Sean won't. She didn't have time to tell me all the details, but she won't be in this afternoon."

"I feel so bad for her, trying to be the only parent," Lainie said.

"Yeah. What that boy needs is a dad who's an actual father."

Thursday, March 14

Once the advertising campaign launched, phone and foot traffic increased, along with Angela's output of Sophie's cookies, and Lainie didn't see John again until the following week.

"Any chance you could get away for lunch?" he asked when he called that morning.

"I think so. I'd like to see what kind of day it is before the sun goes down."

"If 1:30 isn't too late, we could meet then at the Brick Oven."

He reached the restaurant first and smiled when she came in. Most of the lunch crowd was gone now. He reached for her hand. "Hi. Thanks for taking time to get away with me."

"It's a relief to escape the madness at Sophie's Place today."

When they got to the table, Lainie said to the server, "I'll have a chicken Caesar salad."

"Good idea," John said. "Make it two, please, and . . ." He looked at Lainie. "Water to drink?" She nodded and the server went away. John returned his attention to Lainie as they sat down. "Sophie's Place is pretty busy, huh?"

"We have ten more bookings, and the phone rings constantly. We're answering lots of questions and going through dozens of cookie and cake samples."

"I tried to call you three times before I finally got through."

"We're going to have to add another phone line. How's the play going?"

"Really good. Playing the xylophone is a lot of fun. I am having a little problem with costuming, though. I'm supposed to wear one of those old-fashioned undershirts in one scene—you know, like a tank shirt—but I'm reluctant for several reasons. For one thing, I don't want to draw attention to this ugly thing on my shoulder blade."

"Haven't you seen a doctor yet?"

"No, but a little hydrocortisone cream settles the itch. I guess I could cover it with makeup."

Lainie frowned. "John, please don't put it off."

"When I was a kid, I worked on a ranch in Eastern Oregon every summer to earn money for college, and I wore jeans, boots, and a hat from June to September. Had a spectacular tan for a few years, nearly the same color as that mole, but it faded when I started spending time in the law library."

She took a deep breath. "Okay, you exercise your bravado, and I won't mention it again."

When their salads arrived, she unfolded the napkin on her lap. John talked about the fun of rehearsals, and the humor and wisdom of the play, and she told him news of her Sweet Souls and preparations at Sophie's Place.

They were almost finished with their salads when Lainie smiled at him and leaned on one hand. "I know I said I wasn't going to mention it again, but I'm very serious about you having a doctor look at that thing on your shoulder."

"I'm involved in another Legal Services case right now, and with the play and work and my Primary class, I just haven't had time. But really, I intend to see a doctor as soon as possible."

"What kind of case?"

"Divorce proceedings for the parents of that boy in my class."

"But you don't do trial law."

"Actually, things are almost in place for us to do the expansion we've planned at the firm. We both have to do a little more CLE and then we're going to make one of our associates a partner and hire another associate. Many of the businesses we advise involve families, and sometimes they need these kinds of services. This was the next logical step for us."

"But the family of the boy in your Primary class wasn't a client before."

"No. I volunteered to be guardian ad litem for Will and Kendra, and the judge agreed."

"Guardian? They don't come to live with you, do they?"

John shook his head. "In a case where minor children are involved, the court appoints an attorney as guardian ad litem to represent their best interests during the trial." He frowned and put his fork down. "This family moved here last year from out of state. Curtis says his wife told him the marriage was already shaky, and then the husband fell into old patterns with the pressures of the new job. Friends convinced the wife to go to Legal Services for help. When the husband found out, he . . . well, she's in the hospital."

"Oh, no," Lainie breathed. "Poor woman."

"When Will came home from school and found his mother doubled over in pain, he called me because Primary teachers always know what to do, he said. When I got there, I called an ambulance and the police."

"It's a good thing he felt he could trust you."

"Kendra's five or six and has that haunted look too. Will was starting to act like a real kid after the mother threw the husband out and put a restraining order on him two weeks ago. Will actually smiled in Primary last Sunday."

"Where's the dad now?"

"In jail, charged with assault and battery, but he'll probably make bail by this afternoon. He's apparently some kind of genius his company can't function without, so they'll do what it takes to get him back. If the attending physician will corroborate, we may be able to pin attempted manslaughter on him too, and put him away for a good long time."

"When did this assault happen?"

"Yesterday. I was just picking up the phone to call you when Will called me." John frowned. "Curtis and his wife are taking care of Will and Kendra while their mother is hospitalized, and I think I can convince the judge to let them stay there with someone they know instead of sending them into a more formal foster-care situation. We went with the bishop last night to give the mother a blessing." John reached across the table and squeezed Lainie's hand. "This isn't very good dinner conversation. I'm sorry."

She sensed his tender feelings and smiled. "Let's take a walk."

~

John left money on the table and they strolled hand in hand, enjoying the early spring warmth. They climbed the stairs slowly toward the oldest part of the BYU campus. At a landing halfway up the hill they sat on a concrete bench next to a bed of spring bulbs in full bloom.

"John, it's very touching that you care so deeply about this boy in your class."

She put one hand in her coat pocket and he held the other one. "When I was first called to teach Primary," he said, "I had serious doubts about my ability to do it successfully."

"You've taught before, haven't you?"

"Oh yeah—Young Men, elders. I've always liked kids, but I wasn't sure I was the teacher this class needed. So I prayed about it, and the next Sunday at church we sang the hymn "Dear to the Heart of the Shepherd." It's one of my favorites anyway, but that day the text really spoke to me. One of the verses says "make me thy true under-shepherd," and I realized that was the answer to my prayer. I was called to be a stand-in for the Savior in that classroom, to teach the children and love them as He would if He were there. That's how important those kids are, and the Spirit told me I was up to the challenge. It's been a very humbling experience."

Lainie nodded. "That's how I feel about my Sweet Souls. They can be like children too. Sometimes the aging process is frightening and they do things that aren't very lovable. You look at children and see the future. I look at my Sweet Souls and see the past."

John stroked her cheek with his thumb. "You comfort me. Thank you."

"I'm just me. I have no special gift."

He held her chin and placed a gentle kiss on her mouth. "Lainie, you *are* the gift." They sat with their arms around each other until, in a few minutes, a bell rang in a building at the top of the hill. John looked at his watch and sighed. He took her hand and they strolled down the stairs to the Brick Oven parking lot. He embraced her again as they stood by her car. "Thanks for being with me today. Thanks for listening."

"I'm glad I could."

He smiled and felt his spirit lighten. "You look great, Irish."

She hesitated before getting into the car. "That boy is lucky to have you for a Primary teacher. You're a blessing to his mother, too. I'm sure she needs that right now."

He watched her drive away. *Gift. Lainie gives me so much just by being herself. What do I have to give her?* He'd never thought of relationships that way before.

Friday, March 15

Mark Trumbull stretched out across a row of chairs in the parlor at Sophie's Place and sighed. "Okay, today we have to decide who's taking Julie to the prom. Seriously."

Dylan Gregory lay on his side in front of the fireplace. "Yeah. It's crunch time. Somebody's got to rent a tux."

Jane groaned and Julie muttered, "Here we go again."

Mark, Dylan, Jane, and Julie came to Sophie's Place after school to do homework and have cookies most days, or to work for Carrie and Lainie, but today the prom issue distracted them.

"I'm not merchandise with a price tag," Julie said. "I'll go with the person who asks me nicely."

In unison, the boys sat up and said, "Will you please go with me?"

Julie put her head in her hands.

Jane got up. "I have homework. I can't sit around listening to this all day."

Grinning, Dylan jumped up from the floor. "No, wait. I've got an idea." They turned their attention to him. "Let's flip a coin."

"Oh, that's brilliant." Jane sat down again. "I've got to hear this."

"I will not be bargained for," Julie insisted. "I don't have to go with either one of you."

"Wait." Dylan stopped them with a "sit down" gesture. "You haven't heard my guaranteed 'no loser' plan. Here's how it works—we flip a coin and the guy who calls it takes Julie to the prom, but the other guy gets to take Jane on her first date in July."

Both girls groaned and rolled their eyes again, but Mark chuckled softly. "Hey, that might work."

Dylan held up both hands again. "Wait. There's more. Part two."

"Hope it's not 'part duh,'" Julie grumbled as Jane got up again to leave.

"No, seriously, this is what we do. The non-prom-attenders—Jane and one of us—will be the maid and the butler when the other two

67

have dinner before the prom, and the prom attenders will plan Jane's spectacular birthday party. We have a lot of resources for that now, you know. Maybe Mrs. B and Lainie would let us have it here in the dining room."

Jane stood with a hand on one hip. "Think again, party boy. With all the girls at school who want to go to the prom, they need all the boys tuxed and ready to escort. Mr. Salazar is lining people up."

"Yeah, who wouldn't want to go to the prom on a date set up by the guidance counselor," Mark said. "That's bound to turn out well. Just dial 1-800-nerd-o-rama."

Dylan snorted. "Not this boy. I'm not that desperate. Besides, why should I spend all that money on a stranger? I mean, come on. Isn't voluntary servitude more appealing than a blind date to the prom?"

Mark looked at Julie. "It sounds crazy, but this could work. I wouldn't mind being a butler. On a temporary basis, of course."

Julie looked at Jane. "What do you think?"

Jane shrugged. "If Dylan doesn't really care about going to the prom, it's okay with me. Think about it from my point of view, Jules. It gives *somebody* four months to plan the best sixteenth birthday party ever."

They all looked at Julie, who finally relented. "Okay. Who's got a coin?"

Mark pulled a quarter out of his pocket, then tossed and called it. After he read it he did a victory lap up and down the aisle in the parlor, whistling and cheering. Julie sighed and shook her head.

Dylan grinned as he pointed at Jane. "I'll see you in July, chickie babe."

Just then Carrie came and stood at the parlor door. "How soon could you boys get food handlers' permits?"

"How long does it take?" Mark asked.

"You have a training class," Jane explained, "and then you have to pass this dumb little test even a retarded gorilla could pass."

"You can't say 'retarded,'" Dylan cautioned.

Jane punched his arm. "Okay. 'Special needs' gorilla."

"Back to me and my needs," Carrie said.

"Seriously," Julie grumbled, "how hard is it to remember to wash your hands?"

"What's the situation, Mrs. B?" Mark asked.

"We're doing an engagement party in two weeks here in the parlor for thirty people and we'll need some help with prep and serving. Want a job?"

The boys grinned at each other. "Sounds fun," Dylan said.

"Yeah," Mark agreed. "I'm goin' to the prom and I could use a little extra cash."

Friday, March 29

Carrie closed the folder and glanced out the window at a truck parking in front of the house. "Well, I guess that does it. Everything's in place." She handed the shopping list to Angela. "I'm glad you have time to do this today. You're our best shopper."

Angela stood to leave. "I can give myself some leeway at the bakery, but I'm still refining the art of juggling two jobs."

Carrie smiled. "Well, I hope before long it'll be just one job—here."

"I'd like that a lot." Angela turned and ran into a blue-plaid obstacle that had just stepped into the room.

"'Scuse me," it said.

"No, excuse me. I wasn't . . ." She looked up into brown eyes shaded by a baseball cap. ". . . going where I was watching . . ." A slender hand removed the hat, revealing a shock of dark-brown hair.

Carrie stood and reached across the desk. "You must be Kyle. We spoke on the phone a couple of times. I'm Carrie."

He shook her hand. "Yeah. Kyle Kirkwood."

"This is Angela Cavanaugh, one of our employees. She's so multi-talented we're still trying to figure out a title for her."

A teasing half grin crinkled Kyle's stubbly face as he looked at Angela. "Oh, I could think of one real fast." He chuckled while she fumed.

"This cheeky guy is our chief tree-trimmer and grass-cutter," Carrie said. "Aunt Sophie loves him."

"Oh. I'm sure they'll be very happy together." Angela's hands shook as she folded the grocery list and tried to find a pocket to stuff it into.

"He's Mark's uncle."

"Oh." Angela looked once more at the man's face. "My daughter Julie is going to the prom with Mark."

"It'll be okay. He's had his shots now. And that drooling thing? He's getting treatments."

"Kyle, you're scaring her. You're talking about her only daughter."

"Guess I shouldn't joke about that." He offered his hand. "I'm happy to meet you, Angela. Mark's really a nice kid and he thinks a lot of Julie."

"She's l–l–looking forward to it." Angela blinked and let go of his hand. "Bye." She broke away and hurried out the back door.

Carrie sat and pointed to a chair. "I hope you're not going to make a habit of teasing the staff."

"I don't remember when I've seen eyes like that," he said, "exactly the color of blue morning glories, or a blush that red. She can't be old enough to have a teenager."

"She has two of them, just like I do."

"Wow. Does Julie look anything like her mother?"

"Almost an exact duplicate."

"Mark's a lucky guy." He gestured toward the door. "Well, you show me the spaces and tell me your objectives, and Mark and I will start designing gardens."

Saturday, March 30

After a hectic day, Lainie looked forward to some deep and restorative sleep. Just as she climbed out of a hot bath, the phone rang. She put on a warm chenille robe and sat on the bed.

"Hi. How was your day?" John said.

She was glad to hear from him. "It was long and hard and busy. How's yours?"

"Not very good until now. I'm still at the theater. We won't be out of here until midnight. It's coming together, but it can get tedious. What gets me through it is thinking maybe you'll have lunch with me next week."

"I'd love to, but we'll be working with the builders on the final details of the remodeling. Appliances arrived yesterday, and it'll take a couple of days to install them."

"So the end is in sight."

"Uh-huh, and we're having a little celebration to mark the end of the project. Want to come? It's Friday at noon. Our attorney should look closely to see if we got our money's worth."

"I'll be there."

"Great. I'd love to see you. Hope rehearsals go well."

"That gives me something to look forward to while we're waiting for the technical hang-ups to get . . . Oh, they're calling the party game scene. Gotta run. See you Friday. Good night, Sweet Lainie."

She hung up and snuggled into bed, thinking about John's nicknames for her, and remembering that Max had always called her Elaine.

Thursday, April 4

After school, Julie, Jane, and the boys had cookies and milk in the upstairs kitchen, and then Mark found Carrie in the office. "Uncle Kyle said he talked to you the other day about landscaping."

"Yes, and we're eager to see some designs."

"I've been looking at magazines and making a few sketches."

"That's great. Let's talk while we work." Carrie got up and gestured toward the back door. In the kitchen she stopped at the table. "Snack time's over, kids. Let's get that kitchen organized. Lainie's labeling all the spaces for us so it shouldn't take long. We're having the end-of-construction party tomorrow." Carrie herded them toward the door and down the steps now sheltered by a canvas awning in the style of the house, and through the basement door now marked Employees Only.

Lainie, still unpacking a few supplies, stopped to show the teenagers the new sinks and appliances. Freezer and refrigerator space occupied the former bedroom. Worktables with stainless-steel surfaces waited for their first jobs. All of Uncle Walter's paneling was gone, the room now lined with storage units, shelves, racks, and closets. In the bathroom a shower replaced the tub, and a new laundry room had a heavy-duty washer and dryer. A trestle table and benches in the corner gave employees a place to take breaks and plan their work.

"May I point out that this is not a carnival ride," Carrie said as she instructed the kids on using the small freight elevator hidden by the slanted, refurbished cellar door. "It's only for bringing food and equipment outdoors." She also taught them how to use the dumbwaiter next to the furnace room to send food and equipment to and from the butler's pantry upstairs.

While the part-time helpers cleaned the new utensils and equipment and put them away in the designated places, Carrie and Lainie discussed with Mark the details they wanted to include in the gardens. An old-fashioned fountain garden would occupy the north corner at the end of the row of lilacs, and in Sophie's vegetable garden spot, Mark would plant vegetables in groupings and clusters instead of rows.

"I saw the concept in a garden magazine," he told them, "but I'll modify it a bit. Root crops with interesting foliage will give visitors something unusual to see and talk about while they're waiting in line, and you wouldn't have to harvest very much till after the outdoor wedding season is over."

Friday, April 5

At Sophie's Place the driveway and curb parking were jammed with construction vehicles, and John had to park down the street. He left his coat in the car and came up the front steps and into the sitting room, where he found Carrie on the phone.

"If you're not here at eight o'clock Monday morning we'll hire someone else . . . Good. I'm glad we understand each other." She hung up and threw her hands in the air. "Why can't people just do what they say they're going to do without all this drama?"

He grinned. "Welcome to the wonderful world of business."

"Well, we've had a good experience with the carpenter, anyway. He was on time and he's done some beautiful work. They had to redo that end of the front porch for handicap access, but it blends so perfectly into the Victorian style you hardly notice it."

"Looks to me like they refurbished the gingerbread as well."

"Isn't it gorgeous?" She smiled. "There's going to be an English garden in the front too, as soon as Kyle can work it into his schedule." She waited but he didn't say anything else. "Well, what can I do for you?"

"Lainie invited me to the end-of-construction party."

"Oh. She didn't tell me." Carrie got up and started toward the back door, gesturing for him to follow. "When the workers get everything cleaned up, we're going to feed them lunch."

"Well, I'm your attorney and I want to make sure you're getting what you're paying for."

Downstairs, Carrie announced, "Look who just wandered in."

Sitting on a stool arranging a platter of cream-puff sandwiches, Lainie smiled when she saw him. "Hi, John. Glad you could make it."

"Wouldn't miss it." He stood next to her with his hands in his pockets.

"You haven't met Angela." Lainie gestured across the table. "This is the ever-more-indispensable Angela Cavanaugh."

"She made the fabulous petit fours for the spectacular Single Adult party you didn't attend." Carrie put napkins and plates on a worktable at the front of the room.

John winced. "They're never going to let me live that down."

"This is John Marchbanks," Lainie said.

"Hi." Angela smiled, waved, and kept arranging cookies on a large tray.

John found a stool apart from the center of action and sat to watch the final preparations.

Carrie smiled at him. "Did we tell you Angela's also the head of the catering team? She's our first full-time employee. Our calendar is packed and we need her genius."

He watched Lainie interact with other members of the team. Seeing the passion she had for her work, he knew Sophie's Place was her new love. He'd accept it; he couldn't resent something that made her so happy, but he was sorry they wouldn't be able to spend time together today.

When the five workmen came in and lunch began, John chose some food and retreated to the stool to watch as Lainie, flushed with animated excitement, thanked the crew for their excellent workmanship and their diligence in keeping to the timetable.

The men left half an hour later, and Carrie and Angela began clearing things up. Lainie moved a stool near John. "Didn't they do a great job?"

"Looks like it to me." He put his empty plate on the nearby worktable. "Hey, it's good to see you, even for a few minutes. I have a rehearsal Saturday, but I was wondering if you'd come to my place and watch general conference with me Sunday. We could have a late breakfast and make a day of it. Afterward, you could have a nap on the couch while I fix dinner. It's my turn."

"It sounds like a lovely day. I wish I could, but I'm taking a break and spending the weekend with my parents."

"Oh," John said, covering his disappointment. "They'll be glad to see you."

"I've been so busy here I've kind of neglected them lately."

He shrugged. "Well, maybe October conference."

Laughing, Lainie touched his shoulder. "It's a date."

"Well, I'd better get going. I have an appointment back at the office. Everything was delicious. Nicely presented. This is a good thing."

"I'll see you when I get back."

"I'll call you." Walking to his car, he missed her already.

Saturday, April 6

After lunch, Mark, Dylan, Jane, and Julie prepared the garden spot before the afternoon session of general conference began. Jane and Dylan made excuses to go inside the house for a few minutes, where they found Carrie at her desk.

"Mom, we still don't know what we're going to do for Julie and Mark on prom night. Do you have any ideas that go with the Springtime in Paris theme?"

Carrie sat back in her chair. "Let's see, the last time I did anything Parisian was that Single Adult party Lainie and I organized last year."

"I remember that," Jane said. "It was really successful."

"That's where Sophie's Place got started. We had a European café theme, and in the French patisserie we had all the desserts."

"Maybe we could make it like a café." Jane looked at Dylan for approval.

"Or a bistro," Carrie suggested.

"What's that?" Dylan asked.

"A cozy little French restaurant that's casual and friendly."

"Yeah, that's what we want," Jane said. "We'll serve the entire meal before they go to the prom."

Dylan agreed. "Sounds good, and I can sing and dance. I could do *Les Miserables,* the whole thing. That's French."

Jane frowned. "We'll talk. Call me tonight after priesthood meeting and we'll talk."

"I think they'd like a singing waiter. I know the whole show."

"Dylan, you're not going to sing," Jane said.

"Where are you doing this?" Carrie asked.

"Can we do it here? In the dining room?"

Carrie glanced at her calendar. "Sure. I'll pencil you in."

"Angela wants to get pictures of Mark and Julie on the staircase," Jane added, hurrying Dylan back to the planting project in the back yard.

"Really. I can do Act 1 with the salad, Act 2 with . . ."

Jane pushed him out the door. "We'll talk later, I said. Now go dig in the dirt."

Monday, April 8

"How was your weekend?" John asked when he called late that night.

Lainie was glad to hear his voice. "Of all the Sweet Souls in my life, my parents are the sweetest."

"You're a good daughter."

"Mom has arthritis in her knees, and with Dad's wobbly blood pressure, I worry about them taking care of each other."

John paused. "Well, I'm glad you're back."

"Me too, but we have a few tough weeks ahead. How's the play going?"

"We'll be ready for Friday night. These last few dress rehearsals will actually be fun because we all know what we're doing."

"I'm looking forward to seeing you in action."

"I don't think you should come on opening night. It isn't as relaxed. I talked to Morgan and gave him three tickets for next Tuesday. Is that okay?"

"We'll make it okay. That's very thoughtful of you."

"Well, I'll see you then, anyway, backstage after the curtain call."

"Is that allowed?"

"That's tradition."

"And we can't go around breaking traditions. Thanks for the call. Good night, John."

Seven

Saturday, April 13

By Saturday morning, with Mark's design revisions finished and Jane, Julie, and Dylan hired to help, they prepared the fountain garden space while Lainie and Carrie went to Salt Lake on business. Angela tested more of Sophie's cookie recipes in the kitchen. Mark had chosen the plants, and Kyle agreed to deliver them.

Just before noon, Dylan and Jane took orders and went to get lunch for everyone. Mark stopped to show Julie where things would be planted in the vegetable garden, using the blade of a shovel to outline it in the prepared soil.

"Curves are more pleasing to the eye than straight lines," he said, indicating where the poles would be. "Our backdrop will be pole beans with purple pods."

Julie frowned. "Interesting, but poles are straight and you said . . ."

"Well, you can't avoid some lines, but you can soften them—you know—like with rustic poles that have interesting knots and bark. We'll place them in an arc and connect them with two levels of support wires that sag slightly. When the beans grow and start to spread along the wires it'll look almost like the garlands they have in the house."

"Hey, that's impressive. What else?"

He pulled the sketch out of his back pocket and pointed out all the features and details of the plan.

"So where are you going to put the gnomes and flamingos?"

He gasped, pushing the shovel into the ground. "You've got to be kidding."

She laughed. "I am, but you should have seen the look on your face."

"Sophie's Place is classy."

"I know, but marigolds are flowers, aren't they?" she asked as they sat in the rose cottage. "You can eat some kinds of flowers, but not those." Julie turned sideways and put her feet up on the bench.

"Yeah, but they help keep the bugs away, and the vegetables like that." Mark sat at the other end of the other bench. "Bugs don't like onions and garlic very much either, so it's always good to plant a few clusters of those here and there."

She pulled off her garden gloves. "You really know a lot about this."

"Kyle's a good teacher. He made me redo the design five times."

"He must be a nice guy. He sure gives you a lot of attention."

"Yeah. He's had a tough life, but he's so happy all the time you'd never know it."

Julie flattened the gloves against her thigh. "What do you mean?"

"His only kid was killed in a car accident as a baby, and his wife died about a year later."

"That is tough."

"Yeah. She was driving the car when the little boy died, and I guess she never got over it. That's what my mom said anyway."

"When did this happen?"

Mark adjusted his ball cap. "Eight or nine years ago. It was a tough time for the whole family. Kyle's my mom's only brother. I was a little kid then, but I remember how sad everybody was. Anyway, since then, he's taken me under his wing, sort of like another dad."

"And he didn't get married again?"

"Nope. I don't think he even goes out on dates."

"Sounds like my mom, but don't make the mistake of feeling sorry for her."

Mark nodded. "Kyle's like that too."

"You have two parents for seven kids, but my mom has to be both parents for Brandon and me. Sean was out of the picture even before Brandon was very old. I was about five when my parents finally divorced. Mom kept hanging on, thinking he'd change." Julie raised one knee and leaned an elbow on it. "Sean's a genius at making money, but my mom says he never took responsibility for anything to do with the family, and she just got tired of playing house."

"You want your mom to get married again?"

Julie frowned. "I've been thinking about it lately. In a few years Brandon and I are going to leave home, and I'd hate to see her spend her old age alone."

"She seems pretty independent. Maybe she wouldn't mind."

"I just wish she didn't hate men so much. She thinks they're all going to be like Sean."

"You don't see him very often, do you?"

"I'm a minor and he has visitation rights, so we have lunch at the best restaurant in Park City once a month and we talk, and that's that."

"I'm sorry you don't have a real dad in your life, Jules." Mark reached up to touch a bud forming on the climbing roses.

"Oh, I have lots of good substitutes. There's the bishop, and the home teachers and other people in the ward, and Seminary teachers, and Jane's dad. Even some of the boys at school, like you . . ." She smiled and threw her garden gloves at him. "You're not so bad. But yes, I'm disappointed for my mom's sake that there isn't a good man living in our house."

"I'm surprised you don't have a bad attitude."

Julie shook her head. "In spite of Jane's episode with Jason Farrell, I still think there are probably some good guys in the world." Her friend almost being seduced by a predatory boy from school last fall had served as a warning for all her circle of friends. "I realize that not all guys are like that creepmeister."

"Yeah. Some of us are actually trying to be good."

"I plan to get married and it's going to last forever, but I'm not going to choose the wrong guy like my mother did. Besides, I have a lot to do before I settle down, and it's probably a good idea to avoid getting serious till I'm about twenty-seven."

"I know what you mean. I have a lot to do too." Mark smiled at her. "Hey, I'm really looking forward to the prom."

Julie pointed at him. "You know what I like about you? We're friends. We're not taking anything seriously. You're safe. I can trust you. And as long as we're in high school, that's enough, isn't it?"

"Sure. You aren't like most girls at school. Some of them put a lot of pressure on guys."

Jane laughed. "Come on. A prom is just a fancy fashion-show party with dancing. We'll have fun and enjoy ourselves, and it probably won't be the highlight of our lives. No offense."

"None taken. I'd like to think getting married in the temple would be more of a highlight in my life than a high school dance."

"If you're ready for it and you chose the right person." An impish grin turned her mouth up at the corners. "As long as you brush your teeth and excavate all the dirt out from under your fingernails, I'm sure the prom won't be too disappointing."

"Ha. Won't you be surprised when you see I've polished my shoes."

"Really," she said. "I didn't know they had polish for high-tops."

"Just wait till you see your dandelion corsage, miss smarty-pants—dandelions and skunk weed. Count on it." He grinned and threw her garden gloves back at her.

A truck from Hobble Creek Garden Center backed into the driveway, interrupting their playful banter. Kyle got out, a clipboard in one hand. "Hey, Mark," he said as his nephew came toward him. "We got lucky. This place is a gardener's dream."

"Yeah, I know." Mark grinned. "Come and meet Julie Cavanaugh."

"Oh, this is your prom date." Kyle shook Julie's hand. "What do you see in this guy? Couldn't you do better?"

She shrugged. "Well, he flipped a coin for me. No girl could resist that."

"He's a real charmer, all right." Kyle patted Mark's shoulder. "Let's look around before we unload the truck. I want to show you some things I noticed when I was here before." Julie followed as Kyle spoke to Mark, patted tree trunks, inspected leaves, and knelt to feel the soil and assess the grass.

∼

Having prepared dough for three of Aunt Sophie's cookie recipes, Angela set the oven temperature just as the phone rang.

"How are things going?" Lainie asked.

"I've got cookies ready to bake, and kids here to sample them. How about you?"

"We're going to be late. Is Kyle there yet?"

"Maybe. I thought I heard a vehicle in the driveway a few minutes ago."

"Would you let him know we've been delayed?"

"Sure. We're stopping for lunch now, so take your time."

"Okay. We're just leaving Salt Lake. We'll see you soon."

Angela went to check on activities in the yard. Kyle stood when he saw her and took off his hat. His head touched the roof of the rose cottage. She hadn't noticed when they met before that he was lean and bronzed, with broad shoulders and dazzling white teeth. She only remembered his Hershey-brown eyes. He wore jeans, tan work boots, and a green-and-yellow-plaid jacket buttoned halfway up, over a yellow turtleneck. He was clean-shaven today. Very attractive. "Um, I just wanted to tell you that Lainie called," Angela said to him. "Can you wait a few more minutes?"

"Is there a problem?"

She shook her head. "No. They've been delayed. Business, I guess."

Kyle grinned. "Okay. Nice to see you."

Angela looked at him and started to reply but her mind emptied. She hated that this guy made her suddenly stupid. She turned to Julie. "What happened to the others?"

"They went to get some sandwiches."

"Oh. Right." Angela turned to Kyle. "It looks like you're stuck with us, unless you have other plans for lunch."

He smiled. "No. I've been so busy I didn't realize it was lunchtime."

"You know how it is with teenagers," she explained on the way down the stairs. "They can only work for about ten or fifteen minutes at a time before we have to feed them again."

"Yeah, I hire a lot of kids too. These child labor laws can really slow you down."

She did a double take before she realized it was a joke.

Down in the kitchen they washed their hands and sat on stools around a worktable, Kyle at the end, next to Mark, while Angela scooped cookie dough onto a pan and talked to Julie.

When Jane and Dylan came, they unloaded bags of food. Angela stood with her hands on her hips. "Don't you think this is overkill? You've got enough here for a small army."

"We *are* a small army." Dylan shrugged as if that should be obvious. "And we might want a snack later."

"Did you bring drinks or do I need to fill water glasses?"

Jane pointed to the door. "Dylan, we left the drinks in the car."

He snapped his fingers and ran up the stairs, returning soon with cardboard trays of sodas. Then he volunteered to say a prayer, and everyone claimed lunch.

Angela put a couple of cookie sheets into an oven and set the timer, uncomfortable and self-conscious that Kyle might be staring at her. *And you've been out of high school how long?* she chided herself. She turned her attention to putting dough on pans, listening only to Julie, Jane, and Dylan talk about the events of the last few weeks of the school year.

Kyle unwrapped one of the extra sandwiches, opened it to pull out the sliced onions, and glanced up again at the same time Angela raised her eyes. She frowned, thinking he'd been watching her. He took a bite of the sandwich as he turned again to Mark.

"When are Carrie and Lainie supposed to be back?" Julie asked.

Angela sipped her drink. "She said they'd be here by one."

"Kyle has some suggestions for things to do in the yard," Julie said.

Hearing his name, he looked up from his conversation and raised his eyebrows.

"Oh." Angela nodded at him with a tight smile. "Well, they'll want to hear it, I'm sure."

~

When he finished the sandwich, Kyle excused himself and went out to sit in the rose cottage. He couldn't help being fascinated. Angela was pretty. He admired the joy and enthusiasm she put into her work, and the way her long brown ponytail rested on her shoulder as she listened so intently to what Julie was saying. Her graceful neck, slender arms, and delicate hands reminded him of a ballet dancer. *But that's too much ice,* he thought, remembering how she looked at him as if a good idea was more than she could expect from an idiot. *Good thing I don't have to dance with her. She'd probably expect to lead.* He sighed and turned his attention to organizing his notes on the clipboard. *At least the owners are friendlier than that.*

~⌒

Angela glanced up when she heard the door close. *Well, that was rude,* she thought. *He didn't even say thank you.* She dismissed it and turned back to her work.

~⌒

When Carrie and Lainie arrived, they spent about an hour walking through the yard learning what Kyle and Mark planned. Besides severe pruning of the apple tree and putting wrought-iron barriers around all the tree trunks, Kyle suggested replacing the grass with a heat-resistant variety that withstands heavy foot traffic and wouldn't take long to establish. At the same time, they could level out the space and upgrade the sprinkler system.

Then they sat in the rose cottage with Mark to confirm all the tasks to be done for the flower gardens. Carrie and Lainie made plans to choose the sundial, pergola, and benches on Monday morning. Kyle scheduled the apple tree pruning, sod removal, and sprinkler upgrade for next Friday; they'd lay the new sod the next day. Mark and Dylan were out school for parent-teacher conferences those days and would be able to help.

As Carrie and Lainie went into the house, Kyle put his arm around Mark's shoulder and said, "Thanks. I'm usually too busy to get three meals a day. At least let me pay for the sandwich."

"I've got you covered," Mark said. "My treat."

~⌒

Downstairs, over cookies, Carrie and Lainie praised Kyle's expertise and congeniality, while Angela cleaned the worktable with vigorous strokes, remembering her first embarrassing encounter with him, and the way he stared at her today with that amused look. *He's a guy,* she thought, *and guys like to stare. Unfortunately, he'll be here under our feet for a few weeks. Oh well. This too shall pass*

"He's committed to getting everything ready for our first events," Lainie said. "All his suggestions were spot on."

Carrie smiled. "Yes. So, it's too late on a Saturday afternoon to be stuck here. Let's get this cleaned up, and then we'll all have Saturday night to do something fun."

Angela sighed and rinsed the cleaning cloth. "It doesn't matter to me. I have to go home and clean out my fridge."

"What an exciting life you lead," Carrie teased as she and Lainie accelerated the cleanup. Angela shrugged and Carrie added, "You could do something about that, you know."

Angela shook her head. "I'm too busy."

Lainie patted her shoulder. "Well, be sure to stop and smell the roses occasionally."

"Remind me again as soon as they bloom."

Carrie chuckled. "With Kyle and Mark in charge, it won't be very long."

~

Lainie and Carrie had spent the week cleaning the house and learning how to use the new appliances. When John's performances of *You Can't Take It with You* began on Saturday night, Lainie sent him some yellow roses. He called her when he got home.

"You sound excited," she told him. "It must have gone well."

"Yes, it did. Some people muffed a few lines because of nervousness, but that's the way it is sometimes on your first night with an audience in the house."

"You're probably exhausted."

He laughed. "Yeah, but it's going to take a while to wind down from the adrenaline rush. Lainie, I'd really like to see you. Can we have dinner tomorrow?"

"I wish. We spent today making decisions about gardens, and tomorrow I'm making a quick trip home for my dad's birthday."

"Monday then."

"We'll be doing windows and polishing all the wood in the house. I won't be fit to be seen in public. We hired a cleaning service to help us, but we need to be there to supervise."

"You'll stop for lunch anyway. Can't I bring you something?"

"Sorry, John. We're sending out for pizza. There wouldn't be time to talk or relax. Thanks for the offer."

He paused. "I'm sorry. I was hoping . . ."

"We're hit and miss, aren't we."

"But you'll go to the cast party with me, right? It's on the twenty-seventh."

Lainie paused. "Sure. I can take time for that."

"If you're busy . . ."

"I'll go to the party with you. I promise. I'm looking forward to it."

"So am I." He took a deep breath. "Lainie, I miss you."

"I miss you too."

Eight

Tuesday, April 16

As the comedy unfolded, Lainie noticed John had won the costume debate—no tank shirt—and he played the xylophone like he'd played it all his life. His boyish charm made him an audience favorite. Afterward, she and Carrie and Morgan found him in the noise and confusion of backstage and arranged to meet him at the pie shop for a snack.

They arrived first, and when John got there ten minutes later, he slid into the booth next to Lainie and smiled. "Hey, Irish."

"You know, I really like your hair that length," she said, thinking at the same time that the excitement of the performance must be responsible for the light in his eyes.

While they ate, John amused them with stories of his theatrical adventures. Forty minutes later as they finished their pie, Morgan stifled a yawn. "This is too much excitement for me, and I've got an early day tomorrow." He helped Carrie out of the booth. "John, we picked up Lainie, but would you mind taking her home?"

John looked at her as if he'd just won a prize.

On the way, Lainie asked him what the other actors were like and what they did in real life.

"They're all ordinary people who love theater, just like me. Mr. Kolenkhov is a high school French teacher, and Mr. DePinna is a meat cutter in a supermarket. Sue, the girl playing Essie, is a housewife with four kids and a supportive husband. Very talented."

"I noticed things weren't very juicy between you."

"She agreed with me that the script didn't justify it, and finally the director agreed too."

They went inside and shed their coats. "Acting seems like such a risky thing to do," she said, pulling John toward the sofa. "I would never be comfortable with it."

"Nothing is more exhilarating than stepping on stage in front of an audience."

"It was pretty exciting when those fireworks started exploding."

"It's hard to find a play with a more spectacular second-act curtain." He put his arm around her and chuckled. "Life's like that, isn't it. When you least expect it, boom—fireworks. When Grandpa Vanderhof says he has time enough for everything, it really makes me think."

"Yes, that's rather profound. What would you do if you had time?"

"Oh, I could reread all the books in my library and that many more, listen to all the music I'd like to hear, and paint every idea I've ever had." He sighed and brushed a strand of hair away from Lainie's eyes. "But I have to spend most of my time making a living. It's a good thing I like it. How about you?"

"I think about all the people I could help."

He smiled. "Did you make resolutions when you had cancer, when time was uncertain?"

"In some ways I did, and in some ways I still take things for granted."

"You never know how much of your allotted time you've used up, do you."

"Oh, John, it's too late at night to get so philosophical," she protested.

"If I could, I'd ask for more time to spend with you when we're not tired and stressed."

She patted his hand. "We'll have to pay more attention to that when the play is over, and when Sophie's Place is running smoothly."

He pulled her closer and sighed. "I have to go. I have so much to do tomorrow."

"Me too," she said, her head on his shoulder. "Thanks for bringing me home."

He nuzzled the side of her face. They didn't move, just sat in silence. "I wish time would stop, but I really do have to go. I'm so tired I'm loopy."

At the door, she helped him with his coat and put her hands on his chest. "Go straight home, straight to bed," she instructed. "No phone call tonight."

He smoothed her hair back and held her face with both hands. "Good night, Sweet Lainie." He kissed her mouth, the top of her left ear, her forehead above her right eyebrow, and then her mouth again, lingering for a while this time until it became a breathless exchange of ideas. "I don't want to go."

"You have to."

He continued nibbling at her face and mouth. "See you tomorrow. One o'clock."

"What's at one?"

"We're having lunch. Usual place." They stood enfolded now in each other's arms. "But it's such a long time to be away from you."

"Only thirteen hours. You'll sleep through most of it. Can you drive or should I confiscate your keys and call a taxi?"

"Uh-uh. My car knows the way."

"Then go home."

"One more for the road." He held her face to kiss her again. "Oh, I like that."

"Me too," she whispered, then opened the door behind her. "You're a brilliant actor and a great kisser. Now get out." He saluted and she laughed, watching him stroll down the sidewalk doing a giddy sort of dance. Halfway to the street he jumped and clicked his heels. When he got into the car he blinked the headlights twice as a last farewell.

Half an hour later the phone rang. She didn't even bother to turn on the bedside lamp. "Don't you ever sleep?" she complained.

"I just wanted to tell you I found something more exhilarating than stepping on stage in front of an audience."

"What's that?"

"Kissing you."

"John, I'm glad you got home safely. Now stop talking nonsense and go to sleep."

"Tweet dweems, tweet Waynie." He yawned. "See you tomorrow at lunch."

"It's already tomorrow."

"Oh, good. I'll see you this afternoon."

"I'll be there."

He yawned again before he hung up, and she turned over on the pillow, thinking about how much she enjoyed this friendship, and wondering for the first time, *What if he walked away tonight and never came back? What would I do?* Life would be so dull without him. Nobody else called her "Sweet Lainie." Nobody else telephoned late at night just to say "sweet dreams," either. She liked the closeness, and the kissing too. He was easy to be with.

She stared into the darkness thinking how very much she liked him, and then a new thought came into her mind: *What if I love him?* She hadn't ever truly loved a man, and she wasn't sure what it was really like, but she didn't have time to find out now. Launching Sophie's Place took all her time and attention. Besides, John had been in love before and didn't like it. Maybe he wouldn't love her. *And we've only known each other since Tuesday, December 5, 1995, a few minutes past noon. That's a little more than four months. Doesn't it take longer than that to fall in love, if . . .*

Drifting in and out of wakefulness, arguing with herself, Lainie finally decided it was a crazy, impractical, improbable idea and her life was good just the way it was. They could simply be friends—friends who enjoy theater together and admire each other very much, friends who have lunch or dinner now and then and talk on the phone late at night, friends who kiss.

Friday, April 19

Wearing gloves, hard hats, goggles, and ear protection, Kyle directed Mark as they pruned the apple tree Friday morning, being careful where they placed their ladders because the grass was spongy from a long hard rain the night before. "Well, I'm grateful they've got parent-teacher conferences at school today so we can get these two big chores done," Kyle said.

"Yeah. Things worked out well."

Brandon Cavanaugh strolled into the yard. "You guys woke me up."

"Who's this?" Kyle asked, jumping off the ladder.

"Julie's brother Brandon. They live on the other side of the block."

Kyle took off his glove, shook Brandon's hand, and noticed his eyes were the color of blue morning glories like Angela's. "Hi, Brandon." He saw intelligence, curiosity, and pride in the boy's face, and liked him immediately. *He's hungry for something,* Kyle thought.

Mark finished the introduction from his place on the ladder. "This is my uncle Kyle."

Brandon grinned. "Hey."

Kyle moved his ladder to a new spot. "Better sit on the porch. We've got falling branches here. Some of them would hurt or scratch if they hit you." He climbed the ten-foot ladder almost to the top step, waiting until Brandon was on the porch before continuing with the next round.

When the saws stopped again, Brandon asked, "What do you do with the branches?"

"That piece of machinery behind the truck in the driveway is a chipper," Mark explained. "We'll run 'em through there and make mulch for somebody's garden."

"You could build a pretty good bonfire," Brandon said. "That's what I'd do."

Kyle grinned. "Not with green wood."

Mark moved to where Kyle directed him, and again the chainsaws buzzed. When they stopped, Brandon asked, "Hey, do you need any help?"

"What experience do you have pruning fruit trees?"

Brandon snorted. "Well, none."

"All right. Stand over here and I'll teach you." Kyle explained the basic principles of tree pruning and the needs of this particular tree as it related to the purpose of the yard.

"That looks easy," Brandon said.

"I watched for a long time before Kyle would let me use a chainsaw," Mark cautioned.

"I almost wouldn't let him use the chainsaw this morning," Kyle teased. "We don't want him getting hurt and breaking his date for the prom tonight."

"Brandon knows all about the prom," Mark said. "He's going to be some kind of flunky for Jane and Dylan when they serve dinner."

"Well, sorry we don't have safety equipment for you."

"I don't need safety equipment to drag branches to the driveway."

Kyle smiled at the boy's determination. "How old are you, Brandon?"

"I'm not very big yet, but I'll be fourteen in July."

"Okay. We'll wait."

Brandon struggled with a large branch. Kyle encouraged him, and soon he got the branch onto the driveway and returned for another.

"You ought to wear gloves so your hands don't get torn up," Mark advised.

"I've got some extras in the truck," Kyle said. "I'll get 'em for you." He shifted his weight to descend, but one of the ladder feet sank into the soft, moist sod, and he lost his grip on the chainsaw at the same time he lost his balance. His hard hat came off as he fell. With a sharp thud, his head hit the housing of the saw, and the ladder fell the other direction.

"Kyle!" Mark yelled, climbing down to him.

Kyle lay on the grass, not moving at all.

~

"Is anything broken?" Mark knelt beside his uncle. "Are you okay?"

Brandon turned and ran for the driveway. "I'll get my mom! She's downstairs!"

Kyle groaned and sat up. "What happened?" He took off his gloves to hold his head in his hands.

"You fell off the ladder and hit your head on the chainsaw," Mark said.

"Oh, it really hurts." Kyle groaned again. "I don't feel so good."

"Brandon went to get help."

"He's too little. He can't walk yet."

Mark was confused. "Well, he . . ."

"What happened?" Kyle asked.

"I told you. You fell off the ladder. We're pruning a tree."

Mark was beginning to panic when Brandon returned with Angela.

"Nicole!" Kyle began to sob when Angela knelt beside him. "You're here!" He put his arms around her. "You came all this way."

Angela tried to pull his arms away without success. "He hit his head?"

"Yeah. On the chainsaw housing."

Kyle rested his forehead against Angela's shoulder. "My head hurts. Nicole, what happened? I don't remember."

Angela gave up and let him hold her. "He's confusing me with somebody else."

Mark patted Kyle's shoulder. "No, this is Angela, not Nicole."

Kyle groaned again. "And he keeps asking the same questions," Mark said. "This is scaring me."

"It's confusion," Angela said. "Concussions will do that to people. Kyle, listen to me. You're going to be all right, but I can't help you if you don't let go. Come on now. Let me help you."

Brandon knelt by his mother. "What can I do?"

"Should I call the EMTs?" Mark asked.

Kyle relaxed his hold, but continued to sigh and groan, leaning on Angela.

"No, a concussion kind of scrambles the brain and confuses people. Sometimes it messes with the short-term memory, but it's temporary."

Mark frowned. "I don't think we're going to get much work done today without him."

"There's nothing you can do for a concussion but rest and recover. He'll probably have a severe headache. With a couple of painkillers he'll be okay, but if the headache persists, he should see a doctor."

~

Kyle raised his head and looked at the three concerned faces. His eyes and his mind began to clear, despite the pounding headache. He took Angela's hand. "Oh, Angie, it's you. What happened?"

"You fell off the ladder and hit your head."

"Oh, that's why it hurts so much. Shoulder too. Got any aspirin?"

Angela shook her head. "No aspirin. If you have any intracranial bleeding, that could make it worse. I have non-aspirin pain reliever in the first-aid kit in the house, but you have to let go of my hand so I can get it for you."

"Guess I kind of got confused for a couple of minutes. Thought you were somebody else." He relaxed his grip on her hand, but when she tried to pull it away, he held tighter. "Let Mark."

She pulled the keys from her pocket and handed them to Mark, then turned to her son. "Brandon, go with him and bring some water and a bag of ice cubes wrapped in a hand towel."

Kyle let go of Angela's hand. "Thanks for coming to my rescue. That was nice of you."

"Brandon came for me as soon as it happened."

Kyle squinted through the pain. "He's a good kid."

She smiled a little. "Yes, he can be, but at this point, he could go either way."

"When he came into the yard this morning, I felt an instant connection with him."

"That's nice of you." She picked grass off his jacket. "Listen, maybe we should take you to a doctor."

"No, I don't have time. Too much to do here."

"You should go while you're still conscious and able to walk in under your own power."

"Look, you doctor me up a little, and if I'm not feeling better in an hour you can take me to the emergency room."

"Here it is, Mom!" Brandon ran out the back door with the ice. Mark followed with the first-aid kit and a glass of water, and knelt next to his uncle.

Kyle groaned again, leaning against Angela. "Oh. Dizzy."

She opened the kit and found the capsules. "Here's a megadose."

He swallowed the pain reliever with the water Mark handed him. "Thanks."

"Where did you land?" Angela gently probed Kyle's head.

He winced. "Ouch. Right there."

Brandon found the spot and held the ice bag on it.

"Mark, are we done with this tree?" Kyle asked.

"Just a couple more places to trim. I can do it. No problem."

"Call the garden center. If the sod-removal crew hasn't left yet, they need to bring one more guy. That new turf has to be laid tomorrow, and we have to get the space ready today."

Mark righted the ladder and picked up Kyle's hard hat. "I know Lainie and Mrs. B ought to be here soon. They've got a project they're working on in the house."

Kyle held his head and closed his eyes against the pain. "Gotta get this mess cleaned up before the crew gets here. You run the chipper while Brandon drags the branches over to you. He can trim ancillary branches with the small chainsaw if he needs to."

Brandon grinned at Mark. "I can do that."

"Is that okay with you?" Kyle looked at Angela.

"A chainsaw? But he's only . . ."

"I think he can handle it. Mark will teach him."

"I can do it safely, Mom. See? Kyle trusts me."

Angela took a deep breath, but saw assurance in Kyle's face. "Okay. Obviously you need some help."

"Mark, give him my goggles and things, and show him how. When you finish chipping, move the truck out to the curb and let the crew use the driveway when they get here. They'll have that fountain to unload." He gestured with his thumb over his shoulder. "Get it done."

Angela took the ice bag, and Brandon hurried off with Mark. Kyle smiled again as she moved closer and held the ice against his head wound.

"Good kid," he murmured. "Good instincts." He sighed and relaxed, allowing her to take care of him.

Angela smiled. "If you say so." They watched as Mark got some gloves for Brandon from the truck and went inside to make his phone calls, while Brandon began pulling branches over to the driveway. "This grass is pretty wet," Angela said. "You're probably soaked. Can you make it over to the porch?"

Kyle tried to stand but gasped and bent over, his head in his hands again.

"Are you nauseated? That's not unusual with a concussion."

"No, I'm okay. It's gone now. I have a cast-iron stomach."

"Come on, tough guy." She put her arm around his waist to guide him. He wobbled a bit but held onto her shoulders until he got up the porch steps and into a chair. She handed him the ice bag. "You'll need this."

"Yeah. Thanks." He held it to his head.

Mark came out the back door. "All done. We pulled somebody off another job. They'll leave in about ten minutes. And Lainie and Mrs. B are already on the way."

"Good work," Kyle said as his nephew went back to the pruning project. He relaxed, and for a few minutes they watched the boys work.

"How are you feeling now?" Angela asked.

"Like I've been smacked in the head with a brick. Things are still spinning, but it isn't as bad." He nudged her arm. "How do you know about intracranial bleeding?"

"I'm a mother. I've been to the emergency room more than once with a kid who's had a nasty bump on the head."

"I felt like I was in good hands."

"That's very flattering, but you've just had a concussion. Tomorrow you won't even remember what you said today."

"Yes, I will. Try me."

She laughed. "Oh, just forget it."

"Forget it. Now *that's* funny."

She gave him a doubtful frown.

"No, really. I can recite the Gettysburg Address. Right now."

Angela shook her head. "You're impossible."

"Okay, you asked for it. Here it is—1864 Abraham Lincoln Highway, Gettysburg, Pennsylvania, 17325."

Angela rolled her eyes and snorted at the lame joke, but he went on, "See? Zip code and everything."

"That's obnoxious."

"Mark and I made that up when he was nine years old. We both love it."

"You know, I'm getting the impression it doesn't take a bump on the head to make you a little wacko. That's the real you."

Kyle grinned and turned the ice bag. "Does Brandon spend much time with his dad?"

"Too much. Emotionally they're about the same age."

"You know how to pick a winner."

Angela raised an eyebrow. "Keep it up and I'll give you another concussion."

"Can't I leave you kids alone for one minute without you getting into trouble?" Lainie stood in front of them on the sidewalk. "What's going on?" After they explained what had happened, she asked, "What can I do for you?"

Kyle pointed a thumb toward Angela. "She's already worked her magic."

Angela rolled her eyes.

Lainie mounted the steps. "Come inside and get out of the noise."

"My clothes are kind of wet on the back," Kyle said as they helped him into the house.

"You can sit on a towel on a kitchen chair. I'll make hot chocolate to warm you up, and Angela can bring us some cookies."

"Is your stomach really okay, Kyle?" Angela asked.

"Yeah, it really is."

Lainie took a towel from the laundry room and put it on a chair. Kyle sat and reapplied the ice bag to his head. They could hear the chipper at work in the driveway.

"Well, what are you going to do?" Lainie wondered.

Kyle dismissed her concern. "That was a humongous headache, but I'm not so dizzy now. When the crew gets here I'll sit on the porch and supervise."

"We could put it off for a day or two," she suggested.

"No, we can't. I've got a schedule to keep, and if I took you off I couldn't get you back on for three weeks, and that's when you need to be ready to go."

"But you're . . ."

"I'm fine," he insisted. "I'll rest a while and by the time the crew gets here I'll be back to normal. I'll pretend I'm the warden and they're the chain gang. They'll love it."

~◦

Morgan fell asleep waiting for Jane to come home. On the other side of the king-size bed, Carrie thumbed through a magazine as she listened for their daughter. She grinned at the sounds of the front door closing, and feet hurrying up the stairs. "Let's hear it," she said when Jane peeked in the open door of the bedroom. Carrie stretched across to the lump on the other side and kissed his cheek. "Wake up, love. Jane's here to tell us about the prom."

He sat up and leaned against the padded headboard. "How was it?" He rubbed his eyes. Carrie moved over and nestled beside him.

Jane sat on the foot of the bed and reported the color of Julie's dress, the cut of Mark's tuxedo, and the flowers they gave each other. As far as the meal was concerned, Dylan was helpful, "but after Angela took pictures, he got weird," Jane reported.

"What do you mean?" Morgan drew his right knee up, leaned his elbow on it, and stifled a yawn.

"Well, we made the dining room look like a French café, you know, and we had this French dinner with cordon bleu and everything, and as soon as we started serving it, Dylan started speaking fake French, pretending he was a student at the barricade in *Les Miz* and he had to sneak the food past the soldiers."

Carrie and Morgan laughed. "You told him not to do that," she said.

Jane rolled her eyes. "You don't know Dylan. He kept singing and acting out the story until Julie and Mark were laughing so hard they couldn't eat. Finally I told him to go defend the barricade, so he left and didn't come back." Laughing, Jane threw herself down on the bed. "He is so crazy!"

"Did they like the dinner?" Carrie asked.

"Yeah, but later when Dylan did come back to bring dessert, he had a dish towel with ketchup on it tied around his head, like he'd been wounded in the battle, and once he served the dessert he keeled over and died. Mark and Julie had to step over him to get out."

Carrie laughed. "Well, he does have an imagination."

"After they left for the prom, we had the same meal with Angela and Brandon, but with a lot less drama."

"Who's Brandon?" Morgan queried.

"Angela's boy. He's Miranda's age," Carrie explained, then turned to Jane again. "What did you do while you waited for them to return from the prom?"

"We went back to Angela's house and played board games with Brandon but he kept beating us, so we sent him downstairs to watch a ball game."

"What did Mark and Julie say about the dance?" Carrie asked.

"Well, they said the gym was decorated like those fancy French gardens—I forget what they're called."

"Tuileries," Carrie said.

"Yeah, with park benches and lots of flowers and bushes and a fountain and stuff, but after an hour they missed us, so they came back early and we had more dessert, and played some games, and then Mark and Dylan brought me home." Jane got up. "Hey, did you guys ever go to a big dance together?"

Her parents looked at each other. "Only the biggest dance of all," Morgan answered.

Carrie patted his cheek. "We got married."

Nine

Saturday, April 20

Carrie and Lainie worked inside preparing for the open house, but glanced out now and then as the sod project progressed. Kyle kept to the schedule, supervising the crew of half a dozen energetic high school and college boys who seemed to know what they were doing, and did it efficiently.

Angela had spent the afternoon in the kitchen, expecting Brandon to check in before he left for the movie with friends, but she knew he might have been sidetracked by the activity in the yard. She came up the stairs and confirmed her suspicion—her son, the youngest and smallest, worked alongside the rest of the crew.

Kyle saw her sit on the porch and came over. "We're making good progress. Brandon likes being on this team."

"Glad to hear it. He's got two left feet so he's not very good at sports." They watched as the boys set two more rectangles of lush green sod. "You're the Pied Piper."

"He's a hard worker." Kyle sat near her and leaned back on his elbows.

"He told me that he was taking some friends to a movie at the mall."

"Well, he walked into the yard, saw what we were doing, and asked if he could help."

"What do I know? I'm only the mother. At home his room looks like it's been stirred with a great big spoon."

Kyle chuckled. "He's just showing off for his favorite girl."

"Maybe so, but I get a little discouraged sometimes." Angela looked at Kyle. "I almost didn't recognize you without a hat. How's your head?"

"Dull ache, bruise still tender. Not too bad, but without a hat I run the risk of sun stroke."

"Did you see a doctor?"

"Didn't need to. I had you to take care of me."

She rolled her eyes. "Can you still recite the Gettysburg Address?"

"Did I do that?"

"Uh-huh. Complete with zip code."

"I must have been totally crackers," Kyle said.

"I wouldn't know the difference. When are you going to be finished here?"

"In another couple of hours, I guess. Then I'm taking all the boys out for pizza. Is it okay if Brandon comes too?"

Angela shrugged. "Sure, if you think he's earned it."

"I'm paying him for the work he's doing, just like all the other boys, but pizza is one of the perks. And he should be friends with boys like these."

She raised her eyebrows. "You care who his friends are?"

Kyle smiled. "Yeah."

She got up to leave. "Okay. It's a deal."

He returned to the project, yelling directions as he went.

Angela went back to the kitchen, puzzling over this stranger who took such a personal interest in her son's success. He seemed to be a good man and a good influence. She chuckled and decided that whoever Nicole was, she must be a very understanding woman.

Saturday, April 27

Another hectic week went by with progress in preparing for the open house, but Carrie noticed Lainie's distraction. That Saturday, they'd spent a few hours getting ready for a small engagement party, and when the guests left, the two women sat on the window seat in the office to evaluate the event. They didn't get very far. Finally Carrie asked, "Have you seen John lately? I know the play's over now."

"Yes, it closed last night. But we're both still pretty busy. We do talk on the phone and have lunch now and then, or dinner sometimes on Sundays. He took me to an art gallery two weeks ago when we both had some free time on a Friday afternoon. Tonight he's taking me to the cast party, but I'm pretty sure that'll be a mob scene, not very . . . you know, conducive to quiet conversation."

Carrie folded her arms. "I don't know if you realize it, but you're always preoccupied. You talk about him all the time, your eyes light up when someone mentions his name, and you're in a daze for half an hour after he calls. This has been going on for several weeks."

Lainie sighed. "We've become friends."

"You're in denial, but I think what's really happening here is John and Lainie falling in love, which can only be cured with a little gold ring, and that's something I never thought I'd hear myself say about John Marchbanks."

"At our age?" Lainie shook her head. "I like him very much, but it's probably just a crush. I don't know. I've never really been in love to the point of insanity like I've heard so many people describe. Besides, we're not the marrying kind. That would take too much compromise, and we're both too busy with our own lives."

"You're in deep denial, girl." Carrie held up her hands to stop Lainie's response. "When you're together, you don't know anybody else is even in the room, and Morgan says both of you glow bright enough to light a football field. From where we stand, it looks like the real thing. Has he kissed you?"

Lainie shrugged and looked away. "Maybe a couple of times. I'm not keeping track."

Carrie laughed. "No one ever does."

"Like I said, we've become really good friends. He isn't anything like the snob I thought he was when I met him. He's smart and funny and respectful, and he teaches me about art and music and theater. Is he as perfect as he seems?"

"Yeah. He's sort of a cliché I guess."

"Well, he just seems too good to be true."

Carrie smiled. "Every woman should be lucky enough to be married to a cliché."

"I've known lots of men—dated a few, kissed some frogs hoping they'd turn into princes. I can't explain it, but I've never had a friend like John. It's very satisfying."

Carrie patted Lainie's hand. "'Friend' is the operative word. That's how it starts. If it's meant to move beyond that, don't be afraid. Open your life to all the possibilities."

Lainie shook her head. "I don't know. It would probably take a miracle."

Carrie chuckled and pushed her hair away from her face. "Lainie, I think the miracle has already happened. You just need to acknowledge it. We've known John for a long time and we've never seen him like this before. Besides, we took a vote and it's unanimous. He's in love. You're in love. With each other."

Lainie sat staring, absorbing Carrie's words. She was closer to John than she'd ever been to a man before, and when she thought about it, she realized she wasn't afraid of his friendship. But love?

That night at the cast party, Lainie enjoyed the wit and fun, with the actors still displaying the same amazing energy they'd given to their performances. She and John mingled for fifteen noisy minutes of brief introductions and breezy small talk, and never found the refreshment table. Then he leaned over to say, "I know of a better party than this one. Let's go." He took her hand and quickly led her to his car.

"Where are we going?" she asked as they buckled their seat belts.

He started the car and looked at her. "Full disclosure—we're going to my place."

"Another Quail Valley surprise?"

"I hope so."

She quizzed him all the way, but he gave no direct answers. He took her coat and hung it with his in the closet just inside the door, then bowed slightly and gestured to the leather chair with the profile view of the keyboard. "Miss McGuire, please take your seat for the concert."

She smiled and applauded. "Ah, maestro, at last. Thank you."

John sat on the padded leather bench at the piano, ran his fingers up and down the keys and then focused. Lainie recognized the melody. After a few measures he turned and smiled at her. "You've heard this before. 'Moonlight Sonata.'" The song lasted several minutes, and he paused briefly before continuing with another familiar piece. "This is one more little bagatelle from Beethoven." At the end, he smiled as she applauded again.

"John, that's delightful. You play so well, and from memory too."

"Something's wrong with my brain. Once music gets in there, it sticks. Now here's Chopin's 'Minute Waltz.' Takes about two minutes to play. Then we'll have dinner."

With the last note, he turned toward her. "It's intermission." He led her to the table, went into the kitchen, and returned with two large chef salads. He then retrieved a tray of salad dressings, soft drinks, and a basket of bread sticks, and sat across from her.

"John, this is really a good idea."

"Surprises keep life interesting—you know, like fireworks."

"It's all about life, isn't it?"

"Isn't everything? Life is excellent." He reached across the table to touch her hand. "Would you say a prayer, please?" Lainie did, and afterward he cautioned her to save some room for dessert because chocolate was back on the menu. "It's chocolate Bundt cake, my grandmother's recipe. Out of this world."

It was the best she'd ever tasted, and when they finished, John got up. "Intermission's over." He led her back to the chair in the living room. Sitting at the piano again, he started to play a melody she recognized as "Humoresque," then sang in his light baritone voice, "Every evening after dark I kiss the statues in the park—If Cornwall's horse can take it, so can you."

She laughed and applauded, and John winced. "Sorry. I lost my head." Then he launched into a lush, all-over-the-keyboard version of "Begin the Beguine." After the first few measures he looked at her. "This is the pops-concert portion of the program." She watched the pure pleasure on his face as he played. He nodded graciously to acknowledge her applause when the music ended with a glissando and a flourish.

Short compositions by Bach, Mozart, Rachmaninoff, Gershwin, Liszt, and Schumann constituted the rest of the concert, with brief comments about the composer and background of each piece. Lainie applauded again, and John asked if she had any requests.

She smiled. "All I know about music I learned in Humanities 101, and that wasn't much. Why don't you play your favorite piece for me?"

"It's kind of corny and sentimental. Some musical snobs say it's too popular to be good."

"I'm so new at this I'll never know the difference. Please don't apologize. Just play."

He smiled and turned back to the piano. After a slow, rich, melodic opening passage, his fingers flew up and down the keyboard in an impressive display, the music a cascade of anxiety and worry. Then it returned to a thoughtful restatement of the melody and a quiet but triumphant resolution.

Lainie didn't applaud. "Thank you, John. I feel like I'm floating."

"Chopin does that to me too." John's voice was reverent, almost a whisper. "Something about his music speaks to my fingers. And my heart. That was the 'Etude Opus 10 No. 3.'"

"It's very introspective. I felt like I was seeing the real you for the first time."

He smiled. "Maybe you were. 'Tristesse' is the subtitle. That means melancholy sadness. But when it ends, I always feel hopeful."

"I hope this isn't the end."

"It's getting late. Aren't you . . ."

"Oh, don't you have one encore?"

He nodded. "All right. We'll stay with Chopin. I'll say good night with a nocturne." John put his hands on the keyboard and played five more minutes of exquisite music. After the slow resolve of the last two chords, he lifted his hands away from the keys and turned to smile at Lainie.

They stood, and Lainie came to him with open arms. "Thank you so much," she whispered. "Johnny, you're wonderful."

"I'm not usually that good. You inspired me."

"You touched my spirit."

He brushed her cheek with his thumb. "Music does not lie to the feelings."

"That's very insightful."

"That's Franz Liszt. I'm told he was pretty good on the piano."

As she looked into John's very blue eyes, her heart opened and unfolded. "That nocturne means I have to go home."

He helped her with her coat and into the car. They drove in contented silence. She put her hand on the seat between them, and when he didn't need both of his on the wheel, he held her hand.

After they stepped inside her front door, he locked his arms behind her waist and said, "That was the best cast party I've ever been to."

"It's the only one I've ever been to."

"I usually try to do a couple of plays a year, just to keep the edge."

She patted his cheek. "I think you're awfully good on stage, but I'm no expert."

"You're guilty of aiding and abetting, you know, helping me with my lines that way."

"Does that make me an accessory to your performance?"

"Definitely, but you're prejudiced."

"I am a friend of the court, no doubt about that." She reached up and kissed him. "Thank you for the private concert."

"Thanks for being such an appreciative audience." He kissed her. "I certainly have incentive to keep practicing."

She chuckled a little. "On the kissing or the piano?"

"Both." He kissed her again, and then again. The longer it went, the hungrier it became.

She pulled back and put her fingers over his lips. "We're getting carried away, John. Remember the nocturne means good night."

"You're right. I can't think straight when I'm this close to you." He smiled and touched her chin. "Good night, Irish. See you soon."

Half an hour later, after Lainie got into bed and turned out the light, the phone rang.

"Want me to play another nocturne to help you go to sleep?"

"No thanks. I'm not having any trouble with insomnia tonight."

"I'd love to give you another concert. How about next week? I need time to practice."

"Things really get crazy for me the next few weeks."

He sighed. "Well, I'll be thinking about you."

"When it gets chaotic, I'll remember tonight."

"So will I. Good night, Sweet Lainie."

"Sleep well, John." She hung up the phone and allowed his music to replay in her head. He'd given her more than a concert tonight. He'd given her a part of himself.

Monday, April 29

Although Sundays and Mondays were weekends at Sophie's Place, preparing for the open house meant Carrie and Lainie worked on Mondays in April. On the last Monday, preparations increased to borderline madness, and just as the women were about to send out for pizza, John and Morgan appeared at the back door with takeout from China Lily—four entrees to share, and way too much rice.

Morgan greeted Carrie with a kiss and shed his coat. "Since you couldn't come and sit at a table with us there, we thought we'd come here."

She patted his face. "It's a welcome break, much better than our Plan A."

John hung his coat on the back of a chair and helped set out the food. As the four of them laughed, talked, and ate, John failed to teach Lainie how to use chopsticks.

"Can't I just stab the food like this?" She jabbed one chopstick into a piece of chicken.

He made a face. "Not that graceful. Hard to eat rice that way."

"I'm willing to give up rice."

"Want me to feed you?" he asked.

"Thanks, but I'm loyal to my trusty fork." She picked up a plastic one.

"How much longer?" Morgan asked Carrie when they'd finished the meal, and Lainie and John had put the leftovers in the fridge.

Carrie took his hand. "A few hours."

Lainie nudged John. "Want to see what we've done with the house?"

"Sure."

She led the way to the parlor and stood in front of the fireplace, pointing out the decorations for the open house in two days. He stopped her mid-sentence with an eager kiss. "I've been thinking all weekend about doing that, and today I couldn't keep my mind on my work."

"Oh. I can't even think what I started to say just now."

"Who cares? I didn't come here to see the décor." He kissed her again and they stood enfolded in each other's arms. "It's so good to hold you again."

"I could easily get into this habit," she murmured.

"Something's happening to me. I want to be with you all the time."

"Me too. What are we going to do about that?"

"We could stand around like this more often." He went on with gentle, tender kisses. "Do you want me to stay? Maybe I could help."

"No. We'd just end up doing this. Carrie would be shocked. Or maybe not. She thinks she knows something."

"Something we don't know?"

"I know we're getting carried away."

"Seems like that happens a lot lately."

"We should think about setting a quota." He chuckled and her arms went around his waist. "Thanks for bringing dinner tonight. And yourself."

"I had to see you. I couldn't wait any longer."

"Now I have the inspiration I need to get through the rest of this crazy night."

He stroked her cheek. "It isn't fair. You have work to do, and somewhere in my brain, there's a nocturne playing."

She kissed him again. "Maybe I can make it stop."

"I'm sure you could." They held each other in silence until he sighed. "But we'd better listen to the music." They kissed one last time and went back to the kitchen.

Carrie and Morgan still sat with their heads close together, speaking in low voices. Noticing their audience, Morgan said, "Do you think we should tell them?"

Carrie shrugged. "They'll find out eventually."

"Find out what?" John asked. He and Lainie sat again and held hands under the table.

Morgan sighed. "In confidence then, since neither of you live in Orem . . ." He stopped and looked at Carrie. "I don't think I can say it yet. I'm still . . ." He shook his head.

Carrie took a deep breath. "Morgan's been called to be the bishop of our ward."

Morgan sighed. "We were interviewed yesterday by the stake president."

John chuckled. "I'll bet you didn't see that coming."

Morgan looked at his wife. "We've known for a few weeks. We . . . well, that's another story. We both just knew. We're okay with it, but it's still a shock. It'll happen in two weeks, Mother's Day, and we'd like both of you to come if you can." Morgan looked at the sober faces around the table and laughed. "Look, this doesn't change things among us. I'll organize my life so we can all still be friends." He pointed at John. "It might change things a bit at the firm. We'll have another item on the agenda for the next staff meeting."

"I was a clerk in a BYU student ward while I was in law school," John said, "and I saw up close what a tough job it is to be a bishop. It's a five-year sentence now, isn't it?"

"Do we say congratulations, or are condolences more appropriate?" Lainie wondered.

Morgan grinned. "Look, it wasn't supposed to be such a buzz kill. Let's all just pick ourselves up and move on with our lives."

John reached across to shake his partner's hand. "I think you're up to it."

"I was happy teaching Sunday school." Morgan looked at his watch. "Hey, I've got to pick up Jane and Miranda in half an hour. They're taking me to a movie."

"Have you told them yet?" John asked.

"Broke the news last night. They're dealing with it pretty well."

"What's next?" Lainie wanted to know.

"Counselors." Morgan got up from the table. "This is not a job you can do alone. I've got to choose counselors and an executive secretary by the end of the week." He kissed Carrie, whispered something in her ear that made her smile, and went out the back door with John.

Lainie and Carrie went on with their silk flower arrangements, but a little more subdued than before. "Well, what are you thinking?" Lainie asked finally.

"I think I'm quickly going to learn how to be patient. President Stevenson is fairly new on the job too, but from his experience as a bishop he knows that being the bishop's wife is sometimes hard, and there's no handbook. I guess all I can do is smile and love everybody."

"You're good at that. It's what we do at Sophie's Place."

Carrie didn't look encouraged. "Morgan and I have only been together again for a few months, and now I have to share him with the whole ward. I don't know if I'm ready for that."

"Just relax and let the Lord take care of you."

Carrie smiled. "He'll be a good bishop—I'm sure of that. After the refiner's fire we've been through, our marriage is stronger, but he's also learned how to love people in a different way. He's more compassionate than he was before. A bishop needs that. We'll take it in stride and watch for the compensations the stake president promised. Maybe the women in the ward will see me differently too. Maybe I can get out of the box they've always put me in."

Lainie regarded her with pursed lips, then said, "Of course, you know how they really choose the leader of a ward. When my father got the call, he told me they find the most loving, caring, Christlike person in the ward and then they call her husband to be the bishop."

Carrie laughed. "So this is all my fault?"

"Look on the bright side. At least you know you won't be called to be the Relief Society president for the next five years."

"Hmm. Maybe I can request a nice safe job with the girls in Young Women," she joked. "Maybe I have some influence on that now."

"Yeah. I'm sure they'll be taking applications any day."

Finished with her arrangement, Carrie put it aside and said, "Morgan told me it was John's idea to bring dinner, by the way."

Lainie tried to hide the smile on her face. "That was very . . . very thoughtful." She knew John had come because he'd thought all weekend about kissing her. More than thoughtful, he was an opportunist.

"What's that supposed to mean?" Carrie demanded.

Lainie shrugged. "Nothing. John's a very thoughtful man. That's all."

Ten

Friday, May 10

As a featured attraction, the rose cottage gained instant popularity when Sophie's Place opened, sometimes showcasing the wedding cake, other times as the repository for gifts. Carrie and Lainie spent more time in the spring sunshine preparing clients' celebrations.

Julie and Jane started as regulars on the catering team for the summer, with Dylan and Mark as helpers for evening events when needed. They wore T-shirts and baseball caps with the Sophie's Place logo Mark designed, and referred to themselves as Sophie's Kids.

A bouquet of yellow roses from Marchbanks & Burke, sent for the open house, stood on the employee table in the kitchen as the first events unfolded. "So far, so good," Carrie said. "Is this stuff ready?"

"Just needs a sprig of parsley," Lainie replied.

"Hold everything," Angela called as she pushed through the door. "We have a cake crisis! Just look at this!" She opened the door to the elevator and carried the plate to the worktable. With grim faces, the prep crew gathered around to witness the holocaust, their looks of horror punctuated by gasps and soft "oohs."

"It's a disaster." Carrie surveyed handprints amid collapsed layers. "What happened?"

"A kid saw the bride and groom on the cake as something to play with," Angela answered, "so he climbed up to get it. Who brings children to weddings?"

"Must have been the bride," Lainie answered. "Big family. Lots of nieces and nephews."

"And no supervision," Angela added. "We have a dazed bride, and a mother in shock."

"Maybe we need a policy about children being policed," Carrie said with a frown. "Write it into the contract. We can't assume anything."

"Well, what are we going to do?" Lainie gestured to the calamity on the table. "Thoughts? Anyone?"

A silence followed, and then Carrie started to giggle. "Just add a sign that says 'under construction.' Think the guests would buy that?"

Everyone else laughed but soon quieted again. "We have public health laws to consider," Angela reminded them. "Think fast. Even as we waver with indecision, the bride is hyperventilating."

"And guests are arriving in the midst of our debate," Carrie said.

"What would it look like if you just cut away the damaged parts and doctored up the rest?" Lainie suggested.

"That's not a bad idea," Angela mumbled. Everyone looked at her in anticipation. "I'll cut the cake in half, ice the exposed side, and write 'For My Better Half' on it." She looked at the others for approval. "What do you think?"

"What's left is definitely the better half of the cake." Lainie started for the door. "I'll go check with the bride."

Carrie sat on a stool to study the damage up close. "I like it, but what about the shortfall? Maybe we won't have enough cake for guests."

"I have some extra sheet cakes in the freezer, already iced," Angela said. "I could quickly add some flowers, and they'd be defrosted before we need them out there."

Carrie looked up. "You've got extra cakes?"

"Yeah." Angela shrugged. "I've seen these mishaps before. I like to be prepared."

Carrie patted her shoulder. "Extra points for you, girl." She turned to the others. "Okay, people. Move along. Nothing to see here."

Tuesday, May 14

John lamented that he and Lainie were too busy to see each other. "I'll send a summons for lunch next week" was the message he left one day while she consulted with a bride's mother. He was busy when Lainie returned the call but she left her reply: "How about another concert?"

She went home to see her mother on the Saturday before Mother's Day, but came back to attend church with John when Morgan was sustained as bishop. After a goodbye kiss in the parking lot, John and Lainie each had to hurry back to responsibilities in their own wards.

Then other things got in the way—a cancer fund drive in her neighborhood, a funeral, a spring party with her Sweet Souls, and a visit to her father after his emergency gallbladder surgery. Several days of CLE seminars kept John running back and forth between Provo and Salt Lake. Even the late-night phone calls were short because he and Lainie were too tired to talk very long.

"I really miss you," he said when he called that night.

"I miss you too."

"When can we see each other?"

"I'm working sixteen hours a day, including Mondays."

"How about lunch? You still eat, don't you?"

"I haven't had a real lunch since the last time we went to the Brick Oven, but I love these phone calls. That's enough for now, isn't it?"

"Imagining my arms around you just doesn't compare with the real thing."

"Keep the faith. It won't always be like this."

John paused, then chuckled. "I know what we'll do. Get in your car right now. I'll meet you at North Park."

"John, I'm already in bed."

"So am I, but please, Lainie. I need to see you. I'm putting my shirt on right now."

She sighed. "It's closer to my house. If I'm there first, I won't get out of my car."

"That's a good idea. I'm grabbing my keys right now. Oops. Forgot my shoes."

"I'll park in the lot, not on the street." She pulled on her jeans. "Go the speed limit."

"I will if you will."

Fifteen minutes later, he backed in next to her white Volvo. They got out of their cars and he gathered her into his arms. "Thanks for doing this madcap thing with me."

"This just seems like the logical place to be," Lainie replied.

"In the park?"

"In your arms."

They kissed and sat on a bench next to the playground, her head on his shoulder. "I feel like I've been hit by a runaway locomotive, then trampled by a herd of stampeding buffalo," John said, "and I've only felt like that once before."

"When was that?"

He turned to kiss her hair. "When I first met you."

She pulled back. "Now, John, I don't want to be responsible . . ."

He held her shoulders. "But you are, Lainie. I'm so full of you I can't think about anything else. You're in my head and in my heart all the time. I've never felt this way before."

"John, this is not the right time for this conversation. I can't . . ."

"I have to say this."

"Please don't. I'm not ready to hear it."

"When?"

"I can't answer that now. Things are so crazy for me."

It was an impossible question. He'd known all along that he was in competition with Sophie's Place. He got up and went to sit at a nearby picnic table. Lainie followed and sat with him, nestling under his right arm. He pulled her close, kissed her, and said, "I'm sorry. I'm being irrational."

"Things will calm down in a few weeks, I'm sure."

He smoothed her hair. "Yeah. You're right."

"In the meantime, let's enjoy what we have." She held his face and kissed him.

Suddenly a loud voice called, "Hey! Hey! What's goin' on?"

John and Lainie looked up to see a police officer loping toward them with a flashlight. Only then did John notice the squad car on the west side of the park. "Is there a problem?" he said, trying not to sound annoyed that the flashlight nearly blinded him.

"What are you doin'?" the officer asked as he reached them.

"We're having a civilized conversation," John replied. "That's legal as far as I'm aware."

"Hey, lady, you all right?" The policeman shone the flashlight in Lainie's face.

"I'm fine." She coughed, stifling a laugh.

"You're sure?"

"Yes, sir." She looked down and cleared her throat.

"Well, you're here illegally. This park closes at eleven PM."

"What time is it now?"

"About midnight. I'm not sure what you're doin' but you can't do it here. You've got ten minutes to vacate the premises."

"We lost track of time." John glanced at Lainie, who was still fighting the giggles. "We apologize for violating park protocol. Consider us gone."

The officer strode off, and once his patrol car drove away, John and Lainie burst out laughing. Standing at the edge of the grass with their arms around each other, they sighed.

"You'd better go home before *I* take you into custody," she said.

John kissed her. "Mmm. I think I'd like that. I find you very arresting."

Friday, May 17

John coaxed Carrie and Lainie to sit in the rose cottage with him even though they were busy in the back yard that morning. "How's it going so far?" he asked.

Lainie wiped her forehead on the sleeve of her T-shirt. "Very well. We had a couple of close calls, but we were prepared with backups, so disaster was averted."

"Yes. Last week we encountered a kid who tried to climb a cake," Carrie said, "and this week we had a bride with a meltdown. Nothing we couldn't handle."

John laughed. "Glad to hear it."

"It's more than cake and punch around here. We have to be counselors and diplomats," Lainie told him.

"Referees sometimes, too." With her forefingers Carrie pulled her lower eyelids down. "We have bags under our eyes, and our calendar is full. I'd say that's a sign of success."

Lainie smiled. "We don't have any openings until September."

"Good for you." John grinned. "I knew you had the talent for it."

"Says the guy who questioned our motives," Carrie retorted.

"Listen, Sassy, I've been thinking about this for a couple of days. You've got good insurance coverage on your business, but I want you both to see your doctors for checkups and get the best personal health coverage you can qualify for."

"I will if you will," Lainie responded. "It's been three weeks since the play ended. Have you seen a doctor yet?"

"Why does John need to see a doctor?" Carrie asked.

"He has a repulsive mole on his shoulder, and he's pretending it's just a beauty mark."

"How do you know?"

"He showed it to me."

"Oh, just a little game of 'I'll show you my mole if you show me yours.'" Carrie laughed.

"That's enough," John growled. "It was completely innocent."

"Well, he kept scratching back there and I was curious. Besides, I don't have any moles."

He surrendered, his hands in the air. "All right. I'll call today." He pointed at Lainie's skeptical frown. "You think I won't, but I will."

"I'll believe it when I see it."

"Thanks for giving us our five-minute break for this week." Carrie pinched John's cheek. "Come on, partner, let's get these tables ready."

John and Lainie waved at each other, and both went back to work.

"Done," he said when he left a message later that day on her answering machine, "but my doctor's going on vacation and I couldn't get an appointment till June 20. Can you get away Monday afternoon? Let's celebrate your birthday with a picnic. That brief clandestine meeting in the park wasn't enough."

Lainie looked forward to the fresh air, a park with grass and trees, and to being with John for a few uninterrupted hours. She left a message on his machine: "Too bad you have to go to the doctor on your birthday, but the picnic sounds perfect. You're right—I do need a break. Call me Sunday and we'll plan it."

On the phone, he proposed a picnic done the easy way. "Let's stop at a deli and get everything there."

"Sounds good to me, and I'll sneak a few cookies from Sophie's Place."

"You read my mind."

"I'm getting pretty good at that. I knew you'd make that doctor's appointment, too."

"That was easy. If you're so smart, tell me where we're going for the picnic."

"To a park, of course."

John chuckled. "Wrong, but thanks for playing."

"Okay, where are we going?"

"There's a place I know up the canyon. I guarantee you've never been there before, but I know you're going to like it."

Monday, May 20

As the car moved along Provo Canyon Road with that soothing jazz on the stereo, the pressures of Sophie's Place began to melt away, and Lainie relaxed against the soft leather seat. They passed the parks at the mouth of the canyon, so she guessed John might be headed for Sundance or Heber Valley. Quizzing him about it would be fruitless.

Lainie watched emerging signs of spring as the road followed the Provo River. A few miles past Bridal Veil Falls, John turned right into a wide parking area fishermen used, and crossed a wooden bridge almost hidden by overgrown tamarisk. Then he followed an unmarked dirt road winding into a narrow side canyon. Lainie noticed a No Trespassing sign nailed to a fence. In about a quarter of a mile the canyon opened up to a wide, flat expanse of lush pasture. John pulled off the left side of the road and parked under the speckled shade of a gnarled ash tree. "Here we are." He helped her out of the car and opened the sagging gate in an old wood fence.

"Can we do this?" She looked down at the grass and up at the steep canyon wall. "Isn't this private property?"

"Yeah. It's my private wilderness. Welcome to Marchbanks Retreat."

"Yours? How did you find land in this pristine place?"

"After about a decade of trespassing to get out of town and breathe fresh air, I saw a For Sale sign a couple of years ago, and that was that. I've leased it for pasture to keep the grass cut and fertilized, but the rancher died this winter and his kids sold his herd. I've got 53.5 acres here in a deep box canyon." John chuckled. "I don't know what

I'm ever going to do with it. It's too small for the Bureau of Land Management to care about."

By his serene smile and mellow demeanor, Lainie could tell he loved being here. "John, this is the place in your four-seasons paintings."

He nodded. "In the winter I have to hike from the bridge. See that stream over there?" He pointed to the flowing water on the other side of the pasture. "Watercress grows wild. Had the water tested this spring and it's potable." He brought things from the car and they spread the blanket in the six-inch grass under the tree, sat cross-legged, and removed the food from the bag. He smiled at her. "This is nice. Till now I've always been here alone." He prayed and they ate, relaxing and taking their time.

She speared a forkful of pasta salad from a carton. "How's that sad little boy in your Primary class?"

"You mean the divorce situation?" John put down his sandwich. "I'm so disgusted with that judge. Opposing counsel put on such a good show that Her Honor granted a continuance, on the condition that the couple goes to counseling. This is a very lenient, bleeding-heart judge who gives everybody the benefit of the doubt, even if evidence suggests they don't deserve it. But I don't trust that man with his own kids. I recommended they be removed from the home except for regular visitations while the parents are in counseling, and she approved Curtis and his wife for temporary foster care."

"Have you seen any more bruises?"

"No, but I probably will, now that the restraining order has been lifted."

"What does a continuance do?"

"It suspends the trial. It'll be continued after they go to counseling for a few weeks. I met with the judge in chambers and strenuously disagreed, but she's the boss."

"I'm really sorry to hear that, John."

He sighed. "Well, that's what you call due process."

"Thank goodness for Primary teachers." Lainie brightened with a smile. "Hey, I have some good news."

He returned his attention to his sandwich. "I'm always ready for that."

"I got my labs last week, and I've passed my five-year-cancer-free milestone."

"That's great."

She gave him a cheeky grin. "Nicest thirty-eighth birthday present I could have, but we've been so busy I haven't had time to celebrate properly."

Then John frowned at her. "Hey, you're sassy after all. You had that appointment already, before you challenged me to get one."

"Had to get you there somehow. Now you don't have to worry about it anymore."

When they finished with their sandwiches and salads, John took the lunch debris back to the car and returned with a camera and a square plastic box. "I've got a surprise for you."

"What's this?" Lainie asked.

"First-of-the-season Rainier cherries from Oregon. They ripen before the big black Bing cherries do, and my sister Margaret sends me some every year. They're just starting to show up in Utah stores, and they're pricey." Lainie took several. He held one up and she admired its delicate gold-and-pink flesh, scarlet blush, and peak ripeness. "A lot of people like them cold," he went on, "but I think there's nothing better than a cherry warmed by the sun, plucked off the tree, and consumed like a delicate offering, the most delectable sacrifice to Mother Nature."

"I've never known anyone so inspired by fruit."

"Only some," he conceded. "Oregon does have a lot of fabulous fruit, but since I came to Utah I've developed the same reverence for Green River cantaloupe, Cache Valley raspberries, and certain varieties of Utah Valley peaches."

From where they sat on the blanket, they tried, with only moderate success, to throw the cherry pits into rows in the clearing beyond them, perhaps the beginnings of an orchard. When they'd tossed the last pit and wiped their hands, John said, "Now I'm going to take your birthday portrait."

"Is that necessary?"

"Oh yes. It's your first visit to Marchbanks Retreat, and I always take a picture of people when they first come here. You know—recording their responses to my little sanctuary."

Lainie frowned skeptically. "But you said no one else has ever been here before."

He helped her up. "Then we'll start a new tradition."

They walked across the pasture to the stream, and she sat on the grass while he took several shots. He held her hand as they walked back to the blanket. "It's Monday. Want to have family home evening? I have the conference issue of the *Ensign* in the car, and we could take turns reading a couple of talks."

She sat on the blanket again. "You're determined that I'm going to April conference with you, even if it's from the magazine after the fact."

"Actually, I went to the Sunday afternoon session with the eight-year-olds in my Primary class. That little red-haired girl I mentioned is the bishop's daughter, and he had an extra ticket for me." He took the camera and the rest of the cherries to the car, then returned with the magazine.

Lainie stretched out and propped herself up with her left elbow. John sat cross-legged near her and began to read. She hadn't relaxed this way in months, and halfway through the first talk, she fell asleep, her head on her bent arm.

She sank into one of those profound sleeps so hard to awaken from, devoid of dreams, satisfying and restful. At first she thought the irritation on her nose was a fly she couldn't discourage, and then she became conscious enough to open her eyes and see that it was John tickling her face with a small handful of grass pinched together like a brush. She moaned and turned onto her back, out of his reach.

"Wake up, sleeping beauty. You've been zonked out for forty minutes."

"Oh, John, I'm sorry." She sighed. "This is some stimulating family home evening, huh?"

"Well, I have to admit, watching you sleep has a certain appeal."

She sat up and turned to him. "Yeah, like watching snails migrate."

He laughed. "I didn't notice you were asleep until I looked up to make a comment. I slept for about twenty minutes myself, right there beside you. When I woke up I was very busy counting your eyelashes. You have three more on your right eyelid than you have on your left."

"Well, thank you for the eyelash report." She sipped from the drink she'd left at the edge of the blanket. "I didn't realize how much I needed a break from my routine. Thanks for making me take some time away from it."

"You do work pretty hard."

"It's fun and stimulating and creative and everything I promised Carrie it would be. But it is stressful." Lainie smiled at him and stretched out again. "John, I'm honored that you've shared this beautiful place with me. It's a privilege being here."

He lay beside her. "Permission to approach the bench."

"Granted."

He moved closer. "Lainie, lying here watching you sleep, I thought . . . I wondered . . ." He reached over and kissed her. It was gentle at first, but he pulled her closer as the kiss intensified. Then he released her. "I'm sorry. I shouldn't have done that." He sat up and turned away. "Maybe we should go now."

She took his arm to stop him and moved over to sit where she could see his face straight on. "In the interest of full disclosure, I think you should know that I liked it. A lot. I always do."

He shook his head and frowned. "I'll cease and desist before you find me in contempt. We might get carried away again." He tried to stand, but she held his arm.

"John, you pulled away like you're tied to some invisible force that suddenly reeled you in. That's never happened before." Lainie held his face to make him look at her. "This is not the man who persuaded me to meet him in the park at midnight last week so we could hold each other and kiss." She smoothed his hair. "Johnny, what's wrong? Throw yourself on the mercy of the court. Let me in."

His eyes searched hers as if looking for a safe place where his soul could land. He took a deep breath and a long pause. "Years ago at the University of Oregon, I met a girl. I was twenty and hadn't dated very much. She was very bright and pretty and funny—everything I thought I could like. We had the same American lit class that fall semester. She was two years older, and I was flattered by the attention. In no time at all we were a couple. She was a bit moody at times, but I figured everybody is, to a certain extent. I liked it that she organized and scheduled everything because I was still a bit undisciplined. We went everywhere together, and did almost everything except sleep together—not that she didn't want to, you understand. She thought I was old-fashioned to believe marriage is a sacrament and a bed is a place of sacred bonding. I couldn't go there with someone I didn't love, and I wouldn't treat it casually like some of my roommates did."

John pulled his knees up and crossed his arms over them, reaching around to scratch his shoulder. "It went on that way the rest of the semester, but her moods got more erratic and I was ready to break it off. Then she gave me a lot of expensive Christmas presents, which made me even more uncomfortable. When I didn't give her the engagement ring she expected, she threw a spectacular tantrum. That scared me. I told her it was time for both of us to date other people, and then she really had a fit." He sighed and rubbed his chin. "I didn't know enough about it at the time to recognize the symptoms, and then her roommate told me she was bipolar. She felt so good when she was with me, she quit taking her medication."

"Oh, that's not good," Lainie said. "That can be dangerous."

"Yeah. It was. I just wanted some relief from those unpredictable mood swings. Every time I tried to break up with her, she threatened to harm herself, or both of us. I couldn't take it anymore and I hit the wall."

Lainie gave him her hand and he clung to it. "What happened?"

"We had the most terrible argument yet. When she slapped me, I completely lost my temper. In the heat of the moment I used some abusive language to tell her to get out of my life for good." John put his head in his hands.

Lainie gasped. "And she did, in a way that would hurt you the most."

He ran his tongue across his lips and looked away. "Yeah. At a very high rate of speed, she . . . uh . . . drove her car off a very high mountain road into a very deep lake." He swallowed hard. "It was the middle of the day, perfect weather. Accident report said no skid marks."

"And you've felt guilty ever since. Oh, Johnny, I'm sorry."

He shook his head. "I should have seen it coming. I should have encouraged her to stay on her medication. I should have tried to get help."

"You were young and inexperienced. You couldn't have known."

He stared ahead, and Lainie could see his emotions building. "When she died, I was just glad not to have to deal with the craziness of her moods anymore." His voice broke. "What kind of a person thinks like that?"

"So you took a ride on the guilt trip merry-go-round."

"She did everything to please me, and I allowed it because I thought that's what being in love was supposed to be like. But it was really a calculated, cynical trap to make me feel obligated to her. Finally I realized she didn't love me. It was a game she played, her twisted version of love, and the rules kept changing with her illness."

"She used you. That's devastating to a man's ego."

He looked at Lainie, his eyes full of sorrow. "A bright young woman died because of *my* ignorance, *my* insensitivity, *my* inadequacy. A thing like that is with you all the time."

"I don't think there's a person alive who isn't haunted by something from the past."

"But what if I'm not enough? What if something like that happens again?"

"When you're doing your best, you and the Savior together will always be enough."

John stared at her until his eyes welled up and he looked away. "It's a good thing my LDS friends were there to pick up the pieces."

She touched his shoulder to reassure him. "I think you're a good, caring man with a lot of love to give. I'm sorry you've spent so many years being cynical about relationships."

He sighed deeply and caught his breath. "I don't want to go through that again."

"No, I wouldn't either, and I'm no expert, but from what I've seen, not all relationships are like that." She watched his profile as he looked up at the canyon wall. "You've never told anyone else about this, have you."

"What would be the point?"

"Now you think that if you get close to another woman, something bad will happen."

"I know it makes no sense. Lainie, I've never been as close to anyone as I am now to you, and I like it, but today I'm hitting the wall again."

He looked surprised when she leaned forward and placed a comforting kiss on his cheek. "Oh, Johnny, talking about it is the first step to recovery, and you just took a giant step. God knows your heart. You can't change things, and I won't tell you to let it go, as if that were easy to do, because I know it's harder to forgive yourself than another person. But I will remind you that Someone already paid the price for it. His yoke is easy and His burden is light."

When she saw a glimmer of hope in John's eyes, she went on. "Two months before I was diagnosed with cancer, a fireside speaker gave me a whole new understanding of that scripture. His yoke is easy because it's *His* yoke; Christ shares our experience in this adventure called life. I've felt that in a powerful way. On some of my worst cancer days, it was as if He were sitting with me, holding my hand."

John wiped tears from her cheeks. "I hadn't thought of it that way. Lainie, in my head I know you're right, but my heart . . ." He frowned again.

"Sometimes in life, when you have no control over heavy things, you can't do anything but surrender them. Refuse ownership. It doesn't belong to you anyway."

He shifted to put his arms around her. "This is making sense. Go on."

She sat back a little. "What I learned is that His burden is a responsibility, a challenge in life, like adjusting to a handicap or recovering from a trauma, but it isn't oppressive. It's light, not in terms of weight, but in terms of illumination, personal revelation, awareness. It teaches you, if you let it, and you gain greater spiritual maturity because of it. That's how you turn a bad experience into a blessing."

"Thank you for the new perspective," John whispered.

"Thanks for trusting me."

"I do. We're friends."

Eleven

Saturday, May 25

Kyle parked in the driveway at Angela's house and said another prayer before he knocked on her door. He hoped her heart would be soft enough to listen to what he had to say.

Opening the screen door, she looked surprised. "You're out early."

"It's spring. There's daylight to catch." He stepped inside and pulled off his baseball cap.

"Maybe that bump on the head made you forget that Sophie's Place is on the other side of the block."

"I'm pretty good with geography. I came to see you. To talk."

"Oh. Well, we can talk in the kitchen. Would you like some apple juice?"

"Sure. Thanks." It was a comfortable yellow kitchen with lots of counter space, part of the room obviously an add-on to the original home. Through the window Kyle could see that the back door led to a deck and a large back yard. He sat at the table. Behind him a door ajar led to a bedroom that didn't appear to belong to a teenager. "Are the kids gone already this morning?"

"Julie's selling concessions for the debate club at a track meet, but Brandon's still in bed. He was out with friends last night and made it home one minute before curfew. He has till noon on Saturday to do chores, and then in the afternoons he has free time."

"What kinds of chores?"

"His room, the yard, cleaning the bathroom—that kind of thing." Angela put the juice on the table and sat across from him.

"Well, I'm here because I have a kind of proposal, I guess you could call it."

She raised her eyebrows. "That sounds awfully serious."

He took a sip. "Mark told me about the problems you've been having with Brandon."

She got up to start loading the dishwasher. "It's his dad, really. Sean gives him whatever he asks for because it makes Sean look good."

Kyle drew his right ankle up to his left knee and watched her. She looked a little nervous and uncomfortable even in her own territory, and he knew she'd rather not talk about this. "That's understandable. Every dad wants to be a hero to his son."

"But Sean has no discipline or boundaries." Angela was wiping counters now. "He's so indulgent that Brandon turns into a brat over a two-day weekend visit. I can't compete with luxury."

"You don't have to. Give him something constructive to do so there's a visible outcome he can be proud of."

"And how am I going to do that? I work five and a half days a week. He has to govern himself a lot of the time."

"If you'd let me, I could help him." Kyle's tone was gentle.

She stopped and met his eyes. "What do you mean?"

He tapped the other side of the table, so she dried her hands and sat down. "That day at Sophie's Place, before I fell off the ladder, Brandon was eager to get into the project with us, willing to do anything. When I was hurt, he had the presence of mind to bring you to help me. Then he worked with Mark and stayed there all day until the crew finished at sundown, even carried pipe for the sprinkler guys. He didn't stop to go to the movie with friends even though his dad had sent the money."

Angela nodded. "He's never done that before."

"And when we laid the sod, he was right there, pulling his own weight without being asked. I could work with a boy like that."

"He told me how much he enjoyed watching you and Mark trim the apple tree, then helping chip the branches and being trusted to use the chainsaw. He said being part of the sod crew was like a team, and that's an experience he's never had before."

"My team members have to know they can depend on each other." Kyle leaned forward. "Look, Angie, school's almost out. I could give

Brandon a summer job mowing lawns and trimming shrubs. Lots of boys earn pocket change doing that. I'll supervise him myself. It'd teach him how to work and give him a sense of accomplishment. Does he get an allowance?"

"I can't afford much, but Sean is overly indulgent. We live on what I earn because I wanted to be completely free of him, and alimony is a controlling tie. I didn't want anything for myself. But he still pays child support for the kids." Angela looked up at Kyle, defiance in her eyes. "I put all the money in their accounts as soon as the checks come, and they buy their own clothes and shoes. I help them manage it, but I don't use one penny of what he gives them, no matter what. It was hard at first but we've survived."

"Tough choice," Kyle said, regarding her with greater respect. "Look, I'll teach Brandon that it's honorable to work for what he gets."

Angela sat back in the chair and paused to control her quivering mouth. "You don't know how I've prayed."

"You can keep it up. Mothers are good at that, and he'll need a lot more prayers in the next few years." She caught her breath as Kyle went on. "I've been thinking about this since that day at Sophie's Place. Like I told you then, I felt an instant connection with him. What I'd like to do for Brandon will teach him some important things Sean obviously doesn't know. When he's older he can work in the greenhouse and in the store. He'll discover his own potential. He'll learn practical marketable skills and have his own savings, in case Sean isn't so free with his means when Brandon decides to go on a mission."

"And that's your proposal?"

Kyle rested his forearms on the table and smiled. "Angie, you give me your boy for a few hours a week and every summer, and in a few years, when he's ready to leave home, I'll give you back a man who'll make you proud."

She got a tissue from a box on the counter and stood there for a moment. "I don't know what to say. That's a very generous offer, but I don't know."

"I don't expect anything from you. If you're worried about that, you can rest easy. It is what it is—a plan to help a somewhat confused boy grow up to be a good man. No strings."

Angela laughed and sat again, wiping her eyes. "Well, I assume you're not out on parole doing community service because you have to."

He laughed a little too. "You don't know me very well, but here's a summary of Kyle Kirkwood: I'm a church-going Mormon. I honor the priesthood I hold. I have a current temple recommend and use it. I love my family and treat my parents with respect. I pay my taxes, vote in every election, and donate to good causes. I don't abuse people or animals. My worst bad habit is my work. I just love helping things grow, both plants and people, and that's how I spend most of my time. Is that enough of a résumé to qualify me?"

Her eyes brimmed with tears again. "Why? You don't have to do this for a boy you hardly know."

"I read people's eyes, Angie, and looking in Brandon's eyes it's easy to tell he needs a man in his life. Well, I'm a man who needs a boy. Part of the reason I want to do this is because I never got a chance to raise my own son."

She caught her breath. "You have children?"

"My son died in a car accident when he was eight months old. His name was Brandon."

She stared at him. "Oh, Kyle, I'm sorry. I had no idea."

He swallowed and shrugged. "It was ten years ago."

"I'm so sorry," she whispered. "Brandon's in his room. I'll get him for you."

In a minute, the boy clattered downstairs, his pillow face and bed-head hair evidence that he hadn't started the day yet. "Hey, Kyle. Whatcha doin'?" Brandon sat at the table, and Angela moved to stand behind him, her hands on the back of his chair.

"I have a business proposal," Kyle began. "I talked it over with your mother and she said I could ask you about it. You did a great job the day we pruned the apple tree at Sophie's Place, trimming the branches and helping Mark with the chipper, and pitching in with the crew. You learned fast and worked hard the day we laid the sod. I was hoping you'd do me a favor this summer by taking on some other work."

"What kind? I have six weeks with Sean from Pioneer Day to Labor Day."

"Sure. I understand how important that is to you, and we can work around it. I need somebody dependable to do lawn care for five clients. Will you take the job?"

Angela patted his shoulder. "It'd be a way to earn some money of your own."

Brandon turned to her. "Sean gives me what I want."

She sat next to him, her arm around his shoulder. "What if some day you want something that's really important to you and he won't pay for it?"

Kyle waited for Brandon to absorb that. "Besides, that's a handout and it makes you a beggar. There's a lot of satisfaction in knowing you earned the money you spend."

"Remember what you said when you earned money working with the sod crew?" Angela exchanged glances with Kyle.

"Yeah. I liked it. It felt good."

"That's called self-respect," Kyle said.

Brandon frowned. "How much would I get paid for this?"

"It's negotiable. I can teach you the difference between a ten-dollar job and a twenty-dollar job."

"Look, Son, why don't you try it for a few weeks? If you don't like it, you don't have to do it after you come back from Park City."

Kyle glanced at Angela again, impressed with her negotiation skills. "I can agree to that," he said.

Brandon looked at Kyle. "So what would I have to do?"

"I'll give you five clients here in this neighborhood. You might know some of them already—maybe they're in your ward. Some of the yards are bigger than others, and some of the clients may want you to tend the flower beds or trim the shrubs too. Some homeowners want lawn care every week, and others prefer every ten days. You could plan to do one yard a day if you want, and then you'd have the rest of the day for other things you like to do. You have a mower, don't you?"

"Yeah. Mom makes me cut our grass all the time."

"Good. I'll show you how to set up a business of your own. I spend most of my time in Springville every day, but I'll still supervise you. One of your five clients is Sophie's Place. I'll work there with you every Monday morning and you can report on how things are going."

Angela's arm was around Brandon again. "What do you think?"

He sat back in the chair. "I don't know. That kind of ties me down every day."

"That's called responsibility," Kyle said. "That's what adults do."

Angela smoothed Brandon's unruly hair. "Kyle's right. Those hours will come and go whether you're working or playing, and you might as well make good use of the time."

"Just what I was going to say," Kyle added. "Look, I'll show you everything you need to know. As long as you remember what each client wants and follow their directions, you shouldn't have a problem. I know you're capable. We couldn't have finished that project at Sophie's Place on time without you."

Brandon frowned. "I don't know. It sounds kinda hard."

"It's a challenge, like getting to the next level of a video game," Angela coaxed.

Kyle smiled again. "Here's what I'll do to sweeten the deal. You report to me at Sophie's Place every Monday morning about how the previous week went, but if I also get good reports from your mother and from the clients, I'll give you a bonus. And I'll keep you on standby when we need extra help laying sod, so you could earn even more."

Brandon smiled at his mother. "You couldn't ask for a better offer than that," she said.

"And if you like it and want to stay with it," Kyle went on, "you can rake leaves this fall and shovel snow this winter for the same clients. In a few years you can work for me in Springville like Mark does." Kyle detected a light in Brandon's eyes. "What do you think?"

Angela leaned closer to Brandon. "Why not try it until July when you go with Sean."

Brandon smiled. "Okay. Just till July."

"Well, that's a deal." Kyle stood to seal it with a handshake. "Have your mother bring you to the garden center first thing Monday morning and I'll help you get started."

"Thanks for the job."

"Want some breakfast?" Angela patted Brandon's cheek. "We left pancakes on the counter." Brandon went to find the food, and his mother followed Kyle to the front door.

"How's your head?"

"Well, I can wear a hat again." He twirled it in his hand, grinning. "So. Well, uh, thanks for the apple juice."

He saw gratitude in her eyes as she said, "It's the least I could do. Thanks for helping my son."

~

While Brandon had breakfast, Angela made a menu plan for the coming week and started a food inventory so she could compile a shopping list. She asked Brandon for ideas, and by the time he got the lawn mower out of the shed, she was ready to go.

The phone on the end of the counter rang. She picked it up and looked at the caller ID. "What is it, Sean?"

"My, you're charming on a Saturday morning."

"It's my specialty. What brings you out of your cave this early?"

He sighed. "I've been thinkin' about my kids."

"So you're in groundbreaking territory."

"You shouldn't be sarcastic, Angela. Sarcastic isn't pretty."

"I've got things to do, Sean. Did you want to talk to one of the kids? Brandon's cutting the grass, and Julie left a couple of hours ago."

"I'm sincere. I just want to tell you what I've been thinkin' about."

Angela stood at the back door looking out into the yard as Brandon attached the grass catcher to the mower. She wished she could afford a new lawn mower. "As far as I know it was probably 1973 the last time you were sincere."

"That's the year after I was born."

"Just sayin'."

"Be serious, Angela. I've got something important to tell you."

"Okay. You've got about two minutes before I'm headed out for the grocery store."

"Talking with my attorney this week, I realized I haven't really been thinking about my kids' future. Last time I saw Julie it nearly knocked me off my feet to see how grown up she is."

"Uh-huh. Sixteen. She'll do her college applications next year."

"Yeah, and Brandon's not far behind," Sean said.

"You were always good with math."

"I'm planning to put aside some money for a college fund for each of them. What do you think about that?"

It stopped her. Angela felt pressure instantly lift from her shoulders. And then she remembered this was Sean she was talking to. "A college fund."

"Yeah, they'll both probably want to go to college, and they should. They're smart kids."

"Uh-huh. And?"

"Well, you always want something better for your kids than you had for yourself. That's where I'm comin' from. I got too busy with business to finish my degree, and I don't want them to do that."

"Anything else, Sean? There has to be more to it than that."

"Oh, I almost forgot one little proviso."

He's using lawyer language, she thought. This is not a casual decision. "What's that?"

"It's a little thing, really. I have final approval on where they go to college."

"In other words, if you disapprove of their choices, they don't get the money." Angela felt the weight settle on her shoulders again. She took a deep breath and put her head in one hand. "You'll have to talk to them, Sean. It isn't my decision."

"Well, I just wanted to let you know what I'm doing."

"Very thoughtful." Angela felt her forehead heating up.

"I'll talk to them next time they're here."

"You do that, Sean."

"See ya, dollface."

Angela settled the phone carefully in its cradle on the counter before she could change her mind and throw it against the wall. *They're growing up and away from him and he doesn't like losing control.* She stuffed the shopping list in her pocket, grabbed her purse and keys, and headed for the car. *Dear Lord, prevent me from doing bodily harm to that scumbucket who happens to be the father of my children. And forgive me my infinitely bad judgment. Again.*

Carrie and Lainie liked the new turf that withstood heavy foot traffic. As it grew, the vegetable garden always delighted guests. Angela began teaching Jane and Julie how to make Sophie's signature cookies, the featured item so popular with clients.

Carrie's cousins, Iris and Lily, came on Memorial Day weekend to take the furniture and other heirlooms they were entitled to from Sophie's Place. Lily chose the secretary Sophie left in the parlor, and Iris claimed an ornate armoire from Sophie's bedroom. Both took a few incidentals from the upstairs bedrooms and all the items Sophie placed in storage last winter for them and their children. Carrie expressed concern that they weren't taking enough of the things that belonged to them.

"I grew up in this museum," Iris replied. "Enough's enough. You can keep it here as long as it fits in so well with the theme of your business."

"Well said," Lily agreed. "Mementos of my parents and grandparents are all I want."

Carrie nodded. "All right. We'll store everything for you here in the museum. Who knows—maybe one of your granddaughters will turn out to be an incarnation of your mother and will fall in love with it all."

"Oh, perish the thought," Iris moaned.

Lily frowned. "I wish you hadn't said that, Carrie. It's going to keep me awake at night."

Twelve

Monday, May 27, Memorial Day

Angela almost never got to Springville even though it was just a few miles south of Provo, and she never even knew the Hobble Creek Garden Center existed, but she followed Kyle's directions and there it was—with smiling employees wearing red vests, helping people in the greenhouse and store. When Angela and Brandon found Kyle, also sporting a red vest, he was working with a customer but smiled and waved.

For a few minutes, Brandon and Angela wandered down rows of green seedlings in flats that identified the vegetables and flowers, some with colorful blooms.

Kyle caught up with them and nodded at Angela, then gave Brandon a high five. "Good morning. Welcome."

Angela gestured toward the flats and potted seedlings. "You grow all of these in your greenhouse?"

"Quite a few. We have to start some as early as January or February." He motioned toward the back of the store. "Come on. My office is this way."

They went to a small room furnished with cushioned, wrought-iron lawn furniture and cluttered with seed catalogs, industry magazines, and small garden tools. Brandon's attention turned to some charts tacked to the wall above the furniture, showing varieties and seasonal growth patterns of vegetables and flowers. Hanging over the bookcase, a large and thriving Boston fern seemed content with its role as window treatment. On the other side of the room a scruffy wooden desk in the corner had a bookcase beside it and a guitar case next to a computer. Two framed documents hung on the wall nearby.

Angela tapped the glass. "They give degrees in garden center?" One was a bachelor of science degree, and the other a master's, both from Colorado State University.

Kyle sat down at the computer and hit some keys. "Soil science. No big deal. That just means I'm an authority on dirt. I guess you could say I'm well grounded."

"And so down to earth."

"But I have a lot of dirty little secrets."

She tugged the bill of his cap. "You can be such a clod sometimes."

"What's this?" Brandon held the handle of a lawn trimmer.

"That's yours." Kyle took the page that emerged from the printer and attached the sheet to a clipboard. "If you're going to be in this business, you need the right tools. Trimming the edges of your lawns with that gives your work a professional finish. You can use it in your mother's yard, too."

Angela interrupted. "But that's . . ."

"I'm planning to come over tomorrow morning and use your back yard as a school room to teach Brandon the finer points of pruning bushes and planning flower beds. Is that okay?"

She sat in a chair. "Sure. If you think . . ."

"Yeah, I think." He turned back to Brandon. "If you stick with this job past the first frost, this trimmer is a bonus. Otherwise, I'll send you a bill." Kyle exchanged glances with Angela as if asking her permission.

"It's a guy thing, strictly between the two of you," she said.

"Sit here and I'll show you what to do." Kyle handed the clipboard to Brandon and sat on the sofa, his ankles crossed on the coffee table. For the next twenty minutes, he went over the names on the list one by one, describing the particular challenges with each yard. "A lot of things are changing at Sophie's Place, so we'll learn about that together."

"I really like that yard," Brandon said. "It'll be fun taking care of it."

"Some of the other yards haven't had much attention for a while, so they might not be fun at first. Find out exactly what the homeowners want, and set up a work schedule. Call first and introduce yourself as a garden-center employee. Their phone numbers are next to their names and addresses on this list so you can make an appointment. Don't expect your mother to do that for you. This is your job, not hers."

"Okay." Brandon gave his mother a thumbs up.

Kyle tapped the top of the clipboard. "If you have any problems, that's my phone number. It's a private line at the store. I'll see you every Monday at Sophie's Place and bring your pay for the previous week. We'll discuss whether you get a bonus, and if you do, I'll bring it the following week. Okay?" Brandon nodded, and Kyle looked at Angela. "Okay?"

"Another guy thing," she replied. "I have a job already."

"She's right, Brandon. Your job, your responsibility."

Brandon looked up at Kyle. "Yeah. My mom's always had a job. I know how that goes."

Kyle smiled at Angela. "I really admire what your mother does. She goes to work every day and does a good job there, and then comes home and keeps a house going and raises two great kids. That's not easy. She's a wonderful mother."

"Yeah, I know," Brandon said.

Looking down, Angela thought, *That's laid on kind of thick. What would Nicole say?*

Kyle got up and grabbed the trimmer. "Come on. Let's go outside and I'll show you how to use this thing."

When Brandon and Angela left half an hour later, Kyle walked with them to her beat-up-looking Ford Taurus in the parking lot in front of the store. Brandon put the trimmer in the trunk, and then he and Kyle stood grinning at each other. "You've got what it takes to do a great job," Kyle assured him. They did a fist bump, and Brandon got into the car.

Kyle came around to the driver's side. "Thanks for everything," Angela said, letting him see the admiration in her eyes.

He tapped the distinctive finish on the roof of the car. "Too bad about your paint job."

Angela fished the keys out of her purse. "Well, I keep up with the maintenance and it gets me where I need to go. Besides, it's paid for, it's easy to find in a big parking lot, and nobody's going to steal a car that looks like this."

Kyle laughed. "Logical beyond question." She got in and he tapped the roof again and waved before turning toward the building and greeting customers approaching the front door.

Brandon whistled softly. "Look at that place. I'll bet he makes lots of money."

Angela smiled as she pulled out onto the street. "I get the feeling Kyle's business is more about people than plants."

⁓

At the store entrance Kyle turned to watch Angela's car leaving the parking lot. He wondered why a woman like that, so brimming with vitality, had married a man who crushed her spirit and wasn't worthy of her. He sighed and stopped speculating. *None of my business.*

⁓

John and Lainie made a return trip to Marchbanks Retreat on Memorial Day. They ate lunch under a cottonwood tree next to the stream, enjoying the coolness of the canyon, and as they put things away he remarked, "You're very quiet today. What's on your mind?"

She slipped off her sandals and put her feet in the water. "Lots of things. I think it's this place. It's so peaceful here I become more reflective. So many things have changed in my life lately. I'm still adjusting, still deciding what I like about it and what needs to be changed again."

He took off his sandals and dangled his feet next to hers. "Does that have anything to do with me?"

She studied his face; everything about it was familiar now. "Where are you headed in your life? What are your goals?"

"Professionally, we're expanding to a full-service law practice where I'll have more trial experience and new challenges. Personally, I intend to keep teaching Primary until someone takes me out kicking and screaming. I have lots of things to read and paint, and I'm thinking about auditioning for another play. I have relationship challenges with some of my Catholic family members who are still unhappy that I'm

LDS, and I try to show them love and patience. I have lots of friends, one in particular I like very much. That would be you." He pushed some wind-blown hair away from her face. "What about you? Where are you headed?"

Lainie leaned back on her hands. "Since I passed my five-year milestone, the world feels wide open. Professionally, I'm adjusting to being in charge and making decisions at Sophie's Place. It's given me some challenges I didn't anticipate, but every day is stimulating and interesting. Personally, I plan to continue loving my Sweet Souls until someone takes me out kicking and screaming. I have a wonderful family, aging parents I love, and lots of new friends, one in particular I like very much. That would be you."

John took her hand and entwined their fingers. "We seem to be in parallel places, so alike, and yet like railroad tracks, always the same distance apart."

"Until my new livelihood is stable, that's where I'll have to stay."

"Does it have anything to do with the guy who left you when you were diagnosed with cancer? Because I'm not . . ."

"No, you're not a bit like him. I've known that for months."

"He made you afraid, though, didn't he?"

"I think about him as little as possible. That whole episode was an enormous mistake."

"Am I a mistake? Do you want me to go away and leave you alone?"

"Of course not." She shook her head. "John, I really don't know what else I want, what else will fit in my life."

He frowned but said, "I can accept that, as long as we don't lose ground, as long as our friendship keeps growing. I've come to depend on it."

"I'll do my best, but that may not be enough for you. A lot has happened in the five months since we met."

He kissed the back of her hand. "I think about you all the time. And I think about us and all the possibilities."

"I think of us as very good friends who are going to stay on the right tracks."

He smiled. "Come on. Let's hike to the waterfall." She drew back with a skeptical look. "Honest, Lainie. There's one at the end of the canyon. We can just walk upstream."

"You're the only person I know who has a private waterfall."

Playful splashing developed into a thoroughly soaking, no-holds-barred, all-out water fight.

Monday, June 3

Kyle looked up and smiled as Angela came down the sidewalk to the English garden now transforming the front yard at Sophie's Place. Designed to be a natural setting for bridal photographs or a few moments of fragrant peace, the space included a trellis on one side, a pergola with a swing on the other, a bench by the sundial in the center, and a pea-gravel path connecting them. A graceful, well-established sycamore tree, with its distinctive bark, shaded the garden during the afternoon hours. Pots of bushes, greenery, and flats of flowers on the sidewalk awaited the gardener's attention. A border of low shrubs along the front had already been planted.

"This looks great." Angela sat on the bench near where Kyle worked in the far corner of the garden.

He continued digging. "It's the framework. Mark will put in the smaller plants this afternoon while I move on to another project." When the hole was deep and wide enough, Kyle stopped and rested on his shovel. "How's Brandon doing?"

"Well, he's sore from all the walking, and he's going to bed earlier so he can get up and work before the sun gets too hot."

"That's a wise choice." He pulled a lilac bush out of a pot, centered it in the hole, and knelt to loosen the root ball with his gloved hands. "How's his attitude?"

"Pretty good so far. He likes the praise people give him for doing a good job."

Kyle smiled and pushed soil around the plant. "He's a people person, don't you think?"

"Yes. Brandon gets a rush out of doing something that pleases others. That's the way I am. Sean and I were a perfect match—he manipulated, I scrambled around being manipulated, impossibly trying to make everyone happy."

Kyle glanced up. "I think you're your own person."

"What you see is what you get."

"Not always." He stood for a moment, his hands on his hips. "When I got hurt you were nice. Last week at your house you were nice, like you are today. I didn't see that the day I came to Sophie's Place and stayed for lunch. You were afraid of letting me get to know you—all business and not that friendly." With his boot he tamped down the soil around the plant. "It was like you were throwing darts to keep me at a distance."

"I'm sorry. I didn't realize . . ."

"Yes, you did. That's how you keep everybody out of your comfort zone."

Angela huffed. "I have lots of friends."

"All of them women."

"I beg your pardon." She stood with her arms folded.

"Look, if I'm going to help you raise your boy, we're going to have to be friends."

"I can do that."

Kyle grabbed the shovel and another plant and began digging in the other corner of the garden. "I'm the average non-threatening male. Think of me as you would your home teacher."

"I can do that too, but I'm a single woman and I have to be cautious." She went to where he worked and stood with her hands in her back pockets. "What does Nicole think about this?"

"What?" He stopped digging. "What do you know about her?"

"That day you fell off the ladder, you thought I was Nicole."

He took up the shovel again. "Oh. Sorry. I don't remember."

"You don't wear a wedding ring, so I assume you're single and she's your girlfriend."

He stopped for a moment and said softly, "She's . . . she was my wife. She died nine years ago. That's why I don't wear the ring anymore."

Angela caught her breath. "Nine years? Your wife and your son? Oh, that's an awful lot of heartache for one man." He didn't respond. She went on, choosing her words with care. "That day you fell off the ladder, the way you talked, she seemed to be someone you really loved."

"More than she loved herself," he muttered. He pushed the shovel into the soil and tapped the plant on the sidewalk to free it from the pot.

"I'm so sorry."

He dropped the bush in the hole, knelt to center it, and pulled soil away from the root ball. "Not much I can do about it now."

"How long were you married?"

He stopped, his hands resting on his thighs. "About three years." He continued pushing soil around the shrub. "Look, do we have to talk about this? Brandon's more important than . . ."

"Don't snap at me," Angela said. "I'm only trying to be sympathetic."

Kyle frowned and ran his tongue across his bottom lip. "I apologize. Truth is I don't talk about it very much, and I have nothing else to say."

"Well, maybe we've said all there is to say about Brandon, too." She paused. "Anyway, I have to go to work now."

"Look, I'm sorry. Really. I didn't mean to sound like such a jerk." He packed the soil down around the plant. "Fact is, I like you, Angela, and I don't have very many female friends. You've been married before too. You're safe. You're Brandon's mother. He's a great kid and you're doing a wonderful job with him."

"Then why are you angry with me?"

"I'm not." He stood and tamped the soil with his boot. "Not really. It's just that those memories don't sit well."

She hesitated. "Sometimes if you talk about it . . ."

Frowning, he studied her face. He'd already told her most of the story. Maybe he should finish. Then she'd know and understand. He slapped the dirt from his jeans and dropped his gloves on the ground. Sitting next to her on the bench, he took off his hat and wiped his forehead with his sleeve. "It was an accident, but Nicole blamed herself for not fastening the car seat firmly in place." Kyle took a deep breath. "We'd just had a fight, and Brandon was sick with a cold. She was taking him to the doctor. I wanted to go with her, but she said she needed time alone to think. It was raining. A couple of miles from the house she took a turn too fast." He stopped and put his head in his hands.

She touched his shoulder. "Oh, Kyle, that's . . . simply unspeakable. How awful for you."

"Brandon was thrown out of the car and died on impact. Recovery from her injuries took a long time, and Nicole never quite got there. She was so depressed, so obsessed with Brandon's death that she couldn't function, didn't even try to get well. She turned into somebody I didn't know anymore, and we never did resolve the argument we were having that day." He shook his head. "I hadn't realized how fragile she really was." He put his elbows on the back of the bench and stared at the sundial. "I felt so powerless watching her die a little more every day from something curable. Maybe it was my fault. Maybe I didn't love her enough."

"Those are impossible questions to answer." Angela turned to him. "Kyle, how old are you?"

He frowned. "Thirty-six. What's that got to do with anything?"

"You could start over. You don't have to spend your time raising another man's son."

"With you? Is this a proposal, Angela?"

"You know I didn't mean it that way."

"I choose what I want to do. Brandon's a good kid. A man could do a lot worse."

"Is it because his name is Brandon?" she asked, and Kyle frowned at her. "Well," she continued, "I suppose it's easier than taking a chance on getting your heart broken again."

His jaw dropped. "Look who's talking."

"I'm doing just fine. I'll worry about me when I get these two kids launched into life. In a few years it'll be my turn."

"Everybody else comes first. You sacrifice yourself and live through your kids."

"It's what parents do."

"Vicarious life isn't very exciting," Kyle commented.

"I don't expect excitement anymore."

"Don't be so cynical, Angie. You're a good woman. Some good man out there is looking for someone like you, and you're cheating him when you don't make yourself available."

Her eyes flashed with anger. "Listen, if we're going to be friends, don't assume you can micromanage my life." She got off the bench. "I have to go to work now, but when I see you next Monday, we won't talk about anything but Brandon."

"How old are you?"

She stared at him, deciding whether to answer. "Thirty-seven," she said, then stomped away.

"That's not too old to start over," he called after her. She didn't respond. He stared again at the sundial. *Vicarious life,* he thought. *Yeah. What kind of life is that? Look who's talking.* He stuffed his gloves in his back pocket and watered the shrubs he'd just planted, reviewing his own vicarious life over the past nine years. What had it proved?

∽

Trying to forget about what Kyle had said, Angela sat at the desk in the sitting room to double check the grocery order for the week. She was sorry for his loss, but it was none of his business how she lived her life.

Lainie arrived half an hour later. "That English garden is going to add so much curb appeal. I like the way it softens the look of the handicap access at that end of the porch."

Angela didn't look up from her work. "Yeah, it's nice."

Lainie sat on the window seat. "I just came by to look at the garden, and Kyle told me you were here. Isn't this your day off?"

"I wanted to be sure this order is complete."

"You're too conscientious. But we're glad you're on our team."

"So am I." Angela smiled.

"I really appreciate what Kyle's doing for us, too. He's so talented and so busy. He runs the garden center, plays in a band, and helps all those kids."

Angela glanced up and frowned. "What kids?"

"He keeps the lawn-care division of his business strictly to put kids to work who might otherwise go astray and get into trouble. He actually loses money on it."

"How do you know this?"

"A friend of mine lives in his ward. She said the garden center is *the* place for kids in Springville to work. Kyle's sort of like everybody's extra dad, a one-man rescue mission. He had some kind of tragedy in his life—she didn't say what it was—but as a way to work through his grief, I guess, he started brokering lawn-care jobs for kids who need some direction in their lives, mostly kids from single-parent households."

Angela raised an eyebrow. "Maybe someone should nominate him for sainthood."

Lainie laughed and got up. "We're very lucky to have such a good, conscientious man looking after Sophie's Place. Now I'm going home, Angela, and I think you should too. Go out and live a little on your day off. That stuff can wait until tomorrow."

What had Kyle said about vicarious living? "You're probably right. I do still have a life."

Sunday, June 9

When John called that night, he sighed. "Oh, what a day."

"That sounds like not such a good thing." Lainie put a pillow against the headboard to lean on.

"In Primary the kids were so antsy I had to scold them, and then this afternoon at choir practice it seemed like I couldn't do anything right. It's a tough piece of music."

"I'm sorry. Want to talk about something happier?"

"Yeah. What have you got?"

"Let's talk about how we're going to celebrate your birthday."

"Well, I've got the checkup that day."

"And I'm going to have to work that night. All the kids are going to a youth conference for three days, and we'll need all the help we can get."

"Well, let's see . . ." John listed a bar association committee meeting, some CLE, and a guardian-ad-litem consultation in chambers with the judge regarding Will and Kendra.

"How about Monday the 17th?" Lainie said.

"It's a miracle. My calendar is free."

"Oh, I'm glad. Where do you want to go?"

"Why don't we go to Magleby's. Do you realize we met there six months ago?"

"How sweet of you to remember." She sighed in anticipation. "That sounds so nice. Just what we both need."

Thirteen

Monday, June 10

Kyle walked into the kitchen at Sophie's Place feeling a little awkward after his last conversation with Angela. He stood there with his hat in his hand. Preparing a wedding cake at the other end of the ten-foot worktable, she acknowledged his presence with a raised eyebrow.

He cleared his throat. "Hi. Anything to report today?"

She concentrated on her work. "No. What do you hear?"

"Mrs. Merrill says Brandon did a sloppy job on her lawn Friday. He missed some spots and didn't trim around the sidewalks. Mark had to redo it the next day."

"I'm not surprised. He was eager to get out of town with Sean that afternoon."

"Big trip, huh."

"Las Vegas." Angela glanced up. "I wish you'd sit down. You're making me nervous."

Kyle sat on a stool at the opposite end of the table. "That looks tricky."

"It is. I'm a genius. Is that all?"

"So you agree that he doesn't get his bonus this week."

"He knows what he promised to do, but after spending the weekend in a $1500-a-night hotel suite, he's probably not going to be very humble or apologetic about doing an unacceptable job."

"Came home a brat, did he?"

She rolled her eyes. "Let me count the ways."

"I'm sorry, Angie. That must be tough."

She stopped to refill her pastry bag. "You don't know the half of it."

"Well, I'll work him hard this morning here in the yard."

"You'll have to get him out of bed first. When I left an hour ago he wasn't . . ."

Brandon burst through the door, out of breath, holding a half-eaten piece of toast. "Mom, have you seen . . ." He stopped. "Oh, hi, Kyle."

"Morning, Brandon. How was your weekend?"

"Cool. Sean said I was his good luck charm while he was playing slots. He won a hundred and fifty bucks, and he let me keep it."

"Let's see now," Kyle said as they went to the door, "how do you figure tithing on money you won gambling? I've always wondered about that."

Angela watched them leave together. *Rescued by an angel in jeans and a plaid shirt,* she thought. *You don't turn down help from heaven.*

Monday, June 17

"You look delectable," John whispered. He kissed Lainie's cheek as she stepped onto the porch. She wore a long, shimmering, midnight-blue dress with a matching jacket. When he got into the car, he leaned over to focus on a more thorough kiss.

"Mmm. Hello," she murmured. "I've missed you."

He nibbled at her lips. "Yeah. It's been three weeks since the water war at Marchbanks Retreat."

"We're both way too busy. Where have you been?"

"Standing in line, waiting my turn to see you."

She savored another kiss. "Can't do this in a phone message."

He leaned an elbow on the steering wheel and grinned in a lazy, happy way. "It's nice to slow down and see you for a few hours when we're not in a terrible rush to get somewhere else. You look sensational, like a queen, with your hair up that way."

"What a lovely greeting." She smiled, and shifted to buckle her seatbelt. "But we do have a reservation, don't we? I'm starved."

At the restaurant they gave the server their order and then held hands across the table.

"Lainie, you are extraordinarily beautiful tonight."

"It's a reflection of the company I keep."

"Impossible. I'm incompetent, irrelevant, and immaterial. You make me goofy."

"Overruled. Speculation. My sources tell me that 'goofy' is not a bona fide legal term."

They talked and laughed through dinner, then skipped dessert and went to Lainie's house. Complaining of the heat, John took off his tie on the way and left his coat in the car when they got there. Inside, he put music on the stereo, then followed her into the kitchen, where she fixed soft drinks and a plate of cookies.

He stood behind her, gently kneading her shoulders. "I really like your hair this way."

"You've said that twice. I'll take that as encouragement to wear it this way more often."

He kissed her neck. "Mmm. Very tasty."

She shivered with the sensation, then turned and kissed him. "Careful. I might spill these drinks while you're in discovery."

He smiled and took the icy glasses. Lainie carried the cookies and some coasters to put on the coffee table in the living room. They nestled together on the sofa, watching the sunset, kissing now and then.

She sighed as the last rays of color faded and the blue of twilight settled on the horizon. "What a spectacular show. Nice music, too."

"Yeah, it is. Let's dance." John helped her off the sofa and put his arms around her waist.

She put her hands on his shoulders. "I like being held."

"I like holding you, and dancing is a good excuse for an extended hug." Cheek to cheek, they moved to the mellow music in a slow, casual way. "Lainie, I don't know what to do about you," he whispered, his lips exploring the side of her face on the way to her mouth.

"What have I done?"

"You've stolen my heart. I can't think about anything but you."

"Is that petty theft or grand larceny?"

He covered her jaw with kisses. "It's grand for me."

"I deny the allegation. I was the victim of your negligence."

John pulled back. "How was I negligent?"

"It's such a nice, soft, tender heart, and you left it out there where anyone could find it." They stopped moving to concentrate on kissing. "It was beyond my power to resist."

"But judge, I'm the victim, not the accessory."

"You know you're guilty. Confess and you might get time off for good behavior."

"I may have some culpability," John said, "but I will testify that it was a crime of passion." He kissed her again, a long urgent kiss.

Lainie's heart raced in response. "Then I'll have to decide an appropriate sentence right away."

"How about life?"

"You're at the mercy of the court, Counselor."

He crushed her body against his. "Please have mercy." His kiss was hungrier now, seeking, searching, exploring, tasting all the sweetness, savoring her response.

An uncomfortable thrill surged through her and she pulled away. "John, stop. Please stop." He let her go. "Johnny, I want you, I do, but not like this."

He caught his breath. "Lainie, I'm sorry. I'm an idiot. Now I've offended you."

"This isn't what either of us intended. How did we get here?" She switched on a lamp with an unsteady hand and stood in front of the window taking deep breaths to control the awful feeling in the pit of her stomach.

He followed her. "Lainie, I don't know who that guy was just now. That's not like me."

"Yes, it is. We're always getting carried away."

He paused, absorbing her honest assessment. "You're right. I want you too, maybe too much. That was disrespectful and coercive—all my fault."

Her hands still shook. "I was complicit. It takes two to . . . whatever that was."

"I shouldn't have stayed so late." He stood beside her. "I'll go now." She didn't respond. "Please forgive me."

She turned to him. His face reflected a kaleidoscope of feelings. Seeing he was as devastated as she was, she wanted to comfort him but knew it was impossible. Everything had changed. "John, I'm not hurt or offended. Please forgive me."

"Lainie, there's something else, something I know neither one of us has ever felt before. It's new and confusing. I don't know how to handle it." She shook her head. "We can't avoid it anymore," he insisted. "We have to talk about where this is going."

She took a deep breath and let it out slowly. "Yes, you're right. But I'm disoriented right now. I need a couple of days to think it through."

"That sounds so . . . so tentative. Lainie, please, I don't want this to be over between us."

"Don't misunderstand. I still believe there's time enough for everything."

He looked into her eyes. "I'm not afraid. Did you hear me? I'm not afraid of this, and you shouldn't be either. I've never known anyone like you, Lainie, and I . . ."

"John, please, not now."

They turned and went to the door.

"I'll call you tomorrow." He stood with his hand on the doorknob.

She nodded. "Or in a few days. That's all right too, if you need more time."

"I might be rational then. Right now I'm not." His eyes, full of concern, searched hers for some assurance. "Don't give up on us."

"I won't."

"Hold on, Lainie. We'll work it out. Things have to be said." He caught his breath again. "I'm so sorry," he whispered. He touched her chin, then turned and left.

She wandered around the house, trying not to replay the scene in her head, sobbing with frustration. It must have been her fault. If she had talked about this a month ago when he wanted to say how he felt, this might not have happened. But she wouldn't have known what to say then any more than she knew now. Tonight they were both vulnerable at the same time.

She got ready for bed and said her prayers, weeping and begging forgiveness, then settled under the sheet for what she knew would be a fruitless attempt to sleep. She liked her life, and yet something new was happening in her spirit as well as in her body and mind, something good this time. John was different, loyal and steady, not the kind of man to abandon someone in a crisis. She didn't want to retreat from that. She tried to see them together in five years, or ten, or twenty. After praying and pleading again, and shedding more tears, after picking it all apart, analyzing it, and looking at it from every side, she realized hours later that although she wasn't completely sure what being in love was like, if it meant wanting to share his life, to bring him joy, to give herself to him for the rest of forever, then she was in love. And she needed to say it.

Tuesday, June 18

At work the next morning, Lainie received a dozen yellow roses with a note that said, *I've thought about it all night. How can I be sorry and not sorry at the same time? Guilty as charged.* She was sorry and not sorry too. And guilty.

"Is everything all right?" Carrie asked.

"No. Yes." Lainie choked back tears. "I don't know. Excuse me. Time-out." She took the roses and went upstairs to the library, sat on the window seat, and sobbed.

Carrie followed, but said nothing. Holding Lainie's hand she waited for the tears to spend themselves, and then brought a bag of ice to soothe her friend's swollen face.

Saturday, June 22

In the early afternoon, Lainie was preparing for an event in the back yard of Sophie's Place when John parked in the driveway. It alarmed her that he wasn't smiling. "Let's talk," he said. "Right now. It's important."

Glad to see him, she hoped they could work this out quickly because she was prepared to say what needed to be said. She followed him to the rose cottage and sat cross-legged on the bench, wiping her moist forehead on the sleeve of her T-shirt. He sat opposite her, pulled off his sunglasses, and put them in his shirt pocket. He wore jeans, a casual blue shirt, and brown sandals.

"First I want to apologize for getting carried away so often, for forcing myself on you."

"It wasn't force," Lainie replied. "I was a willing participant, but kisses change things between people."

"I've never come so close to breaking my temple covenants. I never wanted that to happen, and I never meant to put you in jeopardy. I'm sorry."

"Does this mean we can start over? Because . . ."

"Lainie, I have something to tell you, and I want you to listen to everything I have to say before you ask any questions."

"If it's about setting limits, I think we should . . ."

"It isn't. Please just listen." He looked into her questioning eyes. "I saw the doctor Thursday and went for tests. Yesterday I went to the oncologist, best in the state. He's a friend of mine, Alan Kurtz. This thing on my shoulder is malignant melanoma."

Lainie knew what it meant. She closed her eyes and began to mourn.

"It's stage two," John continued, "but it's only about a centimeter and a half thick. That's good. It's riding near my shoulder blade, and that could be bad, really bad if it gets into the bone. I'm going for a CT scan Monday afternoon so Alan can see where it's metastasized. He said melanoma sometimes spreads to the heart and brain. It'll be removed on the first of July. My sister Margaret's coming for a few days while I recover from the surgery. Alan doesn't know yet what kind of follow-up treatments he's going to give me. Could be chemo. Could be radiation. Could be nothing if it's . . ." He looked at her again, frowning hard. "Do you have any questions?"

Lainie swallowed a sob. "No. I already know the answers."

"Look, if it's my time to go," John said in a detached sort of way, as if he'd rehearsed it, "at least I've had you in my life. I value everything you are, Lainie. You've made my world so much brighter, so much . . . so much everything. It's ironic that we almost fell in love."

She was incredulous. "Almost? But John, I'm sure now. I want to tell you . . ."

"Lainie, I've made a decision. You can't go through this again because of me."

"But John—"

"You said it yourself. We're all headed for death."

"But I didn't mean—"

"If that's where I'm going, it's better if I go there alone. I don't want you involved. That would hurt us both, and I don't want to watch—"

"Johnny, please don't deny me the chance to love you now that I know."

"No, Lainie." His eyes were icy now. "Don't do that. It wouldn't be smart. Stop it right now before it goes any further. You know I'm right. In a few months you'll get over it. You'll meet somebody else. You deserve that. Look, you've been in my life because I invited you. I have a right to say when the party's over."

"But it's my party too, and I don't have to leave if I don't want to."

"Don't embarrass yourself, Lainie."

"Please don't shut me out. We haven't made promises to each other, but doesn't being a friend count at all? I couldn't get through it alone, and you can't either, no matter how self-sufficient you think you are." He looked away. "I know what you'll need. I can read to you, make you laugh, hold your hand, rub your feet." His silence was frustrating. "Then tell me how you want me to be a friend," she demanded. "Please let me do something for you."

His frown deepened. "I . . . like you . . . more than anyone I've ever known. You're smart and funny and honest and I really enjoy your company." He stopped to collect his logical arguments, now tempered with deep anger. "But I will not be your project, your pathetic, helpless, dying obligation. I don't need charity, and I'm not one of your little blue-haired lady friends who need to be stroked all the time. You're oxygen to some people, Lainie, but now it's too late for me. You know as well as I do that we both have to be realistic."

"Don't tell me how to be realistic about cancer. I've been there."

"It doesn't matter now." He stood, still frowning. "We'll say goodbye here, and we won't see each other again."

"No, John. I won't say it. No one gave you permission to make my decisions for me."

"Don't you know how hard it was to come here? At least I didn't just walk away."

"Now I wish you had," she whispered.

"We had good times, very good times. It's okay to remember them." He touched her chin. "Lainie, I wish things were different. If you want to be my friend, please stay away."

She watched him walk across the grass to the driveway, and then she ran sobbing into the house. Carrie met her in the kitchen. "I just saw John leave."

"He has cancer. He thinks he's going to die. He doesn't want to see me again."

"Oh, no." Carrie embraced her. "And he thinks he has to be cruel to be kind."

"I know now that I love him."

"When you met him you also knew he was an idiot. I warned you."

"But it's cancer, Carrie. I know how to help him."

"How bad is it?"

"It's that thing on his shoulder. Melanoma can be the worst kind."

"Oh, Lainie, I'm so sorry, for both of us. I love him too."

"What'll I do?"

"Don't let him go through this alone. He doesn't know how much he needs you." Carrie smiled and patted Lainie's cheek. "Go upstairs and take a time-out. I'm going to call Morgan and see what he knows."

Monday, June 24

Kyle walked into the kitchen just as Angela took some cakes out of the freezer. He pulled his hat off and sat on a stool at the other end of the worktable. "Hi, Angie. How are you?"

She glanced up and noticed he'd shaved. "Focused on this wedding cake I've got to decorate. What's the word about Brandon?" A large platter lay on the table with some plastic spacers to fit between the levels. She placed overlapping squares of waxed paper around the edge of the platter.

"He's doing a pretty good job. Nobody complained this week."

She centered the first layer on the platter. "He's stopped whining about the hours and how sore he is."

"That's good." Kyle paused. "I was wondering, when does he go with Sean?"

"From July 23rd to September 2nd. School starts the next day." Angela scooped raspberry filling onto the cake and began to spread it.

Kyle frowned for a moment. "He told me his birthday's in July."

"Yeah, the twenty-second."

"And he turns fourteen. What do you think he'd like for a birthday present?"

Angela shook her head. "You can't give him anything Sean can't buy a dozen of, bigger and better. Make it easy on yourself. Just acknowledge the day and call it good."

"Something for a kid who has everything," Kyle mused. "That's a challenge. Something his dad can't give him, something money can't buy. Hmm. What do you usually give him?"

She lowered the second layer onto the stack. "I do what I do best—a spectacular cake. Every year he chooses a movie, and I make a cake with the same theme. Then he and a gaggle of his friends watch the movie and eat the cake. This year it's the enchanted castle from that cartoon. I'm putting the ugly gargoyles on one side, and the happy ones on the other side."

"Really? A cartoon, not an action movie?"

"He likes to think he's all grown up but" —she wrinkled her nose— "not so much."

"That's a nice tradition." Kyle sighed. "I'll be thirty-seven on the Fourth of July."

"Been there, done that last March." Angela began to spread white frosting on the layers.

"A holiday birthday is a real bummer. My family always celebrates it on the third."

"Well, I'll leave you alone in your sorrow while I decorate this cake."

"Is that all you do—cakes?" He came closer.

"People just keep celebrating special occasions, and they pay me well to do this."

He stood next to her with his arms folded. "Brandon and I have some pretty good discussions while we work together every week. He's told me a lot about you, how you've struggled to keep things together. It's impressive."

She frowned. "He's a regular chatterbox. I hope you don't believe everything you've heard from a child."

"Oh, he's not a child, Angie. He understands more than you think, and I've seen maturity beyond his years. He's working hard, doing really well, in spite of Sean. You should be proud."

She looked at Kyle and softened, knowing such growth wouldn't be happening to Brandon without this man's influence. "I am. We both should be."

"Oh, I am. Thanks for helping me make my decision about the birthday present."

"What did you decide?"

"I'll do something I do best." He smiled and put his hat on. "See you next Monday."

Fourteen

Sunday, June 30

Lainie felt empty and lost without John. She missed the phone calls, the kisses, the smiles, the wit, and especially his comforting arms around her. She went through the motions of caring about everything else, occupying her mind mostly in praying for him. All she learned from her prayers was how much she loved him.

Carrie went along with Morgan when he and Troy gave John a blessing. "He seemed at peace," she reported later in a phone call to Lainie, "but his grief was palpable. He thinks he's supposed to be brave and strong because that's what men are, and he thinks he can do this alone, because that's what strong, brave men do."

"And there's no point in trying to convince him otherwise."

"Right. Morgan told me John worked like a whirlwind at the office this week to complete several projects."

"I know that trick. I did it too. If he thinks about work he won't think about cancer."

"He's a proud man, Lainie. He's walked this life alone so far, and there's no reason he can't keep walking. At least he asked his sister to help."

"Yes. He and Margaret are very close."

"His surgery's in the morning. Morgan's going to take him to the hospital. He's second or third on the schedule, I think. He said Margaret will be here late in the afternoon, probably about the time he wakes up."

Lainie took a deep breath. "Thanks. That's what I wanted to know. I've prayed that he'll need me, and I have to be there when he does."

"There's something else I think you should know. Morgan said John revised his will and gave away some of his drawings and paintings. And he signed a Do Not Resuscitate order."

Monday, July 1, early morning

Kyle looked forward to the weekly discussions with Angela about Brandon's progress and felt she did too. He came into the kitchen and stood at the door, waiting until she glanced up from her work and smiled. "Come in. Sit down."

They talked and laughed with comfortable ease as she collected ingredients for cookies and put them in the large mixer. Often guarded and a bit defensive, she sometimes acted like he was her greatest annoyance, but this morning she was relaxed, her sense of humor sharp. Today she told funny stories of last week's events. He liked Angela more every time he saw her and knew they were friends now, but wondered what she might be like outside her kitchen comfort zone. Though he hadn't dated since Nicole's death, he'd been thinking more about it the last few weeks. Maybe he and Angela could help each other get back into the social scene. He was curious more than anxious about it.

In a little while Brandon breezed in, giddy and excited about his trip with Sean. "He called last night and said we're going to Hawaii for two weeks. I'm gonna have surfing lessons and go deep-sea fishing and go to a luau and see a volcano and everything!"

"Sounds like the trip of a lifetime. Mark will take care of your clients while you're gone."

"Well, I'll be back anyway."

"You think so?" Kyle asked. "You like it that much?"

Brandon shrugged. "It's hard and it's hot, but I like the way it looks when I'm done."

Kyle patted the stool next to him. "Listen, there's something I wanted to talk to you about, you and your mother." Brandon sat down. "It's what I want to give you for your birthday. It isn't anything you can touch, but it's something you can feel."

Brandon frowned and glanced at his mother. "What is it?"

"Well, you know I'm the deacon's quorum advisor in my ward in Springville, and on July 20th, we're taking our boys to do temple baptisms in Provo. I want to give you the opportunity to have that experience with us."

Angela sat next to her son and put an arm around him.

Brandon smiled. "My ward's doing that later in the summer while I'm gone and I'm going to miss it." He looked at Kyle. "I've never thought of it as a present."

"Well, it can be, for you as well as those you serve," Kyle said. "I believe people are born to help each other, and a birthday isn't just about you. It's another year of being around to do things for others."

Angela caught her breath. "Something you can't touch, but something you can feel. That's quite a birthday present."

Brandon frowned and looked thoughtful. "I'll have to get a recommend."

Kyle nodded. "You need to take the responsibility for seeing your bishop right away for an interview. This is a limited-use recommend, just for this one visit to the temple, but as I tell my boys in Springville, being worthy isn't just a one-time thing."

"What do you mean?"

"Being temple worthy is how you live from now on. It'll establish good patterns and habits in your life and help you make right choices to protect yourself from bad influences in the world. It's also a way of honoring your priesthood."

Brandon looked at his mother. "You mean even in Hawaii, and Park City."

Kyle answered for Angela. "Yes, at school too, and on the job. Everywhere."

Brandon scratched the back of his head. "I didn't think about it that way. I know Mom always worries about me while I'm with Sean, and I have had problems in the past." He turned to his mother. "Sean doesn't care about the temple, does he, Mom?"

"That's one of the reasons we're not together anymore." Angela smoothed Brandon's hair. "What about you? Is the temple important to you?"

"I just wish we could be a forever family."

She hugged him. "So do I, Son. If we all stay worthy, maybe some day we will be."

Kyle was respectful of this intimate moment. When Angela released Brandon from the embrace, Kyle patted the boy's shoulder. "It's important to keep promises, whether you make them with God or somebody else. But it's especially important to keep the promises you make to yourself."

Brandon nodded. "I heard Bishop Kendall say something like that."

"It's true. You're a really good boy, Brandon, and you have the potential to grow up and become a really good man."

"Thanks. I know I've made some mistakes."

"That's what repentance is for, and because of Christ it's available all the time."

"I'll call Bishop Kendall today."

"Great. Now I want you go out and start weeding the fountain garden while I talk to your mother for a few minutes." Brandon hurried out the door.

Tears streamed down Angela's face, and Kyle moved over to the stool next to her. "Angie, I hope it's okay that I didn't clear that with you before I said anything."

"I didn't know he felt that way." She gasped to control her crying and drew a deep breath. "You have no idea what this means to me. Those are things a father should say to a son, but Brandon's never heard them before. Thank you."

"I didn't say anything I don't believe." Kyle patted her shoulder and she threw her arms around him. It surprised but pleased him and he put his arms around her, feeling like custard inside.

"Thank you, thank you," she whispered.

He felt her love for her son and his throat tightened. He felt the same way. "Sean is his playmate," Kyle murmured, his cheek against her hair, "but I'll be his dad."

Angela wiped her face with a tissue from her pocket. "You're giving him something Sean can't give him, something money can't buy." She looked at Kyle and he saw gratitude in her eyes. "I hope he knows the difference."

Kyle held her shoulders and smiled. "I believe he does. I'm getting to know him pretty well, and I think he meant what he said just now. Sean's lifestyle may be glamorous and appealing, but Brandon's not fooled by that. Have faith in him."

"Kyle, you've given me hope. I needed that." She gave him another brief hug and smiled.

His heart was pounding. He stood and put his shaking hands in his pockets. "Well, I'll see you next week, but after that I guess we won't have a reason to discuss Brandon until he comes back."

She held his eyes with hers. "I'm going to be here anyway."

Kyle nodded, enjoying the morning-glory blue. "Well then. I'll probably see you."

July 1, Late Afternoon

Lainie walked the halls of the medical center while John was in surgery, taking a break in the cafeteria when the nurses brought him to his room. Knowing they'd monitor him for several hours, she wanted to stay out of their way. Margaret would be her protection; surely John wouldn't throw Lainie out of the room when his sister was there. She went to the chapel to pray and meditate. Peace and calm filled her as she returned and stopped at the nurses' station to ask if John had had any visitors.

"I haven't seen anyone," the nurse answered. "I just checked his vitals and he's still too groggy to have much of a conversation. He should be more alert in another hour or so."

Another nurse seated at the desk asked, "Are you Lainie McGuire?"

"Yes."

She handed her a piece of paper. "Here's a message for you." "Miranda broke her arm," it read. "We're at American Fork Hospital. Will try to see John later." There was a number where Carrie and Morgan could be reached. Lainie hurried to call it.

"How's Miranda?" she asked when Carrie came on the line.

"We don't know yet if she's going to need a pin in her elbow."

"I'll tell John when I see him if he's not too mad to talk to me. He's in his room now but still not completely awake. Margaret isn't here yet."

"One of us will try to come over later tonight or tomorrow," Carrie said.

Restless, Lainie paced outside John's room. *It's been three hours,* she thought. *He won't be happy to wake up and find me here, but no one should wake up in an empty room after cancer surgery.* Wanting to bring him something tangible, a peace offering, she found a vase of yellow roses in the gift shop downstairs. She took a few cautious steps past the monitoring equipment next to his bed. He was asleep, the head of his bed elevated. She wanted to reach out and smooth his hair. After putting the flowers on his tray table, she sat in the chair on the other side of the bed and waited, and prayed. She'd missed him so much.

Monday, July 1, almost 7:00 PM

Cold woke him first. *Where's my shirt? Is Margaret here?* He moved his head but didn't open his eyes, just tried to listen and get his bearings. His shoulder blade, cushioned by what seemed to be a rubber donut, still hurt. Pain under his immobilized left arm tried to rise past the receding numbness. His neck ached under his chin, and an IV needle still pierced his left forearm. Oxygen pumping in with every breath annoyed him, and so did the blood pressure cuff on his right bicep as it inflated at regular intervals. With the head of his bed elevated, the sheet wouldn't stay up on his chest. *I need a real shirt. This hospital thing isn't enough.*

When John finally opened his eyes in the evening light streaming through the window, Lainie took his hand. "How are you?"

He pulled away to bring the blanket up over his chest, mumbling, "Where's Margaret?"

"I don't know. I'll wake you if she comes while you're asleep."

"What time is it?"

"Almost seven. How do you feel?"

He frowned. "Thirsty."

She held the mug of ice water from the tray table while he took a sip, swirled the cool liquid around in his mouth, and swallowed. He drew on the straw several more times, then pushed the mug away. "Morgan wanted to be here, but Miranda broke her arm this morning in a bike accident, and they're at the hospital in American Fork," Lainie explained. "It's a bad break. They'll try to come later."

Absorbing this additional disappointment, John busied himself rearranging his immobile left arm in the sling without disturbing the bandaged wound under it or the IV or the monitor connections. He grew more agitated. "Why are you here?"

"It's my day off," she said, thinking the sarcasm fit his mood. "I didn't have anything else to do."

He snorted and looked away.

"Did you really think I wouldn't come?" Lainie asked.

"You have to face facts."

"Not everything you said was fact, John. Some of it was false assumptions, and a lot of it was unfounded fear."

He touched the surgical tape under his jaw. "It's a fact there's a bandage on my shoulder blade, one under my left arm, and one on my neck. It's a fact the labs could be bad."

"Don't you think I know that?"

"I thought you had more common sense."

"More than you have, I think."

"Move on, Lainie. You've got a life and a business to run. Don't bet on a lost cause."

"I'm not going anywhere, and you can't make me," she scolded as he turned and scowled at her. "During your surgery, when I thought about maybe losing you, I realized everything that's happened over the last six months, everything we've talked about—well, I'm not giving up on it. Johnny, I love you and it has to be said."

"No, Lainie, I told you before. Don't love me. It'll be a big disappointment." He took a deep breath as tears started from the corners of his eyes. "What happens to you if I die?"

"What happens to us if you don't die?" She sat on the bed close to him. "I can't change what's happening to you, but I know the way through it. Let me help you."

"I've asked you not to," he said.

"Well, I'm here, and there's nothing you can do about it."

"Lainie, I don't want to play this scene with you."

"That's just the pain meds talking. You don't mean . . ."

He gritted his teeth. "I do mean it." Adrenalin surged, and he took her by the shoulders and shook her. "Don't love me. Don't get caught up in this." He winced from using his left arm and shoulder. Sobbing with pain and the overwhelming uncertainty he faced, he lay back against the pillows and looked away, trying to control the convulsive breathing. "You've got a life. Maybe I don't. Go away. Don't come back. Please, Lainie. Please."

She said nothing, just stood by the bed watching until his breathing, and her own, returned to normal. Then she sat in the chair and closed her eyes, and prayed.

Monday, July 1, about 9:00 PM

While John slept, Lainie left the room to stretch her legs. Coming toward her down the hall was a tall blond woman with blue eyes like John's. She wore jeans and a Cannon Beach T-shirt, and she looked tired. "You must be Margaret." Lainie held out her hands.

The woman smiled as she took them. "You must be Lainie. John told me about your beautiful hair. How is he?"

"Asleep now but anxious to see you."

They sat in the waiting area, and Margaret told her frustrating story. "I missed one flight, and the next plane had mechanical trouble. It was an hour and a half late getting into Salt Lake, and then somebody messed up my car rental, which delayed me another hour. Then there was an accident on the freeway. Traffic was a nightmare."

"I'm sorry, but I'm glad you're finally here," Lainie said. "John hasn't told me about the surgery, except there's a bandage under his left arm, which means they took the sentinel node, and a bandage under his chin, another lymph node. He really wants to see you."

Margaret sighed. "Look, it was wild before I left home, getting three of my boys ready for Scout camp tomorrow, then a crying baby behind me on the plane, and all that traffic. I haven't had three hours of sleep in the last twenty-four, and if I don't get some rest I'll be no good to John. Lainie, as long as he's asleep, let him sleep."

"He'll be very disappointed."

Margaret smiled again through her tiredness. "Me too, but you're here. He doesn't need me right now." They got up and went to the elevator. "That's okay, isn't it? Do you need to go home or go to work?"

"No. It's all okay."

Margaret put her arm around Lainie's shoulder. "When he wakes up, tell him I'll be back first thing in the morning. I'll find a motel close to the hospital."

"I have a spare room."

"This is just for tonight. I'm staying with him but I don't have the key to his condo." Margaret adjusted the strap of her purse on her shoulder. "Thanks for everything you've done for John. You're very important to him. What happens next?"

"We won't know until the doctor gives us the surgical report tomorrow morning."

"Then we'll all keep praying."

"Thanks for being here, Margaret. I know it isn't easy."

"I'll do anything for John. He blessed us so much when he shared the gospel with us." Margaret stepped into the elevator. "See you tomorrow." She waved as the doors closed.

On the way back to John's room, Lainie noticed the clock at the nurses' station said 9:30. John was still asleep. She sat in the recliner and closed her eyes.

Monday, July 1, 11:00 PM

A nurse from the new shift turned on the indirect light over the bed, waking Lainie. John moved his head a little, but his eyes remained closed. "Oh, Mrs. Marchbanks," the nurse whispered. "I didn't realize anyone was still here. I've come to check his vital signs."

"But I'm not . . ." Lainie smiled when she realized she didn't need to give a disclaimer. "I'm not going anywhere without him."

"If you're chilly from the air conditioning, there's a blanket in the closet."

"Okay. Thanks." Lainie smiled and stepped out of the room to get a drink of water, returning as the nurse explained to John about the pain medication in his IV. The blood pressure cuff and the oxygen were gone.

"Your husband is doing really well," the nurse said when Lainie came in. "His blood pressure and his oxygen levels are normal." She turned to leave. "Ring if you need something."

Lainie put the blanket from the closet on the chair at John's bedside. He frowned, his eyes half open. She took his hand, but he pulled it away and lifted the sheet up on his right shoulder. "If you're cold, maybe you need this extra blanket," she offered.

"I need you to leave," he said, his voice shaking. "I need to see my sister."

"She came while you were asleep but she's had an incredibly horrible day and needed some rest, so I'm all you've got until morning."

"You knew I really wanted to see her. You said you'd wake me."

"I'm sorry, John. I know you're disappointed, but she'll be back tomorrow when she's rested." Lainie sat on the bed as he took a deep breath, tightening his jaw, trying to swallow the tears she now realized he wanted to shed only on Margaret's shoulder. She understood. "You have permission to be afraid. That comes with the cancer, no extra charge." Then the tears came and she held him, whispering comfort as he wept. "Surrender it, John. Give it to God. Let it go." He calmed a little. "You can be afraid of everything else—the pain, the treatments, the uncertainty—but you don't have to be afraid that I might leave you. I never will. Oh, Johnny, I love you. I'm sure of it now."

When he was quiet again, she reached over to the tray table and pulled some tissues out of the box for him. He leaned back and mopped up his nose and face, then threw the tissues in the trash can she held for him. "What a baby," he muttered.

"It's okay. We're friends. And you have a good role model. Jesus wept." She drew the sheet up on John's shoulder and tucked it in behind.

"I'm sorry."

"Don't be. Everything's an emotional earthquake for you right now. You have every right to shed tears." Lainie could see he'd worn himself out. "Why don't you sleep if you can? I'll stay right here." He sighed, relaxed, and fell asleep within a few minutes. She silently blessed the sweet relief of pain meds and returned to the recliner.

He couldn't see a clock, couldn't guess how long he'd slept, but when he woke the door was half open and light from the quiet hall fell on the yellow roses he knew Lainie had brought. Looking at her now, dozing in the chair by the bed, he admired her steady wisdom, her sense of humor, and that indescribable hair. He recalled how the strength of her spirit shook him the first time he'd held her in his arms. He hadn't anticipated her ability to climb into the treehouse of his life as if she belonged there, as if it weren't his exclusive club anymore. And then he realized she did belong there. What was it she'd said to him that day at Marchbanks Retreat? *"Sometimes in life, when you have no control over heavy things, you can't do anything but surrender them. Refuse ownership. It doesn't belong to you anyway."*

A glow inside confirmed what she'd said. It was time to let go of yesterday and accept tomorrow. During the last ten days, as he'd anticipated the unknown and prepared for surgery, Lainie's absence had been a massive chasm in his life. He never wanted to feel that way again. Now she was here, his treasured friend, and he realized nothing else mattered. Whatever the consequences, he loved her. She was forever a part of him. It would change his life and it was all right. Tears started and she startled awake when he gasped. He held out his hand.

She took it and sat on the bed. "John, what is it?"

"Lainie, I'm sorry." His voice trembled. "I hurt you, and I'm so sorry, my sweet Sweet Lainie."

"I'm all right, Johnny. You were only trying to protect me." She smoothed his hair and kissed his forehead. "I'm here to stay. I won't leave tonight, and when you wake up in the morning, I'll still be here. Tomorrow we'll do the same thing all over again. That's how we'll get through this."

"And I want you to be here." He touched away the tears on her face. "I love you, Lainie, I do, and I need to say it out loud."

"There's love in everything you do for me." She wiped his face again, and hers too, with another tissue. "I've never been in love before. I never thought it would happen to me, and I'm not going to miss one moment of it."

They embraced and he said, "From now on, neither am I." He sighed and a sense of peace settled over him. "I do love you. I don't want to be alive without you."

"I knew it when you tried to send me away. You were more worried about me than about yourself. That's how love begins."

He held her hand. "That day, after I told you about the melanoma, I went straight to Marchbanks Retreat and prayed and cried and went through all the stages of grieving, and when I was finished, I was right back where I started because you weren't there. I was so lost without you, and I resented that because I'd always handled everything on my own. I didn't want to need anyone, especially you, but I did. I do."

She stroked his cheek. "I didn't realize until I said it how very much I love you." They held each other and both laughed and cried a little more. "Now tell me how you are. I hope you didn't tear any stitches back there."

He skimmed his hand across his left side. "This thing under here is pretty tender. Had to shave my armpit." He looked at her and tiredness overwhelmed him again. "A plastic surgeon came in to do the one on my neck. It's going to be hard to shave my face for a while. They took two lymph nodes. What does that tell us?"

"It means our prayers have been answered. It probably isn't as bad as we thought it might be. Try to sleep, John. That nurse will be crashing around again in three more hours."

He smiled as his eyelids drooped. "Will you tell her your name?"

Lainie straightened the pillows and tucked the sheet behind his shoulder. "Lights out. I'll be right here in this chair if you need me." She reached up to turn off the light and he caught her hand again in the dark and held it against his lips.

"I need you."

"Already?"

"I'll always need you."

All the tension of the last two weeks burst within her, and now it was her turn. As tears came, she tightened her hold on his hand. "Oh, Johnny, you're going to live," she sobbed on his shoulder. "You're not going to die."

"I'm pretty happy about that too," he said as he held her.

"I've never loved anything or anyone the way I love you."

"I love you, Lainie. I'll always love you."

She held his hand until he went to sleep and his grip relaxed. A miracle had happened. She was grateful for it, but they would need several more tender mercies before this was over. She wrapped up in the thermal blanket and sat in the chair smiling, listening to John's steady breathing, offering prayers of thanks before she fell asleep.

Fifteen

Tuesday, July 2, 3:00 AM

Another nurse, a balding young man with a fair complexion and compassionate manner, came later to check John's vitals. Lainie left to give him privacy. When she came back, John was sitting on the side of the bed wearing dark-blue pajamas and a broad smile, drinking a small can of grape juice.

"Look, I'm not tethered to so much equipment, and I even got to brush my teeth. I feel like a new man." His left arm remained immobilized, and he still had the IV.

"Are you ready to go back to sleep?" Lainie asked.

He put the empty can on the tray table and took her hand. "Not now. I want to walk for a while before the pain meds punch my lights out, but first I need to apologize." She sat beside him on the bed and he put his arm around her. "Lainie, I don't know what made me think I could do this without you. I came to the end of everything I'm sure of, and I was afraid. I hit the wall and went into full retreat. It proved again that I'm just a pretentious popinjay. I'm so sorry. I should have trusted you, but I don't want you to be hurt by cancer again."

She smiled and touched his cheek. "I don't think you have control over that. You can't protect me from what I feel for you, whether you have cancer or not."

"I know that now. Thanks for not staying away."

"I'll always need you too. As far as I'm concerned, we're in this together."

They held each other, and he kissed her forehead before taking a deep breath and stepping into his slippers. They strolled from his room to the nurses' station and back, wheeling the IV tree with them.

"What did Dr. Kurtz tell you about chemotherapy and radiation?" Lainie asked.

"Nothing specific yet. He says we'll take it as it comes."

"I'm sure he explained that cancer is mean renegade cells gone berserk. They multiply faster than the normal cells around them. Chemo targets the crazy cells, but it also kills some of the good cells. They're like collateral damage. These are aggressive drugs designed to kill cancer, and they'll almost kill you in the process."

He frowned. "What's radiation like?"

"It isn't painful and doesn't take very long. You might have treatments five days a week for several weeks, and there might be cumulative effects. You won't be hospitalized, isolated, or radioactive since you'll get external radiation, not internal. Treatments are on an outpatient basis so you can go home and rest there, because you will be tired."

"What was your treatment like?" John asked.

"Having chemo to shrink the tumor before surgery meant they didn't have to excise so much tissue. That's kind of a sensitive problem when it comes to breasts that are supposed to be a matched set. They did a little radiation after the reconstruction, but not much. Chemo was worse—more nausea, more pain. On some of the worst days I wished I could die, but something stubborn inside of me insisted on living, and I knew that stubborn something was going to win."

John smiled. "As you know, I can be pretty stubborn too."

"And you're going to need it over the next few months."

They made the circuit twice before he grew tired. He returned to the bed. Lainie sat on the side, facing him. "I'll stay until the doctor comes with your surgical report in the morning, and then I have to go home and clean up and check in with Carrie. She might need to stay home with Miranda for a day or two."

"Poor kid. How is she?"

"I don't know. I haven't heard from Carrie or Morgan."

John took Lainie's hand. "I'm glad you were here to meet Margaret."

"She'll be back in the morning, and I'll check on you later in the day. You'll probably be driving her crazy by then."

He got under the blankets. "It's been known to happen."

Lainie kissed his cheek. "Go to sleep, Johnny. Sleep heals." She turned out the light, wrapped up in the blanket, and put her head down on the side of the bed. With his hand resting on her shoulder, they slept.

Tuesday, July 2

In the early morning light, John's gentle stroking of her hair woke Lainie. She raised her head to smile at him. "Good morning," he whispered. "I love you."

Not fully awake yet, she murmured, "What a coincidence. I love you too."

"You're so beautiful when you're just waking up."

She laughed and ran her fingers through her hair. "And you're still under the influence of anesthesia. Does this hotel have room service?"

"That's what they tell me."

"Did you get any sleep sitting up like that?" She adjusted the blanket, then put her head down again and reached out for his hand.

"Enough. There's nothing else to do all day, so I'll make up for it. Most of the night I've been watching you sleep and thinking about how much I love you. How about you?"

"I'm here with you. That's all I care about."

They held hands and dozed until noises in the hall woke them. Lainie roused and looked at her watch. "I'll be back at seven." She stepped into her shoes, grabbed her purse, and went to freshen up in the restroom. After breakfast in the cafeteria, she returned to John's room and sat outside the privacy curtain as a nurse checked his vitals and incisions. His breakfast arrived just before the nurse left and opened the curtain.

He wiggled the fingers of his left hand and grasped the fork. "I have to use the sling a few more days as a precautionary measure, but I can take it off to eat." He scooped up some scrambled eggs. "I'm not ambidextrous, so you might've had to feed me."

Lainie smiled. "Fine—as long as I don't have to use chopsticks."

Later, a nurse helped him bathe while Lainie napped in the chair. She woke when he kissed her forehead. He sat on the bed, smiling. "It's been an eventful night, my friend."

She sighed, still drowsy. "You could say that. You don't look like a person who had cancer surgery yesterday. How are you?"

"I feel great. Thanks for the roses, by the way."

She stood and put her arms around his neck. "Good morning, Johnny." They kissed and he led her to the window seat, where they sat and held each other.

In a few minutes Margaret appeared at the door with a vase of wildflowers. "Another fine mess you've gotten us into," she said as John stood to greet her.

"Yeah, some kind of mess. Thanks for coming. You met Lainie last night."

"Yes. She's wonderful."

"I think so too."

Lainie took the vase and put it with the roses. "Wait till you see me later. I clean up very nicely." She moved the chair over by the window seat for John.

Margaret reported on family events, and John told her of his cancer diagnosis and surgery.

She took his hand. "I almost forgot the best news of all. Richard and Janine are going to be baptized."

John gasped. "When?"

"I don't know, but they're very close. They wanted to see you again first."

"I wish I could. Let's call them tonight."

Dr. Kurtz came in just after nine, a clipboard under his arm. Not quite six feet tall, he looked young enough to be mistaken for an intern. John introduced Margaret and referred to Lainie as his "cancer guru."

"How's that?"

"I'm cancer-free more than five years now," Lainie said, perched on the arm of the chair.

"Then you can tell John what kind of carnival ride he just signed up for."

"Mine was breast cancer. I don't know as much about melanoma."

Dr. Kurtz nodded at John. "Well, here's the report. Looking at the CT scan, we knew the sentinel node under your left arm had to go, and the node in your neck, but we weren't sure about the melanoma itself. When we assessed it, we found the borders were easy to get, so we went in and took out the trash." He frowned and shook his head. "We were surprised, though, because we found no bone involvement at all. I've never seen anything like it. It was as if somebody put an extra little cushion of tissue in there to protect the bone."

Margaret glanced at the others. "Maybe somebody did."

Neither Lainie nor John could speak.

Dr. Kurtz smiled. "I've seen prayers work all kinds of miracles." He patted John's knee. "Without bone involvement, there's no reason to have radiation. We didn't see anything suspicious anywhere else."

"What's the prognosis?" Margaret asked.

"Very good," Dr. Kurtz replied, "especially if he plays by the rules and doesn't miss treatments. You have an eighty-nine-percent survival rate after five years, John, and an eighty-three-percent chance after twenty. I'm safe in predicting that you'll have plenty of time to turn into a grumpy old geezer and die at ninety-five of orneriness."

John sat for a moment, absorbing the news. "Lainie says you almost have to kill me to cure me."

"Unfortunately, that's about right."

"Alan, I want you to take aggressive action so I can get on with my life. I don't want this to drag on longer than it needs to."

"Good decision. First, we'll let you recover from this surgery for a few days, and then start adjuvant therapy next week. You'll be hospitalized again for about a week so we can monitor your reaction to the chemo. This first course will be strong, and some of these drugs do a different dance at every party they go to. We'll start with what works on melanoma historically, and if that doesn't do what we want we'll send in the second team. I've seen some promising options in clinical trials. In any case, we have to watch closely to see if these drugs are going to play nice with the other systems in your body."

"How long will this treatment take?" Lainie asked.

"John can expect to spend the next four to four and a half weeks focusing on therapy. That's a week or so in the hospital, and two more weeks of chemo at home. Then he'll take a break before having a week of biologic therapy to build up his immune system. It'll feel like you have a nasty case of the flu, John—chills, fever, general rotten feeling. After that you'll have at least six to eight more weeks recovering from the treatment."

John raised his eyebrows. "That's it?"

"By the first of October you should be finished with this science-fair project. We'll keep testing as we go along to see how the drugs are working. Except for the time you need to be hospitalized, there really are no restrictions on your activities. Do what you feel like doing, but start slow. Get Morgan to bring you some things you can do at home between naps. I imagine Lainie has some ideas about that too."

"When will you spring me out of here?"

"I want you to stay at least another day, maybe two, until we're sure these incisions are healing right," Dr. Kurtz said. "You've got three owies, and there's always the danger of infection. Then you can go home and relax before you come back to start the chemo."

"Thanks, Alan." John stood up and held out his hand.

Dr. Kurtz shook his patient's hand and patted his shoulder. "Well, just be glad you got that checkup when you did. Another few weeks and that nasty stuff might have invaded the bone, and then I wouldn't be able to give you such good news."

John glanced at Lainie. Tears came to her eyes again, and she went to the tray table for a tissue. Dr. Kurtz left an instruction sheet about the chemotherapy and went to finish his rounds.

John and Margaret hugged each other again. "I told Mom and Dad you'd call them right after you got the surgical report." She went to the room phone.

"I'll call Carrie and Morgan," Lainie said. She headed to the public phone in the waiting area by the nurses' station. When her friend came on the line, Lainie burst into tears. "Oh, Carrie, he's not going to die," she sobbed. "He's going to be okay."

"What a blessing. What happens next?"

"Hospital chemo, then chemo at home. He'll be well by fall."

"We can give thanks for that," Carrie said. "Morgan headed over there a little while ago."

"John will be glad to see him. Margaret's taking over now. I'm going home soon to have a shower and a nap. Can you get along without me this afternoon?"

"Do what you need to do for John. Our event tonight is covered. Angela found a couple more dependable people for our on-call staff. And Miranda's resting in the rose cottage with a book. She won't need a pin in her elbow after all, which means she won't need another surgery."

"Still, having a cast on her arm is a terrible way for a girl to have to spend the summer."

"Yeah. Poor baby. Pain is one of life's tough lessons."

Lainie heard the elevator signal and turned to see Morgan emerging. "Oh, he's here."

"Good," Carrie said. "Call me later."

Lainie put her arm around Morgan. "It's all good news. He's anxious to see you." As they came into the room, Lainie announced, "Look who I found."

John stood when he saw Morgan. The two friends embraced, but neither spoke until Morgan caught his breath. "It isn't as easy as you think to get out of this partnership." They laughed and wiped tears away. With his arm still around Morgan, John reintroduced Margaret, whom Morgan had met several times before.

A wave of exhaustion washed over Lainie. She touched John's arm. "I think I'll be going now. I've been here all night and I need a shower."

John walked with her into the hall and held her close. "You saved my life," he whispered. "I love you forever."

"I love you, Johnny." She stroked the stubble on his cheek. "Get well."

Later at home she showered, wept, dried her hair, and praised God, thanking Him for sparing John's life. She fell into bed thinking about what would happen to John in the next three months, and surrendered to a sound sleep that lasted well into the late afternoon.

John became impatient by Tuesday night but wasn't released from the hospital until Wednesday morning. Margaret stayed in his guest room, and while he napped or read, she prepared some extra meals and stashed them in his freezer.

Lainie spent time with them when she could get away from work. She and Margaret found they had quite a bit in common. Back home in Washington, Margaret volunteered to assist residents of a care center and worked part-time in a craft store, arranging silk flowers. Lainie brought some materials the next afternoon, and while John rested, the women made a wreath for his front door where they could post messages for the neighbors about his condition.

Thursday, July 4

In the late afternoon, Kyle got into his car and left his parents' house in Payson, where he'd spent the day. Angela had called that morning before he went to the parade with his family and asked him to come for dinner at six thirty. He hadn't thought about it the rest of the day, but now he had twenty or twenty-five minutes in the car to puzzle over this unexpected invitation. Apparently the idea of dating had crossed her mind too. He left the I-15 freeway at University Avenue. Traffic was light now, but it would be a horn-honking madhouse later when people went out to watch the big fireworks display at BYU's Cougar Stadium.

Angela smiled as she opened the screen door. In a bright-yellow casual summer dress, her hair falling in soft curls on her shoulders, she looked like a schoolgirl. Her loveliness made his heart beat faster. "Wow. You look great."

"Thanks. So do you. We're having dinner on the patio. Come in."

He followed her through the kitchen and out the back door to the deck, where a small table was set with two places and two large citronella candles. "Won't the kids be here?" Kyle wondered aloud.

"They went with some friends to watch the fireworks."

"It'll be tough to find a good spot."

"Julie met somebody who lives up on the East Bench and invited some kids to park in the driveway and sit on the lawn. They took drinks and sandwiches and lots of snacks."

Kyle sat in the chair Angela indicated. "Sounds fun. You know, I like watching Julie and Brandon together. They really love each other.

She's nicer to him than some older sisters are to their younger brothers, and I speak as a man who grew up at the mercy of three older sisters."

Angela chuckled and sat in the other chair. "They're fiercely loyal. He's lucky to have so many people standing with him to help fight his battles."

"He's worth fighting for."

She seemed distracted by something. He waited. She shook her head as if trying to refocus her thoughts. "It's hard for me to say things in words, Kyle. I invited you over tonight to show you how much I appreciate what you're doing for my son."

He smiled at her innocent excuse for a first date. "Like a lot of other boys, he just needs permission to act on his good instincts."

She checked the grill behind her, pinching the potatoes to determine their doneness. "I'll put the steaks on now so they'll be ready at the same time as the potatoes." She went inside, brought the meat to the grill, and went back for the rest of the food.

While she was gone, Kyle stood at the edge of the patio and looked at the yard. He'd shown Brandon how to take care of the shrubs, and he was doing a good job. A brick bungalow with classic charm, the house was probably sixty or seventy years old. Some peeling paint on the eaves caught Kyle's attention and he thought maybe he could take care of that for her, but on second thought remembered Angela was a self-sufficient woman who'd been managing things by herself for a long time. He turned when she brought the food out to the table. She seemed to glow, and his heart skipped a beat again.

"Brandon's doing a pretty good job with the yard, isn't he," she said.

"Yes. I think he has a real knack for it. And this is a great old house. It has good bones."

"Julie and Brandon have the two bedrooms upstairs with a bathroom to share, and my room is here next to the kitchen. My luxury is having a bathroom of my own. Sean gave Brandon a big-screen TV for Christmas last year, so he made a man cave in the basement. This year for his birthday Sean's giving him a popcorn machine."

"It looks like a comfortable little nest for the three of you."

"It is." Angela smiled. "Come and pour the raspberry lemonade while I check the steaks."

Kyle poured hers first, then his own. He took a sip. "This is delicious."

"I made it myself. I love raspberries."

"I have some growing in my back yard. I freeze a few for myself and give most of the rest to my mother. She makes raspberry-peach jam that's a little bit of heaven on toast."

They chatted at the edge of the patio and sipped their drinks. When the steaks were done, Angela brought them to the table. Kyle sat and spread the napkin on his knee.

"I don't have a Melchizedek Priesthood holder in my home very often," she said. "Would you say a prayer?"

He smiled and reached across the table, and she gave him her hand. His prayer included blessings on her, her children, and her home. She said amen, then looked up at him and squeezed his hand before releasing it. "Thank you," she said quietly.

Relaxed, easy conversation made the time fly. Kyle liked her sense of humor. He asked about Brandon's performance in school, and she asked about his business and family. "Mark had a good time at the prom with Julie," Kyle said. "He enjoys her friendship."

"That's what she needs right now. They both have so much to do before they can think about . . . you know . . . getting serious with anyone."

They talked long after the food was gone. As dusk advanced Angela lit the candles on the table. Kyle refilled their glasses with lemonade, sat back in the chair, and sipped his drink, smiling at her through the candlelight. *She's so easy to be with,* he thought, *funny and wise and so good at everything she does—a beautiful, graceful woman.* "Will we be able to see the stadium fireworks from here?"

"Sorry. Too many trees, but the neighbors might make up for it with their displays," Angela replied. "We can take a drive later if you want. Actually, we're having fireworks right here."

"In the yard?"

She began clearing the table. "This was a thank-you dinner, but it's a happy-birthday dessert." She went inside for a moment, leaving him wondering. Through the kitchen window he saw a flame, and then sparks, and she came out carrying three firecracker cakes of different heights standing on end, grouped together on the plate, with a burning sparkler stuck in each. She put the plate in front of him and watched his response.

Touched by her thoughtfulness and gratified by her attention, Kyle just grinned. "Oh, will you look at that. You really know how to celebrate a birthday."

"It's only common vanilla cupcakes. It's the sparklers that get your attention."

"Fireworks tend to do that." He watched until the sparklers burned out, trying to think of a way to thank Angela for this pleasant evening.

"We can have some now, or you can take it home and share it with your family."

He smiled at her again. "I want to share it with you."

"Come on. I'll get plates and forks while you choose an ice cream flavor."

He followed her inside. She took some dessert plates from a cupboard and put them on the counter, and as she turned to open a drawer behind her, he slipped his arms around her and pulled her close. "Angie, I haven't been on a date in about twelve years. Thanks for making it so easy. You . . . you're . . ." He suddenly wondered if the questions in her eyes were the same questions he had on his mind. Willing to learn, he leaned forward. A boom of fireworks exploded in the street.

She stiffened and turned away. "Um, ice cream . . ." Taking the plates and forks, she retreated to the patio.

Annoyed at his own ill-timed boldness, Kyle opened the freezer to make a selection, feeling now like crawling in and closing the door. He returned to the table with burnt almond fudge ice cream. Awkwardness settled over them as noise in the neighborhood increased. They didn't say much, just ate cake and ice cream and listened to what they couldn't see.

"It must be about time for the stadium fireworks to begin," he said.

Angela nodded, avoiding his eyes. "I told the kids to come right home after it's over."

"I'm sure they will. They're obedient children." It made him sad that she was more uncomfortable, but knew it was his fault for being so impetuous. When they finished the dessert, Kyle made an excuse to leave. "Big day tomorrow at the store."

She walked him to the door but refused to look at him.

He lifted her chin. "Angie, you have a lot to offer. You need to stop denying that. You should live it up while you're still young enough to enjoy it." He let go and smiled.

"I'm not that young anymore."

"Nobody is, but it doesn't matter. You're a beautiful woman in every way. So far I've only found one thing wrong with you." He paused for effect, and she looked alarmed. "You don't have any raspberry bushes in your back yard."

Angela tried to smile. "And you could fix that too, couldn't you."

"Just say the word." He squeezed her shoulders. "It was a great evening. It's a privilege being here with you. Thanks for everything."

She leaned against the doorframe, tears starting as she listened to him drive away. Did someone so attractive really want to spend time with her? *Kyle's comfortable in his own skin, not full of raging self-doubts like I am.* Putting the food away, she realized he'd left the rest of his birthday cake. *He's right. My life will be over and I'll wonder where it went. I should live it up while I'm young enough to enjoy it. But I'm afraid.* She closed the back door and let the tears come, her heart bursting like the fireworks in the night sky.

Sixteen

Monday, July 8

Angela concentrated so hard on what she planned to say to Kyle that she didn't hear the door open. She startled and turned when he put a small cardboard box at the other end of the worktable, his hat beside it.

"Good morning. I brought you some raspberries."

She looked up from the half-filled pastry bag in her hand. *He's giving me a peace offering.* "You didn't have to do that."

"Look, I didn't mean to make you uncomfortable the other night. I didn't realize . . ."

"You said it's been twelve years since you've been on a date. Well, it wasn't supposed to be a date. I don't know what I was thinking. I just wanted to thank you for what you've done for Brandon. I didn't intend . . . I was just being . . ." This wasn't coming out right. She sat on a stool by the table. "I'm sorry if I sent mixed signals. I'm no good at this . . . this . . . whatever this is."

"I don't care about any of that. In my world, we practice a custom known as dating. It's when two people who enjoy each other's company go out to dinner or a movie, or both, or . . ."

"That isn't a good idea," Angela interrupted. "I have two teenagers and I just changed jobs. You have a business to run and it's your busy season. Besides, it's been eighteen years since I went on a date, and I've forgotten how it's done." He started to protest but she went on. "Look, I'm just me. I'm not very subtle. You'll get hurt." She stared at her hands in her lap.

Sitting next to her, leaning one forearm on the table, he smiled. "I like you, Angie. Don't let that scare you. I think we have a lot in common besides Brandon, and there's a lot more about you that I want to learn. It could be pleasant for both of us, or at least not horrible for you. Okay, eighteen years is a long time. I'll give you that. But if you'll trust me I can make it painless."

She turned to him. "But it doesn't make sense. I'm not looking for . . ."

"Sure, we can go on making excuses to stop living because we've both been wounded by life. That's easy. What a cliché. But it won't make either of us happy. We're friends, aren't we?"

She looked at him. "I . . . I suppose so. We're not enemies."

He chuckled. "We enjoy each other's company. That's enough, isn't it, for now?"

Caught up in the warmth of his eyes, she knew he was guileless, genuine, and right. If he had an ulterior motive, it was to see Brandon through adolescence to honorable manhood, and a boy did need two parents, even if one was only playing the part. "Yes, it's true. That's enough."

They smiled at each other and he touched her cheek. "You have no idea what a good woman you are, Angie. You're funny and smart and refreshing. I like being with you."

"You did say before that we should live it up while we're still young enough to enjoy it."

"I still believe it."

"You're very convincing. You're very . . ." She looked at him again and suddenly she was swimming in his eyes, and yet she felt airborne.

Brandon burst through the door, breathless, stopping when he saw his mother and Kyle together. They turned toward him, the spell broken. "Oh. I thought I was late."

Kyle got off the stool and grabbed his hat. "You are, but so am I. Let's get at it." Brandon went up the steps, and at the door Kyle turned and said, "I'm thinkin' maybe dinner at my house on Sunday. All four of us."

Angela nodded and smiled. "Thank you for the raspberries."

"Fresh-picked this morning." He grinned and took a deep breath. "I'll call you Friday."

Sunday, July 14

Rested and confident from two weeks of healing, John checked into the hospital the night before his monitored chemotherapy began. He and Lainie sat in his room during the preliminary procedures. He looked at her, calm assurance in his eyes, as he rolled up his sleeve and sat with his arm on the arm of the chair while the congenial phlebotomist drew some vials of blood.

When the lab technician left, Lainie pulled a portable compact-disc player out of her bag, along with some music John could use for visualization after treatments. "Cancer recovery is about seventy-five percent mental," she explained. "Listening to this music, you visualize the drugs doing a great heroic battle with the cancer cells, and winning."

John frowned as he rolled down his sleeve and buttoned the cuff. "Why am I paying all these specialists to give me all these expensive drugs if I can just imagine myself cancer free?"

She held his hand as they sat on the bed. "I don't understand the scientific explanation, but the drugs work better somehow with positive-mental-attitude endorphins running around in your system too, like little welcome mats inviting the drugs in to do their job."

John chuckled. "Welcome mats. Must be a new technical oncology term."

"And you need to fortify yourself with food. Your body expends a lot of energy when it heals, and you have to consume more calories. It's the one instance in your life when you'll have permission to practice total self-indulgence and a complete lack of self-restraint."

"What about the nausea? I've heard that can be pretty bad."

"You'll have anti-nausea drugs, but you have to learn what works for you. Sometimes the drugs just make it worse. Ginger tea helped me a lot."

He nodded, quiet for a moment as he stroked the back of her hand. "Lainie, how do I avoid being the victim? I've known a few people with cancer, and I didn't like the way other people treated them. I don't want pity. I want life to go on as usual, for me and everybody else."

"There aren't any rules for having this disease. You have to tell people what you want. I'll help as much as I can, John, but what I think of as helping might just be annoying to you."

"Fair enough. I promise to be candid."

"Another thing that helped me was when I decided to have cancer just one day at a time."

"Very practical."

She leaned on his shoulder. "What did you say to your Primary class?"

"I told them the truth. I'm being treated for cancer and I probably won't feel well enough to teach the next few weeks. I said the treatments will make me look different from what they're used to, but inside I'll still be the same person. I think they understood."

"That's a good way of putting it to children."

He turned and looked in her eyes. "How shall I put it to you?"

Lainie smiled. "Chemo can't change the way people love each other, except to make it more precious. I learned to hold the sweet things closer, to cherish life, to appreciate people, and to love more deeply. And now I'm sitting here completely in love with my best friend."

John leaned in to kiss her. "Well, my friend, what I need you to do is to come and hold my hand and be my rock and my calming influence. Keep me from hitting the wall."

When a knock sounded on the door, they turned to find Carrie and Morgan. John shook Morgan's hand and kissed Carrie's cheek. They had brought him a book to occupy his time between treatments.

They sat on the window seat and he showed them a large, homemade get-well card from his Primary class. Then they talked about all the things they could think of that didn't have anything to do with cancer. Morgan reported on his first bishopric adventures at girls camp in June, and the ongoing challenge of staffing a ward. Carrie talked about Miranda's broken arm, the sixteenth-birthday party preparations of Jane's friends, and the patriotic wedding reception they were doing that week, including red cake with white icing roses and blue punch. All the sheet cakes were decorated like flags.

As they talked, Lainie realized that in being so positive and upbeat, she hadn't really warned John how miserable this week was going to be. He smiled and spoke with good cheer about meeting the challenge, but she knew there would be days he'd want to die. A frightening picture flashed through her mind—John with pasty skin and no hair, depressed and devoid of energy. How could she help him through that?

When they left half an hour later, Lainie asked Carrie and Morgan to wait in the hall.

"Things are going to turn grim very soon," she said to John as he took her in his arms.

"And I won't be very good company." John frowned. "You understand why I don't want you to be here for the worst of it."

"I'll be here whenever I can, but I'll always respect your privacy."

"Thanks. I love you."

With a kiss and one more assurance of her love she left, wondering what he would be like the next time she saw him. Dread crept into her heart again.

They stepped into the elevator, and Morgan pushed the button for the lobby. "I've never been around anyone being treated for cancer, and I don't know what to expect."

Lainie sighed. "It's painful. He'll be miserable and probably not very good company most of the time. One side effect of the drugs is what my doctor called 'chemo brain.' That's where your head is foggy and you can't think well. Anesthesia does the same thing, but chemo brain lingers for a while. Even though it goes away eventually, it's really frustrating while you have it. Of course, it's different with everyone."

"It lingers?" Morgan asked. "You're telling me John may not be able to come back to work as soon as he assumes he can?"

"I probably had more chemo than he's going to have, and I did some silly things at first—decided to sell my house, believe it or not—but my parents pointed out that I shouldn't make any major decisions until my whole brain was working again."

As they left the elevator and started across the cavernous lobby toward the parking lot, Morgan said, "So we should give him something to do that he won't perceive as demeaning busy work, but that won't bring down the firm if he makes an error in judgment." He stopped walking and turned to Lainie. "Does he realize this might happen?"

"I'm sure the doctor talked to him about it, but chemo brain is completely unpredictable. Just monitor him." She took a deep breath. "With everything else that's going to happen, it's . . ." At that moment it all became overwhelming, and she couldn't talk.

"Lainie, come on." Carrie led her to a nearby chair and sat beside her, holding her hands.

Morgan crouched in front of her. "This has got to be a terrible strain on you, Lainie."

"That day in the rose cottage, he said I should walk away and not do this, but I can't, not now." She sniffed. "I'm suddenly reliving my own experience five years ago, and I know what it's going to be like for him. He's being very stoic, but he has no idea what an awful time he's in for. What can I do?"

Morgan stood and took her elbow. "Let's go back upstairs. John and I can help you."

Reading in the recliner, John looked surprised when they knocked and came into the room.

"John, Lainie's having a tough time right now," Morgan said as Carrie closed the door. "I think she needs a blessing."

When he saw her face, John took Lainie in his arms. "I just hit the wall," she cried. "I know what's going to happen, and I need to be stronger than I am so I can help you."

"I'm sorry," he whispered. "I didn't realize it was getting to you." He held her face and looked in her eyes.

"I can do this," she insisted. "I'll do anything for you."

He smiled and wiped the tears from her face. "You've given me so much." With Morgan and Carrie in the room he couldn't say what he was really thinking. He kissed her forehead. "Now let me do something for you."

"I'd like that," she said, sitting on a chair. John stood behind it and paused for a moment with his head down. When he was ready, he nodded at Morgan and they put their hands on her head. Carrie sat on the window seat, lending her faith.

When they left fifteen minutes later, Lainie wasn't so fearful.

Tuesday, July 16

Returning to Sophie's Place after seeing John on the second day of chemo, Lainie came into the office and Carrie smiled. "How is he?"

Lainie tried to talk, but words wouldn't come.

"It looks like you need a break."

Lainie hurried upstairs to the library and kept company with a tissue box for half an hour. She prayed until she felt peace. Then she splashed her face with cold water and went downstairs ready to work again.

~

In another few days, the effects of chemotherapy were full blown. When Lainie came to see John, she'd stay if he smiled. She'd wipe his face with a cool cloth, hold his hand, and whisper encouragement. When he couldn't sustain a conversation, she'd let the nurses take over.

Almost constantly in pain, John was dismayed that the anti-nausea medications seemed to work only half the time. He lay as still as possible, flat on the bed, willing the feelings to pass, but with a basin standing by. Alan came every day to monitor his progress.

Saturday, July 20

Late that afternoon, Brandon rushed into the kitchen at Sophie's Place. "Mom, it was great!" He sat on a stool and leaned one arm on the worktable.

Angela smiled. Before they left, Kyle had talked with Brandon about sacred things and respectful behavior in the temple, just as Angela had hoped he would. She'd spent the day prepping for that night's event and remembering that she and Kyle were dating, sometimes with Julie and Brandon, sometimes just the two of them. Dating. And it wasn't that bad.

"First we were confirmed for about ten people, and then Kyle baptized me for ten more." Brandon grinned. "That's twenty. I helped twenty people today."

"How many other kids were there?"

"I don't know. Maybe about twelve. I kind of hung out with a guy named Riley. He works for Kyle too, only in Springville."

Angela stopped and looked at her son's glowing face. "So how did you feel?"

"It makes you wonder about life. I mean, those people died, but they're still connected to earth because they lived here and they depend on us to be baptized and confirmed for them. It's kind of awesome to help somebody that way." Brandon paused. "Kyle's a nice guy. I like being around him. He said he liked it when we had dinner at his house that Sunday."

Angela smiled, remembering that lovely afternoon. "He's coming to our house for dinner tomorrow." She glanced at her son and saw that he was deep in thought. "What is it?"

Brandon gave his mother a puzzled look. "A kind of weird thing happened. After we put white clothes on, we went to sit in this waiting room until it was our turn. I had a good feeling there. Everything was really quiet and peaceful, and Kyle was sitting on a bench, leaning forward with his head down and his hands folded. He had white clothes on too. I sat by him but he didn't look up. I figured he must be praying. In a little while he sat up and looked at me, and I could see tears coming down. Then he hugged me and kind of kissed my head right there." He pointed to the side of his forehead.

Angela caught her breath. She knew Kyle loved Brandon. "How did you feel about that?"

"Sean never hugs me, but I liked it when Kyle did. It made me feel like he cares about me, and we're really good friends." He shrugged. "I sorta kinda hugged him back."

Angela smiled at her son. "I think he's one of the best friends you'll ever have."

"He never stops talking about how much he admires you, Mom, and how pretty you are. If you want the truth, I think he wants to be your best friend."

She took a deep breath. "It's okay. He's a good man, and a person can never have too many friends." She patted her son's cheek. "Thanks for the report. I'm glad you had a good time."

Brandon turned to go, but stopped. "There's one other thing, Mom. I thought about it a lot today in the temple. I really don't want to be like Sean. I want to be like Kyle."

Angela's happiness soared. "I'm glad you've found a good role model."

Sunday, July 21

Lainie tried to be positive. "It's a different drug. Maybe you'll react to it differently."

John smiled and patted her hand. After ten days of treatment in the hospital, he didn't see how more chemo could be anything other than more misery. "Thanks for saying so, but I'm not as hopeful as you are. It's all a torturous ordeal."

He would start the first of two five-day courses of chemotherapy the next day at home, and Lainie sat on the sofa at his house holding him close. "I wish I could make it all better."

"I can see why some people refuse to do this. I understand how the treatment could be worse than the cancer."

"John, please don't hit the wall. Tell you what. I'll come tomorrow morning and we can have a prayer together. There's a holiday Wednesday and we can spend the whole day doing whatever you want."

They sat and held each other for a long time.

Seventeen

Pioneer Day, Wednesday, July 24

Angela always woke up dejected and worried the day after Sean took Brandon for a lengthy visit. She turned over to check the clock. Only 10:30, way too early to get up on a holiday. She was never sure what adolescent craziness Sean was going to suck Brandon into, so she always spent more time in prayer and in the temple while he was away. Minus a civilizing influence, this vacation would be a scratch-and-belch fest, with Brandon making his own decisions about bathing and personal grooming, which meant he probably wouldn't.

Putting it all out of her mind and closing her eyes again, she snuggled into the pillow and blessed her pioneer ancestors for giving her a day off in the middle of the week. She was just drifting off when the phone rang. She answered, stifling a yawn.

"Are you still in bed?"

"Kyle, are you checking up on me?"

"You've missed a spectacular morning."

"Don't be so cheerful. It's too early."

"I was up at five picking raspberries."

"How diligent of you, but I'm sleeping."

"Well, I hope you're up and around by six o'clock this evening."

"What's at six?"

"I'm taking you to dinner."

"Do I have to?" she whined. "I was planning on feeling sorry for myself and being a slob all day, maybe OD on chocolate. I don't think I can be presentable by then."

"You're gorgeous, Angel. It won't be that hard. Can I bribe you with raspberries?"

"Maybe. Probably. Oh, Kyle, I'm so depressed."

He sighed. "I miss him too."

"I'm worried sick about the bad influence."

"We'll say our prayers and trust Brandon to stick to his principles."

Angela sighed. *He has some now because of you,* she thought. "Okay. You're probably right. See you at six." She hung up and lay on the pillow, smiling at the prospect of seeing Kyle today. As he'd promised, dating wasn't horrible. In fact, she liked it.

~

When the doorbell rang, she found Kyle beaming at her, with about a quart of raspberries in the box in his hands. He was clean-shaven, his hair newly trimmed, and he wore shiny casual loafers, navy-blue slacks and blazer, and a burgundy-and-white-striped dress shirt open at the collar. Angela held onto the door as her knees threatened to give way. How could she ever get used to the idea that someone so attractive wanted her company?

"Hi. I was right. You look highly presentable," he said. She wore a long, oversized red shirt with red shoes peeking out from beneath white pants. They grinned at each other. "Here. Maybe you ought to put these in the fridge."

She took the box of raspberries. "Thanks. Julie and I will bless you as we pig out."

"This is the first installment of my bribe." He wiggled his eyebrows. "You'll get the other part later."

"You're not kidding, I hope."

"I'm always very serious about raspberries." They got into the car, and as they buckled their seatbelts he asked, "Do you like Italian food?"

"Love it."

"Good. We're having dinner and fireworks."

"They have fireworks in a restaurant?"

"They have fireworks in Springville. It's a big Pioneer Day tradition."

"I don't know much about Springville, but I love fireworks."

At a restaurant in downtown Provo, he gave his name to the hostess, who showed them to a small table in a corner. After they ordered, Kyle asked Angela about getting Brandon ready to go with Sean, and she asked him about his family. They relaxed and smiled, their conversation filled with laughter and wit.

An hour later she pushed away her unfinished pasta and groaned. "Oh, that was so good."

"Yes, it was." Missing Brandon brought them together, and being together comforted them both.

"Thanks. You knew just what I needed today."

Kyle smiled. "I needed to be with you today too."

"I've seen so many good changes in Brandon because of your influence. You are very good at making things grow, both plants and people. It's like he's started to bloom."

"God makes things grow, but He expects us to help it along. I'm good at tending."

"It's a gift. I'm glad you have it, and thanks for using it to help my son. I know you don't have to come to Sophie's Place on Mondays to work with him. You could send someone else to do the same . . ."

"Brandon's not a service-club project. I'm very fond of him. But you . . . you're fresh air and a drink of sweet water. Angie, in no time at all I've come to depend on that." He looked in her eyes. "Let's go check out the fireworks."

Kyle made small talk about the meal, the exploits of his pioneer ancestors, and the heat of July and August that was so hard on lawns. It was nearly dark now, and Angela's mind was on the promised fireworks as he pulled into the driveway of his house, an unlit bungalow in a quiet rural Springville neighborhood. In the carport he helped her out of the car and took her into the back yard. Crickets provided commentary. When he pushed his keyless remote, the headlights went on and she could see a circle of what looked like thin sticks, but coming closer she recognized them as two-and-a-half-foot-tall sparklers stuck in the lawn, spaced about a foot apart.

She followed him into the center of the circle. When the headlights went off he pushed the remote again so he could see to light four small sparklers. He gave two to Angela. "Start here and I'll meet you on the other side." She guessed there were fifteen or sixteen sparklers, maybe twenty.

Suddenly the idea of standing in a circle of so many sparklers made her giggle. "I've never been in the middle of fireworks before."

He laughed with her. "Me neither, but we'll probably like it."

When all the sparklers were burning, she gave the small dead ones back to him and he threw them in the grass near the garage. He turned and pulled her into his arms at the center of the circle. "Now that I have your attention, I have something to say." He touched her lips with his, a tender, sincere kiss more breathtaking than the sparklers the longer it went on. She felt pure, joyful discovery. They didn't stop until the last sparkler went out. "Oh, Angie," he whispered, his breath warm on her neck. "I can't think about anything else. I think I'm falling in love with you."

She gasped, stiffened, and stepped away from him. "You can't do that."

"I can't?"

"I don't want anyone to love me. I don't want to love you. I can't go through that again."

"What?"

"It's too hard." She started to cry. "I can't be in love again. I just can't. Don't spoil things."

"Angie, I'm not Sean."

"I know." She caught her breath. "And I'm not Nicole."

"You're not supposed to be." He handed her a handkerchief and held her again.

All the fear, the pain of betrayal, the anxiety of loneliness rose again in her heart where she'd locked them away, intending never to feel their effects again.

When she stopped crying, she sighed and he let go. "Well, I promised dinner and fireworks, but I have a little bonus—raspberry ice cream."

"I don't think so, Kyle."

"Come on," he coaxed. "You'll like it, I promise. I made it this afternoon with the raspberries I picked this morning. Give me a break. It's the second part of my bribe."

He pushed the keyless remote again, and the car headlights illuminated enough of the back yard that he could pull a couple of the now-cold sparklers out of the ground to make space for them to get out of the circle. He reached inside the back door to switch on the light and stepped aside while she went into the kitchen. Just the previous Sunday they'd laughed and talked as they washed and dried dishes together at the sink.

He gestured toward the small table next to a window overlooking the back yard. She sat. He took off his blazer and put it on the back of the other chair, then washed his hands and pulled a plastic box out of the freezer. He took two small bowls out of a cupboard, scooped the pink frozen treat into them, put a spoon in each, and brought them to the table.

"Thank you. I don't mean to be ungrateful. You're very generous." She tasted the ice cream. "Oh, you are an expert at this too," she said, shaking her head.

He smiled. "Glad you like it." He took a bite of his as she broke hers up and stirred it. "Angie, are you okay?"

She stopped stirring. "I don't think so."

"I'm sorry if . . . if this surprised you. I thought there was something happening between us that we both felt. I've seen it in your eyes."

"Brandon is all that's between us."

"I don't think you really believe that. You're beautiful and good, and you're doing a noble thing raising two children alone. You work so hard. But in your heart of hearts, you want more."

"Single mothers aren't any kind of paragon, Kyle. I complain and I get angry and sometimes I ask 'why me?' It's exhausting."

He raised his eyebrows. "Oh, I get it. You wear yourself out on purpose working for Julie and Brandon so you're too tired to think about what you want for yourself."

"I don't want anything for me."

"Yes, you do. You've always wanted a traditional home life, and you thought you only had one chance to have it, but it didn't work out. Now I'm here, and risking it with me frightens you because you don't want to be disappointed again. I get that. You were almost hysterical out there, claiming you don't want me to love you. Angie . . . Angel . . . I believe . . . given a chance . . . we could be happy together."

"I want my children to be happy and not to make the same mistake I did."

"What you want for yourself is valid too. You're worth it."

She tasted the ice cream again. It was delicious. So was Kyle's kiss. "Please take me home," she said.

They rode in silence all the way to Provo. At the door of her house he took her hand. "I'm sorry if it seems like I'm rushing things. Nine years is a long time to deny you have feelings, and I decided to stop doing that. I'm at peace now more than I've ever been."

"Thank you for dinner. And the ice cream."

"But not the fireworks."

"Maybe I don't like fireworks as much as I thought I did."

"What I said is true, Angie. You need to think about yourself sometime."

"I'm putting it off as long as possible."

"It's been so long since I felt anything I didn't realize how much I was missing." He kissed her forehead. "You'll see what I mean. Good night."

Angela wandered around the house thinking, trying not to think, feeling, trying not to feel. Most of all she was afraid, and she hated Sean for that. What she felt for Kyle was more than gratitude for helping Brandon, so much more that it overwhelmed her. But she was afraid of it.

Jane's Sixteenth-Birthday Party, Thursday, July 25

Jane and a group of friends from school and church sat in the back yard on her sixteenth birthday, cheering and laughing, watching the fireworks display Mark and Dylan had arranged.

"Too bad there's not a merit badge for partying," Morgan said with a sigh as he and Carrie cleaned up the leftovers.

She laughed. "Some of those boys would earn it hands down."

Morgan tied up the full garbage bag and lined the can with a fresh one. "I have to hand it to Jane's friends—a Mad Hatter's tea party is a great idea for a sixteenth birthday."

"I didn't know how they were going to fit fireworks into the story, but they did it," Carrie said.

"Fireworks are a great metaphor." He layered barbecued chicken into a refrigerator dish. "Appropriate for any birthday."

She rearranged things in the fridge to make everything fit. "Yes. Life goes along for a while without too much excitement, and then suddenly you hear bursts of sound and see explosions of color in a black sky."

"Uh-huh—spectacular reminders that you're still alive and all your senses are working."

Carrie smiled. "All the most important fireworks moments in my life involve you, when we were falling in love or getting married or having babies."

"Or last New Year's Eve." Morgan reached over for a kiss. "That was downright explosive."

"And the cruise. But there are also personal moments of enlightenment and understanding that come when you need them most, like the ones I had last year as I was preparing myself to come back. When the Spirit speaks to you, it can be like fireworks."

"That's contradictory. It's supposed to be a still small voice."

"Yes, but when I finally knew the answer, the confirmation started still and small and then it began to burst inside of me. It was like the answer came first, and then the celebration of the answer, with the Spirit encouraging me to act on it."

"I see what you mean." Morgan leaned against the counter, looking out the patio door at the party now in the dance phase. Carrie stood next to him and he put his arm around her. "You're thinking about John and Lainie, aren't you."

"He's known Jane all her life and he wanted to be here," Carrie said. "He hates to miss a party."

"He's great with kids. It's too bad he doesn't have any."

"He and Lainie gave Jane a dozen roses and a key chain for her birthday." She sighed and put her arms around her husband. "They love each other so much, and look at the fireworks going off out of control in their lives right now."

"He has another week of chemo coming up."

"Imagine living every day with the possibility that the cancer could come back at any time—what do you think that's like? John's statistics are actually a little bit better than Lainie's."

"It would certainly keep a definite line between what's important and what isn't."

"Lainie says she's grateful for every day, even the bad ones. Maybe we should all have a reason to live like that, with heightened senses, looking for the fireworks."

Morgan sighed. "I gave John some fireworks yesterday. I took him the biggest cactus I could find, with red blooms all over it. It was three o'clock and he wasn't dressed, and I could tell how lousy he felt, but he laughed when he saw it."

"I like it. Honest, candid, symbolic, subtle as a pie in the face."

"Without him, a lot of things are stuck at an impasse at the office." Morgan pulled his wife a little closer. "Keep praying for him, Carrie. Keep praying."

Friday, July 26

"Now remember—we can leave whenever you want. It might be too loud for you." Dylan Gregory held Jane's hand. Like two frightened kindergartners they walked into the church building in Provo for the regional youth dance. It was her first date, and she wore a new dress.

Yes, she thought the music was too loud, but they danced for a while until Dylan asked, "Want to take a break? We could get some refreshments or go out on the patio for some air."

Jane didn't hesitate. "I choose air." Outside the building, they escaped the noise on a small, well-lit patio with a seating area surrounded by low shrubs. "I guess I'm a teenage freak," she said. "I don't understand why it has to be so loud. You can't hear anybody talk. Aren't they worried about somebody suing the Church over eardrum damage?"

"Maybe they're all so shy they'd rather be deaf than have to make conversation."

She laughed with him. "I never thought of it that way. I figured people would want to talk to each other. Isn't that how you get acquainted?"

He stretched out his long legs and crossed his ankles. "So, how's your first date so far?"

"It's good—much better than the experiences I've had with other boys up to this point."

"Maybe I shouldn't say this, but I really hate that slimy guy who tried to . . . you know."

"'Slimy' doesn't begin to describe him." She sighed. Jason had only wanted one thing from her, something she wasn't ready to give. She'd been so foolish to listen to his flattery and believe his lies. "I really learned a lot, though, the hard way."

"What do you mean?"

"He tried to take advantage of me because I was so inexperienced. That makes him a monster. My dad gave me a birthday blessing yesterday and told me if I can always have the Spirit, I'll be able to discern dangerous situations and people who don't have good intentions."

"That's good. That'll really help you."

"I know, and while we're on the subject of goodness, I just want to say—"

They both turned when someone else came out of the building. "Jane? Is that you?"

Her heart sank. What was Jason doing here?

"We came out here to sit alone and talk, Farrell." Dylan stepped forward. "Alone."

"Don't get so excited, Gregory. I just want to talk to Jane. It's important."

"Then do it from there."

"It's okay, Dylan." Curious about what Jason's next lie was going to be, Jane knew she was immune to him now, but here was a chance to speak her mind. "Go ahead and get some refreshments for us while I listen to what Jason has to say. I'll be all right."

Dylan didn't move until she waved him away. "Five minutes," he told her as he went into the building. "That's all."

"What are you doing here?"

Jason stepped out of the shadows. "I'm coming back. I mean . . . That is . . . They wouldn't let me come to a dance for a long time. I can't go on dates but I can go to dances and see people if I help with the refreshments and the cleanup. That's all they let me do."

She hadn't expected a humble Jason. "I heard you were seeing a therapist."

He laughed nervously. "Yeah. I go to a shrink a couple of times a week. Imagine that." He took a step closer, and his voice changed to a whisper. "It was those magazines. My dad shouldn't have given them to me. That started everything bad. I'm supposed to talk to all the girls I offended and ask them to forgive me."

"Did you?"

"You don't know the others, but Kassie laughed and Suzanne cried, and Liz . . . well, she wasn't really too offended."

"So they didn't forgive you?"

"Not all of them. Will you?"

"My bishop said I should, but I'm not there yet, Jason. I'm still pretty mad."

"Oh. Well, I understand why."

"Yeah. Don't get me started." Now the angry words wouldn't come. Where was Dylan with those refreshments?

"You're a nice girl, Jane. I did some bad stuff. I'm sorry. I didn't know it was so bad."

"Well, thank you for saying that."

"So you can't—"

"No, I can't. Maybe someday I will, but not today. When somebody takes advantage of you that way, sometimes it hurts longer than you think it's going to. I'm working it out."

He nodded and turned to go inside, passing Dylan on the way.

Dylan gave her a glass of punch and put a plate of cookies between them on the bench. "Why did you need to talk to that creep?"

"It's okay, Dylan. He victimized me once, but I won't let it happen again. Maybe I can forgive him someday, but I don't have to trust him. I just ended some unfinished business, locked it up, and threw away the key. He's not going to spoil my first date." Jane changed the subject. "This is good punch, don't you think?"

"Not as good as the kind they make at Sophie's Place."

"And between you and me," she whispered, "Aunt Sophie's cookies are better too."

They laughed and made small talk, finished their refreshments, and then stood to return to the dance. "Well, I like being out on a date with you," Dylan said, "but I'm sorry that jerk spoiled it. I really hate that guy."

Jane stopped at the door. "I don't waste time hating him anymore, Dylan. He's a sick, pathetic person, but if we're going to be truly

Christlike, we have to see him as God sees him. We don't have permission to hate anybody, no matter what they've done."

Dylan paused. "Yeah. You're probably right."

Jane reached up and patted his face. "What I started to say before we were interrupted is thank you for being somebody I can trust, and thank you for respecting me. I love you for that, and I always will."

Monday, July 29

"How many surgeries did you have?" John asked Lainie as they walked unhurried around his neighborhood that quiet morning. He would start the third and last course of chemo that day.

"Just one, but I have plenty of scars because it was a two-for-one deal. They removed the tumor and reconstructed my breast at the same time. I won't need another surgery unless the adipose tissue they transplanted from my belly loses its blood supply." She patted her abdomen.

"So you have one that's false and one that's true?"

"They're both my own tissue. Of course, the right one is completely normal, and the left one is about eighty percent normal. With the transplanted tissue they're equal volume."

"That's why they feel the same."

"What?" She stopped and frowned at him.

"It's kind of obvious. Breasts are right out there, and I notice every time we hug."

"I didn't realize."

"Hey, I have cancer but I'm not brain dead."

"Well, I don't have cancer anymore but I'll never wear a bikini."

John laughed as they walked on. "Isn't medicine just another word for magic?"

"Sometimes medicine's just another word for miracle."

They returned to his house, where they knelt and said a prayer. Then he took the drug and they held each other for a long time.

After Lainie left, John settled in a comfortable chair and opened his scriptures to read until the pain and nausea overtook him.

⁓

"How's John." Carrie asked when Lainie came in the next morning.

"I haven't heard from him yet today, which means he's not up to having company."

"This must be stirring up lots of memories for you."

Lainie sat at the desk. "At this point, it's unpredictable. On a very good day he paints or goes to the office for a couple of hours. Sometimes when I visit he feels like going for a walk."

"Is that a good sign?"

"If he's having a good day I find him dressed, trying to keep up with things at work."

"On a bad day?"

Lainie shrugged. "He stays in bed. Sometimes I pray with him, but I always know when it's time to leave."

～

With Brandon away, Angela hoped Kyle would send someone else to work in the yard, but it was wishful thinking to believe he'd stay away. She'd avoid this confrontation if she could. On Monday morning she sat at the table in the corner of the kitchen, studying the schedule for the week, trying to focus on all the petit fours she needed to ice and decorate for Tuesday night's event.

When Kyle came in, he took off his hat and sat across from her, frowning. "Angie, I haven't been able to think about anything else for the past five days. I should have called, but . . ."

"I'm glad you didn't."

"Yes, it's better to talk about it after we've had time to think. I didn't mean to hurt you."

"Kyle, I've thought about it for five days too, and there's no reason for us to see each other again until Brandon comes back. It's just not going to work."

"After Nicole died, I shut the door on all my feelings. But you made me want to open it again, to remember what it's like to be close to someone."

Angela shook her head. "Don't . . ."

"If you open your heart to the possibilities, something good is bound to happen, Angie. It's what I did, and before I knew it I had a whole functioning heart again."

"Stop trying to convert me."

His frustration spilled over. "Angela, what are you so afraid of?"

"*I'm* the one I know I can depend on. *I'm* the one who won't fail me."

Kyle studied her face. "Fear is bigger than anything else in your heart right now, so you shut out everybody. You refuse to believe you might be able to love someone again, a dependable man who really loves you and won't betray you. Somewhere inside you must know that's the kind of love that can heal your heart. What can I do to help you?"

"Nothing."

"Please don't do this to yourself."

"That's enough, Kyle. Don't . . . please just don't say anything else."

Anger swept through him, and then understanding. He got up and paced away from her. "I know what it is. You couldn't trust Sean, so you think you can't trust me."

"It isn't that simple."

"It's exactly that simple. You *can* trust me. You know it's true."

"Lots of things are true that are never acted upon."

He went back to the table and held her chin, forcing her to look at him. "I know, Angie, and it's such a pity, isn't it, because whether you like it or not, I do love you."

She looked away. "Please don't."

At the door he turned to her again and spoke in a softer tone. "And I'll miss you, more than you can ever imagine."

She cried when he left, but scolded herself. *He's a man. He'll get over it. That's what men do. So will I. That's what women do.* She dried her eyes and went on with her work.

Eighteen

Tuesday, July 30

John gave Lainie a key to his house so she could come by whenever she wanted. She arrived at lunchtime the next day with some groceries and a plan to fix an irresistibly appetizing meal. She found him in bed, curled into a fetal position, with the pillow over his head and the sheet half on the floor. He wore a T-shirt, cutoff sweats, and mismatched athletic socks. She made a mental note to check on his laundry.

"Rough day?" she asked, standing over him.

"How could you tell?"

"What can I do for you?" She put the sheet over him but he kicked it off.

"Nothing, unless you have a magic cancer wand."

"I brought some ginger tea. I'll leave it in the kitchen in case you want to try it."

"I don't do chemo the same way you did." He turned over in the bed. "I thought we agreed you'd let me be sick in private."

"I'm sorry. I didn't know today would be so bad." She turned to go but noticed his hospital water bottle. She shook it, found it empty, and refilled it in the kitchen with ice and water. "Be sure to keep pushing liquids so you don't get dehydrated," she reminded him as she returned the bottle to the nightstand. "Call me later, okay? I can come back tonight and fix dinner, maybe do a little laundry."

He groaned, "Oh, Lainie." and turned to look at her with a pained frown. "I love you madly. Please come back tomorrow."

"It's all about *life*. Remember that."

"Yeah, what you said," he muttered, returning to the fetal position.

"I love you, John."

"It's a good thing," he mumbled into the pillow.

Thursday, August 1

At lunchtime, Lainie turned the key, knocked, and came in the door with caution. "Is it safe?"

John smiled and pulled off his reading glasses. "Thanks for taking a chance and coming back." Wearing his BYU Law sweats, he sat in a living room chair barefoot reading a brief. He took her hand when she came to kiss him. "I'm sorry I was so awful yesterday. You were right about the ginger tea. I do feel a lot better."

She scratched the ragged stubble on his chin. "It's nice to see you upright, but you're not so friendly with your razor this morning."

"It hurts to shave my face."

She sat at the end of the sofa. "Yeah, well, it hurts to kiss your face."

"I'm giving it up."

"Kissing?"

He frowned at her. "Shaving. My beard isn't that heavy, and it's all going to fall out anyway. You should see my pillow, and the drain in my shower."

"I defied the cancer," she boasted. "I shaved my head before the drugs had a chance."

"Oh, all that beautiful hair." John shook his head. "With mine it doesn't matter as much." He stretched and yawned. "Maybe I'll shave what's left of it so I don't scare my Primary class when they visit me Sunday. You haven't met them yet. You want to come too?"

"Can't. I'm substitute teaching in Sunday school." She pulled her legs underneath her on the sofa and hugged a pillow. "I hope you'll be on your best behavior."

"Me too. I do the last of the drugs on Friday, so I should be okay for a while Sunday morning."

"I'll be glad when it's over for your sake as well as mine. Sometimes just talking to you is like crossing a minefield. I'm never sure what to do or say to please you."

"You're an absolute saint, Lainie."

"Case in point. Frequent sarcasm."

"No, I mean it. I appreciate your patience. You're the only one who knows how really lousy I feel." He leaned back and entwined his fingers on the top of his head, staring at the ceiling above the piano. "Alan said I could have sex. Maybe that'd make me feel better."

"Excuse me?"

"I said the doctor says . . ."

"I heard what you said. Why do doctors think they can supersede the laws of God?"

"I thought it was funny. Just look at me. How likely is that to happen, even if I had a willing partner?"

"It's a cruel 'guy' joke."

"I guess having cancer makes some people go a little crazy, but Alan knows that's not me. He's in the stake presidency, Lainie, and his signature is on my temple recommend."

"Yes, I know that, but why did he even bring it up?"

John took a deep breath. "In the interest of full disclosure. Sometimes chemo causes sterility, and sometimes that's temporary, sometimes permanent. He told me I could bank some sperm before the treatments began if I wanted to be certain of having children later on. I'm still young enough." He stared again. "It didn't seem right. I didn't do it."

"My doctor never mentioned sex or children, but I didn't bring it up either," Lainie admitted. "I was afraid. And at that point, it was probably already irrelevant."

"In all fairness, he should have discussed it with you anyway."

"He was an 'old school' kind of doctor, and I suppose my status as . . . well, an older single woman was a foregone conclusion. Maybe he thought bringing it up would be too much."

"You could sue him for discrimination, gender bias, and malicious negligence."

"You think so?" She played along. "Would you represent me?"

Reaching out to her, John leaned forward. She sat on the arm of the chair so he could hold her. "There's your retainer." She kissed him. "Now build a case."

He rested again in the comfort of her embrace. "Oh, Lainie, I'm going crazy. When am I going to be well?"

"I know how hard it is. Remember the first time we had dinner here, when you brought me to Quail Valley on false pretenses?"

He laughed at her painful but accurate characterization of their first date. "We never imagined we'd be here like this now, did we."

"We said parties are what we both do best, and we'd always find something to celebrate. John, what are we waiting for? We need to live it up, to celebrate your milestones. Every fraction of an inch toward recovery deserves a ticker-tape parade."

He raised his eyebrows. "Well, when I picture myself well again, I see us back in Marchbanks Retreat with a picnic on a blanket."

"That's simple enough. When do you want to go?"

"I don't know when I'll feel strong enough for that."

"I'll plan the picnic, John, and you work on the part about getting stronger."

He shook his head. "Oh, I'm so glad nobody else found you first."

Monday, August 5

When she came up the walk at eleven that morning, Lainie found a large envelope leaning against the front door. It was marked "Brother John" in two-inch childish scrawl. Inside the house, she put the envelope on the sofa and smiled to hear John singing in the shower at the other end of the hall behind the closed bedroom door. It meant he was feeling good today. She checked the fridge to see how much of yesterday's food was gone. Only about half, she noted—not nearly enough. A few minutes after the shower went off, she knocked on the bedroom door. "I'm here now, so don't go wandering around in your skivvies."

"Thanks for the warning."

"I found a special-delivery package on the front porch that I think you're going to like."

"Give me two minutes."

Back in the living room Lainie stood at the window looking at the tops of the mountains. By the end of the month, signs of autumn would start up there, yellows and oranges, browns and reds creeping down the steep terrain day by day, the first reminders of another change of seasons. She heard the bedroom door open.

"Good morning, Irish," he called as he came down the hall. "I love you." She met him halfway and they embraced. He wore black walking shorts, sandals, and a gray Gleneden Beach T-shirt. He'd even shaved.

"What did you have for breakfast?" she asked.

"A chocolate shake with a banana and a handful of raspberries, like you said. I liked it."

"That's good. You can't afford to lose any more weight. As soon as the peach harvest gets going I'll make you a cold peach soup with fresh cream."

He kissed her. "Sounds delicious."

"Except for the shaved head, you're almost back to normal. It's a good day."

"I think I might go to the office for a couple of hours this afternoon."

"That's great. Would you like to read your fan mail now?"

He sat on the sofa, opened the envelope, and took out several homemade cards. First was an eight-and-a-half-by-eleven piece of green construction paper folded in half, with a drawing of the class seated on chairs in a semicircle around John. On the inside it said, "It's a good thing you didn't die. I love your choklit chip cookies." Inside another card, illustrated with a bright-yellow sun, a child wrote, "Thank you for being my Primary teacher. I'm glad Heavenly Father didn't release you."

Oddly, the next card opened left to right. "He's dyslexic and left-handed," John explained, but the message, "thanck fro tetchin em abot Jesus," was decipherable.

In another card, the youngest child in the class reminded her teacher that he promised to give a talk at her baptism in November. "And she'll hold me to it. She's that determined little redhead, the bishop's daughter."

John lingered over each card from the nine children expressing love to their Primary teacher, and then put his head back on the sofa and let the tears go. "They're great kids, and I'm going to live to teach them another Sunday."

"Yes, you are, and I for one am very grateful." Lainie stroked the back of his hand. "I can stay for lunch, John. Is there anything you need me to do while I'm here?"

"Yes. I need you to sit here and let me hold you."

And so she did. They cried a little more and laughed a little and kissed a little, and then fixed a frittata for lunch.

Monday, August 12

Angela blinked with surprise when Kyle came into the kitchen that morning, dressed in brown Dockers and a brown-and-yellow plaid shirt. A wide grin on his clean-shaven face revealed him to be in an extraordinarily annoying good mood. She frowned with suspicion.

"How are you, Angie?"

"Who wants to know?"

He laughed. "How's Julie?"

She sighed and dropped her angry pose. "Growing up and growing away, claiming her own life. I know it's supposed to happen like that, but I never expected to have to make appointments to see my own daughter." Angela had just been thinking about how much she missed Kyle and regretted getting angry when he declared his growing feelings for her, but she found herself saying, "Look, I thought we agreed—"

"This trumps all your lame excuses, cookie. Look what I got Saturday."

She took from his hand a large postcard of the recognizable Diamond Head crater towering above Waikiki Beach and turned it over. In Brandon's tiny block printing, it said:

Dear Kyle,

Sean and I are having fun I guess. He's in meetings a lot. I like surfing but got seasick on the fishing boat and ralphed over the side. I liked the volcano. A little lava was coming out. Sean ate raw fish at the luau. Yuck!!! We go to Park City next Monday. I miss taking care of Sophie's Place with you. See you soon.
Love, Brandon
P.S. I'm still worthy.

Angela turned to Kyle with a look of disappointment. "He wrote to you, not to me."

"Are you jealous?" He put his hat on a stool and folded his arms.

She sighed. "No. I'm just glad one of us heard from him."

"Well, I confess I sort of bribed him. I gave him address labels and postcard stamps."

"You're some kind of genius with bribes." She frowned and sat on a stool.

"It usually works with kids." He sat next to her. "Not so much with adults sometimes." He waited, watching her mood soften as she read the card again. "Do you still have a 'mad' on?"

"I'm sorry. You were right, but I wasn't ready to hear it and needed time to sort out my feelings." She put the card on the table. "You know I'm always frantic all the time Brandon's gone, but you did something about it, just like a real . . ." She stopped herself before she said "dad." No, he wasn't Brandon's father, but now she wished he had been. On an impulse she hugged him. "Thank you." When she let go, he didn't. "Kyle . . ."

"Can't I hold you for a minute? I've missed you."

She relaxed. "Okay. Maybe a minute, but just because I'm a little bit sad."

"How about two minutes? One for you, one for me."

"Whatever."

He smiled and caressed her cheek with his chin. "You are such a beautiful woman, Angie, in every way. I admire so many things about you. My heart keeps doing these little flip-flops whenever I'm around you, and I . . ."

"Don't start with me." She pulled away but he held her elbows. "I don't want to fight with you today."

"That's a fight I think I'd like to have," he teased with a half grin.

She shook her head. "Thank you for showing me Brandon's postcard. It does relieve a lot of my anxiety."

"It has my name on it, but it's for both of us. You know he'd want me to show it to you."

"I get so depressed, Kyle. He doesn't even miss me. He never calls when he's away with Sean, and Sean doesn't encourage him to. I surrender my son to that egomaniac who knows nothing about parenting, and I'm never sure what Brandon's going to be when he comes home six weeks later. Lots of times I have to start all over with civilizing him."

Kyle stroked her jaw with his thumb. "I'm sure that's hard."

"By the time he gets home I'll be a basket case."

"He's *our* son, Angie. You almost said it just now. Sean takes him to Never Never Land occasionally, but Brandon knows that isn't home. He can't articulate it yet, but I think deep in his heart he knows that with Sean, love equals money."

She nodded. "But with us, love equals discipline and security."

"It says right there on the card that he's still worthy. He knows that's important to us, but it's becoming more important to him too, and he wanted to reassure us. It sounds to me like he doesn't really want to play both ends against the middle anymore."

"That is a big change," Angela said.

"It means he's depending on us to raise him the right way. He knows we'd never teach him anything that isn't true because we love him and we want him to be happy."

"He told me before he left that he wants to be like you. He does love you, Kyle."

He lifted her chin to look in her eyes. "It's all about love, isn't it?"

"Most things are."

"Maybe someday you'll see it the way Brandon does." Kyle kissed her then, with love, concern, and comfort. She didn't resist this time, and he lingered.

Eyes still closed, she sat up, pressing her lips together to savor the taste. At last she swallowed and whispered, "Please help me. Please go away."

He relaxed his hold on her arms. "If that's what you really want." He got up, grabbed his hat, and went to the door, turning to smile at her. "It's good to see you again."

"Kyle, wait." He came back and stood next to her. "I'm sorry. I'm so confused. For sixteen years I've just been somebody's mother. I don't know how to be me, or even who I am."

"It's all right. I know who you are, and I'm happy to be here while you rediscover it."

She smiled, grateful for his patience. "You're a good man, Kyle. I don't know how to deal with that. I've never been . . . well, appreciated by a good man before."

"Get used to it." He held out his hand. She took it and stepped into his arms. "There's no mystery to it. How do you feel now?"

"Good. You always make me feel good, Kyle. That night with the sparklers . . . well, it really was fireworks, and I didn't know what to do."

"Do you think if you gave yourself a chance you could learn what to do?"

"I could, if you'd help me."

"It's a deal. I feel good too when we're together. Maybe it doesn't make sense for either one of us, Angel, but there it is. Sometimes good things come at an inconvenient time."

"How do we start over? Shake hands, exchange phone numbers—" He stopped her with a kiss.

"That works for me," she murmured.

They held each other until they startled at the sound of a lawn mower powering up in the back yard. Kyle chuckled. "I think Mark's trying to tell me something."

Angela patted his chest. "I'll be here all morning. Come and see me again before you leave."

Wednesday, August 14

John's biologic treatment played out exactly as Dr. Kurtz said it would, with chills and fever and other flu-like symptoms. "At least you know when it's going to be over," Lainie remarked on Wednesday morning as she massaged John's feet.

He sat in bed, a cold cloth over his face. "But when this is over, will it really be over?"

"John, you sound like a three-year-old who didn't get what he wanted for Christmas."

"You don't know anything about three-year-olds."

"I'm learning from you."

He moaned. "I've got to get back to work. Morgan's carrying me, and I'm dead wood."

"Morgan knows healing takes time."

"And this is your busy time. Carrie's shouldering it all when you're here so often."

"Oh, stop it, John. Sometimes I wish I could press the mute button when you start talking this blather. None of us would step up if we didn't love you."

"I'm just so sick of being sick."

Lainie stopped the foot massage, moved closer, and took the cloth off his face.

He frowned. "Don't."

"Don't what?"

"Don't kiss me. My mouth feels like the bottom of a birdcage."

She rolled her eyes. "Nothing wrong with your ego."

"Weren't you going to kiss me?"

"No."

"Then why did you get my hopes up?"

"I was going to have you repeat the mantra."

"What if I don't want to?"

"Tough. I'm not leaving till you do. Say it for my benefit." She squeezed his hand. "Say it like you mean it. Life is good."

John snorted and stared at the ceiling.

"Come on. Life is good. Remember, it's all about life—about living."

"It's all about life," he repeated with a noticeable lack of sincerity. "Life is good."

"Once more, this time like you mean it."

He sighed. "Life is good. It's all about life."

She smiled. "That wasn't so hard, was it?"

He looked at her and kissed her hand. "My life is good with you in it. Sweet Lainie, I'm sorry I'm so . . ."

"Sorry for what? For being sick?" She kissed his forehead. "Just get well. That's all I want. I love you, John, in a way I've never loved anything or anyone in my life."

Now he smiled. "I understand. That's the way I love you."

"I have to get back to work. Get some rest and I'll see you tonight."

He grinned and adjusted the pillow. "I'll brush my teeth in anticipation."

Lainie stopped at the door. "Yeah, yeah, promises, promises."

Tuesday, August 20

With the biologic therapy behind him, Lainie knew John was eager to take on additional activities like going to the office, teaching his Primary class, playing the piano, and painting more. But it was frustrating for him to be so tired all the time and to have such a short attention span. *Aha,* she thought when she saw him come to Sophie's Place that Tuesday afternoon. *It's a good day.*

Busy with a client, Lainie moved around the yard to explain all the possible arrangements for the wedding reception the week after Labor Day, and John sat in the rose cottage hiding behind sunglasses. He wore a tropical-print shirt in bright blue and white, denim walking shorts, and sandals. A white cap protected his bald head from the sun.

When the client left, Lainie walked over and greeted John with a kiss. "So you've escaped from the asylum," she teased, "but they'll catch you if you don't lose that uniform."

"Now I fit right in at your asylum." He pulled her down to sit on the bench with him, then took off his sunglasses. "Jerry won a vacation in the Bahamas from the company he works for, and Margaret sent this shirt to cheer me up."

"It worked. You look like you feel good enough to take that trip to Marchbanks Retreat."

"Yes, I do. I haven't felt this good in a long time."

"We can have lots of parties and outings to celebrate your recovery," Lainie said.

"Let's plan the first one for Labor Day, just the two of us."

"You're on, and so are the peaches, by the way." Lainie turned and leaned on the back of the bench, loving him with her eyes.

John grinned. "I love peaches."

"You're kind of peachy yourself."

"You're only saying that because it's true."

They laughed and she caressed his cheek. "What have you been up to this morning?"

"I spent a couple of hours at the office," he said, "grinding away at my usual tortoise-like speed, accomplishing an infinitesimal and inconsequential amount of work."

"You're the champ."

"I have to run some errands right now, and then this afternoon I'm going to lock myself in my studio and try to finish that project."

"Is this that same one you've been working on for so long?" Lainie asked.

"Uh-huh, and I need a little inspiration, so I came to the source."

"How can I inspire you? What do you need?"

He held her shoulders and kissed her mouth. "A little of this." He kissed her again. "A little of that." He kissed her once more. "And another for medicinal purposes."

"Wow. Now I'm inspired too. What kind of painting is this?"

"I'll show you someday." He held her close. "Someday soon."

"I've heard that before."

"Just you wait." They kissed again. "I'll call you later. Say hi to the sassy lassie for me."

Nineteen

Friday, August 30

"I'm so sick of weddings!" Jane pounded the table when Carrie put another pan of watermelon cubes on the table in front of her.

"Me too," Julie grumbled.

They sat on stools around a worktable, making fruit kabobs for that night's event, which marked the saturation point for both girls. In fact, they agreed the charm had worn off somewhere around the middle of June.

Carrie chuckled. "Does that mean you don't want a wedding reception when you get married?"

Jane pulled open another pack of skewers. "I'd rather elope."

"It's pretty hard to elope to the temple," Carrie said on her way to the cooler with a tray of finished kabobs. "You have to let them know a few weeks in advance that you're coming."

Jane rolled her eyes. "I'd like to try."

"You know, sweetie, I don't think that's a decision you have to make today."

Julie said, "I think what I've learned about weddings this summer is that it's about more than the food or the presents or the dresses. That's all for show. It's really about the people."

Carrie sliced open a cantaloupe. "How did you learn that?"

"I've watched the brides and grooms." Julie pulled some grapes off their stems. "They come here and have a party to celebrate their marriage, and everybody's happy for them, but then they go away together on their own. Some of them look really scared."

"Well, that's marriage," Carrie said. "It can be scary sometimes."

"But some of them are getting married for different reasons."

Carrie frowned. "What do you mean?"

"I remember one couple especially—really pretty girl, really sharp guy—but you could tell they weren't getting married for the same reason. She was crazy about him, but he was marrying her just to have a pretty girl on his arm, eye candy for his friends. It didn't seem right."

Jane shifted on the stool. "Okay, what would be the right reason to get married?"

"Well, some couples are really nice to each other," Julie said. "I like that. I think you have to be considerate and thoughtful—to want to make each other happy. And you have to really love each other."

"Jules, most people get married because they think they're in love," Jane commented, "but how do you know for sure?"

"I figured that out too, and I'm not getting married until I find somebody I can look at the same way John and Lainie look at each other," Julie replied.

Carrie's eyebrows went up. "You've been watching John and Lainie?"

"Last week I saw them together in the rose cottage and thought I was going to melt. It's just so obvious they love each other."

"Why aren't they married, Mom?"

Carrie chuckled. "Let me know if you figure that out."

Julie gasped. "Wouldn't it be fun to throw a wedding reception for John and Lainie?"

"Yeah," Jane said. "For that I'd even be willing to make more kabobs."

"I wouldn't even mind throwing a wedding reception for my mom."

"Is she interested in someone?" Carrie started on another cantaloupe.

"I'm not sure. She's been out with Kyle Kirkwood quite a bit lately," Julie said.

"From the garden center?" Jane reached for another piece of fruit.

"He's a great guy. He calls her Angel sometimes. It's so sweet. But I don't think she knows what she wants."

Carrie put a pan of fruit cubes on the table in front of the girls. "Having a man in her life is quite an adjustment."

Julie smiled. "We have family dates sometimes, and Brandon and I think he's terrific. I just hope my mom is smart enough to see that. She ought to live it up while she has the chance."

"Guest alert," Angela announced as she burst through the door. "They're coming down the sidewalk. Are you people working or schmoozing?"

"Careful, girls," Carrie warned. "She's got a pastry bag and she knows how to use it."

Monday, September 2

Lainie prepared the Labor Day picnic, and in the early afternoon she and John drove to Marchbanks Retreat. It was a warm day in the canyon. When they finished the meal he leaned over and kissed her. "Thank you. That peach soup lived up to all the hype."

"Your recovery inspires me." She stroked his head as if he had hair. "What happened with the family of that boy in your Primary class?"

"For obvious reasons, I had to withdraw as guardian ad litem, but our associate Chad Remington volunteered to take over for me, and the judge agreed. Chad has a lot of family-law experience."

"That's good. And he can keep you informed."

"Yeah, this is one I definitely want to follow. We prepared the doctor to testify but some technicality wouldn't allow it, so we didn't get the attempted manslaughter charge. The judge granted the divorce and sent the abusive dad to jail but she only gave him one to five years. With the extenuating facts of the case I thought it warranted more time." John lay back, joined his fingers behind his head, and crossed his ankles.

Lainie stretched out next to him. "At least the kids and their mother are safe."

"Maybe for a little while. We advised her to leave the state and not to tell anyone where she was going. He'll probably get out early on good behavior and come after them."

"And now two more children will be raised without a dad."

"Yeah. Lots of rotten ironies in this world."

"At least he can't hurt them anymore."

"Unfortunately, the damage has already been done."

"You did everything you could, John. Think where they might be without you."

He studied the passing clouds and the tic-tac-toe grids of airplane vapor trails in the sky. "I just wish I could have done more." He sighed and looked at her. "Lainie, what have you done in the past five years that you might not have done if you hadn't had cancer?"

"I learned to look for and enjoy the pleasures of every day. I nurture my Sweet Souls because I love them and they need someone like me. I chose to partner with Carrie at Sophie's Place because I love her and what we do brings people together for happy occasions. And I fell in love with you, John. That's the best thing that's happened to me so far. Ever. In my whole life."

John smiled and turned toward Lainie. "My latest lab report was good. All the evidence leads me to believe I'm a survivor. I'm still processing what that means."

"Yes, it's as hard to be a survivor as it is to be a patient. Some people feel so guilty, so 'why me?' when other good people didn't make it. I guess if I've done anything different it's deciding to live deliberately, like Thoreau said when he went to Walden Pond. I don't do anything I don't really want to do, and when I die I'm going to be all used up."

"You see headlines all the time about spectacular feats of courage by cancer survivors," John said with a puzzled look, "like sailing around the world alone or taking up bull fighting."

"Why do you have to do something heroic just because you survived cancer? Doesn't it take courage simply to resume your life? John, there's no one as awesome as an ordinary person who simply tries to bloom where he's planted. To me, that's the definition of a hero. Cancer has nothing to do with it."

"That minimizes cancer and defuses the fear."

"Cancer might remove a person from this life, but it doesn't erase memories or cancel relationships." She moved closer and put her hand on his chest. "Cancer can make you feel lousy, but it doesn't take away your capacity to give or accept love. I was in God's hands no less when I had cancer than I am now. When I surrendered, it wasn't to the disease; it was to the healer of the disease. I chose love."

John kissed her hand and held her in his arms. "Lainie, you *are* love." After a long time his hold relaxed and he lay smiling at her until he fell asleep, their hands still joined.

When he awoke, he saw that Lainie had cleaned up the picnic things and was sitting under a tree by the stream, dangling her feet in the water. He sat beside her, splashing her feet with his, and leaned over to kiss her left cheek. "You've done it again, Lainie. It's been a perfect day."

"So what's it going to be, sailing or bull fighting?"

"I've still got chemo brain. I can't make any important decisions right now. I'm doing well just to choose what socks to wear."

"I take it, then, that you probably won't sell out and become a wild-eyed recluse just to prove you're not worthy of survival."

"Even on a bad day I know I have a lot to live for." John rubbed his eyes. "I had a letter from my brother Brennan the other day. From the basis of practically no experience whatsoever, he's giving me advice about recovery and still trying to rescue me from my errors in thinking."

"You'd think, being a priest, he'd understand what it means to be hopelessly converted."

"He's convinced that my *telos* is in Catholicism."

"What's telos?" Lainie asked.

"It's a philosophical term that means 'ultimate end,' and since Brennan teaches philosophy, we're all the recipients of his endless wisdom and free advice."

"He sounds arrogant."

"No, he's just terminally sincere and doesn't want any of us to be misled. In Greek, 'telos' means fundamental purpose, the end of existence. Without telos there's no meaning to life. Everything has a role, something it's foreordained to be. In French, it's *raison d'être,* reason to be. An acorn's telos is to become an oak tree. Brennan found his telos with the Jesuits. Aristotle said our telos as human beings is happiness, but St. Augustine said it's to love God."

"Brennan has a hard time accepting that your telos is to be a Latter-day Saint."

"And a priesthood holder and Primary teacher and attorney. From what I know of the gospel plan, I'm Aristotelian and Augustinian."

"Why is your telos so important to Brennan?"

"He's always trying to coax me back to where he thinks I belong. Besides, if he's wrong about his telos that means his whole life is a lie. I think the central question is whether we decide on our own purpose or accept the one God gives us."

"So you're rethinking your own telos," Lainie said.

"In some ways I suppose I am. What do you think I should do?"

"Look, I'm no telos expert, but I do know you're not required to make sweeping changes in your life just because you survived. Remember that wacky family in *You Can't Take It with You.* They only did things that made them happy. It isn't complex Greek philosophy, John, but take a lesson from it. Follow your passion, whatever it is. Isn't that why you studied law? If you still feel the same fire, if it still makes you happy, then stay with it."

"Morgan's like a brother to me, and I really enjoy the practice of law, but maybe I'll find something else to do with my life once I'm able to resume it. I've thought lately about victims advocacy or maybe seeking an appointment to the bench." John raised his eyebrows and grinned at her. "I could even work harder at painting, open a cooking school."

She giggled. "You can play the xylophone now."

"Yeah, there's a big demand for that, you know. And there's always acting."

"You're pretty good at that."

"Or I could move to Gleneden and become a professional beachcomber." They looked at each other, and John took her in his arms and sighed. "Lainie, I know we haven't finished that conversation we started in June, but I'm still trying to collect my thoughts, and they're still getting lost in the fog."

"Chemo brain."

"Yeah. All I know for certain is that I love you."

"I know, John, and I love you, but I don't want to talk about the telos of our relationship until I'm sure your head is completely clear."

After supper on her deck, Angela and Kyle walked around the block while waiting for Sean to bring Brandon home. They stopped in the English garden at Sophie's Place to make the trip last longer, sitting for a while in the swing.

"Why didn't you have a temple marriage?" Kyle took out a pocketknife and cut one of the late-summer roses climbing the pergola.

Angela shook her head. "Sean's promise of a temple marriage was his first and biggest lie. He said he believed in the Church, and I trusted that, but it was just the idea of it he liked—eternal perfect families with eternal perfect wives to cater to eternal demands from husbands with authority. He had it skewed, and he only stayed with it long enough to trap me. But I wasn't perfect, so it was my fault that the marriage didn't work. He's a razzle-dazzle artist, an eternal con man. I was so blinded by his charm that I didn't see the fraud for what it was."

Kyle frowned, slicing the thorns off the stem of the rose. "You couldn't see that he wasn't good enough for you?"

"I was always worried about being good enough for somebody else." Angela stared ahead. "Kneeling at the altar with someone I loved had been my goal since I was a little girl, but when I found out what Sean really was, I was glad it wasn't a temple marriage."

"To my way of thinking, the temple is personal. You go there for individual covenants and blessings before you go there to create a family." Kyle put the knife away and held her hand.

"That's true, and I honor my covenants because they taught me who I am. I went to the temple for myself the week after my divorce was final. It erased a lot of the bitterness I felt and helped me focus on the responsibility of raising two children alone. I don't think I could have survived if I hadn't been endowed with temple blessings. I'm still grieving, though, because my children aren't mine forever."

Kyle stopped the swing. "Paying child support is one thing, but it isn't the kind of steady emotional support you need most."

"No. I hated depending on Sean for anything. I left him twice before I finally filed for divorce. Brandon was born after our first attempted reconciliation."

"But having a baby couldn't bring you closer if the marriage was beyond saving."

Angela sighed and leaned against Kyle's shoulder. "I realized later that Sean didn't really want children at all because they drew attention away from him."

"What an ego."

"But once he had them he wanted other people to believe he was a concerned, attentive father. It's all as phony as he is. He never plans a father-son trip just for the two of them. Brandon gets dragged along on business trips for Sean's amusement. I don't know how much time Brandon spends alone in Park City."

Kyle frowned. "That's despicable."

"Sean could afford more lawyers than I could, so I didn't even ask for alimony, just for the house and the kids. I wanted to sever as many ties as possible, and I paid a huge price for his freedom. It guaranteed that the three of us would be on the edge of poverty until I could support us. My parents helped a lot with child care, and money now and then."

Kyle pushed Angela's wind-blown hair away from her face. "I'm sorry it happened that way."

She shrugged. "That's the hand I was dealt. At least Julie's bright enough to see Sean for what he really is."

"She's remarkably well adjusted."

"It gives me hope that someday Brandon will see through Sean's deceptions too." Angela turned to Kyle. "You had a temple marriage, didn't you?"

"Yes. We were happy, but Nicole changed after the baby died. She became a physical and emotional invalid, like she was punishing herself for the accident. Or me. But the most frustrating part was that she wouldn't help herself recover, and she wouldn't turn to me for strength. She gave up on everything. I don't know. Maybe, after time to think, she'll decide she doesn't want to be married to me for eternity."

"I'm so sorry."

"That's the hand I was dealt. It'll all get sorted out later. But other good things have happened. I'm very fortunate to be able to do for a living the thing I like most. I have a chance to work with kids, too, and I like helping them grow."

"Like my son. He needs you to show him the way."

They stood and walked toward the sundial at the center of the garden. "Angie, I want you to need me, too. I want us to feel connected. I want you to love me for who I am, not because of Brandon."

She sighed. "Kyle, I'm still afraid."

"Fear isn't your friend. It delays the good things that could be happening in your life."

"But fear is persistent."

He smelled the rose, then gave her his hand. "Come on. Let's go back and wait for Brandon."

"Everyone enjoys the English garden," she said as they closed the gate. "You made a beautiful thing happen."

"I like to think I'm in partnership with the Creator. It was important to Him that all the things He made were beautiful and pleasing for His children to enjoy. Besides, the two most consequential events in human history have taken place in gardens."

They walked on in silence in the fading light. As they approached the broad front porch, Angela chuckled. "You know, with Sean's sense of timing we could play a couple of rounds of Monopoly before he gets here." She turned on the light and they sat on the wicker love seat.

"I'd rather sit here and look at you." Kyle tickled her chin with the fragrant flower before giving it to her.

Taking the rose, she looked at him—the smiling face she'd seen across several tables at dinner over the last three weeks, and in the temple twice—and realized he was giving her back the self she'd lost while focused on raising two children. *What is there to be afraid of?* She snuggled close to him and enjoyed the comfort of his arms.

A few minutes later a car drove up. Brandon scrambled out, waving.

As Angela and Kyle left the porch, she said, "Sean's on time. He probably has a late date."

"Well, a man has to have priorities," Kyle muttered.

Sean took three bags from the trunk and gave Brandon a high five. Then he stood on the curb, leaning against the car with his ankles crossed while Brandon gave his mother and Kyle eager hugs.

"Wow, what a tan," Angela marveled as she kissed her son's cheek.

Kyle grinned and ruffled Brandon's shaggy hair. "I think you've grown at least an inch." He grabbed two of Brandon's bags. Brandon took the other one, and they headed for the house.

Angela turned to Sean. "Thanks for bringing him home safely, and on time. Points for you. He'll see you in a couple of weekends, I guess."

Sean licked his lips. "Yeah, I guess."

"Well, if it doesn't fit your schedule we can . . ."

"Who's the guy?" Sean pulled off his sunglasses and nodded toward the porch.

Angela watched as Brandon and Kyle went inside the house, chattering like old friends. "That's Kyle. He owns a nursery in Springville, and he gave Brandon a job doing yard work. Isn't that okay with you?"

"Kid couldn't talk about anything else. Kyle this, and Kyle that." Sean shifted his feet and put a hand on his hip. "Even made me take him to church."

Angela's jaw dropped. "You went to church?"

Sean shrugged and leaned against the car again. "Dropped him off, picked him up later."

"Well, thank you for that. It's important that he attend his meetings."

"Is that what Kyle tells him?" Sean drawled out the name.

"He's been very good to Brandon the past few months."

"Is he *very good* to you too? Using the kid to get into your . . ."

"That's none of your business, Sean." Angela smiled. "Don't you have someone waiting for you in Park City? Should be a nice drive up the canyon."

Inside she found Brandon and Kyle on the sofa. She sat next to her son and put an arm around him. "Did you have a good time?"

Brandon shrugged. "It was Hawaii. It was Park City. What can I say?"

The circles under his eyes reminded her he'd been living on Sean Standard Time. In the middle of a story about surfing, Brandon yawned. "How long has it been since you've had a full night's sleep?" Angela asked.

"Well, not last night."

"School starts tomorrow, you know."

"Oh yeah." Brandon stifled another yawn and turned to Kyle. "Thanks for holding my job for me. I'll talk to Mark tomorrow about taking over again."

"That's great. Grass isn't growing as fast now. You'll have six or eight more weeks of lawns before the first frost. Then you'll be into raking leaves and shoveling snow."

Brandon grinned and nodded. "And I'm still worthy."

"Your mother and I prayed for you every day. We knew you could do it."

Angela hugged and kissed Brandon again and walked him to the foot of the stairs. "You have a choice. You can shower tonight or in the morning. You remember what a shower is, don't you?"

He laughed, starting up the stairs. "You're so funny, Mom."

"I love you, Son," she said.

Brandon turned and smiled at them. "I love you, Mom. You too, Kyle. It's good to be home. Is Jules here?"

"She's in her room. I'm sure she'd love to see you."

"Oh, I forgot to give you the souvenir I bought."

"I'll get it tomorrow. Go see Julie."

Brandon knocked on Julie's door. Angela and Kyle stood looking at each other, smiling at the reunion of the brother and sister upstairs. "He's home," Angela whispered as Kyle took her in his arms. "He's safe." They walked to the door. "He's never brought me a souvenir before. What do you think that means?"

"He wants you to know he recognizes everything you've done for him."

She met Kyle's kiss with enthusiasm. When they stopped, she stood enclosed in his embrace, listening to his breathing and his pounding heart, wishing they could go on holding each other like this. "It wasn't so bad this time while Brandon was away. You were here."

"It's what I wanted too. Good night, Angel. I'll call you tomorrow and we'll plan something for this weekend with the kids." He kissed her again and went out the door.

Twenty

Friday, September 6

Just before John left at noon, Morgan came into his office and closed the door. "How are you?" He sat in a chair and leaned forward. "I mean, how are you *really*?"

John smiled. "Alan said I should be well by October. I'd like to believe that."

"Well, things are beginning to spin out of control around here. In the last few months, since we changed direction, business has grown. I think it's time to make these associates partners and find some new associates. Will you think about it?"

"We knew that would happen eventually. How's the new paralegal working out?"

"Great. She ought to be in law school."

"How soon do you need an answer?"

"As soon as possible. That's why I'm asking how you really are."

John shook his head. "It sounds like a good idea, but honestly, Morgan, the chemo brain hasn't entirely gone away yet. I spend too much time rereading papers I just read."

"I don't want to push you, John. Do what you can. These people have been with us quite a while. They need a career move, and we need them to stay with us."

"That's right. They've been good associates, and they'd be good partners."

"And they fit so well into our master plan."

"I will think about it."

When Morgan left, John stared out the window at the hint of fall in the trees. His inability to resume his life discouraged him. He could hide his persistent depression from everybody but Lainie. With his hair uneven as it grew back in, he kept his head shaved. He couldn't stay at the office more than half a day three or four times a week, couldn't concentrate when he brought work home and often fell asleep reading it.

John left the office and drove up the hill to his condo, thinking too much of his life was vacation. He needed to become exhausted by physical or mental labor, to be refreshed again by sleep, but he didn't have the energy. Except for Lainie and his Primary class, very little held his interest. At home he made a milk shake for lunch and then stared out the living room window. He closed his eyes for just a few minutes, and when he awoke it was nearly time to go to bed.

Tuesday, September 24

Arriving in Quail Valley at John's mysterious phone invitation, Lainie saw a blue van with a Washington license plate in the driveway, and then she understood. John stood on the porch before she could get out of her car. She hurried to him.

"What took you so long?" he teased, kissing her. "Come and meet my brother."

Richard was a little taller than John, a little broader, with the same eyes and hair. He ignored the hand she offered when John introduced them and hugged her like an old friend.

"And this is Janine." John's sister-in-law was tall and strawberry-blond. She hugged Lainie too. "They didn't even tell me they were coming," John said. "They just popped in, all the way from Vancouver."

Richard sat with Janine on the sofa. "It's only a fourteen-hour drive."

"And we left the kids with my mother," Janine explained. "They love that."

"What a nice surprise," Lainie said. She sat in the armchair, and John sat on the ottoman in front of it, his forearm on her knee. "How long are you staying?"

"Just till Thursday. Classes begin next week," Janine replied. Lainie knew Richard and Janine taught English, literature, and humanities at a community college in Vancouver.

"And the missionaries are coming Friday," Richard said. "We need to be home then."

"So where are you with them?" John asked.

"We're coming to the end of the instruction. I've never encountered anything that makes such perfect sense. I wish we'd done this years ago when you and Margaret gave us that first Book of Mormon. We read it then, but we weren't ready to commit to it as completely as we are now. I was never a very good Catholic anyway . . ."

"And I was a Jew in name only," Janine added.

"If we're going to be Mormons, we want to do it right."

"That's the only way," John said.

Janine smiled. "To think we can be an eternal family is so thrilling. We've started having family prayer, and it really has made a big impression on the kids. There's such a sweet feeling in our home now."

"How many children do you have?" Lainie asked.

"Alex is eight, Bailey is five, and Callie is three." Janine rubbed her belly. "We don't know yet who the new baby is."

Richard looked at Janine. "We're reading the Book of Mormon together now. It's powerful. So many obvious parallels to modern society, and such elegant language."

"Alex isn't too young to read it. My Primary class loves it," John said.

"We've been reading some of the stories with him, and we can see what an impact it has. He loves the adventures of Lehi's family, and the story of Christ's visit to the Nephites."

"So you're going to do it? You're going to be baptized?"

Richard paused for a deep breath. "We really want to, John, but we have the same problem you did—disappointing Mom and Dad."

"My parents don't care," Janine added. "They celebrate both Hanukkah and Christmas."

John leaned forward. "Doesn't the problem really belong to Mom and Dad, not to you?"

"We want to make peace with them somehow. I know they were so mad they were ready to disown you, and then when you corrupted Margaret too, they almost didn't recover. But she doesn't care. She just snaps her fingers at it and loves them anyway."

"I visit them whenever I make a trip to Gleneden, and Mom still serves coffee at every meal, thinking this time I'm going to drink it." John chuckled. "I don't even say 'no thanks' anymore, but now the smell ruins my appetite."

"She's doing that to us too," Richard said.

"She's looking for a crack in our resolve, Brother. She'll never stop testing us."

Janine shook her head. "We don't like that adversarial feeling."

"I know exactly what you mean," John said. "But you have to do what's right for you and your family. That's your first consideration. If it's true, it's true, and nothing else matters. It's that simple."

Richard looked at his wife. "Maybe we've been making it too hard."

"Exactly," John said. "Mom and Dad are so stuck on being mad about it they won't listen to explanations that might answer their questions. We talk about restored doctrine they don't understand yet, and it's confusing and frightening. Maybe with enough examples in the family they'll soften up. Maybe that's what your baptism can do for them. If we keep an eye on eternity, everything else will work itself out."

Richard nodded. "That's what Margaret and Jerry told us, and I appreciate your optimism, but on the other hand—"

"Richard, I've been 'on the other hand' for twenty years. Believe me, I know what that means. Think of that cup of cold coffee by my place at Mom's table."

Lainie looked at her watch. "Hey, I have to get back to work. We don't have an outdoor event tonight, so we're picking apples this afternoon. We have a big old tree in the corner of the yard that adds a lot of ambiance, but it still has to be harvested." She leaned forward and put her hand on John's shoulder. "What are your plans?"

He looked at Richard and Janine. "That's up to you two."

"Of course we want to go to Temple Square while we're here," Janine said. "What else will we have time to see?"

Lainie recommended the Church's and BYU's museums and galleries. "And we could take a ride up the canyon to Marchbanks Retreat. We already have some fall color up there."

"What's that?" Richard asked.

John explained, and Lainie added, "You'll love it," just before she excused herself. "Choose a restaurant where we can go for dinner," she suggested as John walked her to the car, "and I'll escape with you."

"Okay. We can help you with the apple harvest and you can show them Sophie's Place." He kissed her.

"Keep an eye on eternity," Lainie said. "That's good advice."

Friday, September 27

John's emotional state deteriorated from euphoria into depression after Janine and Richard visited. Lainie came at lunchtime and found him angry and frustrated at the piano, music strewn all over the floor. He wore cutoff sweats and a T-shirt, and he hadn't shaved. She sat beside him on the bench.

"I can't play anymore." His voice shook. "I've forgotten the Chopin etude."

She put her arms around him. "John, you know it'll come back. This is temporary."

"So is life, but I don't want to spend it not remembering Chopin." He closed the cover on the keyboard and leaned on it. "Lainie, this is never going to end. I can't take it anymore."

She held him close and prayed for the right words. "When I was recovering, I decided to sell my house. I thought it was too big, too nice, I didn't deserve it, and somebody else needed it more. My parents advised against it, but I signed a contract with an agent and told her to make a deal with the first buyer she found, regardless of price. In about three weeks, I realized what I'd done and called the agent in a panic. 'Don't worry,' she told me, 'I tore up the contract as soon as I left your place. I did some crazy things like that when I had chemotherapy too, and I knew you didn't mean it.' It was the kindest thing anyone could have done for me, John, and that's what I'm going to do for you. I'm going to tear up all the self-destructive and hopeless things I hear you say because I know that isn't you. That isn't the John Marchbanks I love, but I'll wait for him to come back, no matter how long it takes."

Tears filled his eyes and he clung to her. "I love you so much. What would I do without you?" When he was calm, he continued to hold her.

"Lainie, I've hit the wall again and I'm scared. I'm afraid I'll never be able to think straight. What am I going to do?"

She stroked his shoulder. "First, you need to exercise some faith. Have someone give you another priesthood blessing. Yours helped me so much."

"I didn't think of that. I'm so foggy even the obvious things don't get through."

"You also need to exercise your body more." She took his hand and led him to the sofa. "Walk along the river trail or in a park. Get a bike and keep it with mine in my garage. We can ride out to the lake or the airport together. Don't you have a health club membership?"

He nodded. "It's lapsed now, but I used to run or swim three times a week."

"You also need to eat, John. You'll never get your strength back unless you feed your brain to wash away all the toxic waste of the drugs and make it work again. You don't have a big appetite, but you're still entitled to total self-indulgence and a complete lack of self-restraint."

He patted Lainie's hand. "You'd think that would be easy."

"You could come to my house once in a while even when I'm not there and get the comedy cure from my video collection. Laughter's good for you."

"Yeah. That would help."

"Most of all, you need a change of scenery. Don't hang around here and get depressed. Come to Sophie's Place after school when the kids are there and have some milk and cookies with them—help them with their homework. That'll energize you, and they'd love it."

John put his arm around her. "Was that four or five things you suggested? I should have had you write them down."

Lainie chuckled softly. "Like a prescription—Dr. McGuire's Genuine Bona Fide Never-Fail Chemo Brain Cure."

"Is it guaranteed fast-acting and dependable?"

"Mmm-hmm. And contains no snake oil."

"I hope not. I've got enough bizarre substances running around in my system already."

She patted his cheek. "I have to go back to work. Are you okay?"

He kissed her hand. "I think so, but if I'm not I know where you live. Thanks for being my safety net. Again." He helped her off the sofa and they walked to the door.

"Why don't you get dressed and bring a book to Sophie's Place for a while this afternoon? I'll fix a fresh-peach milk shake and you can sip it in the window seat and read while we set up for a party. Then I'll take you to dinner later."

"What kind of party?"

"Fiftieth anniversary."

"Fifty years. Imagine that."

"My parents had their fiftieth anniversary last year," Lainie said.

"Still crazy in love?"

"Even crazier, if that's possible."

"Well, I'm crazy in love with you." John held her close. "A little more now than when you walked in a while ago. Thanks for tolerating my nonsense."

She held his face and kissed him. "Get well, Johnny. I want you back. Do whatever it takes to get well."

He smoothed her hair and touched her chin. "I will, Irish, I promise. I'm sorry it's been so awful for you."

She hugged him again. "But look how awful it's been for you." She gave him a fierce, decisive kiss. "Just come back, Johnny. I love you."

Saturday and Sunday, October 5–6

John and Lainie watched both days of general conference together at Quail Valley and were inspired by the proceedings. He dozed between sessions or puttered with her to fix meals. Sunday morning she made buttermilk pancakes, which they smothered with spicy homemade applesauce and whipped cream, and ate accompanied by the Mormon Tabernacle Choir.

After the last session Sunday afternoon, they had a long, unhurried dinner, reviewing the talks and proceedings, then sat at opposite ends of the sofa eating chocolate Bundt cake.

"Well, we said back in April we were going to do this," Lainie pointed out.

"I remember. You went home to visit your parents that weekend."

"And you were in the play."

"I was so disappointed. I just wanted to be with you all the time."

"Me too." She made tiny circles in the air with her fork. "We were just getting Sophie's Place going then. It was hard to concentrate on anything else."

"I think I knew then that I was in love with you. I just didn't know what to call it yet."

She swallowed another bite. "And look what we've been through in the meantime."

John chuckled. "I do know what to call that."

Finished with her cake, she put the plate on the coffee table. "What do you think Alan will tell you at your checkup tomorrow?"

"I hope it's something encouraging, but regardless, I'm going back to work this week."

"You can take naps on the sofa in your office."

"Yeah. It's October and I still don't feel completely back to normal, but I'm tired of doing what I'm doing."

"I understand." Lainie took their dessert plates to the dishwasher. "I'm going home now. Come to my house early tomorrow and we'll walk out by the lake and say goodbye to the ducks before they head south. Then I'll fix breakfast before you go to your checkup."

He walked her to the door. "Okay. Tantalize me."

"How about a spinach omelet with artichoke hearts and several kinds of cheese, and—"

"Say no more." He gave her a long good-night kiss. "See you in the morning."

Monday, October 7

They walked in the brisk autumn air, laughing and talking. John was playful and in good spirits. They fixed breakfast, and with half an hour to spare before his appointment, he wrapped his arms around Lainie and kissed her thoroughly.

That hectic morning she tried to please a bride's mother who didn't want to be pleased, and then ran errands, consulted with Carrie and a new client, and straightened out an incorrect shipment of supplies. Late that afternoon Lainie called John's office, anxious to hear about his appointment.

"He's going to be away for a while," the secretary said. "He's gone to Oregon."

Lainie had a hard time finding her voice. "Is Morgan there? This is Lainie McGuire."

"Yes. Please hold."

She realized John was in unfamiliar territory; there were no handbooks or checklists for cancer survivors, but when did he decide to do that? He wasn't impulsive. Was this chemo brain?

"Hi Lainie. I think I know what you're calling about," Morgan said when he came on the line.

"Why did he leave like that, without an explanation? I don't even know what happened at his checkup."

"We didn't get any warning either. He said you told him he needed a change of scenery, so he went to Gleneden."

"That isn't what I meant." Lainie sighed. "Why would he isolate himself from people who love and support him?"

Morgan chuckled. "Think of it as a time-out. Carrie did that once. Remember? I didn't understand at first when she told me what she needed, but John gave me some good advice. He said I should have faith in Carrie's love. I did, and it turned out to be a good thing for both of us. That's what John needs from you right now. He doesn't talk about it, Lainie, but it's obvious to everyone around him that he loves you, and you need to have faith in that."

She was silent.

"Lainie, are you okay?"

"I don't know. I'll figure it out and tell you later."

She hung up the phone and stared at the wall in front of her, wavering between anger and forgiveness.

Twenty-One

Thursday, October 10

While replaying scenes of last weekend in her mind, Angela prepared frosting for the cake on today's agenda. She was getting used to the idea that Kyle was increasingly a part of her life, and Julie's and Brandon's, too. He spent both days of general conference with them, helped prepare meals, took Brandon to priesthood meeting Saturday night, and napped on the couch between sessions. It was almost like they were a family, and it felt comfortable. Last month Brandon had begun refusing weekends with Sean to spend more time with Kyle, which made Angela happy. She turned with a welcoming smile when he came in.

"Good morning." Kyle took off his hat and kissed her cheek. "Do you love me yet?" She laughed. "Just checkin'."

"What are you doing here? It's Thursday," she said. He usually came to Sophie's Place only on Mondays—five sweet Mondays now since Brandon had come back from his time with Sean—and sometimes on Monday nights for family home evening. They'd been out to movies and high school basketball games, gone hiking in the autumn splendor, and had board game tournaments with the kids. They talked on the phone in the evenings, but there was no substitute for a smile and a touch.

Kyle sat on a stool near her. "I have business in town. I'm allowed. And we don't even have to discuss Brandon today."

"I didn't mean that the way it sounded." Angela leaned over to kiss him. "I'm always glad to see you."

"Welcome to fall. We had our first frost last night."

"I noticed. Is this a great cause for celebration?"

"Well, it has been a busy growing season. It doesn't leave me much time to do anything else, but now the pressure's off and I can relax a bit. We've shut down the greenhouse, set the poinsettia starts, and today we got out the snow blowers and changed to winter opening hours."

"What do you do during the winter?"

"Read seed catalogs, catch up on professional journals, and plan for next spring with Jeff and Phil. I manage the store, Jeff does the contracts for sod and sprinkler systems, and Phil runs the greenhouse. It's a well-oiled machine. We've known each other since high school when we were in the Future Farmers of America club. In January and February we hire a crew to start spring seedlings. I'll involve Brandon in that if it's okay with you."

"Sure. But that's work. Don't you do anything for fun?"

"My parents want me to take them to Mexico and show them some of the places where I served my mission."

Angela looked up from her work. "How long will you be gone?"

Kyle grinned. "We've been talking about it for five or six years. I don't think it'll ever happen, but we still talk. We'll be in danger of actually going if one of us buys tickets."

"I see."

"I also have a little dance band with Jeff and Phil—the Hobble Creek Ramblers. Jeff plays the fiddle and Phil's on keyboard. I play the guitar. We only take bookings from October to February, but it's fun and keeps us from going stir crazy."

"When do you have time to practice?"

"A couple of nights a week, Jeff's wife and Phil's wife come with food at closing time and bring the kids. After dinner we practice and they all dance in the aisles."

Smiling, Angela filled a pastry bag with frosting the color of pyracantha berries, adjusted the tip, and began to squirt small flowers onto individual sections of a sheet cake. Kyle watched with fascination until she stopped and stared at him. "You guys played at the Single Adult party last November."

"Were you there?"

She went on with her work. "I did all the bread and French pastries and spent most of the time in the kitchen because I didn't know anyone to dance with."

"Well, you do now."

"We've had our last outdoor events here at Sophie's Place, and the indoor parties will be much smaller and less stressful, so maybe . . ."

"Let's have dinner tomorrow night, the four of us, and then we can play games and dance. I have CDs of big-band music."

"Sorry. All of Sophie's Kids are going to a BYU basketball game, so I have to work."

"Okay. Next Friday. If the kids are busy, we'll dance alone, have a prom for grown-ups."

Using a pastry bag with frosting the color of buttercups, Angela began squirting tiny centers into the flowers on the cake. "Kyle, do you realize how much time we're spending together?"

"That's not such a bad thing, is it. We're friends. Very close friends."

"You've made it easy," she said. "I'm getting used to having you around."

"Maybe all my scheming hasn't been in vain."

She laughed with him. "No, not at all. It's comfortable. I like being with you."

"Good." He stood to leave. "Then you can tolerate more frequent visits this winter."

She put the pastry bag down and slipped her arms around his neck. "What time tomorrow?"

"I'll pick you up at six." He kissed her and held her close. "And I'll be here Monday for family home evening. It's my turn to give the lesson. Have a good day, Angel."

Friday, October 13

Lainie sorted through a pile of mail on her desk in the afternoon and found an envelope with a return address from John T. Marchbanks at a post office box in Gleneden, Oregon. He wrote:

Tiring trip, due to late plane and bad traffic. Stayed with the parents last night. Mom cried when she saw my bald head, and said they were sorry they couldn't get to Utah when I was sick. This time there was no coffee by my place at dinner, but Dad toasted my health with a glass of wine. He smiled and said I turned out to be a decent kid after all—no criminal record or anything. That's either his weird sense of humor or he's beginning to forgive me for not being a priest or a doctor. Or maybe he's finally surrendered me to what I believe.

I'm headed for Gleneden right after breakfast and want to get this into the mail before I leave town. Sorry for such a hasty exit from Provo, but like you said, I need a change of scenery, and Gleneden is good for me. I'll be here for a while. I love you, my sweet Lainie. I don't know what I would have done without you these last few months.

She read it again, still wavering between anger and understanding. They'd shared some grim and difficult times the past few months, talked about everything and had come to know each other well, and yet she still didn't know a simple thing like his middle name. Maybe he would always be a mystery.

Carrie bustled in and stopped at the desk. "Why the scowl?"

Lainie sat back in her chair. "John went to Oregon."

"Without telling you?" Carrie sat in the chair in front of the desk. "Is somebody sick?"

"Just John."

"How do you feel about that?"

"At first I thought he might have gone home to die."

"Lainie, that's—

"Silly. I know. I understand why he did it. He's still got chemo brain and . . ."

"But how do you feel?"

"Well, I miss him, of course."

"No, Lainie. I want you to tell me how you feel."

"Sad, sorry, lonesome, confused, left out of the loop—"

"And angry."

Lainie put her head in her hands. "Yes, angry. I know I shouldn't feel this way, but—"

"But you do, and it's okay. He didn't discuss this with you. He did a 'guy' thing, chemo brain not withstanding, so don't make excuses for him. You have every right to feel angry."

Lainie sighed. "He wrote to me and explained it all." She read the short note to Carrie, whose face kept a skeptical frown. "There it is."

Carrie pursed her lips. "Doesn't say when he's coming back. What are you going to do?"

"What *can* I do? Go to Oregon and drag him back?"

"You could always find a boy toy and have a fling. That would serve him right."

Lainie laughed. "I guess I do sort of sound ridiculous. But this is just so . . ."

"Unfair. You've been so supportive and then he does this, leaving you out of the equation." Carrie sat, elbows on the desk. "Well?"

"I'll write a nice, supportive reply, but I don't want to have a war in letters. I'd say something he'd misunderstand, something that would be misconstrued and blown all out of proportion. What do you think I should do?"

"Take a trip, spend a weekend at a spa, get a new hairdo, go shopping."

"What?"

"You've fasted for John so often over the past few months your pants are baggy."

Lainie's eyebrows flew up

"If your friends won't tell you, who will?" Carrie went on. "You really do need some new clothes. All I'm saying is that when he comes back, make sure you look sensational."

Lainie shook her head and stared out the window. "I don't know how to play this game, but in a strange, convoluted way, that actually makes sense. Clothes this week, facial next."

"Exactly. You've had disappointments before and you've always forged on. That's what I love about you. Just live life. Don't put yourself in suspended animation."

Late that night, when she'd thought it through, Lainie replied to John in a brief note. If she knew anything about having cancer it was that recovery can't be rushed. She wouldn't ask why he left without any warning, and she wouldn't overwhelm him with lengthy letters. He didn't need any more pressure. Wanting to keep it light, she wrote:

It was great to hear from you. How's the coast? We've had a blustery October day. With temperatures falling, the world is shutting down for winter. Indoor events are smaller and less stressful.

Everyone asks how you are. My Sweet Souls had a party last week and they thought you might come with me. Sophie's Kids still hang out after school, lured by Angela's cookies, but they're having hot chocolate now instead of cold milk. Carrie sends best love from the sassy lassie. She and I are going shopping this week and hope to find some classy new clothes. How's your appetite? Just don't OD on clam chowder. Johnny, all my love is yours.

Tuesday, October 15

When Lainie heard from John again, he wrote:

All I've done since I've been here is sleep, read, walk on the beach, consume gallons of clam chowder, and think about you. And sketch. This place is inspiring for that. Ocean air clears my head. Went to the Columbia River Maritime Museum in Astoria on Friday—more than everything you've ever wanted to know about boats—and then climbed the Astor Column to see the spectacular view. It's always windy where the river flows into the ocean.

Stopped at the cheese factory in Tillamook on the way back for a double-dip ice cream cone of Wild Mountain Blackberry and Tillamook Mudslide (i.e. chocolate heaven). Talk about total self-indulgence and a complete lack of self-restraint! Almost as delicious as having my arms around you.

On Sunday the Primary of the Lincoln City Ward gave their annual presentation and they let me sing with them. I went to church feeling empty and realized that before I fell in love with you I was never lonely. Now my love for you can't be measured or confined, and neither can my loneliness when we're apart.

Lainie replied:

You're a little-people person. That's a talent I haven't developed. Life around here isn't nearly as exciting as the Oregon coast. I went to the dentist Friday (no cavities) and I'm getting my car serviced tomorrow. Ho-hum. One night last week while Morgan was involved in bishop business, Carrie and I went to see A Man for All Seasons *at the university—excellent production. Afterward we ate pumpkin pie and debated which part you would have liked playing. We also brainstormed new party ideas we can offer to clients.*

Would have loved seeing that view from the top of the Astor Column. Maybe someday. When you get a chance, have one of those ice cream cones for me—sounds blissful. What does the "T" in your name stand for? What are you reading? Went to Marchbanks Retreat yesterday—magnificent autumn color. Remembered the times we went there together, and prayed for you. Nature may be dying, but loving you makes me feel more alive than ever before.

Thursday, October 17

Lainie,

I'm rereading the McConkie Messiah series. Finished the second book last night. It makes me ask myself if I'm really as Christlike as I could be—I think about it while I'm walking on the beach every day and looking at this magnificent ocean. It has such power, and I've learned to respect that. I remember so many of our conversations. You were right when you said I don't own that trauma of the past. Letting it go has brought me closer to the Savior, and His power to save always brings me to my knees.

Went to a small art gallery Monday in Seaside. They bought some of my pieces a few years ago and asked if I had more. I came up with several that have been taking up space in my storage closet but decided to frame and keep a series of seashells I did a couple of summers ago.

You'd love the kites here—there are so many colorful and creative designs. Stopped for lunch in Rockaway Beach and walked for a while. Sat on a rock and watched some college kids building a sandcastle while their kite, anchored by a log, sailed in the wind. Knew you'd love doing that. October is the perfect time to be here—not too hot, not too cold, not many storms.

Took my sketch pad and drove down to the Devil's Punchbowl yesterday. It's a shaft in the rocks that forces incoming water into a spout. It's quite spectacular when the flow crashes in at high tide. Had dinner at a little Chinese restaurant in Depoe Bay on the way back and sketched some fishermen at the end of the jetty silhouetted in the sunset. Brave souls—the wind was vicious out there.

I'm feeling better every day. Next week I'm going to visit Richard and Janine. Lainie, you make me happy. I love you with all my heart.

She knew it was good for John to be there in that familiar, peaceful place and she couldn't resent that, no matter how much she missed him. Finally, she wrote:

Glad you're feeling good and getting around to see family. I visited my parents last week. They're doing well, though the arthritis in Mom's knees and hips is giving her a lot of pain as the weather cools. Our events at Sophie's Place have slowed down a bit before the December rush, but I'm glad for the break. Angela, Carrie, and I need time to regroup and reevaluate what we're doing.

Angela has been dating Kyle Kirkwood, the owner of the garden center that grooms our yard. Her kids are crazy about him. She's in love with him too, but is either in denial or hasn't figured it out yet. Does that remind you of someone you know?

Our summer profits were excellent. We sent Sophie's Kids to a concert as a bonus for their hard work—a country-western heartthrob the girls love and the boys tolerate. I've been thinking back on my ordinary life, to the dark ages of last year when I didn't know you yet. I love you, John, and I love how we are together. It's my personal renaissance. I thank God for you every day.

Lainie mailed the note on the way home from work and couldn't help wondering how long this would go on.

Twenty-Two

Friday, October 18

Kyle and Angela pushed back some furniture and moved throw rugs out of the way, and after they danced for nearly an hour to some lively Glenn Miller tunes, beads of sweat covered their foreheads.

"Come on. We could use some raspberry lemonade," she said.

"I'm glad it worked out this way." Kyle sat down at the kitchen table. "We can spend Sunday with the kids."

Angela smiled as she poured the drink. "They look forward to that." She sat across from him. "Where did you find all the old tunes on CD?"

"That kind of music never dies. It just gets reformatted."

"You dance well."

"We dance well together." He sat back in his chair, watching her sip the drink. "I'm alive again, Angie, and it's because of you. I learned that if you unlock the pain, it sets you free." He studied her for a moment. "I want to tell you what happened. I think you deserve to know."

"Thank you for trusting me. I think I'd like to know."

Kyle folded his fingers on the table in front of him. "I was young when my baby son and my wife died, and so numb I walked around like a robot. A few months later my bishop called me in. He knew I needed counsel even though I didn't realize it myself. We reviewed the whole ordeal and the grief I still felt. Then he opened the scriptures and read to me about Joseph Smith's suffering in Liberty Jail."

"I know that passage. It really tears your heart out."

"I'd read it dozens of times before, but this time I heard it in a different way. It seems oversimplified when the Lord said, 'Thine adversity and thine afflictions shall be but a small moment,' and 'All these things shall give thee experience and shall be for thy good.' It doesn't appear to recognize the magnitude of the pain, but then I realized pain isn't really the point."

Angela reached for Kyle's hand. "What do you mean?"

"Joseph Smith was able to make something good come out of something terrible, and the bishop challenged me to do the same." He squeezed her hand. "I realized then that I didn't carry that little casket from my car to the gravesite alone. I had help. That's what Isaiah means when he says 'Surely he has borne our griefs.' That's what Gethsemane means. It won't happen on our timetable, but eventually justice and mercy will be answered."

She nodded. "Some things are too heavy to carry alone."

"Nicole was still in intensive care and I didn't know if she'd even make it. Honestly, I thought I'd never stop crying." He reached over to wipe a tear from Angela's cheek.

She caught her breath. "How awful. Your whole life was shattered."

Kyle stopped for another sip of lemonade. "But it wasn't over. When Nicole died almost two years later—my beautiful Nikki—I allowed my emotions to shut down, thinking that would make the pain go away. But Angie, nobody suffers the way Christ did in Gethsemane or on the cross. Now I understand what the Lord told Joseph Smith. Having pain isn't negotiable, and it doesn't entitle us to immediate explanations. Regardless of what I'm called to endure, I still have the responsibility for whatever I was sent here to accomplish. That's the point. I'm still in school to learn how to be an eternal person. If I reject or deny any of the experiences the Lord gives me in my human phase of life, I reject and deny Him and what He wants me to learn. There's pain and there's pleasure, and it's a package deal."

She leaned on one hand. "I haven't thought of it that way before."

"This life is a rare, sweet moment, Angie, bittersweet sometimes, but it's only a moment and we only get one chance at it. I don't want to waste any more time."

"Is that what you think I'm doing? Wasting my life?"

"No, I didn't mean it that way. Being a good mother, a good friend is never a waste of time. But you need to apply the Atonement to your situation."

She sighed and wiped the condensation off the glass with slow, methodical strokes. "What happened to me didn't involve death. I still have to deal with Sean and it's like having a third child, only I don't have custody of him."

Kyle frowned. "No, I think it did involve death. A relationship died. Trust died. Intimacy died. Your marriage was destroyed. It isn't easy to recover from such an enormous loss, but the Atonement still applies."

She took another sip of the cold drink, considering his words. "Maybe you're right. When I married Sean I thought those things would be mine forever."

"He killed them when he betrayed you and the kids and the Church. That's got to be devastating. What he wanted for himself was more important than the spiritual and emotional needs of his family. Selfishness kills love, and it's natural for you to resent that."

Angela looked at him, a new understanding pouring into her heart. "Yes, and when those things died, I died too. I didn't realize that."

"You know, you don't have to get stuck in that time warp."

"Is that what you think I've done?"

He smiled. "Angel, the trouble with you is that you don't believe in spring." She was startled by the look of love in his eyes and the tenderness in his voice. "You don't think you can bring trust and intimacy back to life again. You don't realize you're just dormant."

"And I'm not sure I want to risk it again. Can you understand that?"

"You don't have to die anymore. You can get past the hurt. Do you understand that? You trust me with Brandon. Now trust me with yourself." She shook her head. "Yes, I love you, Angie. It's a settled feeling, right here." He put an open hand on the center of his chest. "If you're honest with yourself, I think you'd have to admit you have some fondness for me. You can't hide it. I can see the truth of it in your eyes. You know I won't fail you or betray you. I love your children too, and I want to enjoy them with you and help you launch them into life. Angela, marry me, and before spring comes you and your good, generous heart will understand what a joy it is to be fully alive again."

"You *are* trying to convert me."

"Look, the door is open. Have the faith to walk through it. With me."

She shook her head. "We've only known each other since the spring."

"One growing season, and look how much we've both grown."

"I like the way things are, Kyle, safe and familiar. I need more growing seasons."

He studied her eyes again. "I know you're still afraid."

Angela glanced down at her hands on the table and took a deep breath. She didn't want to tell him how awful it was to be married to Sean; he didn't need to know the humiliating whys and wherefores. "I'm not afraid of you. I know that. But Kyle, I can't . . . I just can't risk it again."

"What can you risk?"

She looked up at him and extended her arm across the table. "Here's a hand of friendship. That's all I can give right now."

"That's the beginning of trust." Clasping her hand, he swallowed and frowned. "If it's what you want, I'm willing to wait for the rest until another season."

They finished their drinks and went back to the living room to dance again, more subdued now, skipping past the fast-tempo numbers to the slow ones that gave them an excuse just to hold each other. She listened to him sigh, his cheek against hers, and wondered what it would be like to trust him with her whole life—to have his arms around her every day, to share her life and her children, and her bed.

After another hour Kyle said, "It's getting late. I'd better go." They moved the rugs and furniture back into place and walked to the door where he held her again, buried his face in her hair, and kissed her neck.

"Come for dinner Sunday," Angela said, her hands on his shoulders.

"I will. I'll call you tomorrow."

She kissed him, wanting to give him some comfort. "Please don't worry about me."

"Angie, think about what we've said. Sooner or later, whatever's bothering you, you're going to have to give it away. Give it to the One who already paid for it. As you said, some things are too heavy to carry alone. Don't do it for me. Do it for yourself. Free yourself to be happy again." He held her close and said softly, his lips on her forehead, "And please pray about us. I know that's asking a lot, but we both need to know the answer, whatever it is." He left her with a reassuring kiss.

Angela prepared for bed, then prayed for a long time, weeping and giving thanks for Kyle. She poured out all her anger about Sean in a way she'd never been able to articulate before and realized at last that hating and resenting him meant expending more energy on him than he deserved. Kyle was right. She did want to be alive again. Sean's betrayal had destroyed her trust, and to be a complete human being she needed to trust again.

Sometime in the middle of the night she surrendered all the pain, the humiliation, the betrayal, and wept again to feel the burden lift. When her heart was rid of the ugliness, all that was left in it was love. And Kyle. Knowing him and having him in her life was a blessing from the beginning. She could trust this man. She slept in peace the rest of the night.

Saturday, October 19

"Mom, can I talk to you?"

Julie's knocking roused Angela from a sweet dream about walking through the greenhouse with Kyle. Flowers grew and bloomed before their eyes, and he gathered bundles of them for her. Angela smiled to remember it; she'd never dreamed about him before and wished she could go back to it. She glanced at the clock. Nine thirty. "Sure. Come in." She moved over as Julie sat on the side of the bed. "What are your plans for today?"

"We have that seminary service project cleaning Sister Bedford's windows in half an hour, but I can't leave until you tell me about your date last night."

Angela laughed and leaned against the headboard. "It was fine. He dances well, we drank raspberry lemonade, he went home—end of date."

"So what do you think? You've been going out for a few months. Do you like him?"

"Of course I like him. He has a quirky sense of humor, and he can be a little bit crazy sometimes, but he's very nice."

Julie's jaw dropped. "Nice? Did you say 'nice'? Nice is nothing."

"Nice means he's considerate and thoughtful and easy to talk to."

"So what do you talk about?"

Angela raised her eyebrows. "Well, aren't you the pushy little miss today?"

"You're my mom. For all I know, you don't know how to talk about anything but whose turn it is to do the dishes."

"He told me about the death of his son and his wife and how hard it was to recover from that. But things have happened this summer, and he's ready to go on with his life."

Julie's eyes grew wide. "Go on with his life. Does that mean what I think it means?"

"Well, he's thinking about getting married."

"Mom, don't play games with me."

Angela smiled. "Yes, he thinks I'm the one."

Julie screamed and jumped and ran halfway up the stairs, pounding on the walls. "Brandon! Brandon! Get down here! Emergency family meeting in Mom's room! Now!" She bounced back to where Angela sat on the side of the bed, laughing and shaking her head.

Several seconds later, Brandon clattered down the stairs. "Huh? What's all the screamin'—"

"Kyle asked Mom to marry him!"

"Cool." Grinning, Brandon sat at the foot of Angela's bed. "That's really cool."

"Hold on. I didn't say yes."

Julie stopped bouncing. "What? Why not?"

Brandon frowned. "Mom, you've been eatin' ditzy flakes."

"You've got to call him," Julie insisted. "Call him right now and tell him yes."

Angela sighed. "When you're older you'll understand."

"No. I want to understand now," Julie said.

"Kyle's a great guy, Mom." Brandon's voice cracked. "I've been praying for you."

Angela looked at them. She'd been so busy providing the necessities for them that she hadn't thought about giving them the one thing they seemed to want most—a man in their lives, one they could respect and admire. She took a deep breath. "He does love all of us, but I don't know if I'm ready for such a big change in my life. I'm doing fine on my own."

Julie looked horrified. "Is that what you told him? Oh, Mom, please, *please* tell me you didn't say that."

"I told him I need more time. We've only known each other since the spring, one growing season, and we've both been too busy to date very much, and get acquainted, and . . ."

"What's that supposed to mean?" Brandon asked.

"It means I recognize what a big step it is. I'm not going to make that kind of decision in a hurry or under pressure. He said he'd be patient until I'm ready to, you know, consider—"

"Does that mean six months? A year?" Julie looked at her brother.

Brandon moved closer. "Mom, do you love him? I know he loves you, and that's all that matters."

Relaxing her defenses, Angela touched Brandon's face and listened for the answer to her prayer. "Yes, I suppose I do. I love him for the way he's helped you." She looked at Julie. "I love him because he's a good man, a good example, and because he's respectful and dependable and funny and wise and patient. And because he keeps his word. Because I can trust him." She shrugged. "And because we dance well together."

Brandon shook his head. "Then what's the problem?"

Julie knelt and took her mother's hands. "Look, Mom, you have to think about Brandon and me. We've never lived in the same house with a dad who could bless us when we were sick, or let us beat him at Monopoly, or give us advice, or help us with homework. Mom, Kyle's more than a good man. He's a good dad."

Angela was momentarily speechless. "I guess I didn't realize how much that meant to both of you."

"Maybe you don't feel ready but we do," Julie said. "Please, Mom. This is an answer to my prayers. He treats you so well because he truly loves you. Anybody can see that in the way you look at each other. What are you waiting for?"

Brandon knelt beside his sister. "When I work with him every week at Sophie's Place, he teaches me stuff about life Sean doesn't know. It's like Kyle's my real dad." He shrugged. "I guess waiting one more season is okay with me as long as it's a short one."

"Yeah, maybe the Thanksgiving season," Julie said.

"A month from now?" Angela blinked. Four weeks.

"Then instead of Christmas cards this year, we'll send out wedding announcements," Brandon said. "Hey, Jules, how about that? Julie and Brandon are pleased to announce the marriage of their mother Angela to Kyle Kirkwood, the greatest guy in the world."

"Call him." Julie handed the phone to her mother. "Get married now, get acquainted later. You'll have a date for the rest of your life."

Brandon stood with her. "Mom, all I want for Christmas this year is a real dad. It's something money can't buy."

Angela took the phone and stared at the keypad. "I don't remember his number. I've only called him once. He's always just been here."

"And he always will be, Mom. You know you can count on that."

Brandon said, "I call him every week. Just dial 'good guy.' That's his personal line at the store."

"And tell him you have a deadline," Julie added. "No later than Christmas."

Angela's hand shook as she tried to dial, and she had to start over.

"Here, I'll do it." Brandon dialed the phone and handed it to his mother.

Her heart jumped when she heard Kyle's voice. "Uh, hi. Are you busy?"

"Not too busy for you."

"Well, I have two answers for you."

"Answers?"

"Last night. Did you ask me to marry you? Did I misunderstand?"

"No. I mean, yes, I did, and I still think it's the best idea I've ever had."

"Well, I just wanted to say—"

"Look, I'm sorry, Angel, I didn't mean to force the issue. I just—"

"Kyle, if you don't stop interrupting I won't be able to say this."

He paused. "What would you like to say?"

"First of all, Julie and Brandon said yes."

"I always knew they were smart kids. What about you?"

"Positively, absolutely, definitely, without a doubt, and in all other ways, yes."

He gasped. "I'll be right over."

She laughed. "Give me an hour. I'm not out of bed yet, and I—"

"When next you see me, I'll be pacing in your living room."

"You'll recognize me right away." She smiled at her children. "I'll be the tallest one who's in love with you."

Twenty-Three

Thursday, October 24

John wrote:

Finished the Messiah series and started through my collection of Maxwell books. They're small but packed with "nutrition," like consuming a spiritual energy bar. This morning in sacrament meeting our high council speaker gave a great talk on faith. I love you for always having faith in me, even on the days I wasn't very lovable. Sometimes it seems like I've always known you, always loved you. Nothing is more important to me than that. Thursday I'm headed for the city.

He must be all right if he's talking about survival, Lainie guessed. She wrote:

Hope all goes well with the family visits. Be safe on the road.

We had some snow last night, but it melted quickly this morning when the sun came out—no shoveling required. I thought about your winter painting of Marchbanks Retreat. Maybe this moisture will encourage our cherry pits to sprout and you'll have to paint new pictures. Carrie and I went to a day spa for facials and massages this week, and now I'm thinking about getting my hair cut. What do you think?

Johnny, my little world was so narrow, so bland and colorless before you came into my life. You've opened doors and windows in my soul that I didn't know were there, and you've changed how I see the world. Thank you for loving me and letting me love you.

Friday, October 25

Not ready to leave this sacred place, John stepped into the atrium just off the lobby after the temple session. He dodged photographers and brides and grooms before he found a place to sit. Cool Oregon rain kept the wedding parties in this muggy warmth that encouraged these tropical flowers. Anthuriums and orchids of every shape and color bedazzled, while tree-like ferns and philodendrons reached to the glass roof. Bromeliads bloomed, some waxy red flowers growing on a spike out of sword-like leaves, others from thorny rosette foliage of variegated maroon and cream. John smiled and wondered if the north forty of the Garden of Eden might have looked something like this.

In a quiet corner he pondered what he'd seen and heard in answer to prayer. In fact, he couldn't remember when a prayer had been answered with such force. Reviewing it, he realized it was more like a command. Knowing the expected change in his life involved Lainie gave him a sense of peace. A wheat motif in the celestial room décor represented the staff of life. Wheat. Bread. Eternity. Jesus Christ. John acknowledged the Bread of Life as the reason he felt so alive in that room, just as he felt so alive with Lainie. She always said "It's all about life." And now it would be all about their life together, sanctioned and sanctified by God.

Margaret and Jerry found him there, smiling to himself. "Are you okay?" she asked.

John took a deep breath. "I'm about as okay as a guy can get."

~

Later at Margaret and Jerry's house, Richard and Janine came over. While the children took possession of the family room for videos and games and Ping-Pong, John sat with his siblings in the living room and answered questions about his battle with cancer.

"Is chemotherapy as bad as they say?" Janine asked.

"And worse. I had surgery in July and chemo in August, and I'm just now beginning to feel good again, almost like my old self, but I'll never be the same. It makes you think about how delicate life really is."

Richard took Janine's hand. "As we studied the gospel, we've been amazed at the beauty and simplicity of the plan of salvation. It gives us a different perspective on life and death and human relationships."

"I know what you mean," Jerry said. "When I learned that one of the most important purposes of life is to create an eternal family, I knew the doctrine was true. It resonated and it still thrills me right here." He put a fist on the center of his chest.

"It just makes sense." Richard looked at his brother. "You've believed all these years about eternal families, John, but you still don't have one. Why not?"

Everyone looked at John in anticipation. It was a question no one in his family had asked before. "What is this—the Inquisition?" he said.

Richard shook his head. "Wrong century."

"Wrong church," Janine added.

"Wrong answer," Margaret chimed in.

John laughed. "Well, I wanted Lainie to be the first to know—she'll have to agree—but yes, I'm going to ask her to marry me."

They all cheered and Jerry whistled.

Janine asked, "Will you be married in the Salt Lake Temple or come back to Portland?"

"Probably Salt Lake, but I'll let you know."

"We're really looking forward to the time when we can have temple blessings," Richard said. "What are you doing tomorrow?"

"Why? What's going on?"

Richard smiled at his brother. "We're going to be baptized, and we thought maybe you could do that for us."

Wednesday, October 30

Lainie's week was crammed with planning meetings and decisions, designs and consultations, and coordinating with Carrie and Angela to gear up for December weddings. That meant arranging the schedule so they could all participate in Angela's marriage to Kyle Kirkwood the Saturday after Thanksgiving in the Provo Temple, and giving her time off for a honeymoon in Mexico.

John's letter came Wednesday, full of good news.

> *Saturday I baptized Richard and Janine and their boy Alex in Vancouver! I can't tell you how humbling and marvelous it was! I could hardly get the words out. I stood in the circle with Jerry when he confirmed them. Margaret invited Mom and Dad, and they surprised us by coming. I know they both felt the Spirit. Dad said he didn't realize I'd become a priest after all. Mom just cried, bear-hugged me, and couldn't talk. I went to church with all of them this morning, and Mom and Dad came too. It was so satisfying to be there with my family, take the sacrament together, and see Richard's family introduced as the newest members of the ward. Jerry and I stood in the circle when the bishop ordained Richard to the priesthood.*
>
> *Their new baby is a boy, due in February, and they're going to name him Douglas, after Dad. Maybe that will help soften hearts too.*
>
> *It was also a great day on Friday when I went to the Portland Temple with Jerry and Margaret. I spent time afterward thinking and praying. I now know some significant things about you and me that I didn't know three weeks ago. We'll talk about them when I get home. Got back to Gleneden tonight just as the sun was going down in a spectacular display of glory.*
>
> *By the way, DO NOT, under any circumstances, cut your hair.*

John's simple report of this tender time thrilled Lainie, but she felt curious about the "significant things" he mentioned. She replied immediately.

> *What a blessing you've been to your family! I'm so happy for Richard and Janine, and I can imagine how satisfying that must have been for you, Margaret, and Jerry. Maybe this signals a change in your parents' attitude.*

I've spent some time in the temple too. Peace, tranquility, and joy encompass me when I'm there. I sat for a while thinking about us and felt so close to you, so loved and cherished by God. It's probably obvious to everyone else, but it finally occurred to me that a temple is a monument to love, both the love in families and God's love for us.

Angela's still a little preoccupied. After what she's been through, she deserves this happiness with Kyle. They are so much in love, and Julie and Brandon are beside themselves with excitement to have a dad they can depend on.

Carrie and I keep the celebrations going at Sophie's Place, but I'm happy because every day I wake up thinking "I love John Marchbanks," and I rejoice and thank God.

Saturday, November 2

John replied:

I've been sketching and writing a lot. It's turning colder and it rains more, but I'm still running twice a day most days. I've also done a few home improvement projects around the place and they're taking longer than I expected. Morgan sent me some work I can do from here. Our clientele has grown this year. One of our associates is leaving to go into business, but the other one, Chad Remington, is staying to become our new partner. We'll bring on one or two more associates who specialize in family and trial law, and then our expansion will be complete. Interviews begin in December. We had a conference-call staff meeting last week and I'm up to speed with everything now.

Went to the Oregon Coast Aquarium in Newport yesterday to sketch starfish, coral, and sea cucumbers. Several busloads of school kids were visiting too. I miss my Primary class. And I miss you. Have I mentioned that? All my love to you, Sweet Lainie, forever, amen.

Lainie knew that if John was making business decisions again he must have recovered, and she wished he would give her some clue about when he was coming home. She wrote a reply Sunday evening, essentially a business report. December wedding plans occupied her time and Carrie's, Angela was priceless, and word of mouth was the best advertising. Sophie's Kids were still with them, and Sophie's signature cookies were their most popular offering. "What are you writing? John, I love you," Lainie concluded her note. She mailed the it on her way to work Monday morning.

Thursday, November 7

While Carrie and Angela went downstairs to coordinate schedules and order supplies, Lainie took time to reread the note she'd received from John in that day's mail.

> *Too turbulent and cold to go out on the beach yesterday, so I stoked the fire, made hot chocolate, and watched the weather from the window. There is no drama quite like a stormy sea. Whether calm or tempestuous, the consistent movement of the tide is like the surging love God has for us no matter where we are in life. I feel that every day. When the sky cleared and the ocean rested, I thought about Jesus calming the Sea of Galilee for the frightened fishermen.*
>
> *Testimony meeting on Sunday enriched me, calmed me, filled me to the brim with love for the Savior and love for you. You've both stood with me through the bad times and the good this year. I know now that I'm better and stronger when you and I are together and the Savior is with us. We three are a good combination. I can't imagine my world any other way. You said it once before—believe in life before death. It all descended on my heart today and I am joyful.*
>
> *Drove down the coast this afternoon, sketching and savoring God's creations. I've filled two sketch pads now with lots of subjects to paint when I get home. Lainie, I love you.*

She hurried to reply so she could mail the note on her way home.

Sketching heals—sounds like a medical breakthrough. Wait till the health care system hears about this. But I don't care about anything else, Johnny, as long as you're well. I walked around Marchbanks Retreat yesterday and realized that my heart is so full of you I can hardly think about anything else.

As she wrote the last sentence, she heard the front door open and footsteps in the entry. When they stopped, she turned from her desk to see John standing there smiling at her.

"Hey, Irish, you look fabulous."

She laughed and caught her breath. "So do you. You know, the lumberjack look doesn't work for everybody." He wore jeans with two-inch cuffs, a red-plaid flannel shirt, a dark-blue sleeveless down vest, hiking boots, and a red ski cap. His eyes were bright and full of love. He pulled off the cap and pushed it into the vest pocket.

She stood and stepped toward him, but he held up a hand to stop her as he unsnapped his vest and reached inside to take something from his shirt pocket. "Wouldn't want to break this." He placed a sand dollar on the desk. "A dollar for your thoughts."

"That's highly inflated I'm sure," she said, melting into his arms.

"I found it on Gleneden Beach. It's perfect, just like you."

She touched his face. "When did you get back?"

"Just now. I haven't even been home yet." He kissed her tentatively at first, then settled with the familiarity of it. "But now I'm really home."

"So am I."

"I'm never going anywhere without you again, I promise. I missed you."

"I missed you too, Johnny." She giggled softly. "You know, you just saved me a postage stamp." She retrieved the note she'd been writing, folded it, and pushed it into his pocket where the sand dollar had been. "You can read it later."

"I love to get letters." He wrapped his arms around her again and kissed her once more. She didn't want him to stop, but he let her go and touched her chin. "Sweet Lainie, we have so many reasons to celebrate. I want you to come to my house for dinner tomorrow night."

"Not tonight?"

"How about dinner tonight at the Brick Oven."

"Sounds good."

He grinned and raised an eyebrow. "But for tomorrow I have a few things to prepare."

"I love a party, especially when it's a Quail Valley surprise."

"I'll pick you up at six." He looked at her as if she were something good to eat. With one more kiss he was gone.

Twenty-Four

Friday, November 8

John and Lainie lingered over dinner, and once each got home they talked on the phone until late into the night. He called her three times at work the next day. When he picked her up for dinner—charming, animated, and funny as ever—Lainie couldn't stop smiling. His eyes were more alive than she'd seen them in a long time. The month he'd been in Gleneden, though good for him, had been so hard for her. Yet being with him again now, she realized time and space didn't matter. Her love for him had grown and ripened in ways she couldn't measure.

When she walked in the door at Quail Valley, the Mt. Timpanogos painting was gone from the mantel and in its place was a portrait of her. She caught her breath. "Oh, John, this is what you were doing all that time."

They stood in front of the fireplace, his arm across her shoulders, her cheeks wet with tears. "You're my muse, my inspiration in every way, Lainie. I started that the night you told me about your breast cancer, and finished it with pictures I took that first day we went to Marchbanks Retreat." She turned to hug him. "I've wrestled with that hair color for months. I can't decide how to describe it—maybe burnt sienna, more sienna than burnt."

She sniffed and laughed. "Maybe a bloodshot carrot."

"Or auburn corrosion . . . maybe even a little copper pumpkin cake."

"John, it's the highest compliment I've ever had. Thank you." She kissed and hugged him again, and loved him more.

He served the meal and they held hands across the table as he said a prayer. Then he smiled and asked, "How are things at Sophie's Place?"

"We're busy and getting busier, paying the bills, and having a lot of fun. We have eighteen events to prepare for next month."

"That *is* busy."

"Carrie and I realized that since we opened we've hardly had a break, so we blocked out ten days around Christmas and New Year's, like they do at Marchbanks & Burke, when we're taking no bookings. Besides, the last six months have been so hectic for Carrie and Morgan that they decided to spend a week in St. George."

"They deserve it, but the last six months have been hectic for you too," John said. "Look at everything that's happened."

"I do plan to relax. I just haven't planned exactly how. Maybe I'll make some baby quilts for the hospital or something, just rely on serendipity."

He chuckled. "So I might get to see you occasionally."

"I guess there's no avoiding me."

"Two of the kids in my Primary class are being baptized tomorrow. Will asked me to baptize him and I'm giving a talk. I'd like it if you came too."

"I'd be honored. I've heard so much about these little people this year it's almost like they're my kids too." Lainie paused to watch him, so grateful he was here again. "How about going with me to the Thanksgiving dinner my Sweet Souls are having in a couple of weeks?"

He nodded. "I'm thankful you asked. This time I promise to behave myself."

After dinner they took slices of chocolate Bundt cake into the living room and settled shoeless on the sofa. When they finished with the cake, she nestled under John's right arm and kissed his cheek. "Thanks for the yummy dinner."

"Bachelor fare—nothing like the fancy stuff they do at Sophie's Place." He turned to kiss her cheek and then her mouth.

She kissed him back. "I could just kick myself when I think of the years I wasted not doing this."

"It wouldn't have been as good with somebody else."

"Where have you been all my life?"

"All wrapped up in my convoluted, pathetically myopic self."

Lainie chuckled. "Your hair is coming back nicely."

"Uh-huh." He pulled her close and settled with his arms around her, his head on her shoulder.

"John, why did you go to Gleneden without telling me, and why did you stay so long?"

He sighed. "What did you think about when you had cancer, besides the obvious regrets and bemoaning the fact that life's too short?"

"Oh, lots of crazy things ran through my mind—chocolate and giraffes and crocuses and whipped cream and burgundy velvet and everything I hadn't done that I always assumed I'd get to do in my life. I thought about how sweet life is, how much I love it, and how much I'd miss the beauties and pleasures of this world. Mostly I wondered what it would be like to actually pass . . . you know, go home to God."

"That about covers it for me too."

Lainie pulled back to look at John. "But it doesn't answer my questions. I thought you were getting well, and then you had more tests and suddenly you were gone. For all I knew, chemo brain had stolen you away, or you really hadn't told me everything about your test results. To be honest, at first I was afraid you'd gone home to Gleneden to die, and I didn't want you to die alone."

"Oh, Lainie, no."

"It's irrational, I know, but—"

"I'm so sorry. I thought you understood. You told me to do whatever it took to get well, and I did. At that last appointment with Alan, he told me not to be so impatient. Recovery takes time. It wasn't what I wanted to hear, but Gleneden has always been a spiritual health spa for me, so I went there."

She smiled. "You left me with a mystery. You gave me lots of clues—weather reports, news flashes, book reports, a travelogue. You seemed to be fine, but I didn't want to assume anything, and I didn't feel free to cross-examine you about your motives."

"Actually, I intended to call, but decided against it when I realized those little notes were the first love letters I've ever had and I didn't want them to stop. Now I have written proof that you love me and I can reread them anytime you're not around to take the witness stand."

"I confess I saved yours too, for the same reason."

John took both of her hands and looked into her eyes. "Lainie, there's no mystery. I stayed in Gleneden until I was well, until I was sure I had things between us completely clear in my mind. I don't want to alarm you, but I wrote my obituary because I wanted to think about what I'm going to do with the rest of my blessed, treasured, precious life."

"We talked about some of those things the last time we went to Marchbanks Retreat."

"We did. I told you in my letters how much I sketched and read and ran on the beach, but in fact, I spent a lot of time on my knees to get more of that kind of strength, too. I told the Lord I wasn't going to leave there until He gave me the answer."

"What was the question?"

John gave her an impish smile. "I had to be sure who to invite to my New Year's Eve party."

Lainie rolled her eyes. "Oh. Nothing frivolous at all."

"For me, New Year's Eve has always been a serious time of contemplation and reevaluation, where I review the past and set goals for the coming year. It's an exclusive party with a very short guest list. Until now I've been the only one on it. But then I met you, Elaine Thomas McGuire, and it's overwhelmingly obvious that this year I need to change my tradition and have a much different kind of party. This year you're invited too."

"Well, I'm honored. A party with two people is definitely more interesting."

"And the possibilities multiply when those two people are married."

Lainie raised her eyebrows. "Like having rings and a two-car garage? And the same name?"

"Yes, that kind of married—decisively, confidently, eternally tied." He reached into his back pocket. "You always ask about dress standards, but the attire for this affair is very simple. All you need to wear is this." He opened his hand to reveal a gold ring. "I admit it's kind of small, but it covers the essential parts."

"Oh, Johnny," she whispered as he put the ring on her finger. He kissed it and then kissed her mouth. "I'd like to go to that party with you," she said. "It'll never end."

"I don't remember when I didn't love you, Lainie, and I don't know how to measure the heights or depths of it. You're the greatest blessing of my life." He took her in his arms. "I want you now and always. I want to spend the rest of my life celebrating and living it up with you. That's what I learned when I went to Gleneden."

Unable to speak, she felt warm tears run down her cheeks onto his shirt.

"Hey, Irish," he said, his voice breaking, "don't start or I'll go too. This is supposed to be a happy occasion."

"I know and I'm so happy it spilled out my eyes." They laughed and hugged and kissed, and now some of the tears on her face were his. "This is not an easy thing we're going to do," Lainie said, "but I've prayed about it since the moment I knew I loved you. Something happened to me too, while you were in Gleneden. With my whole soul I love you deeply, totally, and irreversibly. You're my oxygen. Without you I can't breathe."

"Lainie, we're both high-risk people. We'll have to live entirely on faith."

"Everyone does, even if they've never had cancer. I have faith in us, John. It's all about life, and it's right for us to spend the rest of this life together. And then forever."

He smiled and squeezed her shoulders. "Well, you're the wedding expert. What happens next? We only have a few weeks before New Year's Eve."

"I don't know. I've never been in love before." She laughed. "First, I think we should definitely go somewhere tomorrow and find something like this for you to wear to the party too." She looked at the ring on her finger. "It's perfectly beautiful. And we'd probably better tell some other people, like our parents, for instance."

"My Primary class. Your Sweet Souls, the immediate world."

"Carrie knew before I did that I was falling in love with you."

"I think Morgan had a few clues too. They deserve to be the first to know." John got up and pulled Lainie off the sofa. "Let's go see them right now." When they had their shoes on, he turned and wiggled the fingers of his left hand at her. "Come on. Give it back."

"Oh, just kidding, huh?"

"Now we know it fits. I'll return it to you in the temple, right after the wedding, and then you'll never take it off again."

She removed the ring and started to put it in his hand, but withdrew it. "Okay. You're so smart. What day will this marriage take place and in which temple?"

"December 28th."

"I think I can clear my calendar."

"Which temple do you like?" John asked.

"Where will you be?"

"Salt Lake."

"Then I'll be there too," she assured him.

"Good, because the Wednesday before I left Gleneden I called and scheduled it."

"You did what?"

"It's at eleven o'clock. You'll get a letter in the mail any day now."

Lainie sank onto the ottoman and laughed and cried some more. He knelt beside her, a silly grin on his face. "You can change it if you want."

"Wasn't there a date sooner than that?"

"It was the earliest I could get. Somebody else canceled."

Still laughing, she threw her arms around his neck. "I'll take it."

"Since I chose the day and place for the wedding, you get to choose where we have the New Year's Eve party. Want to have it at your house?"

She shook her head. "Too many noisy neighbors. How about Quail Valley?"

"Okay, if you like fireworks in your driveway at midnight."

She frowned. John stood and helped her up. "What happens if we go to Gleneden?" she asked.

"We drive to the airport, fly to Portland, rent a car, and drive to the coast. It usually takes seven or eight hours on a good day, if the weather cooperates. I checked the long-range forecast. It's good."

She debated the question, then said, "Gleneden it is. We'll be alone and far away from everybody we know. I think I'm going to love it there as much as you do."

"I'll call tonight and get plane tickets for Mr. and Mrs. John Marchbanks."

"I'm surprised you haven't done that already too." She gave him the ring. "Take good care of this. I didn't have it on very long, but I like the way it feels."

"I like the way it looks." He put the ring on the mantel next to her picture. "Lainie, two things we need to do from now on are pray together every day and go to the temple as soon and as often as possible. We have to talk over some important things there."

She wasn't sure what he meant, but she followed his lead. "We can go tomorrow afternoon after we find a ring for you."

Both were silent in the car, and then Lainie asked, "John, where are we going to live? I love my house, and I know you love yours." After debating the pros and cons of each place, they concluded that neither was adequate.

He looked at her when they stopped for a traffic light. "What about our finances? We've both been independent for a long time, and we're each encumbered with a lot of material things." Comparing notes they found that besides retirement savings and a few investments, she owned her house, and he had stocks and some real estate besides Marchbanks Retreat, Quail Valley, and the house in Gleneden. Both supported missionaries.

"I'm a 'close is good enough' sort of person when it comes to balancing the checkbook," Lainie confessed.

"I like to be precise. We'll use my accountant." They were silent again for a few minutes. "Another thing you should know about me is that I have season tickets to nearly every local theater and concert series you can name."

"That might conflict sometimes with my work schedule." She looked at his profile as he drove. "I'm curious, John. Where do you keep your toothbrush? I don't remember seeing it in your bathroom."

"In the drawer. Do you like a soft or firm mattress?"

"Firm. Who's going to cook?"

"We'll take turns. Will you try to correct all my bad habits?"

She gasped. "You have bad habits?"

"Maybe a few."

"Well, I'm shocked, just shocked."

"I told you I'm a garden-variety guy."

She laughed. "Hey, I'm signing up to be your wife, not your mother. Anyway, if you snore, I'll just smother you with my pillow."

"You're creating a threatening environment with that kind of talk."

"It's a bed. I'll be there. How threatening could it be?"

"Okay, well, you might as well know I like to sit in the back at church," John went on. "That's where all the kids are."

"I like to sit in the front where I can pay attention."

"I'm a neat freak."

"I'm creatively sloppy."

"Two holidays we're never going to celebrate are Valentine's Day and Halloween. They're both profoundly stupid and based on shameless emotional blackmail."

"Can't we compromise?" Lainie asked.

"Okay. Choose one."

"Valentine's Day."

They didn't speak for a few minutes, and then John pulled into the empty parking lot of a dental clinic and turned off the car. "Is this the sound of second thoughts? From what I've heard, that's not supposed to happen until the day before the wedding."

"We're getting married so soon we'll have to telescope everything in."

"Well, if you're going to have second thoughts, have them now and get it over with."

"John, after what we've been through, second thoughts are a lack of faith."

He took her hand. "Such a pretentious popinjay like me finding the perfect woman at this point in my life—I can't take it all in. And after having cancer, when the future looked so bleak, it's the second chance I never thought I'd have."

"Me too. I may be thirty-eight and single, but I'm not desperate. I choose you, Johnny." She kissed him to emphasize the point. "I've never been so sure of anything in my life."

"I thought about it all the way back from Oregon. This is an eternal merger, not a hostile takeover. We'll put everything in the Lord's hands.

Everything's on the table, expendable. I'm ready to surrender it all, Irish. I choose you now and forever. Nothing else matters."

They shivered and held each other and kissed for a few more minutes, and then she began to giggle. "I have no second thoughts, John, I promise, but I am getting chapped lips."

"So that's what that is. I've never had chapped lips from kissing before."

"Get used to it." They buckled their seatbelts, but she put her hand on the steering wheel to keep him from driving away. "John, there's something you have to tell me right now. I can't be Mrs. Marchbanks until I know my husband's middle name."

"It's Thomas." He started the car and steered back onto the street.

"Really? That's why you laughed when I told you my legal name."

"Thomas is my father's favorite saint, and I think Dad likes you already," John explained. "Your name came up in the conversation a few times. Did I tell you that?"

Lainie smiled. "My parents invited you to come home at Thanksgiving and meet the whole family."

They talked excitedly of their plans the rest of the way to Carrie and Morgan's home.

"How are we going to tell them?" Lainie asked as they hurried to the door.

"It's too late to send a singing telegram." John rang the doorbell and pulled her into his arms. "We'll break the news this way."

"But I thought you had chapped—"

"It's about time," Morgan muttered. Then he turned and called to his wife. "Carrie, you've got to come and see this."

Aunt Sophie's Very Best Brownies

What can I say? These are well named. You could bribe anybody to do anything if you offer them these melt-in-your-mouth treats. —Sophie

¾ cup cocoa
½ teaspoon baking soda
⅔ cup melted butter, divided
½ cup boiling water
2 cups sugar
2 eggs
1⅓ cups flour
1 teaspoon vanilla
¼ teaspoon salt
1 cup semi-sweet or milk chocolate chips (raspberry flavored,
    if you can find them)

Heat oven to 350°F. Grease a 13 x 9-inch baking pan. In medium bowl blend ¾ cup cocoa and baking soda. Stir in ⅓ cup melted butter. Add boiling water; stir until mixture thickens. Add sugar, eggs, and ⅓ cup melted butter. When smooth, add flour, vanilla, and salt. Blend completely. Mix in chocolate chips. Bake 35 to 40 minutes. Cool completely before frosting.

Frosting
6 tablespoons softened butter
½ cup cocoa
2⅔ cups powdered sugar
⅓ cup milk
1 teaspoon vanilla

Cream the butter. Add cocoa and powdered sugar alternately with milk. Add vanilla. Beat to spreading consistency. Frost and cut into 36 bars.

Aunt Sophie's Sour Cream Banana Bars

These are so moist and flavorful you can even emit the frosting, and it's a good way to use up those old bananas turning brown in your fruit basket. —Sophie

1½ cups sugar
1 cup sour cream
½ cup softened butter
2 eggs
1½ cups mashed ripe bananas
2 teaspoons vanilla
1 teaspoon salt
1 teaspoon baking soda
2 cups flour
½ cup chopped nuts (optional)

Heat oven to 375°F. Grease and flour a jelly-roll pan. In large mixer bowl, mix sugar, sour cream, softened butter, and eggs on low speed for 1 minute. Scrape bowl. Add vanilla and mashed banana; beat 30 seconds. Add salt, baking soda, and flour and beat at medium speed for 1 minute. Scrape nowl. Stir in nuts. Bake 20 to 25 minutes, then cool on a rack.

Browned Butter Frosting
¼ cup butter
2 cups powdered sugar
1 teaspoon vanilla
3 tablespoons milk or cream

Heat butter in a saucepan over medium heat until it is a delicate brown color. Remove pan from heat and stir in the powdered sugar. Add vanilla and milk and mix until smooth, adding more powdered sugar or milk until you get the right consistency for spreading. Spread on cooled cookies and cut into 1 x 3-inch bars.

Aunt Sophie's Oatmeal Raisin Cookies

You can't beat the combination of oatmeal and raisins. If you like grapes, you ought to like raisins. Took me years to figure out that baking powder wasn't bacon. —Sophie

3 cups brown sugar
1 cup regular shortening
1 cup butter-flavored shortening
4 eggs
1 cup buttermilk or sour milk
1 tablespoon vanilla
3½ cups flour
1 teaspoon nutmeg
2 teaspoons cinnamon
½ teaspoon salt
2 teaspoons baking soda
2 teaspoons baking powder
6 cups regular rolled oats
1 cup cinnamon chips
2 cups raisins

Heat oven to 375°F. Cream brown sugar and shortening. Add eggs, buttermilk or sour milk, and vanilla. Stir in spices, salt, baking soda, baking powder, and flour. Add rolled oats, cinnamon chips, and raisins. With a cookie scoop, drop dollops of dough 2 inches apart on a baking pan. Flatten each raw cookie with a glass dipped in sugar. Bake for 10 to 11 minutes. Cool on a rack.

Meridee's Macaroons

That's Walter's sister. She always brought him some of these on his birthday. —Sophie

1 cup softened butter
1 cup brown sugar
1 cup white sugar
2 eggs
1 teaspoon vanilla
2 cups flour
½ tablespoon baking soda
1 teaspoon baking powder
1 teaspoon allspice (We like to use half nutmeg and half cinnamon.)
2 cups rolled oats
2 cups crisp-rice breakfast cereal
1 cup flaked coconut

Heat oven to 350°F. Cream butter and sugars. Add eggs and vanilla; mix well. Stir in flour, baking soda, baking powder, and allspice, then oatmeal, crisp-rice cereal, and coconut. Using a cookie scoop, drop dough onto a baking pan, spacing cookies 2 inches apart. Bake for 10 to 12 minutes. Cool on a rack.

Lainie's Florentine Minestrone

10-ounce package frozen chopped spinach, thawed and well drained
1½ pounds lean ground beef
⅓ cup fine dry Italian seasoned bread crumbs
1 egg
1 teaspoon salt
¼ teaspoon pepper
7 cups beef broth (or use bouillon cubes and water)
1 large onion, chopped
16-ounce can diced tomatoes (Italian seasoned if you can get it)
1 cup sliced carrots
1 cup sliced celery
16-ounce can cannellini (white kidney) beans with liquid
1 tablespoon chopped fresh basil
1 tablespoon chopped fresh oregano
1 cup shell or other small macaroni

Heat oven 350°F. Mix ground beef, bread crumbs, egg, spinach, salt, and pepper. Shape into 1-inch balls and bake on a rack set inside a pan for 20 to 25 minutes. (Meatballs may also be cooked on the stovetop. Be sure to drain on paper towels.) Place chopped onion and broth in large soup pot over medium-high heat. Add tomatoes, carrots, and celery. Cover, bring to boil. Turn to medium-low until carrots are cooked through, 30 to 40 minutes. About an hour before serving, add macaroni, beans, fresh herbs, and meatballs. If using dried herbs, reduce to 1 teaspoon each. Serve with a sprinkle of grated Parmesan or Romano cheese, and bread sticks.

Tips: Wear plastic disposable gloves to mix and shape the meatballs. Minestrone may also be made in a slow cooker.

John's Mother's Best Chocolate Bundt Cake

¾ cup softened butter
1⅔ cups sugar
2 eggs
¾ cup sour cream
1 teaspoon vanilla
⅔ cup sifted unsweetened cocoa powder
2 cups flour
½ teaspoon salt
1 teaspoon cinnamon
2 teaspoons baking soda
1 cup buttermilk or sour milk

Heat oven to 350°F. Grease and flour a 10-inch Bundt pan. Cream butter and sugar in mixer bowl. Add eggs, sour cream, and vanilla. Mix ⅔ cup cocoa with the flour, cinnamon, and salt. Stir baking soda into buttermilk or sour milk. Add flour and buttermilk to creamed mixture alternately. Beat 2 minutes at medium speed. Bake 45 to 50 minutes. Cool 10 minutes on rack. Remove from pan to rack to finish cooling.

Glaze
2 tablespoons butter
¼ cup sifted unsweetened cocoa powder
3 tablespoons water
1¼ cups powdered sugar
½ teaspoon vanilla
½ cup mini chocolate or cinnamon chips (or ¼ cup of each)

Over low heat, melt 2 tablespoons butter in a small saucepan. Add ¼ cup sifted cocoa and water. Cook, stirring until thick, but do not boil! Remove from heat and add powdered sugar and ½ teaspoon vanilla, then beat until smooth. Pour over cooled cake. Garnish with mini chips.

Discussion Questions

1. Does the first meeting between John and Lainie bode well? How do their stereotypes and preconceived notions change over time?
2. What do you like about John's friendly relationship with Carrie?
3. Most people don't like to be bothered with late night phone calls. What do John's late night calls mean to Lainie?
4. What are the similarities and differences between John's relationship with Lainie and Kyle's relationship with Angela? How is love different when it's experienced for the first time at forty than it is at twenty?
5. Why is it important that Lainie learned the language of John's profession? How does this contribute to their communication?
6. What happened that night in June at Lainie's house that left both of them so shaken? What does it mean about their future?
7. Why does John break up with Lainie when he's diagnosed with cancer?
8. Why does Angela refuse to see Kyle again after he kisses her and professes his love?
9. What is the turning point for each character that allows them to let love into their life?
10. How does John's patience work in his favor while Lainie is getting her business started? How does Lainie's patience work in her favor when John leaves unannounced for Oregon? What part does patience play in the developing relationship between Kyle and Angela?
11. Parents are important role models as their children observe what it's like to be married. How does John's relationship with his family influence his relationship with Lainie? What have Lainie's parents taught her about marriage without saying anything?
12. Kyle and John use nicknames and terms of endearment for Angela and Lainie. What do nicknames mean in a romantic relationship?
13. Kyle falls in love with Angela's children, as well as with Angela. How important is that in step-parent families?
14. Humor is an important part of the book. Which character has the best sense of humor? Why is humor important in a relationship?

About the Author

Pamela Stott Williams has been a newspaper reporter, writing teacher, tutor, poet, playwright, essayist, editor, and novelist. She has won contest prizes for her work from the League of Utah Writers and the American Night Writers Association. She loves writing about the challenges of being a believing Latter-day Saint. A native of Portland, Oregon, Pam now lives in Provo, Utah with her husband Roger, but they have also lived on Guam, in Iran, in Navajoland, and most recently spent thirty-three years in Richfield, Utah. They are the parents of three, grandparents of seven, and have a grand-dog, Doug. Her first novel, *Living It Down,* was published in May 2014.

Join in the conversation about John, Lainie, Carrie, and Morgan at auntsophiesays.blogspot.com or facebook.com/JohnandLainie.

Photo by Mindy Gonzalez

If you liked *What Took You So Long*, catch up with Carrie and Morgan's story in *Living It Down*.

Carrie Burke has it all—marriage to a successful lawyer, two lively teenage daughters, a beautiful home, the gospel. Why isn't she happy? Confused, joyless, and depressed, she questions her own worth and decides to take an unorthodox "time-out" to reevaluate her life. Her husband Morgan calls it selfish. Carrie calls it self-preservation.

Renting the basement apartment in Aunt Sophie's vintage Victorian home brings its own set of challenges, but also advantage of friendship with vivacious, creative Lainie McGuire. Coincidence brings an old flame, Todd Kendall—a man Carrie never wanted to see again—back into her life. To guide her daughter through a moral crisis with a predatory boy, she realizes she needs the help of both Todd and Morgan.

In her spiritual quest to reconnect with her values and reclaim her best self, Carrie yearns to find joy again, and in the process discovers that maybe there's no such thing as coincidence.